'Hello.'

Sandy hadn't heard anyone approach. He had set up his easel in the park and soon become engrossed in his painting. He turned round in amazement to see the French woman, Sophie.

'Hello.'

'Don't let me disturb you.'

'That's all right.'

Sophie stared at the canvas he was busy with. 'I thought you were a medical student, not an artist?' she queried.

'I am. The art side is just a hobby.'

She studied the canvas with a knowledgeable eye. 'Hard to tell at this stage, but I think it's going to be very good. The brushwork is particularly fine. I live in Montmartre – everyone there seems to be an artist and I have modelled for many of them. Picasso was the last one. Have you heard of him?'

Sandy nodded vigorously. 'And seen his work produced in magazines. I found it rather disturbing.'

She frowned. 'How so?'

'Well, it . . . it's hardly conventional.'

'Is that what you are, conventional?' she teased.

Sandy couldn't help blushing. 'Is there something wrong with that? And you, Sophie, what are you?'

She stared at him, eyes dancing with amusement. 'A bit perhaps. Conventional . . . and not so . . .'

Finding Happiness

Emma Blair

sphere

SPHERE

First published in Great Britain in 2003 by Time Warner Books
This edition published by Time Warner Paperbacks in 2003
Reprinted by Time Warner Books in 2005
Reprinted by Sphere in 2007

A CIP catalogue record for this book
is available from the British Library.

ISBN 978-0-7515-3195-4

Papers used by Sphere are natural, recyclable products made from
wood grown in sustainable forests and certified in accordance with
the rules of the Forest Stewardship Council.

Typeset by Palimpsest Book Production Ltd,
Polmont, Stirlingshire

Printed and bound in Great Britain by
Clays Ltd, St Ives plc
Paper supplied by Hellefoss AS, Norway

Sphere
An imprint of
Little, Brown Book Group
Brettenham House
Lancaster Place
London WC2E 7EN

A Member of the Hachette Livre Group of Companies

www.littlebrown.co.uk

Finding
Happiness

Chapter 1

Sandy McLean glanced up from the book he was studying when there was a soft, tentative, tap on his bedroom door. He frowned at the interruption. 'Come in!'

It was his younger sister Laura who entered, her expression one of uncertainty. 'Am I disturbing you?'

Sandy sighed. Of course she bloody well was. 'That's all right,' he declared magnanimously. 'I was about to take a break anyway.' That was a lie. He waved in the direction of the bed. 'Take a pew.'

A glance at the clock on the mantelpiece told him it was just after nine-thirty p.m. He'd had his head down for over two hours now, and it felt like it. The beginnings of a headache were starting to pulse inside his skull.

After she'd sat Laura gazed curiously around her. It had been a long time since she'd been in her brother's room, several years in fact. It was as messy as ever, she noted, tidyness certainly wasn't one of his finer points. In one corner an artist's easel had been set up, displaying a half-finished landscape in oils.

It suddenly struck Sandy how much his sister had grown of late. Why, she'd become quite the young lady, with a nice figure too, even if it was still in the budding stage. As he saw her nearly every day he wondered why he hadn't noticed that before. 'So, to what do I owe the honour?' he asked.

Laura shrugged. 'I don't know really. I just thought I'd come and talk to you, that's all. We so rarely get a chance.' When she saw his puzzled look, she added, 'Talk properly that is. Not just good morning, goodbye and that sort of thing.'

'I see,' he murmured, amused by this.

A silence followed during which she twined and intertwined her fingers in her lap.

'There must be something in particular?' he prompted.

'Not really. It's just . . . well, although we're brother and sister we seem such strangers at times. I mean . . . I mean . . .' She trailed off, frowning. 'I've no idea what you actually get up to. Who your friends are. You know?'

For some reason that rather touched him. And she was right, they weren't exactly close. Not apart, but not close either. The usual brother and sister relationship, he supposed. 'I'm flattered,' he confessed.

Laura's face lit up, the tension between them suddenly broken. 'How are your studies coming along?'

How indeed, he thought bitterly, for he was in that sort of mood. How indeed! 'All right I suppose,' he replied non-committally.

'Just all right?'

Sandy bit back a waspish retort. Leaning sideways in his chair he pretended to yawn. 'Sometimes you can't see the wood for the trees.'

Laura slowly nodded. 'I understand. I find it the same with Latin. There are occasions in class when my head feels it's so crammed full nothing makes sense any more and that at any moment it might just explode.'

He regarded her with new interest, having forgotten she was even taking Latin at school. It dawned on him then how right she was about knowing so little about one another. 'Same with me,' he laughed.

Laura relaxed even further on hearing that, believing a bond, if only a tenuous one, had been established between them. '*Amo amas amat, amamus amatus amant,*' she recited and giggled. 'Round and round like a dog chasing a cat.'

How old was she now? Sandy wondered, desperately trying to work it out. Fifteen, yes that was it. Or was she fourteen? No, fifteen some months previously. 'Do you enjoy school? Overall that is?'

Laura considered that. 'Parts of it.'

'Like what?'

'English for example. The books we have to read. They can be fun.'

'And what else?'

'Art.'

A warm glow filled him. 'Are you any good?'

Laura shook her head. 'I'm rotten. No flair at all, at least that's what Mr McCormack my teacher says. And he's right. I can't draw or paint to save my life.'

Her eyes strayed over to the half-finished canvas on the easel. 'Unlike you. Now *you* have real talent. Everyone thinks so.'

Sandy couldn't resist it. 'Except Pa of course. And even if he did think I had something he'd never admit it in case it distracted me from what he wants me to do. Has decided I shall do.'

Laura could hear the bitterness in his voice. 'Is medicine so awfully bad?'

'Oh come on,' he chided softly. 'You've heard Pa often enough. He doesn't just want me to be a doctor but an eminent surgeon into the bargain. The goal he was never able to achieve himself.'

'You hate the idea, don't you?'

'Damn right I do,' he spat. 'But what choice have I? I can't go against Pa. That would be unthinkable. People like us don't go against their parents' wishes.'

'Poor Sandy,' she sympathised.

'The fact is, I totally loathe medicine. As for being a surgeon, eminent or otherwise, how ghastly having a job like that. A human butcher and plumber in other words.' He shuddered at the thought. 'No, whatever happens I'll be a family doctor the same as Pa, which is bad enough. Imagine having ill people around you every working day, especially horrible, smelly ones. Showing you their tongue, varicose veins, lumpy bits.'

'You're hardly being fair,' she countered. 'Medicine is about curing folk, making them better. Relieving pain and anxiety. I can't think of anything more rewarding than that.'

'Then *you* become a bloody doctor,' he snapped viciously. 'That might let me off the hook.'

Laura lowered her gaze, the cold fury of his eyes having frightened her. 'Sorry,' she mumbled. 'I was only trying to help.'

Sandy's anger subsided at the sight of her contriteness.

'I'm sorry too. I shouldn't have lost my temper like that.'

Laura reflected that Sandy had no idea he'd always been her idol, something of a God in her book. Her handsome big brother who, at least so it seemed to her, had always had something of an aura about him. She'd always wished she was as pretty as he was handsome. But, sadly, that would never be. Though she was certainly not unattractive, and hopefully would improve as she got older, she'd never be as good looking as Sandy whom over the years she'd worshipped from afar.

'Can you keep a secret?' Sandy queried earnestly.

The abrupt change in conversation took her aback. 'Of course.'

'No, I mean it, really. Cross your heart and hope to die. All that sort of muck?'

Laura nodded, wondering what on earth he was about to confide to her.

Sandy got up from his desk and crossed over to where his painting things were, delving amongst the mess and clutter that was there. He grunted when he produced a nearly full half-bottle of whisky. 'If Ma or Pa knew I kept alcohol in the house they'd have a seizure,' he grinned.

Laura watched, a little in admiration she had to confess, as he poured himself a large one which he topped up from a bottle of lemonade standing on his desk.

'Bottoms up!' he toasted.

Sandy took a deep breath and then slowly exhaled. 'That's better. First of the day.'

He sat down again and smiled at her. 'Shocked?'

Was she? 'More surprised.' She gestured towards the

bottle. 'That stuff is expensive. Where do you get the money from? I thought the allowance Pa gives you was only a small one.'

'It is,' Sandy confirmed. 'But I have ways and means. Other irons in the fire, so to speak.'

This side of him was a revelation to Laura. 'What sort of other irons?'

He winked conspiratorially. 'Ones that make me a fair old income on the side.' And with that he had another swallow.

'Can I try it?'

He stared at her in amazement. 'Don't be daft! Women don't drink whisky. At least, respectable ones don't.'

'Maybe not. But I'd still like to try it. I've only ever had sherry and that was nice.'

'Whisky is very different, Laura. Extremely intoxicating.'

'I appreciate that,' she replied patiently. 'I'm not asking for a glassful of the stuff, just a sip to find out how it tastes.'

Well, well, Sandy thought. There was more to his sister than he'd given her credit for. He'd always considered her something of a mouse. 'Are you absolutely certain?'

Laura's eyes were twinkling as she slid from the bed and made her way over to him. 'Absolutely. So what about it?'

With a shrug, he handed her the drink. 'Not too much mind. A sip, that's all.'

The fiery liquid, thankfully diluted by lemonade, almost made her choke. 'Not altogether unpleasant,' she pronounced eventually. 'In fact, I rather like it.' And with that she took a second, larger, sip.

'Here, hold on!' Sandy admonished, coming to his feet and taking the glass from her. 'I don't want you getting drunk.'

She giggled, already a little light-headed. 'It certainly beats sherry. By a mile.'

Sandy saw off what remained in the glass and promptly poured himself another. He suddenly realised he was enjoying her company.

'So, tell me about these irons in the fire you have,' Laura prompted.

In for a penny in for a pound, he thought. He'd already let her into his secret about keeping booze, why not the rest of it? Staring into her face he reckoned she'd keep shtum. 'I run a book amongst the other students,' he informed her.

Laura frowned, not comprehending. 'What kind of book?'

'A racing book. I take bets on horses and dogs. It's extremely lucrative. Most of the time anyway.'

She was dumbfounded. 'Isn't that illegal?'

He shrugged. 'There's a need and I provide for it. Look at it that way. It doesn't harm anyone except the poor mugs who lose money and that's their fault for betting in the first place. Some of those chaps have pots of boodle coming from very well-off families. They can afford to lose.'

'But they don't lose all the time, surely?'

'Of course not. But overall they do. When it comes to betting there's only one person makes a profit at the end of the day, the bookie. *Me*, in other words.'

Laura, her mind whirling, returned to the bed. This was fascinating, exciting too. 'So how much do you make a week?'

Sandy pulled a face. 'Depends. It varies. And occasionally I'll be out of pocket. But on average, evening it out, I'd say roughly six quid a week, give or take a bob or two.'

Laura gasped. That was the weekly take-home pay of a working man. More actually. Considerably more in some cases. 'How long have you been doing this?'

'About a year now. Good idea, eh?'

She had to admit it was. 'As long as you know what you're doing.'

'Don't worry on that score. I do.'

She regarded him with now undisguised admiration. 'What do you spend it on?'

'This and that. And what I don't need I put in the bank. I've already put by a tidy sum, thank you very much. It just grows and grows.'

'Well done you,' she acknowledged. 'And what else?'

'How do you mean?'

'You said irons, plural.'

Sandy shook his head. 'Then it should have been singular. That's the one and only thing I have going on the side.'

'You're incredible, truly you are,' she stated wonderingly. 'And terribly clever.'

The compliment pleased him, enormously. He reflected on how liberating it was to have his own income and not have to rely totally on handouts from his father, who could be parsimonious to say the least. The very epitome of a tight-fisted Scotsman if ever there was.

'You won't breathe a word, will you?' he queried. 'You promised.'

'Not to a single soul,' she assured him.

'Good.'

Laura dropped her gaze, suddenly shy and hesitant again. 'I'm glad I came in to visit.'

'I'm glad you came in too. I was bored witless poring over these musty old books.'

'Can I come another time?'

Why not? he thought. Particularly if it gave him an excuse to stop studying for a while. 'If you like.'

'Then I will.'

Sandy glanced at the clock on the mantelpiece and decided he'd had enough 'work' for one night. He'd have another dram after Laura had gone and then take himself to bed.

As though reading his thoughts Laura pushed herself off the bed. 'I'd better go downstairs and say goodnight to Ma and Pa.'

'Just don't let them smell that whisky on your breath,' he warned. 'There'll be hell to pay if they do.'

'I hadn't thought of that,' she acknowledged. 'I'll make sure they don't.'

Laura headed for the door, then paused. 'Sandy?'

'What?'

Crossing quickly to him she kissed her brother on the cheek. 'Thanks.'

He didn't reply to that, merely smiled.

Moments later Laura had left, the door snicking quietly shut behind her.

Sweet, Sandy thought. He hadn't realised how sweet his sister could be. And how grown up she'd become. Well . . . almost. For some reason he felt extremely happy, certainly better than he had before she'd appeared.

* * *

He couldn't sleep. He didn't know how long he'd been lying there, his mind churning. Instead of tiredness all he felt was a restless energy.

He idly toyed with the idea of getting up and painting. He hadn't touched his present canvas for five days now, thanks to all the damned studying he had to do for the forthcoming exams, which his father would be expecting him to do well in.

Sandy groaned in the darkness. There was about as much likelihood of that as there was of him sprouting wings. The trouble was he had no interest in Medicine, none whatsoever. And without interest how could he possibly learn and excel, the sense of application simply wasn't there. Duty, yes. But not application.

Christ, if only things were different, if only his father wasn't so insistent on his career, if only his father didn't expect so much of him, was more approachable – which he wasn't in the least – about a different profession.

If the choice had been up to him there wouldn't have been any contest. None at all. He'd have become a professional artist or at least had a damn good try at it.

All right, he knew what the odds were against success in that field, especially living in Glasgow where the arts weren't exactly given prominence. Token gestures were made, the art gallery for one, the theatres for another. Although in the case of the latter it was mainly shows of a variety and musical nature that were put on with the accent, literally, very heavy on the Scottishness of them. Harry Lauder would pack a theatre every time, he and other acts of the same, and similar, nature.

Ballet? That was a laugh. Not that he was very keen on it himself, but then how could he be as he'd never seen any. Despite this omission he was certain he would have hated it.

The most amazing thing as far as he was concerned was that Glasgow had a first-class art school housed in a beautiful building designed by Charles Rennie Mackintosh.

Given the choice that's where he would be, learning about and practising a subject he adored, instead of reading Medicine, being taught how to be a human butcher and plumber as he always described it, though never in the hearing of his father who would have been outraged and probably had apoplexy on the spot.

Of course, Father apart, the burning question to which he didn't have an answer, was if he was good enough ever to be a professional painter. There were times when he thought he might have enough talent, others when he considered it a ridiculous idea. An absurd presumption on his part.

One thing was certain, he'd have to work very hard at it, and learn a great deal, before he could ever possibly achieve such a lofty ambition.

A professional painter, living off the proceeds of his work! He sighed at the prospect. Following in the steps of Constable, Turner, Degas, Monet, Titian, and so many others. His skin felt prickly all over at the thought.

If only he could have gone to Art School then the question of his talent, or possible talent, might have been resolved one way or the other. But that wasn't to be; for the rest of his life it would merely remain a dream, the question of his potential forever a mystery.

No, his lot would be to be an amateur, painting for fun in his spare time, never as a livelihood.

Despair filled him; deep, black despair. That and anger that he couldn't have what he wanted above all else.

Sandy turned over onto his side to stare into the darkness, a darkness that seemed to reach deep inside him to the very depths of his being.

A Glasgow doctor with some pretty little mouse of a wife in time, and then no doubt children, all chaining him to the pillar of respectability that he so shied away from. He wasn't cut out for that, never in a million years. His soul was the rebellious sort, not destined to be confined by the restrictions of cosy hearth and home. His soul wanted to soar free, to wing its way wherever it wanted.

He groaned, knowing he was about as near sleep as he'd been earlier, in other words miles away. What torture it was lying there thinking about things, so desperately desiring something other than had been given him in life. He knew he should be thankful; his parents loved him, if in that peculiarly cold Calvinistic way; his father was well-to-do – money, within reason, was never a problem, there was always good food on the table and a roof over his head. Far removed from the life of many in Glasgow where there was so much grinding poverty and where the men, even when lucky enough to be in work, toiled in backbreaking graft in heavy industry such as the shipyards, steelworks, foundries and factories. Their only relief in life was to get roaring drunk on a Friday night, as they spent most of what they'd earned during the previous week, while at home the anxious wives fretted about how much of the pay packet would be left when their man finally came stumbling, usually incoherent, through the door.

And yet such men and women had a majesty about them, an incredible dignity etched indelibly on their faces. Pain, passion, sorrow, bewilderment, hope and anguish, anger and even, on occasion, the sheer joy of being alive. The indomitable human spirit showing through despite the crushing burden that was their day-to-day existence.

Like a bolt out of the blue it came to Sandy that that was what he should be painting, the working-class folk of Glasgow in all their grim reality.

'Oh!' he breathed aloud, excited at the thought. More than excited, exhilarated. He would sketch them, then come home and execute what he'd sketched in oils. Dull colours, greys and blacks and weak yellow, the colours that were Glasgow. No reds and blues here, or if so only sparingly, just the colours of dirt, grime, soot and flame.

He'd start sketching soon, he promised himself. That very weekend! Every available minute he could find.

And then his heart sank again, remembering the forthcoming exams he had to study for.

He swore long and vehemently.

'I'm worried about Alexander,' Harriet McLean declared to her husband Mathew across the breakfast table. Sandy and Laura had already excused themselves to go to university and school respectively.

Mathew, a tall thin man with a bony face and pencil-thin moustache, glanced at her in surprise. 'Why's that?'

Harriet considered her words carefully. 'He's so . . . well, restless of late. Forever fidgety. And he doesn't look well, he's decidedly peaky.'

Mathew snorted. 'Speaking as a doctor, and his father, let me assure you there's nothing wrong with him. No doubt he's simply distracted about his exams. Perfectly natural, my dear. Perfectly. And even if it isn't his exams, boys of that age are quite often odd, it's part of the growing-up process.'

'Do you really think so?'

'I'm certain of it. I seem to recall behaving somewhat similarly when I was twenty or thereabouts. It's just a stage, no more.'

Harriet remained unconvinced, though she didn't say so. Mathew hated being contradicted in any way. An iron tonic, she thought. Perhaps that might help. She had an appointment for a corset fitting later that morning. She made a mental note to drop into the pharmacist's directly afterwards.

It had been a good day for Sandy from the betting point of view. His net profit, after all bets had been settled, was seven pounds two and six for the week. Terrific.

He stopped outside The Clachan, a pub he often came to on a Saturday night as it was frequented by art students whom he enjoyed mingling with. Other medical students invariably went to the Union, the university bar where drinks were cheaper than elsewhere, but he much preferred The Clachan despite it being more expensive. He plunged into the heady atmosphere of cigarette smoke and loud conversation.

He went downstairs where the younger people gathered; upstairs was for the locals and older generation.

Right away he spotted Grant Bell, an acquaintance

of his who lived out on the southside where he worked as an apprentice engineer. The pair of them had got talking in the pub one night, about philosophy of all things, and since then kept one another company when there.

'You all right? You're late,' Grant said, eyeing the large and ornate clock behind the bar.

'I'm fine. Got held up, that's all.' He'd been delayed waiting for one of his punters he had to settle up with.

The barmaid, an ancient crone who must have been in her seventies, had dyed orange hair and a face like a prune. Her name was Myrtle. Sandy waved to catch her attention. 'A pint and a hauf,' he ordered when she bustled over. The hauf meant whisky.

Grant glanced about him. 'There's no decent talent in yet, but it's early. Something might turn up.'

Sandy grinned. Grant, not exactly the best-looking of men, was always trying to chat up the women who came down there and, to Sandy's knowledge, had never succeeded in getting off with one. 'Aye, you never know your luck.'

Grant's eyes flicked back to Sandy. 'Do I detect a hint of sarcasm in your voice, you cheeky sod?'

Sandy assumed an expression of innocence, knowing this was only good-natured banter. 'Not at all. As if I'd be sarcastic.'

Grant grunted, thoroughly enjoying himself. 'There's a table free. Do you fancy sitting down?'

It was unusual to get a table so late. 'You grab it and I'll be over in a mo'.' He drained the whisky as Grant moved away and instantly beckoned to Myrtle for a refill.

'This is Martin Benson, a pal of my brother's. They

15

went to school together,' Grant said, introducing Sandy to a chap who appeared to have joined them.

Sandy placed his drinks on the table and extended a hand. 'Pleased to meet you, Martin. I'm Sandy McLean.'

'Aye, Grant just mentioned.'

Sandy took an instant liking to the man who had dark auburn hair and pale blue Celtic eyes. 'I see from your scarf you're at the Art School,' Sandy said as he sat down.

'That's right. Second year.'

'Enjoying yourself?'

Martin shrugged. 'I don't know about enjoying, but it's good. Aye, definitely that.'

Sandy was filled with envy and jealousy which he did his best not to show. How he wished he was there.

'And yourself?'

'Medical School.'

Martin nodded, but didn't make any comment.

'Holy fuck, will you look at what just walked in,' Grant swore softly.

Sandy followed Grant's gaze to fasten his own on the most stunning of women who was with a chap slightly older than herself. Sandy guessed her to be in her mid-twenties. She was absolutely gorgeous. A real knockout.

'Lucky bastard, whoever he is,' Grant said, meaning the chap with the woman.

'You should see her stripped, she's really something then,' Martin declared in an offhand manner.

Both Sandy and Grant turned to stare incredulously at him. 'You've seen her naked?' Grant croaked.

'Quite a few times.' Martin grinned. 'The last being this afternoon.'

Sandy was dumbfounded, not knowing what to say to that.

Martin was enjoying his little tease, all the more because it was true. 'She's French, all the way from Gay Paree. And her name's Sophie.'

French, Sandy mused. Now that he thought about it she did have a foreign look about her.

'How . . . how . . . ?' Grant sort of spluttered.

Martin laughed, deciding to put them out of their agony. 'She models for us in life classes.'

'Oh my God,' Grant whispered.

Sandy went back to staring at the French woman, trying to envision her nude. The picture he conjured up made his throat constrict.

'If I get a chance I'll introduce you later,' Martin declared. 'She's very nice. You'll like her.'

'*Like* her? I'm already in love,' Grant sighed, causing the other two to laugh.

As it transpired that chance never came. Minutes later, Sophie and her male companion left.

Sandy's gaze followed her up every inch of the stairs until she disappeared from view.

Chapter 2

'Can I ask you something?'

Laura turned to look at her friend, Madeleine Abercrombie. The pair of them were out for a Sunday stroll in Kelvingrove Park, something they often did when the weather was good. 'Of course, Madeleine.'

Madeleine cleared her throat, horribly aware that she was blushing. She and Laura had been best pals since their first-ever day at Laurel Bank School, and they were now as close as sisters. 'It isn't easy,' she mumbled. 'I mean, I'm embarrassed.'

Laura frowned. She indicated a nearby bench. 'Would you like to sit down?'

'Please.'

Once seated Madeleine fiddled with the fancy umbrella she was holding, which was similar to Laura's. As it was a beautiful day the umbrellas were for purely decorative purposes, part of a well-brought-up young lady's ensemble on such an occasion.

'So?' Laura prompted.

Madeleine glanced sideways at Laura, her cheeks now flaming scarlet. 'I wouldn't ask another single soul this. Honest.'

When her friend didn't go on Laura nodded, urging her to do so.

'I mean, I just couldn't,' Madeleine added in a tremulous voice.

'I'm flattered.'

Madeleine took a deep breath, and slowly exhaled. 'It's about men. I know absolutely nothing about them. What . . .' she gulped. 'What goes on between them and women to make babies?' She turned away, breaking eye contact. 'I thought, well, you coming from a medical family, your father being a doctor and Sandy studying to be one, you were bound to know.'

'I see,' Laura replied quietly.

'I have tried to . . . well I did broach it with Ma once, in a sort of roundabout way, but she wasn't forthcoming at all. In fact she couldn't have been more evasive.'

Laura could well believe that. Her own mother would have been just the same.

'Is it something to do with kissing and tummy buttons?' Madeleine queried.

Laura shook her head, her own knowledge on the subject extremely scant. 'No, it isn't. First of all, do you know the difference between men and women?'

'Sort of. Don't they have some kind of "thing" between their legs?'

'That's right. At least, so I understand.'

Both girls pondered this mystery.

'How big is it and what does it look like?' Madeleine queried eventually.

'I don't exactly know,' Laura confessed. 'Although my father's a doctor he's about as tight-lipped on those matters as your mother. *My* mother too come to that. It's a sort of forbidden subject, as far as I'm concerned.'

Madeleine was momentarily distracted as a seagull flew overhead. At times there could be quite a few seagulls in the skies over Glasgow, it being built on a river and not far from the sea. She brought her attention back to Laura. 'What does he do with it, when making babies that is?'

Laura shook her head. 'I haven't the foggiest, but I'm certain it's nothing to do with your tummy button. And it can't be kissing, I've seen lots of people kiss.' She hesitated. 'Well, not many kiss in that way. Husband and wife so to speak. Kissing just wouldn't make any sense at all. Not if you think about it.'

'I suppose so,' Madeleine sighed.

'It's my belief, and I'm not sure where the idea came from, that a man's "thing" as you call it, is something like a spigot.'

Madeleine's eyes opened wide. 'A spigot?'

'Like you get on a barrel.'

Madeleine tried to imagine that between a man's legs, and couldn't. It was too ludicrous for words.

'A spigot,' Madeleine repeated, fighting back the urge to laugh.

This was a subject Laura had thought about herself from time to time, but how to find out details? 'Why are you asking anyway?' she queried.

Madeleine shrugged. 'Just curious, that's all.'

'What made you think about it now, today?'

Madeleine shrugged again and didn't reply.

They sat in silence for a little while, each lost in thought and conjecture. The silence was finally broken when Laura proposed they resume their walk.

'If I do find out I'll tell you,' Madeleine suddenly declared.

'And I you.'

'Promise?'

'Promise.'

Madeleine shivered slightly. 'I just hope it isn't too horrible, that's all.'

Laura hoped so too. Somehow she didn't think it could be. Or could it?

While Laura and Madeleine were taking their stroll, Sandy was down at the Broomielaw, right on the River Clyde, where the ships were loaded and unloaded. A hive of activity during the working week, now it was quiet with an air of serenity about it. Dotted around the quayside were tall, motionless cranes, like skeletal beasts having a well-earned rest.

Groups of men stood on the street corners chatting amongst themselves, passing the time of day. This was customary on a Sunday when there was absolutely nothing else to do. Glasgow entirely closed down for the Sabbath. Not a single pub, shop or any other convenience would be open; so strict was the rule that even the swings in the parks remained chained together.

Sandy was sitting on an empty wooden crate, sketch book in one hand, pencil in the other. The object of his attention was a circle of men opposite, each in a flat cap, collarless shirt, and standard black, or dark blue, 'Sunday best' suit. From the little he could overhear they appeared to be in a heated argument about the merits of various football clubs. One man in particular had caught Sandy's eye. He was old with a leathery, weatherbeaten face, the lines on it etched so deeply they might have been chiselled. It was a face with incredible character.

Suddenly one of the men broke away from the circle and strode across the road, coming to a halt in front of Sandy to glare suspiciously at him.

'You. What the hell are you doin'?'

Alarm flared in Sandy, he hadn't expected this. 'Just drawing.'

'Drawin' what?'

Sandy prayed there wasn't going to be any trouble. The chap confronting him looked as if he could eat him for breakfast. He wasn't a big chap, but undoubtedly was as hard as nails, as most of these dockies were. 'Well, that man over there actually,' Sandy explained, pointing. 'The one smoking a pipe. Is that all right?'

'What do you want to draw him for?' The voice crackled with belligerence.

Sandy realised the group had fallen silent and were now, without exception, staring at him. 'He's got an interesting face. At least, I think so.' Sandy was doing his best to try to sound as friendly as possible.

The man was still glaring at him. 'Are you anythin' to dae with the Polis?'

That took Sandy aback. 'No, nothing,' he stuttered.

'Are ye sure?'

'Positive.'

'They come down here out of uniform sometimes trying to find things out. Snoopin' like, the bastards.'

'But why would they do that?'

22

The glare became an expression of foxy cunning. 'No ideas meself. Maybe they think there's the odd bit of jiggery pokery goes on from time to time. If they do they're barkin' up the wrong bloody tree.'

The man extended a rough and callused hand. 'See's that here.'

Sandy gave him the sketch book which the man looked at. After a few seconds he nodded his approval. 'That's Archie right enough. A good likeness.'

'Thank you,' Sandy acknowledged in relief.

The man flicked through the book, briefly studying the other sketches it contained. 'You have a talent, son, I have to admit.'

The eyes were suddenly back boring into Sandy's. 'And ye're nothin' to do with the Polis or Excise?'

'I'm a medical student,' Sandy explained. 'This is just my hobby.'

The man grunted. 'Wait here.' And with that he rejoined the others, the sketch book being given to the man Sandy had been drawing, and then to each man in turn.

The one who'd addressed him now returned and handed the book back to Sandy. 'Archie says his nose isn't as big as that, but otherwise thinks it's jim dandy.'

Sandy gave Archie a brief wave and was rewarded with a thumbs-up.

'If you want to draw faces and characters, then that pub down the road there, Betty's Bar,' the man said, pointing, 'is where you should be on a Friday and Saturday night.' The man laughed, a rasping rumble. 'Oh, you'll see some interesting faces in there awright. It's full of them.'

'Thank you. Maybe I will try it one weekend.'

'If you do and anyone attempts to gie you trouble just tell them you're a pal of Mick Gallagher. Got that?'

Sandy nodded. 'Got it. Thanks.'

'Same if you come here again on a Sunday. Any hassle then mention my name and you'll be awright.'

'Thanks again.'

Mick regarded him shrewdly. 'What's yours by the way?'

'Sandy McLean.'

'And where do you live, Sandy?'

'Lilybank Gardens in Hillhead.'

'Off the Byres Road?'

Sandy nodded. 'That's it.'

'Right then. Good luck to you, Sandy. Maybe see you in Betty's Bar.'

'Possibly.'

Sandy sketched for a while longer until the men broke up and went their various ways, Mick giving him a cheery wave as he walked off. Sandy returned the gesture.

Betty's Bar, Sandy mused as he headed for the nearest tram stop. It sounded a right dive. And fascinating.

It was later that week, during which Laura had often mulled over her conversation with Madeleine, that the idea popped into her head. Of course, she thought. Obvious really. The only question was, when would it be safe?

'What are you doing in here?'

Laura started, not having heard Sandy come in, engrossed as she was in one of his many art books. 'Sorry,' she mumbled.

Sandy closed the door behind him, angry at having found her in his bedroom without permission. 'I don't go into your room, so why come into mine?' he accused, eyes glinting his anger. Inviting her in when he was there was one thing, but this was quite another. It surprised him she'd taken the liberty. He waited for an explanation.

Laura closed the book and laid it on his desk. 'You're not usually home this early on a Sunday night.'

So this was planned, he realised, still mystified. 'The pub wasn't very good. Just one of those things. I got fed up and decided to leave.'

Laura was desperately trying to think of something other than the real reason for her being there.

Sandy crossed to his desk and stared at the book she'd been holding. 'Why the sudden interest in art?'

She shrugged.

Sandy went to where he kept his bottle of whisky hidden and proceeded to pour himself a large one. As far as he could remember it was at more or less the level he'd left it so it didn't appear that that was the motive behind her intrusion.

'I'm waiting,' he demanded harshly.

Laura felt completely wretched. It had taken her ages to get the opportunity to sneak off upstairs and now she'd been caught in the act. How on earth could she possibly tell Sandy why she was there? She would absolutely die of embarrassment if she did.

'Was it that book in particular?' Sandy probed.

She shook her head.

He was becoming exasperated. This just didn't make sense and was quite out of character for Laura. At least, as far as he knew it was.

Picking up the book he opened it and started to flick through some of the pages. For the life of him he couldn't work out what she'd been after.

'Can I go please?' she croaked.

'Not until you explain yourself.'

Tears appeared in her eyes. 'Please, Sandy?'

'If you're after something and I let you go then you'll just come back another time, so it's best dealt with here and now. Out with it, Laura.'

She couldn't look him in the face. This was awful. 'You'd laugh at me.'

'No I won't.'

'You would.'

He sighed, this was getting him exactly nowhere. But his curiosity had been aroused and he wasn't about to let her off the hook. 'Come on,' he cajoled. 'It can't be that bad. And I am your brother, don't forget. If there's something you want just say and you can have it.'

It was out of the question her taking any of his books to her own room, certainly not the ones she'd been searching for. There was too big a chance of discovery for her to do that.

Sandy decided to change tack. 'Would you like a sip of this whisky?'

Laura swallowed hard. 'If you don't mind.'

'Not in the least. But just a sip don't forget, apart from anything else you're under age.'

She had a sip and moments later felt better. Even that small amount of alcohol made her body relax and calmed her somewhat. On impulse, and despite what he'd said, she took a proper swallow.

'Hey!' Sandy exclaimed. 'I told you not to do that.'

She found herself smiling as he took the glass from her. She could get to like whisky and lemonade she thought. She could get to like it a lot.

'I can just go,' she stated. 'You can't keep me here.'

'No?'

'No.'

True, he reflected. He could hardly have a tussle with his own sister. Nor was there a lock on the door. 'Fine,' he replied. 'Leave. I'll simply have a word with Ma and you can explain to her what you were doing rummaging around in my room.'

'I wasn't rummaging,' she protested.

'I'd call it that. Going through my things is rummaging.'

'I wasn't going through your things,' she retorted fiercely. 'I was glancing through some of your books.'

'But why? That's the question.'

Would he tell Ma on her? She quite believed he would. 'Sod,' she whispered.

He wagged a finger at her. 'That's not a word a supposedly good little girl like you should use.'

'I'm not little,' she snapped back. 'I'm grown up.'

'At fifteen?' he mocked.

'Well almost,' she conceded.

He was beginning to enjoy this.

Laura knew she'd been cornered. If she didn't tell Sandy why she was there then she'd have Ma to deal with, a far more daunting proposition. It was impossible to lie to Ma, she always saw right through you.

Laura took a deep breath, admitting defeat. How humiliating this was going to be. Totally and utterly. 'Let me have another sip,' she requested.

'No.'

'I need it to get the courage to speak.'

Sandy was now intrigued. He returned the glass to her and watched her have another swallow rather than the sip she'd asked for. Christ, he thought, half in admiration.

Laura went slowly to the fireplace and stood facing it, her back to Sandy. It would be easier this way.

'I'm still waiting,' he urged.

'Promise not to laugh?'

'I said I wouldn't.'

'You swear?'

'Oh for God's sake, Laura, I swear. Now get on with it.'

It was now or never, she thought, steeling herself. 'Madeleine and I were having a chat on Sunday, and we discovered . . . discovered . . .' She gulped. 'That we didn't know how babies were made. Or what a man's "thing" looks like.'

Sandy was stunned, this was not at all what he'd been expecting. Laura was right, his first impulse was to laugh, but, keeping to his word, he didn't.

'I see,' he murmured.

'It's so difficult to find out anything,' Laura went on. 'It's all such a mystery.'

Well, Sandy thought. Well, well, well. He finished off what remained in his glass then, returning to the bottle, poured himself a huge one to which he didn't add lemonade. He needed this one neat.

Laura remained silent, her back still to her brother.

Sandy was at a loss what to reply, wishing he hadn't persisted in making her confess. 'It is something of a taboo in polite circles,' he admitted. 'People just don't discuss it.'

'So how are we supposed to learn?' she queried.

Good question, he reflected. He'd heard of cases where women had gone to their wedding night blissfully unaware of what was about to happen. He was certain it must be different amongst the working classes where such matters would surely be more open, living as they so often did in overcrowded rooms with no privacy.

'I tried several of your medical books but didn't know what to look under,' Laura stated. 'Then I started leafing through your art ones trying to find a nude male. I couldn't. Females yes. But no males.'

A right pickle he'd landed himself in, he thought ruefully. What now? Explain what he could, or leave her in the dark?

'Sandy?'

Half the whisky in his glass vanished down his throat. He was becoming a little drunk, he realised. Good. Good. More whisky went the way of the other.

'Sit down,' he instructed. 'At the desk would be better,' he added when she moved towards his bed.

First things first, he thought, having decided to go through with this. It took him a few minutes to locate the book he was after, drawings by Michelangelo. Opening it at the appropriate place he laid it in front of Laura.

'That's a man's "thing", as you call it. The correct name for it is penis. It's referred to, especially amongst men, by many different pseudonyms, but penis is the correct, and medical, term.'

Laura was gazing at the drawing in fascination. How small it looked, she thought. Not at all frightening. 'So what does he do with it?'

Sandy cleared his throat. 'Have you, eh . . . started having periods yet. Your monthlies?'

Her face flamed. 'Yes.'

'Well, you see . . .'

When he'd finally finished Laura was staring at him in absolute horror. 'That's disgusting,' she whispered huskily.

More whisky, Sandy told himself. He needed it.

'I mean, it can't be right.'

'I'm afraid it is.'

'And it . . . gets a lot bigger?'

'When it fills with blood, engorged, which it does when the man gets excited.'

'And he actually . . . inside?'

Sandy nodded.

'Surely it must hurt?'

'A bit the first time. But after that it's quite pleasurable. Certainly for the man, and often, I believe, for the woman. Though there are those who don't like it at all, the women that is, and only do it through a sense of duty. Or to simply procreate.'

Laura couldn't imagine . . . She gave an involuntary shudder. 'Ma and Pa . . . ?'

'Had to have done otherwise you and I wouldn't be here.'

Laura was aghast. She didn't know what she'd expected to hear, but never this. She couldn't understand why such a barbarous act could possibly be pleasurable for either gender.

'So there you have it,' Sandy declared, glad that was over. Relieved in the extreme, to be exact.

'I still can't believe it,' Laura murmured.

'Well, it's true.'

'Laura! Where are you, dear?'

Laura instantly came to her feet. 'That's Ma calling. She must want me for something.'

She had one final look at the drawing in front of her. 'Thanks for explaining, Sandy. I appreciate it.'

'Glad to be of help.'

He watched her hurry from the room, allowing the door to close before his face split into a huge grin. Her expression, when he'd got down to the nitty gritty, had been absolutely priceless!

'If you don't get a move on you'll be late for surgery,' Harriet admonished Mathew who was engrossed in the morning newspaper.

He didn't bother glancing up. 'If I am late they can just wait. I want to finish this.'

Harriet gave an exasperated sigh. 'What's so important?'

'A house advertised for sale in Kelvinside. I'm reading the details.'

So that was it, Harriet thought. How many years was it now Mathew had coveted a house in Kelvinside, an area where the well-to-do lived? Certainly many of the hospital specialists had houses there.

The trouble was, and why they'd never buy a house in Kelvinside, Mathew simply didn't earn enough money for them to do so. That didn't stop him desperately wanting one though.

'How much is it?'

'Doesn't say.'

'Whatever, it'll be outside our pocket.'

He lowered the newspaper a little to stare stonily at her over the top. 'There's no need to state the obvious.'

'Perhaps one day,' she smiled, trying to placate him. 'When our ship comes in.'

His reply was a grunt, both of them knowing that would never happen since there wasn't any ship to come in.

Mathew closed his eyes for a brief moment, living his dream. A dream that would never, could never, be.

'I do believe I'll have another cup of tea,' he declared, opening his eyes again. Now he certainly would be late. Truth was, he didn't give a damn. Let the hoi polloi wait, he'd see them when he was good and ready, not before.

Professor Leishmann might be a brilliant surgeon, but his lecture delivery was the most boring imaginable. He intoned, dropping the ends of his sentences in the way that many ministers often do. Sandy, listening to him, was having the utmost difficulty in not dropping off to sleep.

Leishmann droned on. 'Mechanically, the thorax resembles a syringe; the diaphragm acts as the piston, or plunger, being pulled down by its own contracting muscle and recoiling upwards as it relaxes. By an alteration of the ribs . . .'

Sandy had long since stopped taking notes, idly doodling instead. Suddenly the memory of the French woman in The Clachan that night flashed into his mind and before he knew what he was doing he was attempting to draw her likeness.

What a cracker, he recalled as his pencil flew. He paused every so often to scrutinise his effort.

That jammy bastard, Martin Benson, he thought, having her as a nude model in life classes. He'd have given anything just to attend a single one.

When he had her face to his satisfaction, the eyes particularly good, he thought, he began drawing what he imagined she might be like with her clothes off. All sheer speculation of course, but fun.

The rest of the lecture just whizzed by.

'I found out,' Laura announced to Madeleine, as the pair of them walked home from school.

'Found out what?'

'How babies are made and what a man's "thing" looks like.'

Madeleine stopped walking to stare at Laura. 'How?'

'My brother told me and even showed me a picture of a man's thing, the correct name for which is penis, by the way, in one of his art books.'

'He did!'

Laura nodded.

'What's the penis like?'

'A spigot, as I said. At least that's the best way I can describe it.'

'And what does he do with it to make babies?' Madeleine demanded eagerly.

Laura took a deep breath. 'I still find it hard to believe this is true myself, but Sandy swears it is.'

Madeleine listened open-mouthed as Laura recounted what Sandy had told her.

Chapter 3

Now that he was actually here Sandy wasn't at all sure it had been a good idea. The Broomielaw at night was a darkly menacing place, with the threat of danger lurking all around.

Come on, don't be such a big jessie, Sandy told himself. If it's too awful you can just turn round again and leave. He pushed open the badly chipped door and went inside.

The smell that hit him was a combination of spilt beer and rank human sweat. Was it his imagination or had every eye in the place suddenly focused on him?

There were three barmen, all tough-looking characters. The one he approached had what he surmised to be a razor scar running the full length of his cheek down to his mouth. The flesh around it was puckered and drawn.

The barman appeared mildly surprised to see him. 'Aye, what do you want?' the barman demanded.

'A pint and a hauf please.'

'Which beer?'

Sandy, heart thumping, glanced at what was on offer and selected one.

'Never seen you in here before?' the barman queried as he poured the pint.

'First visit. It was recommended to me by Mick Gallagher.'

The barman's expression changed to something approaching friendly. 'Are you the artist chap?'

Sandy liked that, being called an artist. 'Yes, I am.'

'Mick warned us you might be coming in. Said we were to look out for you.' He lowered his voice fractionally. 'It can be a wee bit rough in here at times, if you get ma meanin'.'

Sandy got it all right. 'Thanks for the tip.'

The barman looked him up and down. 'You do stand out in those posh clothes.'

Sandy hardly considered them posh. But there again, they weren't a workman's clothes. 'They're all I've got,' he apologised.

'Mick'll be in later. He'll no doubt want to say hello.'

'Do you know him well?' Sandy inquired as the barman placed his pint in front of him.

The barman grinned, a grotesque leer on account of the scar. 'I should do since I'm married to his sister Kathleen. Me and Mick are great pals.'

'So you're his brother-in-law.'

'That's it.'

Sandy paid and the barman moved off to serve another new arrival. Glancing round Sandy spotted an empty table in a corner and decided to sit, thinking to make himself as inconspicuous as possible.

He was amazed at the number of single women present, which was very unusual for a Glasgow pub. Normally they would only come in with their husband or boyfriend, or in groups, two at the least. Single women were rare. And then he had a thought. Unless . . . ? That could be a possibility, he decided.

As it got towards eight o'clock the pub began to fill rapidly, the men clearly intent on enjoying themselves after a hard week's graft.

Mick had been right, there were some extremely interesting faces and characters here. A tall blond man was speaking to an equally blond male companion in what sounded to Sandy like Swedish, or possibly Russian. The man would have made a splendid Viking, Sandy decided.

A couple of brown men burst in through the door, Laskars off one of the ships Sandy presumed. They seemed good natured enough.

A fat woman caught Sandy's attention. Her face was raddled with old smallpox scars while one of her eyes had a cast to it. Her bosom was absolutely enormous and she was drinking pints. Another first for Sandy who'd never seen a woman drink pints before.

'It's yersell, Bella,' another woman called out, swaying drunkenly over to the fat woman and plonking herself down beside her. They immediately fell into an animated conversation peppered with swear words.

Mick and a couple of his cronies came in and went straight to the bar where his brother-in-law immediately muttered something to him. Mick glanced over, spotted Sandy and waved. Sandy acknowledged him.

A few minutes later Mick came across carrying two full pints. 'You made it, I see,' he smiled.

'I did that.'

'What do you think?'

'It certainly lives up to what you said.'

Mick laughed and pushed a pint to Sandy. 'That's for you.'

'Thank you. You're very kind.'

'And you're helluva polite,' Mick laughed again. 'We're no used to that in here.'

Sandy didn't know what to reply to that, so said nothing.

'There's someone I want you to meet,' Mick went on. 'He'll be out in a minute or two. Tommy's gone to tell him you're here.'

Sandy was mystified; who would want to meet him, and why? 'Is Tommy your brother-in-law?'

Mick nodded.

'He says you and he are great pals.'

'We are that. Used to work alongside each other, but then he got this job which he prefers because of his rheumatism. Indoors see.'

Sandy wanted to ask how Tommy had got his scar, but decided that might not be wise. It could be construed as offensive. He was about to ask, instead, who wanted to meet him when a middle-aged and reasonably well-dressed, in the sense that he wore a collar and tie, man emerged from behind the bar heading in their direction.

Mick came to his feet. 'Aye, there you are, Bob. This is that Sandy McLean I mentioned.' To Sandy he explained, 'Bob owns the pub.'

Sandy also came to his feet. 'Pleased to meet you, Bob.'

'And me you, son. Sit down, sit down, no need to stand on ceremony.' He caught one of the barmen's eye and held up three fingers.

'I hope you don't mind me joining you,' Bob smiled, sitting alongside Sandy.

'Not in the least.'

'It's just that Mick says you're a bit of an artist, like?'

There it was again, being called an artist. He loved it. 'I'm really a medical student, art is merely something of a hobby.'

Bob regarded him shrewdly. 'Mick tells me you did a right good likeness of Archie. I don't suppose you have it with you?'

'As a matter of fact I have.' He'd brought along his sketch book in the hope he might be able to use it while there.

'Can I see it, son?'

'Of course.' Again Sandy was mystified. He leafed through the book till he found the page with Archie on it, then handed the book to Bob.

Bob studied it for a few moments. 'Aye, right enough. It is good. Archie to the life.'

'I told you!' Mick stated triumphantly.

Bob focused again on Sandy. 'I have a wee proposition for you, son.'

'Proposition?'

'Mick's idea. I've spoken to some of the lads, regulars like, and they all agree.'

The conversation was interrupted by a barman who laid three drams on the table, one of which Bob placed beside Sandy's pint, another alongside Mick's. 'On the house.'

Mick lifted his glass. 'Slainthe!'

Sandy and Bob followed suit.

'My own bottle, best malt,' Bob explained to Sandy, and chuckled.

'It's certainly good stuff,' Sandy acknowledged.

Bob became businesslike again. 'Archie has been coming in here man and boy, long before I ever bought the place, and the owner before me. Well, the thing is he's due to retire next month and we wanted to do something a bit special for him. Something more than just getting him pissed for the night. That's where Mick comes in, he suggested we get you to do a proper portrait of Archie which we'll have framed and hang on the wall. He'll be dead chuffed with that, so he will.'

'A portrait,' Sandy mused, taken aback.

'No' an oil thing, but pencil like you've already done. Though this time proper like and a decent size. What do you say?'

'Will you do it, Sandy?' Mick urged.

Sandy didn't see why he couldn't. 'Next month?'

Bob nodded. 'Three weeks the night to be exact.'

That wouldn't give him long, Sandy thought. Not if the drawing was to be framed as well. 'Will Archie be in later?' he queried.

'Should be,' Bob replied. 'Usually is on Fridays.'

'I need to get closer to him, get a better look at his face. What I did before was from a distance. To do it properly I'd need more detail.'

'So you'll do it?' Mick smiled.

'Honestly, it would be my pleasure.'

'That's settled then. Except for the money,' Bob declared.

Money? He hadn't expected that.

'What will you charge?' Bob asked.

Sandy hadn't the faintest notion, never having been paid for a drawing or painting before. His brow furrowed as he thought about it. 'Tell you what,' he said at last. 'Let's wait and see what you think of what I produce. If you don't like it, fine. If you do, then you can decide what it's worth. How's that?'

'Fair enough. It's a deal,' Bob declared, extending a hand which Sandy shook.

'Talk of the devil,' Mick said quietly, and nodded towards the door where Archie had just appeared.

Mick came to his feet. 'Leave this to me, Sandy. I'll get him close enough for you, and keep him there for a while. Awright?'

For the rest of the night pints kept turning up on Sandy's table, compliments of the management.

Sandy was smiling broadly as the tram taking him home rattled along its rails. A commission! Well, that's what it was. Of course it was. A real commission, his first ever.

What a night it had been, he couldn't remember the last time he'd enjoyed himself so much. And most of it for free too, a bonus if ever there was.

True to his word Mick had manoeuvred Archie close to where Sandy had been sitting giving him plenty of opportunity to study the older man's face. Without it being noticeable he'd even managed to make a few rough line sketches to go from when he came to do the job properly. And Archie had been right in his original criticism, his nose wasn't as big as Sandy had initially thought, as viewed from across the street!

A commission! He couldn't wait to get started. All

going well he'd deliver it the following Friday night which would leave Bob enough time to get it framed.

Providing Bob liked it that is, which Sandy fervently hoped he would.

Mathew sighed in annoyance as he laid aside the latest edition of the medical journal *The Lancet* he'd been reading.

'Are you aware you've been staring at me, on and off, for what must have been the past hour?' he accused Laura.

Laura blushed. 'Sorry, Pa.'

Harriet, who'd also been reading, glanced up at them both in surprise. 'Were you staring, Laura?'

'I wasn't aware of it, Ma,' she lied.

'Well, you were,' Mathew snapped. 'Most disconcerting. I was beginning to think I must have sprouted horns for you to find me so fascinating.'

'I suppose I was just daydreaming,' Laura lied further, mortified at having been caught out. The truth was she'd been trying to imagine her father and mother doing what Sandy had described you had to for making babies, and totally failing.

It was simply so absurd, obscene almost. Pa putting his penis inside Ma didn't bear thinking about, and yet that's exactly what must have happened.

Sandy had said some women found it pleasurable, did Ma? And what about Pa, did he?

Surely that sort of thing was long in the past now she and Sandy were here. How old were her parents, after all? Pa was somewhere in his late forties, Ma a few years younger. Yes, they had to be well past that kind of business.

Unless they wanted another child, but, at their age, it was most unlikely they did. At least to her way of thinking. Quite ridiculous.

Her thoughts were interrupted by the sound of the telephone ringing outside in the hallway. During the day Morag, their maid, would have answered it, but she'd gone home some hours previously, as had Cook, as neither of them lived in.

'Probably for me,' Mathew grunted, heaving himself out of his chair where he'd been most comfortable. He left the room, still somewhat irritated by Laura having been staring at him for so long. A strange child, he thought. Always had been. And certainly far too wilful for her own good. He had no idea where that had come from. Not him, nor Harriet either. Harriet could be strong minded, stubborn even, but never wilful.

'Oh dear, I hope he hasn't got to go out,' Harriet said to Laura. 'But there we are, it's a doctor's lot I suppose if he has. People don't realise how disruptive these things can be to home life. They just haven't any idea.'

Laura smiled in sympathy, wondering why her mother still made a fuss over something that had been happening regularly for as long as she could remember.

Mathew returned a few minutes later. 'Mrs McEvoy's baby is arriving and the midwife wants me there as she thinks there are going to be complications.'

'I don't suppose you know how long you're likely to be?'

Mathew shook his head. 'These matters are a law unto themselves.'

'You'll miss supper then?' That was a snack the Scots have usually around nine-thirty to ten shortly before going to bed. It invariably consists of sandwiches and savouries accompanied by tea or coffee.

'I should imagine.'

Harriet shook her head sadly. 'Pity. Cook has left out a particularly nice one too.'

'I may have a bite when I get back, so don't throw out what's left.'

Mathew went to Harriet and pecked her on the cheek. 'Toodle-oo then.'

'Toodle-oo, darling.'

For the rest of that evening Laura made a point of hardly looking at her mother, then only when spoken to, and certainly not staring.

It was finished, Sandy thought triumphantly. And he was pleased with it, even if he said so himself. He decided to put it up on his easel, covering the painting of the landscape which he still hadn't completed. Now that he came to think about it, he doubted he would. He'd lost all interest in the subject.

He frowned when there was a tap on the door. 'Who is it?'

'Laura. Are you studying?'

He was about to reply that he was, then changed his mind. 'Come in!'

'I hope I'm not disturbing,' she apologised as she came in the room.

'No, you're not.'

She caught sight of the drawing, and smiled. 'I say, that is good,' she declared, pointing.

'Do you think so?'

She went closer and peered at it. 'Yes, I do. Who is he?'

'My first commission,' Sandy couldn't help boasting.

Her eyes opened wide. 'Commission! You mean someone is actually going to pay you for it?'

'Well, don't sound so surprised,' he replied, a trifle miffed.

'Sorry. But as you just said it is your first ever. Don't be so touchy.'

He ignored that. 'His name's Archie and he's a dock worker. I've been commissioned by the landlord of his local pub. It's a retirement present from the landlord and the regulars.'

'How much are they paying you?' she queried, both fascinated and curious.

'That hasn't been decided yet,' he admitted. 'It depends on whether or not they like it, and if so, how much they think it's worth.'

'About a hundred pounds, I'd say.'

Sandy burst out laughing. 'I wish!'

'Well, it's as good as any professional artist could do. I've seen the paintings in the art gallery and they're certainly no better.'

'You're talking nonsense, Laura,' he protested.

'No I'm not. I mean every word.'

If only it was true, he thought. It would be a dream come true.

Laura rightly interpreted the look on his face. 'Would you really like to be a professional artist instead of a doctor?' she queried quietly.

Sandy took a deep breath. 'More than anything. Medicine bores the pants off me. Always has done. I wouldn't be at medical school if it wasn't for Pa.' He shrugged. 'But I've already told you all that.'

'Poor Sandy,' she sympathised. 'I knew you enjoyed

your drawing and painting but never guessed you felt that way about it.'

His expression became melancholy, the elation of her compliment seeping out of him. 'It's just not to be, that's all. All there is about it. Sadly.'

She went to him and touched him ever so lightly on the arm. 'I am sorry.'

'Not as sorry as me. I suppose it's simply that some things in life just aren't to be.'

Laura looked at the drawing again, marvelling at how lifelike the portrait was. She half expected the man to open his mouth and speak to her. 'Maybe you'll draw me sometime,' she heard herself say.

'Maybe,' he prevaricated.

The tone in his voice told her he was reluctant. 'I shouldn't have asked. Very presumptuous of me,' she apologised.

'No no, that's all right.' He could see he'd hurt her feelings, after her being so kind to him too. He decided to explain.

'Perhaps in a few years, Laura, when your face has acquired a few lines. At the moment it's bland because you're so young. Can you understand that?'

'You're saying it's not interesting enough?'

'Let me put it this way, I think it will be far more so when you're older,' he replied tactfully.

She accepted that, realising he was trying to be gracious. 'Well, I still think that old man is wonderful and I can't see how these people can fail to like it. And, in my opinion, no matter what they pay you they'll be getting a bargain. So there.'

He grinned, touched by her words and sentiments. 'I think this calls for a drink,' he announced.

'From your secret cache?'

'Exactly,' knowing that her comment was meant to tease.

Laura watched him as he hunted out his bottle and poured himself one, adding the usual lemonade.

'Cheers!' he toasted.

'Can I have a sip?'

He wagged a finger at her. 'You're getting a taste for this stuff,' he admonished.

She knew that to be so. 'A sip won't harm,' she argued.

'Last time you were here you were having swallows instead of sips,' he reminded her.

Her reply to that was a broad smile.

'Anyway,' he went on. 'Why are you here? It wasn't about my drawing.'

'Can I sit down?'

'If you wish.'

'After a sip?'

How could he refuse when she'd been so nice about his drawing. 'Just one then. And I'm holding onto the glass so make sure that's all you have.'

When she'd had that she took herself over to his bed.

'Well?' he prompted.

'It's to do with our last chat.'

He inwardly groaned. Not that again!

'I'd like some more information.'

'Go on,' he said slowly.

'It's detail really.'

'I'm listening.'

'You said a man's penis gets bigger when he's about to . . .' She trailed off.

'Yes.'

'How big?'

Christ, he thought. What a question. He couldn't believe he was actually having this conversation with his young sister. Or any woman, come to that.

'I suppose it depends,' he said evasively.

Laura looked puzzled. 'Why?'

'They vary in length. Some can be longer than others. Or so I'm led to understand.'

'You don't really know?' She frowned.

'Bloody hell!' he muttered in exasperation. 'No, I don't. Men don't exactly go around comparing their willies with one another.' He glared at her. 'Willies, that's one of the many pseudonyms I mentioned.'

Willies, willy? A far nicer word than penis. Less threatening somehow. And certainly less clinical. 'Don't get cross with me, Sandy. I'm only trying to find out about these things. Surely there's nothing wrong with that?'

He couldn't disagree, but it was so embarrassing.

'So what would an average be?'

He returned to the whisky bottle and topped up his glass, praying this was the last time she'd come to his room asking questions like these. 'Average?'

'Show me.'

That alarmed him. 'How do you mean, *show* you?'

'With your hands, silly. Hold them apart at the appropriate length.'

Relief rushed through him. For a horrible moment there he'd thought she was asking him to expose himself. Heaven forbid! He was only too well aware how intently Laura was studying him. 'Is this necessary?'

'Please, Sandy? I'm curious,' she pleaded, voice loaded with cajoling femininity.

There seemed to be nothing else for it. Laying down his glass he held his inwardly turned palms roughly the right distance apart.

Laura had paled. 'That can't be right.'

'Well it is. Satisfied now?'

She gulped. 'And that's what . . .'

'Yes,' he interjected.

It was impossible, she thought. Something that large could never . . . Her mind was reeling.

Sandy suddenly smiled, struck by the ridiculousness of this. Picking up his glass again he had another swallow. The whole thing was somehow surreal. 'Don't forget that where a willy goes in is where the baby comes out. It expands. All quite natural, I assure you.'

When he saw the expression on Laura's face he went to her. 'Here, have another sip.'

'Thank you,' she whispered when she'd had it.

'Anything else? If so, let's get it over and done with.'

Laura shook her head.

'Are you sure?'

Laura slid off the bed. 'I'd better go.'

'Thanks for being so complimentary about my drawing.'

She nodded, but didn't reply.

'Bloody questions,' he muttered when she was gone. Talk about being put on the spot!

He glanced over at his desk and the books piled there. The exams were only a few weeks away, he really should get down to a bit of study, but as always was reluctant to do so.

But he had to, he reminded himself. Simply had to. But that didn't make it any the easier.

* * *

Nervous as anything, Sandy halted outside Betty's Bar. He'd come to deliver the drawing which he was carrying rolled up inside a cardboard cylinder. 'Oh well,' he thought, 'best get on with it.'

He was greeted by a smiling Tommy when he went up to the bar, the scar making Tommy's grin as grotesque as ever.

'Is Bob around?'

'Aye, he's out the back.'

'Could you tell him I'd like a word?'

'Of course.'

Tommy returned a few moments later with Bob in tow. 'Hello, son.' Bob nodded.

Sandy held up the cylinder. 'I've brought it.'

The pub was near deserted as it had only been open a short time. 'Let's have a dekko then,' Bob replied.

Sandy shook the drawing free and unrolled it.

'Excellent,' Bob pronounced after what, to Sandy, seemed an eternity. 'You've done a grand job there. Done Archie proud.'

Sandy almost sagged where he stood. His first commission and it had been approved! Elation sang within him.

Bob clapped him on the shoulder. 'Couldn't be more pleased. This will look terrific when it's framed and up on the wall. Now what do you want, on the house?'

When Sandy left the pub a little later he felt as if he was walking on air.

Chapter 4

Sandy was ambushed the moment he got home by Laura, who had been keeping an eye out for him and listening for the door. 'Well?' she demanded. 'Did he like it?'

Sandy, still euphoric, nodded.

Laura squealed with delight. 'That's wonderful! I told you he would.'

On impulse he gathered her into his arms and swung her round. When her feet touched the floor again he kissed her on the cheek. 'Thanks for saying what you did the other night, about it being good.'

'But it was true!' she replied, eyes shining.

'I can't wait to see it framed.'

'I wish I could too.'

Sandy laughed. 'That'll never be, I'm afraid. Betty's Bar isn't exactly the kind of place for you. Far too rough.' He lowered his voice. 'You should see one of

the barmen, a razor scar from here to here.' He indicated the length of the mark on his own face.

'Really!'

'All sorts goes on in there, though I haven't seen
that side of it yet. They're all hard as nails.'

Laura's expression became one of concern. 'You will
be careful, I hope?'

'Don't worry, I'm protected. Firstly by my new
acquaintance Mick Gallagher, secondly by the landlord
and his barmen. If anyone tried anything on they'd
soon be out on their ear.'

'How exciting,' Laura enthused. 'I'm quite jealous.'

It *was* exciting, Sandy reflected. 'The people are all
so . . .' He groped for words. 'Different to what I'm
used to. These are real people, workers who graft with
their hands for a living.'

'Do women go there?'

'Oh yes, and you should see them. Scary to say the
least. And I do believe some are . . .' He suddenly hesitated, was this what he should be confiding in his sister,
and would she even know what he was talking about?

'Go on,' she urged.

'Prostitutes.'

Laura had vaguely heard the expression, but wasn't
at all knowledgeable about what a prostitute did. 'I see,'
she replied gravely, pretending she did know. Or at least
had an inkling.

'At least that's my guess.'

Something else she was going to have to find out
about, Laura thought. She'd look the word up in the
dictionary.

'What are you two up to?' Harriet demanded,
appearing in the hallway.

'Nothing, just talking,' Sandy answered.

Harriet's eyes narrowed. 'It looks to me as if you're up to something.'

Sandy laughed. 'What on earth would we be up to? That's nonsense.'

It was still a bit peculiar, Harriet thought. Normally that pair didn't have much time for one another, far less being deep in conversation as they appeared to have been.

'Well, you'd better get ready for dinner. It'll be served shortly,' Harriet stated as she swept away.

'I am delighted for you,' Laura smiled to Sandy. 'Let's just hope this was the first of many commissions.'

Sandy matched her smile. 'I doubt it. But it's a lovely idea.'

'See you at dinner,' Laura said and headed after her mother. Later she intended getting out her dictionary.

'I'd like you to meet the wife,' Mick Gallagher declared. 'Beryl, this is Sandy who I've told you about. And Sandy, this is Beryl.'

Sandy had already risen from his chair and now shook hands with Beryl Gallagher. Considerably younger than Mick, Sandy noted. And pretty, in a rather obvious way. He couldn't help notice, well it was rather on display, how well built she was in the bust department.

'Pleased to meet you,' Sandy said.

'And me you. I'm dying to see this picture of yours. Mick says it's terrific.'

'You sit with Sandy for a minute while I get them in,' Mick nodded to her. He eyed Sandy's nearly empty pint. 'Another?'

'Please.'

'And a dram to go with it?'

Sandy's expression was affirmitive.

'Right, won't be a tick.'

Sandy found Beryl's cheap scent almost over-powering. Despite the vulgarity of it he thought it was very sexy. As was Beryl herself.

Beryl pulled out a packet of cigarettes and offered Sandy one.

'No thanks, I don't.'

'Nasty habit, but I love my fags. I go mental when I haven't got any. Wednesdays and Thursdays usually, just before pay day. First thing I do when I get his money is shoot off down to the shop for some Woodies.' She laughed, a surprisingly deep sound. 'Pathetic, isn't it?'

Sandy decided to be diplomatic. 'I can't say really as I don't smoke, and never have. But I do know it can be quite addictive.'

'Aye, too bloody true,' she laughed, her green eyes sparkling.

Like Mick, she was of Irish descent, Sandy realised. She had an Irish look about her. And Catholic too no doubt, the minority in Glasgow, and hated by many Protestants.

Beryl leant a fraction closer. 'Mick tells me you're going to be a doctor. Is that right?'

'Hopefully.'

'That's fabulous,' Beryl enthused. 'I wanted to be a nurse mesell, applied to a few hospitals too when I was younger. But they didnae want to know. Turned me down flat. I don't think I was posh enough for them.'

She was probably right, Sandy reflected. Hospitals were notoriously snooty about who they took to train as nurses. Beryl's broad Glasgow accent would have ruled her out straight away.

He was saved replying to that by Mick returning with their drinks. 'I'll join you both in a minute,' Mick said. 'I just want to speak to someone first.'

Sandy watched Mick move away, edging his way through the crowd that was rapidly beginning to gather. 'Good man, your husband. I like him,' Sandy declared.

Beryl picked up her gin. 'Oh, he's a good man right enough. One of the best. Mind you, he hasn't been the same since his accident.'

Sandy frowned at her. 'What sort of accident?'

'At work. It happened a couple of years ago. He got crushed when an eejit operating a crane dropped a wooden crate on him. He was laid up for three months and more. Hard times those.'

'He seems all right now though.'

'Still got a wee bit of a limp, especially when he's tired. And both his legs are scarred.'

Sandy's expression was one of sympathy. 'At least you can both be thankful it wasn't worse.' He said that knowing men were killed on the docks, an ever-present occupational hazard.

'Aye, there is that,' Beryl replied slowly. 'The worst part was it wasn't only his legs that got crushed, if you get ma meanin'. As I said, he's never been the same since.'

Sandy realised the implication of that and was absolutely appalled she'd confided such intimate information to him on such short acquaintance.

'It makes life difficult,' Beryl added quietly, staring into her gin.

Sandy could well imagine. He had absolutely no idea how to reply to what he'd just been told.

In a catlike way Beryl glanced sideways at him. 'Tragic, huh?'

Sandy nodded, not meeting her gaze.

'It gets me down at times. I'm so young too. Only twenty-five. Just twenty-five in fact, last month.'

Sandy would have thought her older by several years at least. But then the working class often looked older than their actual age due to the conditions they lived under, which were often harsh to say the least. He enjoyed a life of ease and luxury by comparison.

'Do you have a ladyfriend yersell, Sandy?' she asked, apparently innocently.

Christ, he wished Mick would get back. He shook his head.

'That surprises me. A good-lookin' chap like you. I'd have thought the lassies would have been fallin' over themselves. Apart from anything else a budding doctor is quite a catch.'

'I don't have any time for girls. I seem to be either at medical school or home working,' he lied. Of course he had time to spare, otherwise he wouldn't have been there.

Beryl leant even nearer, affording him a view down her cleavage. 'That's a cryin' shame, so it is. Some poor lassie is missing out. And you such a big strappin' lad too.'

Strapping lad! He'd hardly have described himself as that. Her scent was so strong this close it was beginning to make his head swim.

'I hardly think so,' he muttered in a strange, strangulated voice. Mick! he silently screamed. Get back here!

Beryl reached across and laid a hand over his. 'Well, I do.'

A pint was suddenly plonked down on the table. Mick had rejoined them. Thank God for that, Sandy thought in relief. She'd have been propositioning him next.

'Sandy's just been tellin' me he disnae have a ladyfriend,' Beryl said smoothly, switching her attention to Mick. 'Maybe we can do something about that.'

'Don't be daft, woman. There's nobody round here would interest the likes of him. He's a cut above this lot. Educated properly and that. Well spoken. So get a grip.'

There was amusement reflected in Beryl's eyes as she lit another cigarette. 'Aye, you're probably right.'

'Of course I am. Stands to reason. That so, Sandy?'

How did he answer that without causing offence? He didn't reply, merely shrugged and had a long pull from his pint.

'Archie!' the call suddenly went up. 'The old bugger's here at last!'

Sandy could just make out Archie through the crowd, people clapping him on the back and shaking his hand as he made for the bar. From what he could see Archie looked both moved and surprised.

Bob appeared from the rear of the pub carrying the framed drawing wrapped in brown paper. A few moments later he cried out in a foghorn voice for silence.

The speech was relatively short, reminding everyone that Archie had been coming into Betty's man and boy and was a model customer to boot. A glare intimating that many of them weren't got a loud laugh.

Eventually Archie was presented with the drawing which he unwrapped with hands that trembled with emotion. After staring at the drawing in astonishment for almost a full minute he held it up for all to see, earning a huge round of applause.

'And it's to go on the wall above Archie's favourite seat!' Bob informed everyone, which received another huge burst of applause.

Bob placed the drawing behind the bar where it could be viewed by all and sundry as the night wore on. Tommy meanwhile slipped out from behind the bar holding an empty pint pot.

'I think we can safely say your drawing is a success.' Mick beamed at Sandy.

'Aye, look at Archie, he's right chuffed,' Beryl added.

'Mick's idea in the first place,' he informed her.

'Aye, he mentioned.'

Tommy was going from customer to customer, having a quiet word with each. As Sandy watched he saw money tinkling into the pot, in one case a ten-bob note.

'I'm goin' for a gander at the drawing,' Beryl announced. 'I could use another gin in the meantime.'

'That's my shout,' Sandy said quickly, also rising. It was with relief that he went one way, Beryl the other.

When Sandy returned it was to find Archie waiting for him, the old man misty eyed.

'I believe I've got you to thank for yon drawing, son,' Archie stated gruffly.

'I did it, yes.'

'It's one helluva retiral momento. Although it's stayin' in the pub I'll treasure it to my dyin' day. I just wanted you to know that.'

'Thank you, I appreciate it,' Sandy replied humbly.

'You're sure talented, by God. Good luck to you, son. Good luck to you.'

Archie stuck out a gnarled and callused hand which Sandy shook. 'My pleasure entirely.'

Archie sniffed. 'I'd better get back tae the bar. They're linin' them up for me.'

'We'll be carryin' you home the night, Archie,' Mick laughed.

Archie winked. 'I hope so. I certainly hope so. It's no every day you retire.'

'What will you do now?' Sandy inquired.

'Sweet fuck all, if I have my way. Sweet fuck all, and enjoy every moment of it.'

Mick was sombre after Archie had left them. 'By the end of next week he'll be wishing he was back at work again,' Mick prophesied. 'I've seen it before. They spend years looking forward to retirement then when it comes it's a complete let down. They wander the streets not knowin' what tae dae wi' themsells. Lost souls. I'm guessin' mind, but Archie probably started when he was twelve and knows nothing else.'

'Maybe he's got a hobby?' Sandy suggested.

Mick shook his head. 'I doubt it! If he's got one at all it's coming in here. Well, he'll have plenty of chance to do that in future, only he won't have the money to indulge hissell. No, not on what he'll have in his pocket from now on in.'

Mick raised the glass of whisky Sandy had just bought him. 'I hope I never come to that. If it was up to me I'd die in harness. So help me, God, and I would. Retirement's a curse in my opinion.'

Sandy stared after Archie's retreating back, hoping Mick was wrong in his prediction.

'So what do you make of the wife?' Mick asked, changing the subject.

'Very nice.'

Mick's chest expanded. 'Fell on my feet there. Quite a "looker", eh?'

'Very much so,' Sandy agreed. In a common way, he qualified silently. But yes, Mick was right.

'A real bobby dazzler. Every day I thank my lucky stars that I met her. Yes, sir, every bloody day.' And with that Mick turned and beamed in Beryl's direction, to where she was chatting to someone at the bar.

The man was obviously besotted, Sandy realised. He wondered if Mick had any idea of what Beryl had implied she got up to behind his back. He hoped not.

It was growing very hot and stuffy in the pub, Sandy reflected, which was only to be expected with the number of people present. The bar was doing a roaring trade.

Beryl rejoined them a few minutes later to light up yet another cigarette. She took a quick swig of gin before smiling broadly at Sandy. 'I really am impressed. That drawing's the bee's knees. Mick wasn't exaggerating when he said it was good.'

'Thank you,' Sandy acknowledged, feeling uncomfortable at the intense scrutiny from her green eyes. He decided he was going to get out of there as soon as was politely possible. Beryl was definitely trouble, with a capital T.

'Tell us more about yersell. I'm interested,' Beryl prompted.

'Ach, leave the lad alone. I'm sure the last thing he wants is to give us his history,' Mick admonished.

'No, no, that's all right,' Sandy assured him.

He hadn't been speaking for long, Beryl listening in

rapt attention, never taking her eyes off him, when Bob came over to the table.

'The collection's been taken and there you are,' he announced, placing a sheaf of notes in front of Sandy. 'I changed it up for you, thinking that would best.'

Here it was, his payment for the drawing. Sandy lifted the sheaf and counted it. 'Eighteen quid!' he gasped in amazement.

'And worth every penny,' Bob nodded. 'There isn't a single person in the pub doesn't think you haven't done a grand job.'

This was far more than Sandy had expected. A fiver at most, he'd thought, and that would have been generous. But eighteen quid! It was unbelievable.

'Thank you,' Sandy spluttered, quite overcome. What a wonderful first commission! And only a drawing too. He couldn't have been more delighted.

'You're welcome. And I hope you'll spend some of it over the bar before you go,' Bob joked.

Sandy, staring at the notes, was in a daze.

Laura woke with a start. What was that? Something had roused her from sleep. Moments later she heard a sort of retching sound coming from somewhere close by.

There it was again. Someone was . . . being sick, she realised. Quickly she slid out of bed, switched on the bedside lamp, and reached for her dressing gown.

She found Sandy in the lavatory with his head in the bowl, vomiting noisily. The stench made her stomach contract.

She knelt beside him. The reason for his condition was obvious, for he stank of alcohol.

'Christ,' he slurred. 'I'm pissed as a newt.'

'Try to be quieter,' she urged. 'You don't want Ma or Pa getting up. They'd go through the roof.'

His head was spinning wildly, while his insides were . . . He vomited yet again. Strangely, all he could smell was Beryl's cheap scent.

There was vomit on the outside of the bowl as well, Laura observed. And a splash on the linoleum. She'd clear it up after she got him into bed.

'Feel terrible,' Sandy groaned.

'I'm not surprised. Look at the state you're in.'

'They paid me eighteen quid for the drawing, Laura. Eighteen quid! Can you imagine?'

'That's a lot of money,' she agreed.

She grabbed a hand towel and gave it to him. 'Here. Wipe your mouth if you're finished.'

Was he? He didn't know. He wiped his mouth anyway.

'How did you get home?'

'Taxi.'

'I'm surprised they picked you up like this.'

'I wasn't so bad then . . .' He broke off and gulped in air. 'My head's just going round and round.' He took another deep breath. 'It was during the ride I began to feel ill. The night air, I suppose.'

'How much did you drink?'

'Too much,' he groaned.

She studied him grimly. 'Are you going to be sick again?'

He considered that. 'I don't think so.'

'Then let's get you through to bed.'

With her assisting him he came unsteadily to his feet where he swayed.

'Lean on me,' she instructed.

He had to, he'd have fallen over otherwise. 'Sorry, Laura. Truly I am.'

'You're the one who'll be sorry in the morning.'

'I think I'll probably die before then.'

That brought a smile to her face. 'I doubt it. But from what little I know of hangovers you're going to have an awfully sore head.'

He moaned in agreement.

'Let's go, one foot in front of the other. And keep it quiet.'

It wasn't easy, even for such a short journey, and at one point she thought, despite her holding him, that he'd still collapse. But eventually she got him into his bedroom and sitting on the bed.

Kneeling, she began undoing his shoelaces. She was just pulling his second shoe off when he, still upright, closed his eyes and started snoring. Ever so slowly, he toppled onto his side.

Laura wondered about taking his trousers off to make it more comfortable for him, then blushed when she realised what she was considering.

It would give her the chance to take a peek at his willy, she thought, blushing even more. It might be the only opportunity she'd get before her wedding night, whenever that might be. She was dying to see what one actually looked like in the flesh and to touch it.

She couldn't, simply couldn't. What if Sandy woke up while she was doing it? And, worse still, remembered in the morning?

Fat chance of that, she thought. He was out cold. But still she couldn't bring herself to do it. He was her brother after all.

After a bit of heaving and manipulating she managed

to get his quilt out from under him. When she finally left the room he was nicely tucked up.

'The morning mail, sir,' Morag announced, presenting a silver salver to Mathew who'd just sat down to breakfast.

'Thank you.'

He flicked through the various items, pausing when he came to one postmarked Canada. 'For you, dear,' he declared, handing an envelope to Harriet. 'From your sister, it would appear.'

Harriet's face lit up. 'I haven't heard from Cakey in ages. How lovely!'

Mathew frowned. 'I wish you wouldn't refer to her by that ridiculous nickname. She was christened Margaret.'

Harriet laughed. 'She'll always be Cakey to me.'

Laura, toying with some scrambled egg, knew the story of how her Aunt Margaret had come to be called Cakey. It seemed that as an older child she'd been forever in the kitchen baking all manner of cakes, which she simply adored doing. It was her grandparents' cook who'd given her the nickname that had stuck down through the years. She'd met Aunt Cakey only once, a long time ago when she was little. Cakey had been married to a man called Herbert who was now dead. She knew her father had disapproved of Uncle Herbert, considering him to be a 'shady character'. When Uncle Herbert had passed on, from pneumonia, he'd left Aunt Cakey a very rich woman indeed.

Harriet had opened the envelope and begun to read. 'Oh my!' she exclaimed. 'Cakey is coming to visit.'

Mathew's fork stopped halfway to his mouth. 'You mean *here*?'

'Of course, silly. Next month. Isn't that wonderful?'

'Can we have a fresh pot of tea, Morag,' Mathew suddenly snapped. 'This lot is cold.'

'Sorry, sir. Right away, sir.'

Morag collected the offending pot and scurried away.

'And where is Alexander?' Mathew went on in the same bad-tempered tone. 'He should be down by now.'

'Yes, he is rather late,' Harriet agreed without glancing up from her letter.

'I suppose Margaret wants to stay with us?' Mathew queried.

'Well, naturally, dear. I wouldn't expect my sister to book into an hotel. We have plenty of room after all.'

Mathew snorted. That would cause disruption round the house which he hated. He was a very orderly man and loathed being put out in any way, which this impending visit was bound to do.

'Cakey says she plans several excursions round the country,' Harriet informed him. 'And definitely a trip to London for some shopping.'

'Nothing wrong with the shops in Glasgow,' Mathew protested. 'There's no need for her to go to London. She can get anything she might want right here on our doorstep.'

Harriet smiled, thinking how little he knew about women. There was all the difference in the world between Sauchiehall Street and Bond Street. At least so she believed. She had never been to the latter, and knew it by reputation only.

Mathew felt his entire day had been spoiled. He had nothing personally against Margaret, except the man she'd married, of course, but he could have done without her descending on them like this. 'Where is that damned boy?' he grumbled.

'Shall I go and see what's keeping him?' Laura offered, only too aware of the reason why he hadn't appeared for breakfast. 'I've finished anyway.'

'You've hardly eaten a thing,' Harriet protested.

'I've had enough, Ma. Honestly.'

'On you go then.'

'And give Morag a shout,' Mathew added waspishly. 'Tell her to hurry with that tea.'

Laura excused herself and left the room, bumping into Morag outside in the hall. 'Pa's in a right old mood this morning,' she whispered to the maid, who rolled her eyes heavenwards before continuing on her way.

Upstairs Laura halted outside Sandy's bedroom and listened. No snoring, nothing. She tapped. 'Sandy, are you awake?'

There was no reply.

She tapped again, this time louder. 'Sandy?'

Again no reply.

Opening the door, she peeked in. Sandy was lying curled in a semicircle, eyes firmly closed. Crossing to him she shook his shoulder. 'Sandy?'

'Sod off,' he rasped.

'It's breakfast time and Pa's asking for you.'

'Can't get up. Can't even open my eyes. Make an excuse for me, Laura, please?' he pleaded.

She stroked his forehead, her fingers coming away covered in sweat. 'I'll try.'

'Thanks.'

On returning to her parents she reported that Sandy had been up to the early hours studying and now wanted a lie-in as a result. Surprisingly, Mathew not only believed her but was actually pleased Sandy was being so diligent with his work.

It was well after noon before Sandy did surface, by which time both his parents were out and not there to see his ashen pallor and pink-tinged eyes.

He couldn't have been more grateful to Laura for covering for him. He was beginning to appreciate his young sister.

Chapter 5

Sandy was sitting at his desk engrossed in working out the odds he was prepared to give for that weekend's horse and dog racing. Every few minutes he consulted one of the various sporting journals and papers he was surrounded by.

It always amazed him how good he was at this, and how profitable a business it was. Or usually was. There were the occasional times when he made a loss but, thankfully, they were few and far between.

He smiled, thinking of the lads at medical school who were his customers, most with more money than sense. Idiots, he thought of them as. Total idiots.

Sighing, he sat back in his chair, allowing himself a brief break. When he'd finished this he'd have to get his head down and study, the exams being only a couple of weeks away.

He was dreading them, absolutely dreading them,

and just knew he was going to do badly. If only he had more of an interest in medicine it might have been different, but he didn't and that's all there was to it. The whole thing left him cold.

His gaze strayed over to where his whisky was hidden and he was tempted to have a quick dram. Later, he promised himself. Later. It was far too early to indulge when he had so much to do.

He wondered what Laura was up to? Sitting downstairs with Ma no doubt, Pa having been called out earlier. He'd have enjoyed her knocking on his door and asking if she could come in for a chat. It was surprising how close they'd become of late, and a revelation on his part the excellent company she could be.

Didn't she have a birthday coming up? For the life of him he couldn't remember the date, but was certain it was soon. He must ask Ma so he could get her a card. Present too, a first on his part. Something nice, but not too expensive or his parents might wonder where he'd got the money from to buy it.

And then he knew what he'd give her. Something she'd already asked for and which he'd refused. He'd draw her and have it framed.

He recalled his argument for refusing her in the first place and it still held true. Nonetheless, that's what he'd do.

He bent again to his task, a pleasure compared to the studying afterwards.

That was tedious in the extreme.

'Where the hell have you been?' Grant Bell demanded, as Sandy entered the downstairs bar at The Clachan.

'Haven't seen you in ages, me old china.' China was short for china plate, rhyming slang for mate.

'I've been busy. Got the exams coming up,' Sandy replied. He didn't see any reason to explain about Betty's Bar where he'd been doing his recent drinking and which he'd decided to give a miss for a while because of Beryl Gallagher.

'Oh!' Grant nodded, understanding that.

'But I need a night off. All work and no play et cetera, et cetera.'

Grant grinned. 'You can say that again.' He glanced around. 'No talent to speak of here yet. Still, there's plenty of time.'

Women, always women with Grant, Sandy thought. And no success with any of them.

'Martin Benson's about somewhere,' Grant went on. 'Must be in the cludge.' The latter was a Glaswegian word for toilet.

'How's he?'

'Fine. As far as I know. Haven't spoken to him tonight yet. He's with some of his pals from Art School.'

Myrtle was busy but Sandy managed to get the attention of another barmaid, one he'd never seen before, and placed his order.

'God, she's ugly,' Grant whispered, nodding in the direction of the new barmaid. 'Got a face like a pissed-on cabbage.'

Sandy couldn't even begin to imagine what a pissed-on cabbage looked like. Still, it was a descriptive phrase.

'So how have you been?' Sandy queried, making small talk.

Grant shrugged. 'The same. Just chugging along.'

69

Martin Benson came strolling over clutching an empty pint pot. 'Hello, lads.'

'Hello,' Grant replied. Sandy nodded.

'What are you doing tonight?'

'What does it look like?' Grant retorted, his idea of humourous repartee. 'Drinking here, what else?'

Martin winked. 'Fancy coming to a dance? Should be lots of talent there.'

Grant was suddenly very interested. 'A dance where?'

'At the Art School.'

'You're going then?' Sandy queried.

'Oh aye. Wouldn't miss it. But not till later, I want to get a few bevvies down me first.'

'Are you on for it?' Grant asked Sandy.

Sandy wasn't at all sure. It was one thing mingling with art students, another actually going into the Art School itself. He had been in it once before, out of sheer curiosity, but the visit had upset him because he so desperately wished to be attending there rather than where he was. He could remember the feeling, mainly jealousy, quite clearly.

'I don't know,' he prevaricated.

'Oh, come on,' Grant urged. 'As Martin says, there'll be plenty of talent there. It's bound to be a laugh if nothing else.'

For you maybe, Sandy thought sourly. 'Is that French woman . . .' He pretended to mentally search for her name. 'Sophie, wasn't it? Will she be there?'

Martin shook his head. 'No idea. She might be. It's possible.'

'You took a right fancy to her, didn't you?' Grant teased.

'Didn't you?'

'True,' Grant admitted. 'I did that.'

'Anyway, you don't have to make up your minds right now. I'll give you the nod when I'm off and you can come, or stay here, as you please,' Martin said.

Sandy had a sip of his pint, and speculated about talking to and dancing with the delectable Sophie. He knew then, despite his misgivings about the place, that he'd give in to temptation and go.

If she wasn't there he could always leave straight-away.

Sandy recognised many of the faces from The Clachan as students who drank there, but there were many more he didn't.

'Holy shit, just look at some of those birds!' Grant swore softly. 'I think I must have died and gone to Paradise.'

Sandy smiled, there certainly were a lot of good-looking women present, some of them dressed out-landishly to say the least. There again, they were art students, he reminded himself, a breed that liked to be different.

The band, in evening wear, were playing a slow number and the dance floor was packed. Sandy looked around for Sophie, but failed to spot her. Which didn't mean anything, she could still be there somewhere, out of sight for the moment.

'Here goes,' declared Grant, and headed in the direc-tion of a group of women standing talking amongst themselves. The one he chose to ask up, from what Sandy could see anyway, was the least pretty of the lot.

He moved around a bit, edging through the crowd, trying to spot Sophie, but to no avail. Then, all of a sudden, there she was on the dance floor, laughing at something her male companion had obviously just said.

Handsome bugger, Sandy thought morosely. As for Sophie herself, his memory hadn't deceived him, she truly was sensational. A real knock out.

The dress Sophie had on was a shimmering black creation of all silk Charmeuse. It had a scoop neckline, mandarin sleeves and was heavily beaded, in a combination of black and pearl, both front and back. It was finished off with a matching tie round the waist that fell to her knees. Her hair was fastened in a French pleat, quite distinctive from any of the hairstyles of the other women present.

Sandy gnawed a thumbnail as he watched her glide gracefully round the floor, the very epitome of femininity, he thought. In his opinion there wasn't another woman at the dance who could hold a candle to her.

That particular number came to an end and those who'd been dancing applauded politely. Sophie took her partner by the arm and together they walked off.

'Damn!' Sandy swore. She was here with someone. At least so it would seem. All he could do was hang on and see if that really was the case.

He lost sight of her, as she and her dancing partner disappeared into the throng.

'Any luck?'

Sandy turned to find Grant beside him. 'She's here, but with someone, I think.'

Grant pulled a face. 'Too bad.'

'How did you get on?'

'Nice lassie, but she wouldn't stay up. Pity that.' Grant glanced around. 'I don't know what I expected of an Art School dance, but not this. It's all so very ordinary somehow. I'd have thought it would have been a bit more . . . well, lively.'

Sandy agreed with that. 'Me too.'

'The lassie was telling me that a lot of these birds aren't students here either, a lot of them are just ordinary working girls simply here for the dance. Surprised me that.'

It surprised Sandy also.

'Well, here I go again,' Grant declared, and strode smartly away. This time it was a red-haired girl he asked up.

Sandy started in the direction of where Sophie had left the floor when suddenly she reappeared with a different chap. The band struck up again and the man took Sophie into his arms.

And so it proved for the rest of the night, Sophie no sooner coming off than she was asked up by someone else. Sandy did everything he could but was thwarted at every turn. No matter where he positioned himself he was never in the right place, and when he finally did get there it was already too late.

Then she came off and disappeared altogether, Sandy unable to find or spot her anywhere. Eventually, thoroughly dejected, he came to the conclusion she'd left.

'Have you managed to get her up yet?'

It was Grant without anyone in tow. Sandy shook his head. 'I think she's gone.'

'Tough luck.'

'And how about you?'

'I'm beginning to get a complex. Is there something wrong with me, Sandy. Something I don't know about?'

That made Sandy smile. 'Not that I'm aware of.'

'I've had eight lassies up, a couple of them crackers,

and not one was interested enough to stay and have a second dance.' He shook his head in bewilderment. 'Maybe I say all the wrong things.'

'Maybe.'

'I don't have bad breath, do I?' he asked anxiously.

Sandy laughed. 'Not at all. A bit beery perhaps, but not bad.'

'Well, it isn't that then.'

Sandy made up his mind. 'I'm going home. I've had enough.'

'Have you danced at all?'

'No, I just didn't fancy it.'

'Unless with the French bird, eh?'

Sandy clapped Grant on the shoulder. 'You're hanging on, I presume?'

'Oh aye. Try, try and try again, that's my motto.'

'Then get to it.'

Sandy made his way from the hall, stopping at an open-doored sideroom where a great many drawings and paintings of all sizes were hanging on the walls. The room's lights were on. Curious, he stepped inside.

It was obviously an exhibition of the students' work, each picture having a small card with the artist's name on it pinned beneath. Fascinated, Sandy slowly made his way round the room.

Some of them were terribly good, others not so. At least not in his opinion. He stopped abruptly when he came to an oil of a nude woman whose face was partially turned away from the viewer. He had no trouble recognising Sophie.

What a body, he marvelled in total admiration. Full breasted, a little bulge of tummy, and gently rounded hips that brought his heart into his mouth.

God, you're beautiful, he thought. Absolutely beautiful. He stood, gaze riveted to her naked form, amazed that such a creature should exist. He'd thought her wonderfully good looking fully clothed, but like this, naked . . . Words failed him.

He peered at the card beneath the oil which bore the name B. Tanner. Whoever B. Tanner was, he'd done Sophie proud. He was also one lucky bastard to have such a subject to paint.

Eventually Sandy roused himself from his reverie. He couldn't stay here all night, though he might have done if he'd been allowed to.

He had one last look at the painting from the doorway, then headed on down the corridor towards the main entrance. In his mind's eye he was still seeing Sophie in all her glory, quite bedazzled by it.

He decided to walk home as it wasn't that far away, and it was a lovely night, with a myriad of stars gracing the heavens.

Sandy had hardly gone any distance at all when he was halted by the sounds of a scuffle along the lane he was passing. Two figures, a man and woman, were struggling, the woman appearing to be trying to beat the man off.

'M'sieur, stop! Stop it!'

The accent was unmistakably French, the word *m'sieur* a giveaway anyway. Sandy knew beyond the shadow of a doubt, albeit the lane was dark and unlit, that the woman was Sophie.

He didn't consider himself a particularly brave or courageous person, but he didn't hesitate. He ran towards the struggling couple and, reaching them, grabbed the man by his jacket collar and pulled him off.

'What the fuck do you think you're doing?' the young man spat, balling a hand into a fist.

'Are you all right, Sophie?' Sandy demanded, for that's indeed who it was.

'He's drunk,' she replied, voice quivering.

'I think you'd better hop it, pal,' Sandy said to the young man who was glaring at him, adding with a bravado he didn't quite feel, 'while you have the chance.'

If the young man had been about to lash out he now changed his mind. 'Fuck you! Whoever you are.'

Sandy didn't reply to that, as he continued to stand his ground.

Swearing again, the young man abruptly turned and hurried off. 'She's nothing but a bloody French whore anyway!' he shouted back over his shoulder.

'I asked, are you all right?' Sandy queried again.

Sophie's chest was heaving. 'I am. But thank God you came along when you did.'

Her English was good, Sandy thought. He glanced in the direction the young man had taken, then gestured the opposite way. 'I'll walk you down to the street where there are lights,' he offered.

'Thank you.'

They fell into step together, and Sandy noted that she was almost as tall as he. 'I hope he hasn't ruined your dress,' Sandy said. 'It's a lovely one.'

She stopped and stared at him. 'How do you know that? And how do you know my name?'

He laughed, more a release of tension than anything else. 'I was at the dance.'

'Oh! But that still doesn't explain how you know my name.'

'You came into a pub I was in once and the person I was with told me. He's one of the art students.'

She glanced sideways at him. 'You're not. At least, I've never seen you there.'

'I'm studying medicine myself.'

'Ah! You want to be a doctor. A physician?'

'That's the idea.'

He could smell her in the darkness, a rich, warm intoxicating fragrance. Whatever her perfume was, it suited her. Presumably something French. And there was certainly nothing cheap or vulgar about it like Beryl's.

When they reached the main road Sophie immediately opened her coat and examined her dress in the light from the streetlamp.

'Is it torn?'

'No,' she replied in a relieved voice.

'Good. It is pretty.'

She smiled at him. 'You're very kind.'

'Not at all.'

She reached up and touched her hair which had become partially undone. '*Merde!*' she swore. 'I can't fix it here without a mirror.'

Her make-up was smudged, but Sandy decided not to tell her that as it might only upset her further. 'How on earth did you come to be up a dark lane with that chap anyway?' he queried instead.

She shrugged. 'He's one of the students. When I was leaving the dance he offered to escort me home so that I didn't come to any harm. He told me the lane was a . . .' She frowned as she searched her memory. 'How you say, short cut?'

Sandy nodded.

'That would save time. It never crossed my mind he might try and do what he did. He's always seemed such a quiet and polite young man.'

'Well, you're safe now, so may I walk you home instead?' Adding quickly, 'And I promise not to do anything untoward. My word of honour.'

Sophie realised she was more shaken than she'd thought. 'That would be nice . . . ?' She trailed off and raised an eyebrow, the unspoken question obvious.

'Sandy. Sandy McLean.'

'That would be nice, Sandy.'

'Where do you live?'

He knew the street. It was about ten minutes from there. 'Shall we then?'

His stomach turned over when she slipped an arm through his.

'You're very gallant. A gentleman,' she said as they set off.

The compliment thrilled him.

'Here we are,' she announced.

The tenement was old and run down. One of the windows on the ground floor was boarded up from inside with planks, the glass in front of them broken. Sandy thought the whole street looked hideous and was appalled she lived there.

He looked up at the four storeys, knowing there would be three apartments, or houses as Glaswegians referred to them, on every floor. 'Which one are you?' he asked.

'The top middle.'

He nodded, trying to think of something else to say, not wanting to let her go.

'Thank you again, Sandy. I appreciate what you did.'

He found himself flushing slightly and hoped she didn't notice. 'It was nothing,' he declared modestly.

'Well, I thought it was.' She sighed. 'I must leave you now.'

Come on, he urged himself. Ask her out. Now's your chance, the opportunity you've been waiting for! 'I was wondering . . .' he began slowly. What gorgeous green eyes she had, he thought. He ached with the wish to paint them. Them, and her. He swallowed hard. 'If you'd care to go out with me one evening? The pictures perhaps, or a drink. Or both?'

She dropped her gaze. 'I'm afraid not,' she replied in a small voice.

He couldn't have been more disappointed. 'I see.'

'No you don't.'

'Of course I do. What do you know about me after all? Nothing, apart from my name being Sandy McLean and the fact I'm a medical student.'

'I know enough,' she whispered. 'If things were different, then yes, I would go out with you. But I can't.'

The penny dropped. 'There's someone else?'

Sophie shook her head. 'Not now. But there was until recently. I still . . . have feelings for him. It wouldn't be fair to go out with anyone else. Not fair on them you understand.'

'How long since you split?'

'You mean parted?'

Sandy nodded.

'Only a few weeks.'

'And you're still in love with him?'

'Yes,' she whispered. 'I'm so sorry.'

Not as much as he was. Not by a long chalk. 'I can't make you change your mind?'

'No.'

That was it then. 'In which case I'd better be off,' he said reluctantly, but that was the last thing he wanted to do.

'Goodbye, Sandy. *Au revoir.*'

'*Au revoir.*'

Her hand fluttered up to his cheek and briefly touched it. Wheeling round she walked into the dimly lit close mouth, the communal entranceway to the tenement, and rapidly vanished upstairs.

Hands in pockets, Sandy trudged back along the street. If the pubs had still been open he'd have gone into one and got roaring drunk.

Life could be terrible at times, he reflected. Now was one such time.

Sandy woke with an all-consuming feeling of dread and impending doom. The fatal day had arrived, the start of his exams.

'Christ!' he swore softly, wishing with all his heart he'd put more into his studying, that he'd listened more intently at lectures and in the lab. Wishing all manner of things.

Get up, he told himself. But his legs and torso remained exactly where they were. 'Get up!' he said out loud. And still nothing happened.

Closing his eyes, he groaned, a groan from the very depths of his being. Disaster loomed, he just knew it. He couldn't bear to think how his father would react if he didn't do well. All hell, and then some, would break loose.

He lay where he was for another five minutes before managing to summon up the willpower to pull the bedclothes back and swing his legs over the side.

As he dressed he felt he was doing so in preparation for his own execution.

'Morning, Alexander!' Mathew beamed when Sandy sidled into the room for breakfast. 'A big day ahead, eh?'

Sandy nodded, thinking he wasn't the least bit hungry but had better eat something. To try and settle his stomach, if nothing else.

Laura shot him a sympathetic smile, well aware of what must be going through his mind.

'A good night's sleep, son?' Harriet inquired anxiously.

'Fine, thank you, Ma.' It hadn't been at all, for he'd continually tossed and turned, drifting in and out of consciousness, worry gnawing his insides like a dog at a bone.

'Just toast please. And tea,' he instructed the hovering Morag.

Mathew frowned. 'Nonsense! Bacon and eggs for you, lad, you can't go skimping on a day like today. That right, Harriet?'

'That's right, dear.'

'Yes, Pa,' Sandy agreed meekly. 'Bacon and eggs then please, Morag.'

'Mushroom, tomato and fried bread as well,' Mathew added to the maid. 'The full shebang.'

The thought of eating all that made Sandy feel decidedly queasy. But what could he do? As always, Pa had to be obeyed.

'I remember my exams,' Mathew reminisced, dabbing the corners of his mouth with a napkin. 'One poor chap, can't remember his name now, looked at the paper on the first day, fourth-year exams I seem to recall, and keeled over in a dead faint. Was ever so funny.'

Except for the chap in question, Sandy thought. Poor bugger. He just prayed that didn't happen to him. What a humiliation that would be.

He thanked Morag when she brought him a fresh pot of tea, telling her he'd pour it himself. A mistake he soon realised when his hand shook. Thankfully no one seemed to notice.

'Right!' declared Mathew, rising from the table. 'Must get on. Lots to do.' He glanced at Sandy and smiled. 'Good luck, son, though I doubt you'll need it. You'll sail through your exams, I'm sure.'

'I'll do my best, Pa.'

'That's the stuff to give the troops. Right, Harriet?'

'Right, Mathew.'

'You can tell me all about it when I get home this evening, Alexander,' he said.

'Yes, Pa.'

'I'll be looking forward to that.' He focused on his wife. 'Are you going out today?'

'Perhaps. I don't know yet.'

'Well, if you do don't spend too much. You do have a tendency in that direction.'

Harriet didn't reply, knowing the accusation to be true.

When Sandy's breakfast arrived he bravely tried to eat it, but couldn't. When his mother wasn't looking he hid the fact by draping his napkin over the remains.

Laura caught him at the door as he was leaving. 'I want to say good luck too.' She smiled.

'Thank you.'

'I'll be thinking of you.' Going up on her tiptoes she kissed his cheek. 'Now on you go. And forget about Pa and Pa's expectations. Just do your best as you promised and I know you'll be all right.'

What a smashing girl she was, Sandy thought. He was lucky to have her as a sister.

Laura stood in the doorway waving him off down the street.

The first day of the exams was over and Sandy was exultant. The two papers he'd sat had been nowhere near as difficult as he'd feared. They hadn't exactly been a piece of cake, far from it, but far easier than they might have been.

A glance at his watch told him the pubs would be opening soon. He'd treat himself to a pint, he decided. He'd earned it.

His relief was palpable.

Chapter 6

'You'll never guess what I heard this morning?' Madeleine Abercrombie, Laura's best friend, said to her during morning recess.

'No idea.'

'Well, what happened was, I had to get up early to use the lavatory and I was passing my parents' bedroom when I heard these sounds coming from inside.'

Laura was mystified. 'What sort of sounds?'

'Mainly moaning.'

'I don't understand. Who was moaning?'

'My mother. And every so often my father grunted. Ma seemed to be in pain, as if . . . as if Pa was hurting her. Torturing her even.'

'Dear goodness!' Laura exclaimed, eyes large.

'At one point Ma gave, or started to anyway, a loud cry that was quickly stifled.'

Laura shook her head. This was beyond her. Why

on earth would Madeleine's father hurt her mother? They'd always appeared such a happy couple.

'And then it dawned on me,' Madeleine went on coyly. 'They were making a baby. It's the only explanation that makes sense.'

'Making a baby,' Laura whispered, her eyes, if anything, even wider. 'And you were listening!'

Madeleine nodded. 'I got all sort of goose bumpy and there was a funny feeling in my stomach. It quite upset me.'

Laura had a thought. 'Did you try peeking through the keyhole to watch?'

'That never crossed my mind,' Madeleine confessed, wishing now that it had. She would certainly have done so to witness this mysterious act.

'Maybe your ma just had wind or something,' Laura suggested, thinking her friend's surmise might not be correct.

'Then why would Pa grunt? I doubt they both had wind. I mean, surely if it was due to something they'd eaten I'd have had it too?'

'True,' Laura mused, wishing she'd been there to hear these mysterious sounds.

'Perhaps Ma wasn't in pain,' Madeleine continued. 'Perhaps she was actually enjoying it. Your brother said some women do.'

'Then why moan?'

Madeleine shrugged. 'Maybe it was a moan of appreciation that I mistook for pain. I just don't know.'

Neither did Laura. It was baffling.

'There's another thing,' Madeleine said quietly. 'I found a pamphlet quite by accident. Ma must have put it down and forgotten and I came across it.'

Laura waited for her to go on.

'It's printed by something called the Marie Stopes Clinic, and it's all about "that".'

'Making babies?'

Madeleine nodded vigorously. 'It's only a short pamphlet, so there isn't too much information, but what there is, is fascinating.'

Laura was intrigued. 'Where is it now?'

'In my pocket. I've brought it for you to read.'

Laura glanced around, ensuring they weren't being observed. 'Let me see it then.'

Madeleine groped in her coat pocket to produce a folded single sheet of paper. 'Don't read it here, take it home with you. And for God's sake don't let anyone catch you with it.'

Laura took the sheet of paper which quickly disappeared into her own coat pocket. This was exciting. 'I wonder why your mother had it?' she mused.

Madeleine stared speculatively at her. 'Can you keep a secret? I mean really keep one? Cross your heart and hope to die?'

'Of course silly, would I let you down?'

Laura never had, Madeleine reflected. They were as close as sisters after all. 'Here it is then – my mother is a Socialist.'

Laura was aghast. 'Never!'

'She is, much to Pa's never ending embarrassment. She's been one for years, apparently. Even goes to meetings and the like.'

Mrs Abercrombie a Socialist, one of the enemy? No wonder Mr Abercrombie was continually embarrassed. She could just imagine if Harriet had come home one day and announced to her father that she'd become a

Socialist, a word Mathew could hardly even bring himself to utter. He'd have kittens on the spot and maybe even throw her mother out of the house. 'Well I never!'

'Surprise, eh?'

'It most certainly is. I mean . . .' Laura shook her head. 'How can she be a Socialist with her background?' The Abercrombies were extremely wealthy, he the owner of several factories and sizeable property up north.

'Search me, but she is. She's even tried to get Father to go along to one of her meetings, but there's no chance of that.'

'How do you know all this?' Laura queried with a frown.

'The staff. They know. Nothing is ever said in front of me by either my mother or father, but the staff hear all sorts. Well, you know what it's like. Staff become rather like pieces of furniture round the house, after a while you forget they're there. Or can't hear, or can't understand, that kind of thing.'

'And the staff have told you?'

'Our cook is a great gossip. Never stops. I often go into the kitchen and have a chat with her. It's amazing what you can learn once she gets going. Not only about my parents but other people as well. Mrs Bartholomew knows all the other cooks in the street who meet up regularly for tea and gossip. That's how things get round.'

'Have you ever thought about asking her about making babies and what actually goes on?'

'Oh, I couldn't,' Madeleine protested. 'I just couldn't. She's an old woman after all, old enough to be my granny. Besides, I don't know if I could trust her not to say something to Ma. She just might. Same with the rest of the staff. I'm no more than a child to them, don't forget.'

At that point the bell rang announcing that the recess was over and they had to return to class.

'Don't forget, I want that pamphlet back,' Madeleine reminded Laura. 'I'll replace it where I found it and hopefully Ma will never realise it's been gone.'

'You have my word, Madeleine.'

'And about Ma being a Socialist?'

Laura made the gesture of crossing her heart. 'I promise.'

'Let's go back in then. We don't want to be late.'

Laura couldn't wait to get home and read the pamphlet which was burning a hole in her pocket.

Birth control, this was a new concept for Laura. Apparently there was such a thing, and it was practised by some 'enlightened' (the word used in the pamphlet) couples.

She read on: 'The idea that woman is lowered by sexual intercourse is very deeply rooted in our present society. Both law and custom have strengthened the view that the man has the right to approach his wife whenever he wishes, and that she has no wishes and no needs in the matter at all.'

A fascinated Laura finished that section and went on to the next, a testimony that was headed 1921, three years previously: 'I belong to the working class and know only too well how bitterly the working classes need the help Dr Marie Stopes is giving. I thank God every day that I visited the Clinic when I did . . . What do our lives become? We get broken in health, have sickly babies and too often have to go out to work to make ends meet. And our poor husbands have to suffer for it, you nag at them and then they pay toll at the nearest public house. I wish Dr Marie Stopes was a multi-millionaire so that she could open clinics in every town in Britain.'

Laura sighed, and laid the pamphlet aside, having devoured every word printed on it. What a lot this had given her to think about, she'd had no idea the misery so many people, of both sexes, suffered because of sexual intercourse, as the pamphlet called making babies.

One thing was certain, her appetite had been whetted and she wanted to read more, a lot more, on the subject of Dr Marie Stopes and her work.

It was mesmerising.

Laura arrived back from school to be greeted with the news that Aunt Cakey had docked as scheduled and was in her bedroom freshening up before joining the family. She'd been met at the quayside by Harriet who'd had a taxi waiting. Mathew was unable to be there because of work, and Sandy because today was the final day of his exams.

'It's so wonderful to see Cakey again,' Harriet enthused to Mathew who'd turned up only moments before Laura. He was already helping himself to a whisky. He wasn't exactly looking forward to this as he and Margaret had never really got on. 'I'm sure,' he murmured.

Harriet went to him and put a hand on his arm. 'She's gained a bit of weight. A substantial amount actually. So please don't comment on the fact. There's a good dear.'

'Wouldn't be so rude,' he replied gruffly.

'Well, you might knowing you.'

He allowed himself a small smile. Harriet was right, he was perfectly capable of it, in a humorous sort of way. But now he wouldn't as it would upset Harriet dreadfully. The smile widened fractionally. Margaret too, of course, would be offended.

'A sherry, dear?' he proposed. 'It is an occasion after all.'

'A small one then, thank you.' Both of them were moderate drinkers, Harriet particularly so.

Laura looked at the whisky decanter, wishing she could have one. Naturally that was impossible. Her parents would have been scandalised if she'd even suggested a sherry for herself.

'How was Aunt Cakey's journey over?' she asked her mother.

'Not too bad, though there were a couple of days when the ship rolled a bit keeping some of the passengers in their cabins. Cakey said it didn't affect her in the least. In fact, she rather enjoyed the experience.'

'A robust woman,' Mathew declared, handing Harriet her drink. A remark that earned him a warning look.

'And how was the surgery today, dear?' Harriet inquired, as she did most evenings.

'Busy. But then when is it anything else?' Mathew joked.

Harriet frowned. 'I do hope you're not overworking, Mathew. I don't want you laid up like you were last year.'

'That was influenza, darling,' he reminded her. 'Nothing whatsoever to do with work. Though I probably caught it there.'

'You were ever so poorly. Thank goodness none of the rest of us got it. That's all I can say.'

'Yes, that was fortunate,' he agreed.

'It's steak and kidney pudding for dinner tonight,' Harriet informed them. 'I ordered that especially as it's always been Cakey's favourite.'

Mathew had a sip of whisky. Steak and kidney certainly wasn't one of his which is why it was rarely served in their household, usually only when he wouldn't be present for dinner. Harriet knew that, which infuriated him now.

Sandy appeared, but before he could say anything Mathew asked, 'Well, how did it go?'

'All right, Pa. At least I think so.'

'Just think so?'

'Don't get alarmed, it went well. At least, as far as I know it did. That's all I can tell you.'

Mathew snorted. He'd wanted to hear that it went swimmingly. 'Care for a dram?'

'Please.'

Mathew poured a very small amount of whisky into a crystal glass, then topped it up with water, completely drowning it. He'd never quite accepted the fact that Sandy was old enough to drink.

It was another twenty minutes before Cakey put in an appearance, sweeping into the room with a broad smile on her face and carrying an armful of presents. 'Hi!' she declared in a deep, husky voice. 'How are you folks?'

A flicker of distaste flashed across Mathew's face, and then was gone. 'Good evening, Margaret. How nice to see you again.'

'And you, Mathew. But please, everyone call me Cakey. That's what I'm used to.'

Like hell he would, Mathew thought sourly. It was a ridiculous nickname.

Cakey stared from Sandy to Laura. 'My, how you two have grown. Only to be expected, I suppose.'

She dropped the presents on to the couch then crossed to Laura whom she grasped hold of. 'What a beautiful young woman you've become, Laura. Your parents must be proud.'

Laura flushed. 'Thank you.'

'Mark my words, you'll break a few hearts before you're much older. I swear to God you will.'

Sandy had taken an instant liking to Cakey, not having been sure of what to expect. He only had a dim memory of her previous visit years ago.

What surprised him most was how unlike Harriet she was. For a start she was far larger, twice the size at least of his mother, with an enormous bosom. Facially she didn't resemble Harriet at all, being far prettier, even large as she now was, than his mother had ever been. He guessed correctly she'd been quite a stunner when young. His mother, on the other hand, was neither plain nor beautiful, but something in between.

Cakey released Laura and went to Sandy, her smile a mischievous one. 'Alexander, I take it?' That was a tease, who else could it have been?

'That's me.'

'And studying to be a doctor like your father, Harriet tells me in her letters.'

'That's correct, Aunt Cakey.'

'Well, I'm sure you'll do just fine at that. Just fine.'

'He hopes to be a specialist one day,' Mathew declared proudly. 'That so, son?'

'Yes,' Sandy agreed in a small voice.

Cakey was a shrewd woman and didn't miss the look in Sandy's eyes that told her he wasn't quite in accord with what his father had just said. 'Well, if that's your dream, Alexander, then I hope it comes true,' she smiled.

'Thank you.'

'And don't forget, we always need good doctors in Canada. I have lots of connections there, important people, who would assure you a top-notch career.'

Mathew was outraged by this suggestion. 'Alexander will be staying right here in Scotland, thank you very much,' he spluttered. 'I'm sure he has no ambition to go and practise in some . . .' He groped for the word. '. . . Backwater.'

Cakey realised she'd trodden on sensitive ground. 'Now don't get in a tizz, Mathew. I'm certain, whatever happens, Alexander will do what's right for him.'

Harriet intervened, not wanting this to blow up any further. 'How about a drink, Cakey? What'll you have?'

Cakey eyed what was available. 'Scotch, please. On the rocks, if you have them.'

'Only water I'm afraid,' Mathew informed her stiffly. 'We don't go in for ice cubes in this country.'

'Scotch and water will do just dandy.'

While Mathew was doing that Cakey went over to the couch. 'I brought you all a little something. Now let's see if I can remember which is which. I should have put names on them, but didn't. Silly old me.'

Sandy looked on expectantly, wondering what he was going to get. Laura was doing exactly the same.

'These two are for you, Harriet. I hope you like them.'

'I'm sure I will,' Harriet replied, accepting both presents which, like all of them, were wrapped in gold paper and tied with matching ribbon.

'And for you, Laura.' She received only one present. Cakey laughed. 'And this is yours, Alexander. You were the most difficult to buy for. I think it might amuse you.'

A stony-faced Mathew placed Cakey's scotch on a small table beside the couch, still inwardly fuming at her suggestion that Alexander might consider practising in Canada. A preposterous notion, if ever there was.

'And yours, Mathew.'

'Oh, Cakey!' Harriet exclaimed, having opened a small box to reveal an exquisite cameo brooch that was clearly antique. 'You shouldn't have!'

'Of course I should. Like it?'

'I absolutely adore it.' Going to Cakey she kissed her sister on the cheek. 'Thank you.'

Laura's eyes widened when she saw what she'd been given. It was a dainty chain dangling from which was a diamond encircled in gold. 'Is that what I think it is?' she gasped.

'Sure is, honey. And the chain is eighteen carat, so don't go losing it now.'

'I won't. I . . .' Laura trailed off, never having owned anything of this value before. She was speechless.

'That,' said Cakey, pointing to what Sandy was holding, 'is a genuine Red Indian hunting knife. None of your tourist muck either. When I say genuine I mean precisely that.'

Sandy pulled the knife from its sheath, thinking what a fabulous present it was. He may be twenty-four but still appreciated this sort of thing, none the less.

'It's sharp, mind, so don't go cutting yourself none.'

Sandy laughed. 'It's terrific. Really, really terrific. It shall have a place of honour in my room.'

Harriet had now opened her second gift to discover an intricately patterned black and scarlet, top quality, Chinese silk scarf inside. She thought it gorgeous. 'Thanks again, Cakey. I shall keep this for best.'

Mathew was reluctant to open his present in case, intentionally on Margaret's part, it didn't match up to the others. Or was something awful.

'Well?' Cakey prompted, picking up her glass and drinking.

Mathew needn't have feared. His was a gold Bulova wrist watch, the cost of which he didn't even dare contemplate.

'Try it on,' Cakey urged.

Mathew removed the rather old and somewhat battered watch he'd been wearing for years and laid it aside. The strap on the Bulova was of finest brown leather, the buckle also gold.

'You don't have to say anything, I can tell you approve.' Cakey smiled.

'I most certainly do,' he croaked, quite stunned. 'I most certainly do.' Steeling himself he crossed to Cakey and kissed her on the cheek as Harriet had done. 'A sincere thank you.'

They had time for another round of drinks before dinner was announced.

'I thought you might knock on my door tonight,' Sandy said, when later Laura paid him a visit in his bedroom.

'I came to see what you make of Aunt Cakey?' she queried, sitting on his bed.

He laughed. 'She's different, that's for certain. I like her.'

'Me too.' She indicated his whisky. 'Can I have some of that?'

'Laura!' he exclaimed in disapproval.

'All right, keep your shirt on. Just a little would do. Pretty please?'

He didn't know why, but he relented. 'I don't have another glass.'

She quickly jumped to her feet. 'I won't be a second.'

When she returned she was carrying an empty tumbler. 'Here.'

She'd said a little would do, and that's precisely what he gave her. Adding lemonade the same as in his own. 'I tell you this, you'd never get drunk on what Pa doles out. He's so stingy with the alcohol, except with himself that is.'

Laura had a sip, closing her eyes in appreciation.

'I hope you're not going to turn into an alcoholic when you're older,' Sandy commented wryly. 'Whisky is dangerous stuff that has to be treated with respect.'

She sat down again on the bed. 'That's a good one coming from you. I seem to recall a certain brother of mine vomiting in the lavatory not all that long ago. And it was me who had to clean up after you *and* cover for you next morning when you were hungover.'

'Touché.' He grinned.

'So fewer lectures, brother dear. You're not in the position to be handing them out.'

He picked up his Red Indian knife. 'I really love this. As a present, it was inspired.'

Laura fingered her necklace and diamond. 'This must have cost a fortune. I didn't realise Aunt Cakey was so rich.'

Sandy shook his head. 'Me neither. There again, she's

hardly ever mentioned round the house. At least, not in my presence.'

'I got the distinct impression Pa doesn't care for her all that much. Did you?'

Sandy nodded. 'He was trying to hide the fact, but yes, I agree. I wonder why?'

'Well, I did hear yonks ago that he didn't approve of her husband. A "chancer" was the word I remember being used.'

'I wonder what he did for a living?' Sandy mused.

'There's one way to find out and that's ask Aunt Cakey some time. I'd like to know as well.' Laura stared into her glass, a smile playing across her lips. 'She drinks whisky too, that's another thing I like about her.'

'Not very ladylike.'

'Perhaps it's acceptable in Canada. Who knows?'

'Who knows,' Sandy agreed.

'Can I ask you something?' Laura queried quietly after a few seconds' silence.

'Go ahead.'

'Why do you let Pa bully you so much?'

The question startled him. 'No I don't!'

'Oh, come off it, you do. You're absolutely petrified of him. One word from him and you jump.'

Did he? Yes he did, he realised. 'Pa's Pa, my father. You have to show respect.'

'Respect is one thing, but surely you should stand up for yourself more? Be more of a man.'

Sandy found that deeply wounding. 'Are you saying I'm not much of a man?'

'Not where Pa's concerned.'

He went on the defensive, not enjoying this exchange at all. 'If he bullies me then he also bullies you.'

Laura laughed. 'He only thinks he does, Sandy. I'm a woman, we're more subtle about things like that.'

He frowned. 'How so?'

'Pa's quite happy as long as he thinks you're doing what he wants, as long as he *believes* he's in command and control. I learned a long time ago to agree with him, appear subservient, and then just carry on regardless.'

This was a revelation to Sandy who'd never seen his sister as the devious kind. 'You do?'

'Of course. Ma does it as well, in her own quiet way.'

Sandy poured himself another whisky, thinking about that.

'And when I really want to I can twist him round my little finger whenever I wish,' Laura went on. 'It's easy.'

'That's because he's always had a soft spot for you being a girl.'

'It's an advantage, I admit. But he still tries it on with me as much as you. I simply handle it differently, that's all.'

Sandy was suddenly depressed. Not much of a man! That hurt like hell. He realised then that Laura had far more strength of character than he'd ever have.

'Aunt Cakey certainly isn't frightened of him,' Laura continued. 'If anything she takes the mickey out of him, which is probably one of the reasons he doesn't care for her very much. Did you see that twinkle in her eyes when she was talking to him? I saw it a lot during dinner and afterwards, and Pa didn't like it one little bit.'

Sandy hadn't noticed that. The conversation had seemed quite ordinary and straightforward to him.

Spineless, he thought. Was that really him? Spineless?

'Take you studying medicine, for example,' Laura persisted. 'You've told me yourself you don't want to become a doctor, that you've no interest in it. True?'

He shrugged.

'You're simply at Medical School because Pa wants you to be there, to become what he never could, a specialist, or better still, an eminent surgeon.' She almost glared at her brother. 'Well?'

'I'll certainly never be a specialist, in fact I'll be lucky enough to qualify. As for being a surgeon, eminent or otherwise . . .' He shuddered. 'No thanks. I have trouble enough dissecting frogs, far less slicing up human beings. That's ghastly. I just don't have the stomach for it.'

Laura finished her drink, got off the bed and crossed to Sandy's desk where she refilled her tumbler. He didn't utter a word of protest.

'I think we'll change the subject now,' she declared. 'I'm upsetting you.'

She was, he thought. She most definitely was.

After Laura had gone Sandy sat in brooding silence contemplating what had been said. His sister was right, he knew that. Well, one day he'd face up to his father. One day.

Just see if he wouldn't.

Chapter 7

Mathew came up short when he saw the Rolls-Royce parked in front of their house. It was a beautiful machine, a car he'd always coveted. As he walked round admiring it he wondered to whom it belonged.

'Hello, darling, you're early,' Harriet greeted him when he went inside.

'It makes a change,' he replied affably. 'Hello, Margaret. Had a good day?'

'Very pleasant, thank you. Harriet and I have done loads of shopping. And great fun it was too.'

Alarm flared in him. Did that mean Harriet had been spending money and, if so, how much? He had to watch her like a hawk in that direction as she could get quite carried away.

He bit his lip, not wishing to quiz Harriet in front of her sister. 'I'm glad you enjoyed yourselves. By the way, have you seen the Rolls-Royce outside. I wonder whom it belongs to?'

'Me,' Cakey smiled.

His jaw literally dropped. 'You!'

'I've hired it for while I'm here. Harriet and I drove back from town in it.'

'It's so wonderful,' Harriet enthused. 'Why, I swear you can hardly hear the engine it's so quiet.'

Was that a dig at his little Austin? Mathew wondered. His pride and joy which he'd bought several years previously, the first car he'd ever owned. And a pretty penny it had cost too.

'*You* drove?' He frowned at Cakey.

'Yeah. Anything wrong with that?'

'I, eh . . .' Be honest or not? 'I've never heard of a woman driver before.'

'And judging by your tone you don't approve?'

'Well, no actually, I don't. Driving is a masculine thing, quite an unsuitable activity for a woman to do.'

A broad smile broke over Cakey's face. 'Hell, women drive all the time in Canada. It's common over there.'

Canada, he thought contemptuously. Hardly a civilised country, full of all sorts of ne'er-do-wells. Why else had Margaret's husband Herbert gone there in the first place, other than that he fitted right in with the rest of the scoundrels and misfits.

'Well, it certainly isn't here,' he replied waspishly.

Cakey was amused; trust him to take that attitude. Why, the man was so prim and proper, not to mention hidebound, she was surprised he even went to the toilet. That thought made her suddenly giggle.

'What's so funny? Me?' Mathew snapped.

'Not at all,' Cakey lied. 'It was just something that happened earlier which flashed through my mind, that's all.'

Mathew waited for her to elaborate, but she didn't.

'How about some tea?' Harriet asked. 'I know I could use a cup.'

'Good idea.' Cakey nodded. Then, she simply couldn't resist it, 'I hope my Rolls will be safe out there, Mathew?'

'Safe? Why wouldn't it be safe?'

'Glasgow is Glasgow after all. It does have a certain reputation.'

He was outraged. 'I'll have you know this is a perfectly respectable street where perfectly respectable people live. Your car is in no danger of coming to any harm.' He snorted. 'The very thought.'

'If you say so,' Cakey demurred, looking as though she was still in doubt.

'My car has been standing outside for two years,' Mathew went on. 'And nothing untoward has ever happened to it.'

'And what sort do you have?' she inquired politely, knowing very well as Harriet had told her earlier. She was enjoying this.

'An Austin,' Mathew mumbled.

'Is that one of those baby cars I've heard about?'

He took a deep breath. The woman was infuriating! 'It is sometimes referred to as that.'

'How sweet,' Cakey purred, her expression suggesting that butter wouldn't melt in her mouth.

Mathew was boiling. 'If you'll both excuse me, I have a few things to attend to upstairs.'

'Haven't you got time for tea?' Harriet protested.

'I'm afraid I'll have to forego that for the moment.'

'There are some lovely potato scones, from The City Bakeries, the ones you enjoy so much.'

Even that wouldn't tempt him to stay a moment longer in the room. 'What a pity. Another time perhaps.' And with that he left them.

'Such a charming, understanding man,' Cakey commented, wondering, not for the first time, what Harriet had ever seen in him.

Harriet pulled the bell tug to summon Morag so she could order their tea.

'That's it there,' Laura declared to Madeleine. They were in Partick, a working-class area of the city. What she was referring to was the Marie Stopes Clinic, the address of which had been on the pamphlet Madeleine had lent Laura to read.

Madeleine glanced about her, feeling nervous. She didn't like it here at all. Due to their smart clothes they both looked very out of place.

Going to the clinic had been Laura's suggestion, because she wanted to read more of its literature, as indeed did Madeleine. They'd been full of bravado setting off, thinking this a great lark. But now, faced with the clinic itself and the prospect of going inside, it was a different matter.

'What do you think?' Madeleine queried.

Just then the door opened and a middle-aged woman, very haggard in appearance, came out to hurry on her way.

'I don't know.'

'The thing is, we are only fifteen.'

'I'm nearly sixteen,' Laura pointed out.

'Whatever, we're still awfully young to be going in there. It's going to be so embarrassing.'

Laura could feel her courage rapidly draining away. She'd thought she'd be able to brazen it out, but now knew she couldn't. They were only a couple of schoolgirls after all.

'Well?' Madeleine prompted.

A few seconds ticked by while Madeleine stared anxiously at her friend. 'It'll take a bit of brass neck.'

'I'll say!'

'In fact a lot of brass neck being the age we are.'

Madeleine couldn't have agreed more. 'Let's leave it for now and think about it. We can always come back if we decide to.'

That was true, Laura thought. It had all seemed so easy, and a laugh, when they'd discussed this. The reality, however, was very different.

'Right, we'll leave it,' Laura agreed.

Together, feeling more than a little ashamed of their timidity and lack of bravado, they turned and headed towards their nearest tramstop, Laura thinking how evil smelling this part of Glasgow was. Not at all what she was used to.

Cakey had been wanting a private word with Sandy and now seized her opportunity as he walked past her open bedroom door.

'Alexander!'

He stopped and smiled. 'Yes, Aunt Cakey?'

She beckoned him inside. 'Close that door behind you.'

A mystified Sandy did as he was told.

Cakey came straight to the point. 'That hunting knife

I brought you from Canada was only a token, something to actually hand you at the time.'

'Token or not, I love it. The knife's a wizard present.'

That pleased her. 'Even so, I want to give you something else. Girls are easy to buy for, scent, jewellery, all manner of things. But boys, young man in your case, are different. Far more difficult. Especially buying for one I hadn't seen since he was a little shaver. That being the case I'm going to give you money to put you on a par with what the others got.'

He was completely taken aback. 'That would . . . Well that would be nice. I doubt Pa would approve though.'

Cakey waved a hand in dismissal. 'Then he needn't know. I certainly won't mention it.'

Sandy thought about that. 'Me neither I suppose. What he doesn't know won't harm him.'

'Exactly! Now, do you have a bank account?'

Sandy nodded; that was something his father wasn't aware of either.

'Good. In which case I'll write you out a cheque. I had cash transferred over before I left home so it'll be in pounds, not dollars.'

Sandy watched as she crossed to a chest, opened a drawer and produced a cheque book. Sitting at the table her room provided she proceeded to write.

Sandy gazed curiously about him, taking in all the female paraphernalia and accoutrements dotted around. The air was filled with a smell he recognised as talcum powder. He liked it, finding it strangely comforting.

'This is awfully kind of you,' he said.

'Nonsense. You're my nephew after all, and I can well afford it. So there.'

She signed the cheque with a flourish and tore it from the book. Rising again, she went to him. 'Buy with that whatever you wish, or you could just put it in your account and leave it there. Whatever, it's up to you.'

'Dear God!' he exclaimed on seeing the amount she'd written. 'Two hundred and fifty quid!'

'That's right.'

His mind was reeling. He hadn't known how much to expect, but certainly not this. 'Are you sure?'

'Of course.'

'It's . . . it's a fortune.'

'Hardly,' she smiled wryly. 'You can hardly retire on that.'

'I . . . don't know what to say.'

'How about a plain, straightforward thank you.'.

'Thank you, Aunt Cakey. I'm stunned.'

She laughed. 'I can see that.'

He carefully folded the cheque in two, took out his wallet and placed it reverently inside. 'This'll go to the bank right away. This very afternoon.'

She'd taken a shine to Sandy who, to her delight, she'd found quite unlike his father both in looks and temperament. It was the same with Laura who also took after her side of the family. 'You'd better run along then, I haven't quite finished dressing yet.'

'Thanks again, Aunt Cakey. And mum's the word, eh?'

'Mum it is.'

He was at the door when he hesitated, then turned back to her. 'Do you think you could call me Sandy when Ma and Pa aren't present. Everyone does, except at Pa's insistence. I much prefer it.'

'Then Sandy it is.'

'Another thing.'

She raised an eyebrow. 'Yes?'

'What did Uncle Herbert do for a living? Ma and Pa have never said and I'm curious.'

'Hmmh,' she murmured. 'Good question. It's more like what didn't he do. All sorts to tell the truth. At one point we owned half of a gold mine, on another occasion a small department store. He was forever chopping and changing, a low boredom threshold you might call it. When he died he was heavily into stocks and shares which he'd made a killing on. As his wife – there being no children, we were never blessed in that direction – it naturally all came to me. And a lot of it there was too, far far more than I'd realised he had.' She smiled wistfully. 'So there you have it, Sandy. I suppose if I was to use one word to describe what Herbert was it would be entrepeneur.'

Sandy was fascinated. 'He sounds wonderful.'

'He was,' she replied in a quiet voice. 'I miss him dreadfully. He was one of the most exciting men I've ever known.'

'I wish I'd met him,' Sandy declared softly.

'The pair of you would have got on, I'm certain of it,' she stated, her voice suddenly clogged with emotion.

Sandy didn't know what else to say, so simply left the room, closing the door behind him.

He'd only taken a few steps when he heard what sounded to him like a muffled sob.

'Hello.'

Sandy hadn't heard anyone approach. He had set up

his easel in the park and had soon become engrossed in his painting. He turned round in amazement to see the French woman, Sophie.

'Hello.'

'Don't let me disturb you.'

'That's all right.'

Sophie stared at the canvas he was busy with.

'It's early stages yet,' he apologised.

'I thought you were a medical student, not an artist?' she queried.

'I am. The art side is just a hobby.'

She studied the canvas with a knowledgeable eye. 'Hard to tell at this stage, but I think it's going to be very good. The brushwork is particularly fine.'

That delighted him. 'It's that area over there,' he declared, pointing. 'The trees with the river running behind.'

Sophie nodded. 'Yes, I can see that.'

'Anyway, what are *you* doing here?'

'I decided to go for a walk and the park is one of my favourite places. I find it relaxing.'

That was interesting to know. 'I've never tried painting in the open air before, so it's a new experience for me.'

'And?'

He shrugged. 'Too soon to tell really. But I'm enjoying it so far.'

'Scottish weather isn't good for working outdoors. It's cold and rains too much,' Sophie pointed out, wrinkling her nose.

Sandy laughed. 'Well, that's true enough.'

'Now France, on the other hand, especially in the south, that is perfect for painting outside. The heat, so hot at times everything shimmers, and the colours, completely different to the colours in this country. I don't suppose you know the work of Van Gogh?'

'No, I don't,' he admitted.

'He's dead now. But his landscapes simply burst with colour. It dazzles you just to look at them.'

'Did he sell much?'

Sophie shook her head. 'Sadly no, though I think he is a great artist.'

'You seem to know a great deal about art.'

'I live in Montmartre, *m'sieur*. Everyone there is an artist of sorts, at least so it seems at times. And all nationalities too. French, Spanish, American, lots of those, artists and would-be artists from all over the world. *Tout le monde!*'

He was impressed.

'And I have modelled for many of them.'

'Really?'

'Picasso was the last one. Have you heard of him?'

Sandy nodded vigorously. 'And seen some of his work reproduced in magazines. I found it rather disturbing.'

She frowned. 'How so?'

'Well, it . . . it's hardly conventional.'

'Is that what you are, conventional?' she teased.

Sandy couldn't help blushing. 'Is there something wrong with that?'

'No, if that's what you care to be.'

'And you, Sophie, what are you?'

She stared at him, eyes dancing with amusement. 'A bit of both perhaps. Conventional and not so.'

'I see,' he murmured. God, she was enchanting, there was no other word for it. And despite her excellent English so very French in manner and attitude. He knew he could fall for this woman, if he hadn't done so already.

'I've read about Montmartre,' Sandy went on. 'It sounded a tremendously exciting place. Maybe I'll have the chance to go there one day. I'd like that.'

'Well, be careful,' she further teased. 'If you enjoy painting, and I can see you do, you might like it so much you'll never want to leave.'

'It's that good?'

'More so.'

He closed his eyes for a brief moment, trying to imagine himself living in Montmartre making a living as a full-time painter. The vision conjured up was sheer Heaven.

'Now, I have to go,' Sophie announced abruptly.

His disappointment was obvious. 'That's a pity.'

She gave him a warm smile. 'I have to be at work shortly.'

'Work?'

'The Art School is closed for the summer so I have to make money somehow. I'm a barmaid at the Station Hotel.'

'Oh!' He knew the hotel, but had never been inside. It had always looked to him to be a dreary place. 'When did you start there?'

'I have been employed at the hotel part-time for quite some while, evening shifts only. But now the Art School is closed I'm doing days as well.'

'I see,' he murmured.

'It can be fun. I enjoy it. Now I must go, Sandy. Bye bye.'

'Bye bye, Sophie. Lovely speaking to you.'

'And speaking to you. *Au revoir*.'

He watched her walk away, hips swaying in a most tantalising fashion. If only she wasn't still carrying a torch, he thought. But she was and that's all there was to it.

With a heavy heart he resumed painting. Or tried to. It took him ages, the conversation he'd just had, and images of Sophie, unsettling his concentration.

Mathew waited till the patient had closed the surgery door behind her before sitting back in his chair and sighing. A glance at his Bulova told him that Margaret would have left by now. She had embarked that afternoon on a three-day trip in the Rolls round Loch Lomond and that general area.

An irritating woman if ever there was, who never failed to annoy him. But it had always been the same where Harriet's sister was concerned.

He stared at the Bulova wondering how much it had cost. A lot, that was for certain. If he'd been able to find out the cost of a comparable one he would have done, but Bulova was an American make and not sold in Britain, so all he could do was speculate.

Damn Margaret for being so filthy rich, totally eclipsing him and Harriet. Who would ever have thought that idiot Herbert would do so well? Certainly not him.

He gritted his teeth thinking of the Rolls-Royce, and the stories Margaret had spun Harriet about her wealth and possessions which had been relayed back to him. It was just all so totally . . . unfair. Yes, that's precisely what it was, unfair.

All his life he'd dreamt of being somebody, making his mark on the world, and have been seen to have done so. That's why he'd always so desperately wanted a house in Kelvinside.

Jealousy gnawed at him, giving him the beginnings of heartburn. His only solace was Alexander who could achieve the position, and everything that went with it, that he'd always craved for himself.

Mathew rubbed his forehead. This was getting him nowhere and there were patients waiting outside to be attended to. What a mean and rotten practice this was, he thought, gazing round his surgery, but it was all he could afford at the time he was setting up. He loathed it, along with his patients who could hardly afford to pay him half the time.

His heartburn flared, causing him to swear under his breath. He'd better take something before calling in the next patient.

Whoever it was could damn well wait.

'Would you do me a favour?' Laura smiled at Morag who was busy dusting. Mathew was at work, while Harriet had gone out on some errand or other which left her alone in the house with the staff.

'What sort of favour, Miss?'

'You live in Partick, don't you?'

Morag, continuing to dust, nodded. 'In Purdon Street. Born and brought up there.'

'Have you ever noticed the Marie Stopes Clinic when to-ing and fro-ing?'

Morag paused momentarily to think about that. 'Can't say I have. Though I have heard it mentioned. Something or other to do with women with family problems.'

'That's it,' Laura confirmed. 'Well, I wondered if you'd stop in there for me and pick up some literature.'

Morag frowned. 'Literature? What's that when it's at home?'

'Oh, pamphlets, brochures, printed matter in general. Anything they're giving away.'

'Sort of advice like?'

'That's it exactly.'

Morag was puzzled. 'What do you want that for? You're not married and don't have a family.'

Laura shrugged. 'I'm interested, that's all. So, will you do it?'

'Without telling your ma or pa I take it?' Morag queried shrewdly.

'I doubt they'd be best pleased to learn I was reading such things. You know how stuffy and old fashioned they are, particularly Pa.'

He was that, Morag mentally agreed.

'I'll give you a shilling.'

Morag's eyes lit up. This was different, there was money involved. ''Tain't enough.'

'Then how much is?'

Morag wondered how far she could push this. Not too far, Laura was only a schoolkid after all so wouldn't have a lot of cash. 'How about half a dollar?'

'You mean two and six?'

Morag nodded.

'Make it two bob and it's a deal.'

Morag laughed. 'You little monkey.'

'It's all I have,' Laura said truthfully.

'Then two bob it is. I'll nip in sometime before the end of the week. Do you have the address?'

Laura told her.

'Leave it with me then.'

A satisfied Laura sauntered off as Morag continued with her dusting.

'I simply don't want her along. She'd quite ruin our holiday,' Mathew stated firmly, quite determined about this.

'But it's only for a fortnight, dear. What's the difference between having Cakey with us in Largs and having her staying here?'

Largs was a resort on the River Clyde where they booked the same house every year for their annual holiday. Harriet had suggested on several occasions that they might try somewhere else for a change, Millport perhaps, or even Kirn, but Mathew would have none of it. He liked Largs and the house there.

'Because it's our holiday, Harriet. A family time.'

'But Cakey *is* family,' Harriet protested. 'She's my sister and your sister-in-law.'

'I meant immediate family. You, me, Alexander and Laura.'

Harriet shook her head. 'You've forgotten Alexander has already said he didn't want to accompany us this year, and you agreed. Remember?'

She was right, he had forgotten. 'That doesn't alter matters.'

'It's going to be so embarrassing,' Harriet pointed out. 'And I'm sure she'll be terribly disappointed into the bargain.'

'Nonetheless, my mind is made up. She'll just have to understand, that's all.'

Harriet sat and ran a hand over her forehead, tidying away some stray hair that had come loose. She was quite distraught by this turn of events. 'Please, Mathew, for me if nothing else.'

'I'm sorry, dear. My mind is quite made up. Margaret is at liberty to remain here, or do whatever she might choose to. But I will not have her with us on holiday.'

The prospect of a whole two weeks away from Margaret delighted Mathew, and no matter what pleas Harriet put forward he wouldn't budge on his decision. The damn woman irritated and annoyed him so! She and her money.

'Then perhaps you might tell her, darling. Explain the situation,' Harriet proposed, as that was the last thing she wanted to do herself.

'Of course.' And enjoy every moment of it, he thought gleefully. By God and he would.

'There's nothing more to be said then?'

'No,' he declared roundly, and strode from the room. He'd speak to Margaret later that evening. He was looking forward to it.

That was it, finished, done. Sandy held the drawing of Laura a little distance from his face and stared critically at it. Somehow he'd managed to catch Laura to a T. Nor had it been as difficult as he'd imagined. Despite the lack of character in her face, due to her youthfulness, there was a strength there, particularly round the eyes, that he'd seized and emphasised.

'Not bad,' he muttered aloud, hoping Laura would be pleased with it. He was sure she would.

He'd take it into the framer's the following day, he decided. And he'd buy an expensive frame which he could well afford thanks to Aunt Cakey's money.

His final act was to sign the drawing.

Chapter 8

Mathew had been savouring what he intended telling Margaret all through dinner, anticipating the moment with great pleasure. Harriet was right, he just knew she'd be terribly disappointed not to be accompanying them.

'Would anyone care for a glass of sherry or port?' he asked casually after they'd finished pudding.

Sandy looked at his father in astonishment, this was most unusual, and wondered what the occasion was? For there had to be one.

'Harriet?'

She shook her head. 'No thank you, dear.'

'Margaret?'

'A glass of port would be extremely nice.' She hadn't failed to notice the amused glint in Mathew's eyes all during the meal, or the smug expression that had occasionally crept onto his face. Nor had she failed to notice how uneasy Harriet was. Something was afoot all right, and she suspected it was to do with her.

Mathew rose from the table and crossed to where he kept the drinks. The port, an unopened bottle, had been standing there for almost two years.

'Can I have one as well, Pa?' Sandy ventured to ask.

'Of course, son. Have you ever had port before?'

'Once or twice.'

Laura would also have loved a glass, but it wasn't offered to her.

Mathew began humming as he manoeuvred the cork out of the bottle. The three measures he poured were generous ones which was quite unlike him, at least where others were concerned.

'There we are, Margaret,' he declared, placing a glass in front of her.

'Thank you, Mathew. You're most kind.'

'Not at all,' he murmured, meaning it.

When he'd sat again Mathew cleared his throat. He had considered taking Margaret aside to speak to her, but then decided not to. Far better to do it over the dinner table in front of everyone. More embarrassing for her that way.

'A good one,' Margaret commented on tasting her drink. 'Did you buy it yourself?'

Mathew frowned. Was that an inference that he didn't know a good port from bad? Knowing her, it could well be. A veiled insult. Damn the woman!

'Yes, I did,' he lied. In fact, it had been given to him by one of his better-off patients, of which there were relatively few.

'Excellent flavour, nicely rounded,' she approved, an enigmatic smile on her face.

Did that mean it was the opposite, and bad? He had a quick sip, it seemed all right to him. There again, to his annoyance, he couldn't have told one port from another.

Mathew cleared his throat a second time. 'I don't know if you're aware, Margaret, but next month we shall be going on holiday. To Largs actually, where we go every year.'

She nodded, but didn't reply, noting that Harriet's gaze was suddenly riveted to her empty plate.

'As you will appreciate, this is entirely a family affair.' He broke off to let the ramifications of that hopefully sink in. Also to draw out the procedure.

'I see,' Margaret murmured, her smile never wavering, her expression otherwise giving nothing away.

'You, of course, will be welcome to stay on here in our absence. No question about that.'

He now matched her smile, only his was one of triumph.

Cakey's mind was racing, well aware this was supposed to be some sort of embarrassment for her. 'Actually, Harriet did say something about this last week,' she lied. 'Which gave me an idea.'

She paused to sip her port, making him wait for her to elaborate. Two could play his game. 'I fully intended going to London during my visit to see some shows and shop, which I seem to recall mentioning in my letter. Anyway, I shall plan this little jaunt to coincide with your holiday, which means I shall only miss the family's company for a fortnight rather than the month if I'd done it separately from your holiday. So, if you let me have the dates I shall arrange matters accordingly.'

Mathew's face had fallen. He could have been rid of the bitch for a month which had now, somehow, contracted to a fortnight. He desperately tried to hide his fury.

Harriet was almost shaking with silent laughter. Oh, that was funny, hilarious. Talk about hoisted by your own petard! She fought to bring herself back under control.

'I'd love to go to London,' Laura breathed, eyes gleaming. 'It would be so exciting.'

'Naturally I shall stay at the Savoy or Dorchester,' Cakey went on. 'So central, and relatively close to Bond Street . . .' She broke off, her expression now one of pity and condescension. 'I'd forgotten, you don't know London, do you, Mathew?'

'No,' he admitted through gritted teeth.

'London and Bond Street, sounds like Heaven,' Laura enthused, wishing with all her heart that that's where she was going instead of dreary old Largs which would, as always, be boredom itself. Her parents might enjoy their annual holiday but she hated it, and had done since she stopped being a little girl.

Cakey looked at Laura, reading her mind. Hmmh! she thought to herself.

After dinner Mathew made his excuses and went to bed early. When Harriet finally went on up she found him pretending to be asleep, but knew from his breathing that he wasn't.

She couldn't have been more amused.

Sandy paused in his painting and glanced around. He was back in the park at the same spot where Sophie had happened upon him, and had been there every day since, when weather would allow. He was hoping she might put in another appearance but so far she hadn't.

He scowled as he resumed painting, the canvas almost finished. It seemed he was to be disappointed in talking to her again.

Morag had kept her part of the bargain and brought Laura back various booklets and other printed matter from the Marie Stopes Clinic. Laura, in her bedroom with the door firmly shut, was now poring over one of the booklets.

Although the material didn't appear to be what she'd anticipated she was finding it fascinating and informative, nonetheless. She read on: 'Although this was a poor working-class community, people had a great sense of values regarding moral behaviour. Each woman kept to her own man and would not have dreamed of doing otherwise. Sometimes the men were very cruel to their women, especially when in drink. I have heard many a woman screaming and shouting as a drunken man gave her a good hiding. The following day she would emerge with black eyes and a swollen face, yet would not utter a word against her husband, and woe betide anyone who did! Not a word would she have said against him.'

'What a brute!' Laura muttered in disgust. Imagine having to put up with that sort of thing. It was appalling!

Were the working classes all like this? Surely not. Couldn't be. She turned the page:

THE LAW AND MARRIAGE, FACTS
A husband could lock up his wife – until 1891
A husband could beat his wife – until 1879

A husband owned all his wife's earnings – until 1870

A husband owned all his wife's belongings, clothes, money – until 1882

A husband owned the home and joint possessions – until 1920

'Nineteen twenty!' Laura exclaimed, why, that was only four years ago. She shook her head in dismay. How awful all this was. How very awful.

She continued reading.

'Oh dear!' Harriet murmured. 'I'm afraid Mathew would never agree.'

'I thought it best to speak to you first instead of the pair of you together,' Cakey went on. 'To test the water, so to speak. I mean, how do you yourself feel about it?'

'I think it would be wonderful for Laura to go to London with you, I just know she'd thoroughly enjoy herself.'

'It would be my birthday present to her, don't forget, the whole thing entirely on me. It wouldn't cost Mathew a penny.'

Harriet shook her head. 'I can hear the objections now. She's too young to go gallivanting away from home. Her place is with us on holiday. You know the sort of thing?'

'It would be a tremendous experience for her. Help broaden her mind. We shall see some shows in the West End, take in a concert or two. And then there are the galleries which I particularly want to visit. Herbert was something of an art connoisseur, and patron, in his latter years. It was through him I acquired an interest, and knowledge if I may say so, of art.' She paused, then added, 'Not to mention the shopping. I'm sure we'll be able to find some new, the latest fashion, things for Laura. Again, all on me. That would save Mathew money as I would more or less be supplying a new wardrobe for her.'

'Would you really, Cakey?'

'Of course. She's my niece, don't forget, and a lovely girl into the bargain. I'm much taken with both your children, Harriet. They do you proud.'

Harriet blushed at this compliment. 'Thank you.'

'It's true,' Cakey nodded, then kissed her sister on the cheek. It had always saddened her to think of Harriet married to a man like Mathew, and it made her appreciate all the more having found her Herbert. Chalk and cheese, that's how she'd compared the two of them, chalk and cheese. She knew she could never have put up with someone like Mathew. Never in a thousand years. There again, she wouldn't have made the mistake of marrying him in the first place. She'd often wondered if Harriet had ever regretted doing so, but had never asked. Perhaps if they saw one another more she might have done.

'There is one thing might persuade him,' Cakey said slowly. This trump card, at least she hoped it was, she'd been keeping up her sleeve.

'What's that?'

Harriet laughed and clapped her hands when Cakey told her.

'Come in,' Sandy called out when there was a tap on the door. As he'd thought, it was Laura.

'Can I have a quick word?' she asked.

'It'll have to be quick. I'm on my way out.'

'Oh! Anywhere nice?'

'Just the pub I usually go to on Friday nights. I meet up with a couple of chaps there.'

'Anyone I would know?'

'Fellows called Grant Bell and Martin Benson. And no, you wouldn't know them. They're just pub acquaintances, nothing more.'

She sat on the edge of his bed. 'What's a sheath? And what's a Dutch cap?'

He nearly choked. 'Bloody hell, Laura! Where did you hear about those?'

'In a booklet I'm reading. It says sheaths usually cost three shillings a dozen, Dutch caps two and six.'

Sandy stood goggling at her. 'What sort of booklet gives that information?'

'The sort given out by the Marie Stopes Clinic.'

'The Marie . . .' He stopped and took a deep breath. 'Don't ever let Pa hear you mention that name, it's anathema to him. He totally disagrees with the woman and her teachings.'

That didn't surprise Laura one little bit. 'And what about you? Do you disagree also?'

Sandy hadn't really thought about that. Not that he knew all that much about the subject, only in general.

'Well?' she prompted.

'I haven't actually given it a great deal of consideration, but not really. It's mainly about contraception as I understand it which I do approve of. Though many doctors, and a lot of the male population, don't.'

'Contraception is stopping having babies, right?'

He nodded. 'Otherwise women just go on breeding

123

time and time again, often dying through the experience, which is quite a common occurrence even today, or else having such large families they can't cope, and that includes feeding and clothing them. It also means women can have . . .' he hesitated, then said, 'sex without having to worry about pregnancy.'

'So what's a sheath and Dutch cap then?'

'Methods of contraception.'

'I've already gathered that, but what exactly are they?'

He headed for the whisky bottle, which he seemed to do every time Laura called into his bedroom. He found all this, and her questions, quite unnerving.

'Can I have one too please?' she smiled.

'I only have . . .'

She jumped to her feet. 'I'll get the tumbler,' she declared, interrupting him.

Sandy stared in amazement at his sister, wondering what had become of the innocent little girl who'd first knocked on his door only a few months previously. Here she now was, talking about contraception and about to drink whisky. It was mind boggling.

'Not too much lemonade,' she instructed. 'That spoils it.'

'Does it indeed,' he replied wryly.

'I think so.'

So did he, but wasn't about to say so.

When Laura had her drink she sat again on the bed waiting for her explanation.

Sandy was squirming inside, unable to look his sister directly in the eye. 'A sheath,' he said slowly, horribly aware she was hanging on his every word.

'So, do you understand now?' he queried when he'd finished.

Laura suddenly giggled; what he'd told her seemed so ludicrous somehow. And yet, when she thought about it, it made sense.

'Laura?'

She nodded.

He found the business about a Dutch cap even more difficult to articulate, the cap going where it did after all.

'Inside!' she exclaimed, incredulous.

'That's right.'

'But doesn't it hurt?'

'My information on that is limited, but presumably not.'

'How horrible,' she breathed, and shuddered.

'Better that than babies you don't want and can't afford to raise.'

'I suppose so,' she admitted reluctantly.

'So there you have it.' He drained his glass and immediately poured himself another.

'Could you get one of each to show me? I'd like to see.'

'No, I can not!' he replied in alarm. 'That's going too far. Anyway, where on earth would I get a cap from?'

'But you could a sheath?'

'Of course. From the pharmacist or barber's.'

'Barber's? Why would they have such things?'

Sandy shrugged. 'They just do. After your haircut they ask you quietly if you'd "like something for the weekend, sir?", which means a packet of three sheaths. I suppose gentlemen's barbers sell them because most men would be far too embarrassed to go into the pharmacist. I mean, imagine if you were served by a woman!

Horrendous. Most chaps I can think of wouldn't ask but simply turn tail and walk out again.'

'I can understand that,' she nodded. 'There again, what happens if a woman goes into the pharmacist's shop and gets served by a man?'

'That's different.'

'How is it?'

'I don't know. It just is. They probably view it the same as going to the doctor's.'

Laura's mind was whirling as she tried to digest these revelations. Sticking something, even designed for the purpose, up inside yourself seemed disgusting to her. And surely it must be painful? She couldn't wait to pass on her newfound knowledge to Madeleine whom she'd arranged to meet up with in town the following day.

'Now, scoot,' Sandy declared. 'I told you I was going out.'

She finished her drink, enjoying the warm, dreamy sensation it left her with. 'All right. And Sandy, thanks.'

'Don't mention it.'

He heaved a sigh of relief when the door closed behind her. He'd never imagined having a sister could be like this.

'You're late,' Sandy said to Grant Bell. Then, indicating the chair beside him, 'I kept you a seat.'

Grant glanced around. 'No Martin yet?'

'Not so far. Perhaps he's out somewhere with a woman.'

A strange smile lit up Grant's face. 'Could be.'

There was something different about Grant tonight, Sandy thought, though what he couldn't have said. 'Are you all right?'

The smile broadened even further. 'Fine. Couldn't be better.' He chuckled. 'In fact, couldn't be better at all.'

This was all very mysterious. 'Care to tell me why?'

Grant regarded him steadily. 'Only if you promise to keep it to yourself. And I mean that.'

'A secret, eh?'

Grant nodded. 'Very much so. I wasn't going to mention, but truth is, I'm just dying to tell someone. Bursting with it.'

Sandy had a swallow from his pint. 'I'm listening.'

'Do I have your promise?'

'Of course.'

Grant leant forward slightly and lowered his voice, not wanting to be overheard. 'I've just come from Blythswood Square.'

Sandy stared at him in astonishment. 'Are you saying what I think you are?' Blythswood Square was the area notorious for being the haunt of Glasgow's prostitutes.

'I am.'

'Bloody hell!' Sandy exclaimed. 'What was it like?'

'You mean the actual . . . ?'

Sandy nodded.

'Better than I ever dreamt it would be. Sheer magic.'

'I hope you used a froggy?' Sandy queried, voice suddenly filled with concern. Froggy was the slang name for a condom.

'Of course I did. I'm not daft you know. I don't want to get a dose of the clap.'

Sandy could hardly believe this. Grant using a prostitute!

'I never have much luck with women, in fact I'm a downright disaster with them. And so I thought, why not? And so I did.'

Sandy was curious. 'What was she like?'

'You mean her face or stripped off?'

'Both.'

'Well, you couldn't exactly call her pretty, I'd be lying if I said so. But she wasn't ugly either. No warts on her nose or anything like that.'

Despite himself, Sandy smiled. 'And stripped off?'

'No idea. She didn't do that. We went to a room where she took off her drawers, then just lay down with her skirt pulled up. When she saw me having trouble getting the froggy on she asked if it was my first time. I said yes, so she helped me. Then she sort of . . . helped me with the next bit too. I gave her a tip for being so understanding. I mean, she could have made me feel small, but not her. She was kindness itself.'

Sandy shook his head in amazement. It was certainly a day, or night anyway, for matters sexual. First Laura and her questions, now this.

'I take it you've never . . . ?' Grant queried.

'No,' Sandy admitted quietly, looking away.

'It's terrific. It really is. When I left her I felt as if I was king of the world.'

Sandy thought about what Grant had just confided to him. Could he ever do that? he wondered. He doubted it. He'd find it . . . well squalid. Dirty.

'It was also the first fanny I've ever seen,' Grant went on. 'I suppose you have being a medical student?'

'Only on cadavers. Several of those.'

'That must have been dead interesting,' Grant joked.

Sandy didn't find that funny, quite the opposite. 'Will you go there again?' he asked.

'Darn tootin' I will. Next Friday. I'm looking forward to it already.' He eyed Sandy speculatively. 'Would you like to meet up and we'll go together? There are plenty of women available to pick and choose from. All shapes, sizes and ages.'

'I don't think so,' Sandy replied drily. He found the idea quite abhorrent, especially the bit about the woman not even bothering to take off her clothes.

'Suit yourself.'

For the rest of that evening Grant acted like the proverbial cat with two tails, which irritated Sandy enormously.

'I won't hear of it and that's final,' Mathew stated. 'The girl is coming on holiday with us.'

'But it would be a tremendous experience for her, Mathew. Help broaden her mind,' Harriet continued to argue.

He snorted. 'There's nothing in London to broaden her mind that can't be found right here in Glasgow, the second city of the Empire, I'll remind you.'

'I thought the fact that Cakey is paying for it, and a new wardrobe don't forget, might appeal to you.'

Mathew's eyes glinted with anger. 'Is Margaret trying to insinuate that I can't afford to look after my family, is that it?'

'Don't be ridiculous, dear.'

The impertinence of his sister-in-law, Mathew inwardly fumed. Of course that's what she was insinuating, Harriet just wasn't seeing it, that's all.

'If Laura needs new clothes then I'll buy them for her. Does she?'

Harriet shook her head. 'Not really. But she is getting older and will soon need more grown-up ones.'

'Nonsense! She's still a baby.'

'She's about to be sixteen, dear. That's hardly a baby.'

He knew Harriet was right, but was damned if he was going to admit it. 'Then we'll just have to agree to differ,' he snapped, struggling into his pyjama bottoms.

'As you say, darling.' Harriet smiled, trying to mollify him a little.

'It *is* what I say. I am the man in this house, don't forget.'

The Lord and master, Harriet thought wearily. How tiresome that could be at times. 'I'll tell Cakey in the morning about your decision,' she said. 'Her travel arrangements depend on it.'

Mathew frowned. 'Why do they?'

Harriet played Cakey's trump card. 'Well, if she is going on her own she wants to motor down, but if Laura had been going with her she'd decided to take the train, in which case she did mention that you could use her Rolls while they were away. Go to Largs in it instead of in the Austin.'

'Use the Rolls?' Mathew breathed.

'That's what she said. For the entire fortnight. Of course that won't apply now she's going by herself.'

Harriet could easily have laughed at the expression on Mathew's face.

'Oh Sandy, it's wonderful!' Laura exclaimed in delight. She had just unwrapped his birthday present to her.

'You like it then?'

'Like it, I *love* it!' And with that she went to her brother and kissed him on the cheek. 'Thank you ever so much.'

'You're welcome.'

'But I thought . . . you told me . . .'

'I changed my mind,' he explained.

'It is awfully good,' Harriet commented, gazing at the drawing.

Cakey was looking puzzled. 'Did you do that, Sandy?'

He nodded. 'Yes, I did.'

'I didn't know you drew?'

'And paint,' Laura informed her. 'He's got quite a little studio in his bedroom.'

'Well, well,' Cakey mused. That was interesting, she thought.

'Now Aunt Cakey's present,' Harriet declared.

Laura picked up the sealed envelope with her name on the front and tore it open. Inside was a single sheet of paper which read: TO DEAR LAURA ON HER 16TH BIRTHDAY. MY PRESENT IS A TRIP TO LONDON WITH ME. LOVE AUNT CAKEY

Laura squealed with pleasure. 'Am I really going with you?'

'You sure are, kid. We're staying at the Dorchester while your parents are away on holiday. It's all agreed.'

Harriet looked at Cakey, a hint of amusement reflected in both pairs of eyes. It had taken Mathew a whole day before he'd succumbed and changed his mind about Laura, the offer of the Rolls being just too big a temptation for him to resist.

Cakey had played a trump card.

Chapter 9

'He's the most gorgeous chap,' Madeleine confided to Laura, who had come for tea at her friend's house. 'I simply couldn't take my eyes off him the entire time he was here.'

'So what's his name?'

'Conor Baxter, and he's just started work with his father's law firm. You must have heard of them, Baxter, Bird and McPhail?'

Laura nodded. The names seemed familiar.

'He's got dark wavy hair, dark eyes and is ever so tall. I'm going to marry him one day.'

Laura gaped at her friend. 'You're what?'

'I'm going to marry him one day,' Madeleine stated firmly. 'I knew right there and then he was the one for me.'

'But, Madeleine,' Laura protested. 'You hardly know him. You've only met him once.'

'That doesn't matter. He's the one.'

Laura thought that was a ridiculous notion, but refrained from saying so, not wanting to hurt Madeleine's feelings. 'And he came here on business with his father?'

'That's right. My father employs the firm.'

'Are you telling me it was love at first sight?'

'Exactly. And it was the same for him. It was obvious. He kept looking at me in the strangest way, and blushing, every so often. He was as smitten as I.'

Love at first sight? Laura reflected. How romantic, if there was such a thing. 'So how are you going to see him again?'

'No idea yet, but I'll think of something.'

Laura noted the resolve in Madeleine's voice, a new quality in her. She clearly meant what she said.

'Well, I don't know what to say. You've quite taken my breath away.'

Madeleine laughed. 'Are you happy for me?'

'Of course I am. I just hope, for your sake, you're not reading more into this than actually exists. About him also being smitten, I mean.'

'I was there, Laura, and there was no doubt in my mind at all. He's Mr Right, of that I'm completely and utterly certain.'

'You're still only fifteen, Madeleine,' Laura gently pointed out. 'Don't you think you're a bit young to be falling in love and talking about marriage?'

'Maybe,' Madeleine admitted reluctantly. 'But it's happened, and that's all there is to it.'

Laura fervently hoped this wasn't going to end in tears, which it could easily do if Madeleine was imagining things where this Conor was concerned. 'He does sound handsome,' she said wistfully.

'A dreamboat, Laura. Take my word for it. A real dreamboat.'

'Any idea how old he is?'

'Eighteen or nineteen, I'd say. Not too long out of school.'

A dreamy expression came across Madeleine's face as she fantasised about being alone with him, he kissing her, she eagerly responding. She sighed at the vision conjured up.

Laura poured herself another cup of tea and smiled indulgently at her friend.

Sandy was walking down Sauchiehall Street, on his way to buy some supplies from a little art shop he used, when a woman in front of him stumbled and, with a cry of pain, fell to the pavement. He immediately rushed forward to assist.

'*Merde!*' the woman swore angrily.

'Sophie!' Sandy exclaimed in surprise on recognising her. 'Are you all right? What happened?'

She blinked at him for several seconds before the penny dropped. 'Sandy.'

'Are you hurt?'

'I've twisted my ankle, I think.' She grimaced. 'At least that's what it feels like.'

He went down on one knee. 'There's the problem,' he declared. 'The heel on your shoe has broken off.'

This time she swore more volubly in French.

'Are you able to get up? Here, let me help.'

She pulled more faces as she came to her feet, her chest heaving. 'It's not as bad as I thought,' she declared, after putting a little weight on her injured ankle.

Sandy's mind was racing; what to do? He quickly

glanced around. 'There's a pub about two or three minutes away from here. Can you make that if I support you?'

She nodded. 'You're very kind.'

'Not at all.'

He gathered up the offending heel and slipped it into his pocket. 'Let's go then. Just lean on me as much as you want.'

She flashed him a smile, hobbling as he guided her in the direction of the pub.

Once inside Sandy sat her at the table nearest the door, then went up to the bar where he ordered two large brandies. 'Try that,' he said, placing one in front of her. He was still marvelling at the coincidence of them running into one another again.

Sophie crossed her legs and rubbed the bruised ankle, the bruise having rapidly appeared to swell the surrounding flesh. 'How stupid,' she muttered crossly.

'It was an accident. These things happen,' he consoled her, thinking how wonderful she looked.

Sophie had a sip of brandy, her green eyes staring at Sandy across the rim of her glass. 'I was out shopping,' she explained. 'It's my day off.'

'Lucky I was behind you. Didn't realise it was you until I saw your face.'

'And so we meet again,' she smiled.

'We seem to be fated, don't you think?'

'Fated?'

'Destined to keep bumping into one another. I think somewhere, somebody is trying to tell us something.'

She laughed. 'Perhaps. If you believe in such things.'

'Oh I do, most definitely.'

He took the heel out of his pocket and laid it on

the table. 'You'll need that when you take the shoe in to be repaired.'

'Is there a shoe repairer nearby?' she queried.

'Not that I know of.'

'Or a shop where I can buy another pair?'

He shook his head. 'Not one I've ever noticed. But don't worry, I'll get you home all right.'

'Do you have a car, *m'sieur*?'

'No. I'll put you in a taxi though. How's that?'

She appeared to relax a little. 'How is your painting coming along?'

'Fine. I finished that canvas you saw me working on in the park. But so far I haven't started another. I'm still thinking about what to paint next.'

'And you will paint all summer, no?'

'Hopefully. I really should be studying, even though it's the vac, but I can't bring myself to do so. When it's a choice between studying and painting, painting wins every time.'

From her expression it was clear she approved of that.

'Tell me something about yourself, Sophie, I'd like to know.'

'Such as?'

'Your surname for a start.'

'Ducros.'

'Sophie Ducros,' he murmured. He liked it.

'And in Paris I pose for a living, that is what I do. Sometimes, if money is short, I might work in a bar or restaurant as I am doing now, but mainly I pose. Modelling, they usually call it here.'

He was intrigued. 'Do you make a good living out of that?'

She shrugged. 'So so. I never starve if that's what you mean. At one point I worked in the Circus Fernando as a bareback rider. Circus people are great fun.'

A bareback rider! He thought that was amazing. 'If it was such fun, why did you leave?'

She dropped her gaze to stare into her glass. 'I met someone who wanted me to pose for him, so I gave up the circus, which was moving on, and did.'

'Someone I might have heard of?'

She laughed. 'No, no, he doesn't sell much. Though I think he's very good. So too did Paul, a friend of ours.'

'Paul?'

'Klee.'

'I've heard of him!' Sandy exclaimed. 'He's well known.'

'A nice man, if odd at times. But then they can all be that. Artists are strange, temperamental people. Very exciting to be around.'

Sandy was thoroughly enjoying himself; this type of conversation was meat and drink to him. 'Do you miss Paris?'

Her eyes took on a faraway look. 'Oh yes, especially Montmartre. I shall return soon.'

His heart sank to hear that. 'Not too soon I hope?'

'Who knows? When the time is right.'

'And when will that be?'

'When it is.'

'I see.' He didn't really.

'The man I left the circus for also comes from Glasgow,' she informed Sandy.

'Really!'

'It was he I came here with.'

She looked away, and took a deep breath. 'If you will excuse me Sandy I must go to the toilet and take off my stockings. One is badly ripped.'

'Of course,' he smiled, coming to his feet as she did. He indicated her empty glass. 'Will you have another?'

She thought about that for a moment. 'If you are.'

'I am. Leave it to me.'

Sophie placed a hand on his arm, which sent a delicious tingle through him. 'Can you get me a packet of cigarettes and a box of matches please? I've run out.'

'My pleasure. What sort?'

She gave another of her Gallic shrugs. 'I prefer French, but they won't have any here. Players are nice, or Senior Service.'

'Consider it done.'

He watched in sympathy as she hobbled to the toilet and disappeared inside. So, she'd come to Glasgow with this artist chappie, he must find out more. If she'd tell him that was.

He rose again on her return. 'Better?'

'I bathed the bruise with cold water which has helped a bit. I used my handkerchief.'

'I have to say, your English really is excellent. How did you learn it, from your Glaswegian artist friend?'

Sophie began opening her cigarettes. 'From my grand-mother, who was English. She taught me your language at an early age which came in useful when I was working with English painters in Montmartre. There are so many there.'

'You learnt well,' he complimented her.

'Thank you, *m'sieur*.'

When she'd lit up Sophie inhaled deeply, then let the smoke trickle out from between her lips. Sandy thought this was tremendously sensual to the point of being erotic.

Sophie regarded him steadily. 'You want to know about Jack, don't you?'

So that was his name. 'Only if you want to talk about him. I'm not one to pry into other people's business. That would be rude.' In fact he was dying to find out.

Sophie studied her nails which Sandy now noted were bright red and very long.

She had a sip of her drink, then sat silently for a few moments, her expression contemplative and etched with pain. 'His name is Jack Moore and we lived together for just over two years.'

'You mean . . . ?' He hadn't expected that. It didn't happen in Glasgow, at least not amongst the people he knew. There again, he reminded himself, Sophie had been used to, and was part of, a Bohemian lifestyle. He didn't know if he was shocked or not, his own lifestyle being so utterly conventional.

She was now regarding him with amusement. 'Does that make you think less of me?'

'No, not at all,' he protested, shaking his head.

'But you don't approve?'

He thought about that. 'I neither approve nor disapprove. One should be open to other people's customs and morality. It simply never crossed my mind, that's all.'

'It's common in Montmartre, particularly with artists. They see nothing wrong with being together outside marriage. It's a matter of convenience perhaps.'

'But why did he come back here and bring you with him?'

Sophie took a long pull on her cigarette. 'He wanted

to come home for a while and see his family again. When he asked me to go with him I agreed.'

'Because you were in love?'

'Yes,' she said slowly. 'I never dreamt he would just disappear and leave me.'

'Is that what happened?'

'I returned from Art School one day to find he'd taken his things and left. There was no note or letter, nothing. He'd simply gone.'

Bastard, Sandy thought. How awful for her. 'Did he love you?'

'I thought he did. He said he did.' She shrugged again. 'Obviously not.'

'What about his family. Is he with them?'

'I have no idea. Although we'd been in Glasgow for nearly six months he never took me to meet them. There was always an excuse as to why he went alone. I don't even know where they live. Glasgow somewhere, that's all.'

Sandy thought this was an appalling state of affairs. 'Not very nice for you.'

'No,' she agreed. 'Not very.'

'I am sorry. Truly I am.'

'Thank you.'

'It must have hurt?'

A glint of tears appeared in her eyes. 'I cried myself to sleep every night for a week. And during the day, it was as if I was empty inside. A hollow shell.'

'But you are getting over it now?' he said hopefully.

She attempted a brave smile. 'I think so. I no longer think of him all the time, that has passed.' She stared quizzically at Sandy. 'Have you ever been in love?'

'No,' he admitted. 'I haven't. That's still to come.'

She placed a hand over his. 'I pray it will. Love is the most wonderful thing in the world. It is also the most awful. But better, far better to have had it than not. Believe me.'

He did, thinking how ravishingly beautiful she was like this. Jack Moore must have been mad to let her go, completely insane. Surely she was everything any man could ever want.

'I like you, Sandy,' she said simply. 'You're nice.'

'So are you.'

She took a deep breath. 'I shall have one last cigarette, then I must go home.'

'Must you?'

'No, but I wish to. And you promised me a taxicab, remember?'

'I haven't forgotten.'

'Besides, we can't sit in the pub all day. I would become, as you Scots say, *deid mockit*. Steamboats.'

Said in a French accent Sandy thought those words hilarious. Imagine her not only knowing but coming out with them. They were pure Glasgow. He laughed.

'Did I pronounce them properly?'

'Absolutely.'

'Jack taught them to me.'

Sandy stopped laughing. Bloody Jack again. But what the hell, he was enjoying himself. Every moment spent in her company was a treat.

'Do you mind if I have another brandy while you smoke?'

'*Non.*'

'And you?'

'I've had enough.'

It was while he was back up at the bar that Sandy

had an inspirational idea. But would she agree? There was only one way to find out.

'I was wondering . . .' he said, when he rejoined her. 'And I won't be upset if you refuse, I'll quite understand.' He stopped for a swallow of brandy.

'Wondering what?' she prompted.

'The thing is, I would dearly love to draw you. Honestly I would. There's something about you that makes me want to reach for a pencil or paint brush.'

'You're not the first artist to say that.' She smiled.

'I can imagine. Anyway, what I want to propose is this. Would you object if I came along to the Station Hotel while you're on duty, sat in a quiet corner somewhere, we don't even have to talk, and drew you?'

'In the lounge!' she exclaimed incredulously.

'Why not? There's no reason I can think of. Unless it would be embarrassing?'

She found that amusing. 'It wouldn't embarrass me at all. I'm used to it, don't forget.' She shook her head. 'But never in an hotel lounge bar.'

'You wouldn't have to participate in any way,' he assured her. 'In fact you'll hardly know I'm there. I just don't want to turn up and give you the wrong impression, that's all. I only want to draw you. And maybe paint you from the drawings if I'm pleased with the results.'

Sophie was still amused, her eyes glinting as she studied him while continuing to smoke.

'Well, what do you say?'

She thought of how Lautrec had painted at the Moulin Rouge which made her smile. There was a world of difference between the Moulin Rouge and the Station Hotel in Glasgow. 'You're crazy,' she declared.

'That doesn't answer my question.'

She could see how keen he was, and was flattered by that. Her dented ego needed a little flattery. 'All right,' she agreed. 'But if the management complain then you leave.'

'I promise I will.'

'On your heart?'

'On my heart.'

Sophie ground out what remained of her cigarette, wishing it had been a Gitanes. 'Now I must go.'

He glanced at the clock behind the bar. 'How about lunch?' he queried, hoping to prolong their time together.

She laughed. 'You don't know very much about women, Sandy. I'm not going anywhere, least of all a restaurant, with a broken shoe and no stockings on. What would people think?'

'I don't care.'

Reaching over she stroked his cheek with the tip of a finger. 'Well, I do. So home it is.'

He'd have to settle for what they'd already arranged, he realised, but still felt disappointed. Though not as disappointed as he'd have been if she'd not agreed for him to draw her.

'Right then. If you can make it out onto the pavement again I'll soon hail a taxi. There are always plenty in Sauchiehall Street.'

Unfortunately he was correct about that and a taxi drew up almost immediately when they were outside. 'Quick, tell me your shifts for the rest of the week?' he asked her.

She did and he hoped he'd memorised them. He helped her into the back of the taxi.

'Thank you for everything.'

'My pleasure, Sophie, believe me.'

He gave the driver five shillings. 'Take the lady home and keep the change,' he instructed.

'Ta, pal.'

He watched the taxi drive away, Sophie waving to him through the rear window. He returned the wave.

What a morning, he reflected as he continued on his way to the art shop. He was so ecstatic he could have whooped from sheer joy.

'Sandy.'

He nearly jumped out of his skin having been lost deep in thought.

'Oh sorry,' Aunt Cakey apologised. 'Did I startle you?'

'Just a bit. I didn't hear or see you until you spoke.' He took a deep breath. 'So what can I do for you?'

'I was very impressed with the drawing you did of Laura.'

He flushed slightly. 'Thank you.'

'Very impressed indeed. Laura mentioned you have something of a studio in your bedroom and I was wondering if I could see some more of your work?'

'Of course.' He hesitated. 'My room is in somewhat of a mess, I'm afraid. I've been meaning to tidy it up for a while now.'

Typical of what she knew about young men, Cakey thought wryly. They were nearly all the same. 'We won't worry about that. Now you lead the way.'

He hadn't exaggerated, she thought, when they were inside his bedroom. It was an unholy tip. 'Doesn't Morag clear up for you?' she inquired politely.

'I told her not to, but she still does on occasion. I simply don't like people fiddling around in here. Whether they're cleaning or not. It's just a thing I have.'

Cakey nodded. 'I can understand that. You find it intrusive?'

'Exactly,' he beamed.

Cakey took in the easel and clutter surrounding it. Against one wall were a stack of what appeared to be finished canvases.

'Paintings first I think. If you don't mind, that is?'

'No, not at all.'

He picked out his latest, the one done in the park, and placed it on the easel. Cakey moved closer to get a better look.

'Hmm,' she murmured after a few minutes had slowly ticked past. 'It shows promise.'

That delighted him. 'Does it?'

'I would say so. My Herbert was an art patron in his latter years, you know, and something of a connoisseur. It was through him that I became interested. I even tried my hand at watercolours for a while, but gave up in the end. I was worse than useless. Now can I see another?'

Cakey viewed all the canvases, making positive, and occasionally constructive, criticism of each. 'Interesting,' she nodded when they came to the end of what he had to show.

'Pa's not too keen on me doing any of this,' Sandy explained. 'He thinks it's a waste of time. Time I should be devoting to my studies.'

'Philistine,' Cakey muttered. 'But then your pa always was.'

'Do you still want to look at my drawings? I've loads of those.'

'That's why I'm here.'

She sat, at Sandy's invitation, at his desk and went through the various notebooks and sketchpads that he put in front of her. 'You're particularly good with faces in my opinion,' she commented after a while.

That compliment delighted him.

'And you're very clever with light and shade.' She glanced up at him. 'Do I take it you're self taught?'

'Never had a lesson in my life,' he confirmed.

'Well, you're to be congratulated. You certainly have talent, and a great deal of potential. I like your work enormously.'

Sandy positively glowed from such praise. 'I don't know what to say except thank you again,' he mumbled.

'You're welcome.'

Cakey made a few more remarks about his various paintings and drawings before taking her leave, Sandy's face bursting into a broad smile the moment she'd gone.

To celebrate he poured himself an extra large whisky.

'Are you excited about going to London?'

Laura's eyes glowed with anticipation. 'Oh yes, Ma,' she breathed. 'I can't wait.'

'I'm sure you'll enjoy yourself. Aunt Cakey will see to that. You're very lucky, you know, to have such an opportunity.'

Laura nodded. 'I appreciate that. Madeleine Abercrombie was pea green with jealousy when I told her.'

Madeleine wasn't the only one to be jealous, Harriet thought wistfully. She'd have given anything to be going along with them, London being a place she'd always

146

wanted to visit. But there was fat chance of that being married to Mathew. He'd never entertain the idea, silly man.

'Not long now, eh?'

'No,' Laura agreed, for she'd been counting the days.

'I'll want to hear all about it when you get back, understand?'

'Yes, Ma.'

'The theatres, the galleries, the shops. Everything. You can tell me some time when your father's at work. We won't be interrupted that way.' Or be glared at disapprovingly, she added mentally.

Harriet sighed. In the meantime she'd have to put up with two weeks in Largs, the first time she and Mathew had ever gone on holiday without at least one of the children present.

It was going to be very odd, she reflected. Very odd indeed, just the pair of them together.

Laura might be looking forward to London, but she wasn't at all sure she felt the same about Largs.

Chapter 10

'I've brought you another cup of coffee,' Sophie declared, placing it on the table where Sandy was sitting.

He smiled at her. 'Thank you.'

'How are you doing?'

He turned his sketchpad towards her. 'Judge for yourself.'

Sophie glanced around. So far Sandy was the only customer since they'd opened the bar. Another twenty minutes or so and others would start arriving for the lunchtime session. They'd be busy then for about an hour and a half before it began tailing off again. As the manager was upstairs she decided to take a break.

Sandy's smile widened when she sat beside him to stare at the head and shoulders of her that he'd been engrossed in.

'It's very good,' she acknowledged.

'Thank you.'

'If I may make one tiny criticism?'

'Please do.'

'I don't believe my mouth is as large as that.'

He frowned as he too now stared at the drawing. Damned if she wasn't right. He had made it too large. 'Sorry,' he apologised. 'That's what comes from trying to sketch someone at a distance who's perpetually on the move.'

The more she got to know Sandy the more he interested her, Sophie realised. There was a gentleness about him which appealed, and not a trace of the cynicism that was endemic in Montmartre. He was refreshing, a breath of fresh air as the English said. 'You didn't mind me saying?'

'Not in the least. Now look at the others.'

The sketch he'd shown her was one of three he'd done so far in all of which he now saw her mouth was too large.

'You draw with great loving in your heart,' she smiled.

That startled him. 'Do I?'

'Oh yes, it's obvious. Well, to me anyway. Try never to lose that, Sandy.'

He dropped his gaze. 'Maybe that's because it's you I'm drawing.'

She brushed a hand over his, giving him goosebumps. 'I hope not. I hope it's the way you draw and paint everything.'

'Perhaps,' he prevaricated.

Sophie produced a packet of cigarettes and lit up. When she exhaled the smoke spiralled delightfully ceilingwards.

'What are you thinking?' she asked in a soft, husky tone.

He shook his head.

'Something naughty?' she teased.

'No, no, nothing like that,' he replied quickly, a little shocked that she might imagine such a thing.

His reaction to that amused her; what an unworldly man he was. She found it attractive.

'It was just . . .' He trailed off, and shrugged.

'Just what, Sandy?'

He pulled a face. 'Just wishing that I could paint and draw all the time and forget about medicine.'

Sophie regarded him steadily. 'Do you really wish that?'

'Oh yes,' he breathed. 'Though there's no chance of it. It's only a pipe dream, that's all. It'll never happen.'

'There are many in Montmartre who gave up other professions to become artists, you know. For them it's their overriding passion.'

His eyes gleamed at the thought. If only . . . if only he had the courage. Unfortunately, and he knew himself well enough to admit it, he didn't. He couldn't throw away everything for a pipe dream, it would break his mother's heart. As for his father! Mathew's fury would be unbounded. No, becoming a full-time artist, trying to make his living at it, could never, would never, be. It would remain a fantasy.

'I will visit Montmartre one day. I've promised myself that,' he declared.

'And when you do I shall show you round, introduce you to my friends.'

'Would you really?' he enthused.

'Naturally.'

'But how will I find you? What's your address?'

She laughed. 'I have no apartment there at the

moment, but you would always find me in the Place du Tertre. That is where the artists congregate at night to take their coffee and cognac. They sit outside and talk and argue, who is better than who, who has sold what, who is sleeping with who. It goes on and on and never stops. You would always find me somewhere there.'

'The Place du Tertre,' he repeated, writing it on the back of his pad. 'I won't forget.'

Another customer entered the bar, causing Sophie to instantly grind out what remained of her cigarette. 'I must get back,' she said.

'I'll say goodbye before I go.'

She flashed him a smile, then rose and returned to the bar, her hips swaying provocatively as usual.

Sandy flipped over a page in his sketchpad and began a new drawing, this one from a different angle. When he came to her mouth he took extra care to get it right.

'I'm a little worried about Alexander,' Harriet declared to Mathew. They had just settled down for a night of listening to the wireless which he'd just switched on.

A look of irritation flashed across his face. He wanted to hear the programme about to start on the BBC 2LO service. 'What's wrong with him?'

'He keeps coughing. You must have heard?'

Mathew shook his head. 'No, I haven't.'

'Well he is, and it's worrying me.'

'Probably a summer cold,' Mathew stated knowingly. 'There's quite a bit of it around.'

'Will you give him something?'

'That's quite unnecessary, dear. It'll clear of its own accord. That's what I tell my patients.'

She frowned. 'Don't you give them anything at all?'

'Only if they insist. It doesn't really help but makes some people feel better if they've got some coloured water masquerading as a tonic to swallow.'

Harriet wasn't quite certain about that. 'Do you think it's all right us going away and leaving him while he's unwell?'

Mathew's irritation deepened as the programme began. 'He's young and strong as an ox, darling. He'll soon shrug off whatever it is, so there's no need to be concerned. Anyway, it was his idea he stayed behind, he was always welcome to come along. You know that.'

Harriet was about to speak further when Mathew held up a hand. 'I'd like to listen to this if you don't mind, darling.'

Harriet snapped her mouth shut again. Mathew was a doctor after all, he knew best. And he was right, a summer cold was nothing to worry about, a mere temporary inconvenience. She decided to shelve the matter, remembering that Mathew had accused her in the past of being over protective towards the children. Natural for a mother, she supposed. Certainly the sort of mother she was.

She put it from her mind.

'I'd have thought you'd be tired of drawing me by now,' Sophie teased, coming up to the table where Sandy was.

He shook his head. 'Never. You're inspirational.'

Sophie laughed, thinking that funny. Except the look in his eyes told her he meant it. 'Can I join you?'

'Please do. Fag break?'

'Uh-huh.'

She produced her packet and lit up.

'French I see,' he said, nodding at her packet of Gitanes.

'I managed to get some in a *tabac* I've never been in before. I much prefer them.'

'What you're used to, I suppose.'

She glanced at the drawing lying in front of him, this one a full length version.

'Any criticism?' he queried.

'No.'

'Like?'

It was a representation of her walking in a hurry; he'd caught the sense of movement exactly. 'Very much, as usual.'

That sent a warm glow through him. 'I'm going to start painting you soon.'

'Oh?'

'I haven't quite made up my mind how yet. I mean, what sort of pose I'll put you in. When I decide I'll start. I've certainly got enough preliminary sketches to be going on.'

'I'd like to see this painting when it's finished,' she said.

'You shall.' He peered at her. 'For the life of me I can't fathom out what shade of green your eyes are. It's perplexing. For when I come to do them. I want to get them just right.'

'I'm sure you will.'

He watched her inhale, thinking how fascinating it was to observe her smoke. He didn't know why, but she smoked differently to Scots people, somehow making more of a production out of it. He found it both basic and elegant at the same time. Trust a French woman to be able to do that, he thought wryly.

'Have you ever heard of Harry Lauder?' he asked, thoroughly enjoying her presence, as he always did.

Sophie pouted. 'Should I have?'

'He's a Scottish comedian, very popular. He's topping the bill at the Empire just now and I wondered if you'd care to go along with me on one of your evenings off? I can get tickets.'

Sophie thought about that. It was a long time since she'd had a proper night out, Jack hadn't been very good when it came to things like that. The pub, yes, but not a proper night out.

'Well?' he prompted.

'You know how it is with me, Sandy. I've explained.'

'A night out won't harm, surely? There doesn't need to be any jiggery pokery.'

She laughed. 'Jiggery pokery! I've never heard that expression before.'

'We could have a meal and then catch the second house. What do you say?'

Sophie pulled a face. 'I don't want to be rude, but Scottish cooking is disgusting. Even here in the hotel where you'd think they'd know better it's awful. Vegetables in particular, boiled far too long.'

'Ah!' he smiled. 'But I know a restaurant which has a genuine French chef. And I mean genuine, I've checked.' He had too.

Her eyes opened wide. 'You do?'

'Paris trained, I'm assured. Everyone who goes there raves about him.'

'And the name of this restaurant?'

'Malmaison. Only a short walk from the theatre.'

She sat back in her chair to stare quizzically at him. 'It sounds expensive, Sandy. Can you afford such a place?'

'Uh-huh.'

'You must be rich?'

Now it was his turn to laugh. 'Hardly, but I am in funds at the moment thanks to my dear Aunt Cakey who's over here from Canada. Wonderful woman that she is.'

Sophie was tempted, very much so. It sounded fun. 'And there wouldn't be any jiggery pokery?'

'None, I swear.'

She paused for a few seconds while she had a puff on her cigarette, turning his proposal over in her mind. 'I'm free Tuesday night. Would that be all right?'

Elation filled him – she was going out with him at last! 'Absolutely perfect. Fridays and Saturdays might have been difficult; as I said, Lauder's very popular.'

He made the arrangements there and then.

'Well, what did you make of that?' Sandy asked as they left the Empire Theatre the following Tuesday night.

'It must have been funny, everyone was laughing,' Sophie replied, tongue firmly in cheek.

'Except you.'

She gave one of her Gallic shrugs. 'How could I? I didn't understand most of what was said.'

Harry Lauder, good as he was, had been a mistake, Sandy thought. The trouble was, there was nothing else on in Glasgow that wasn't also very Scottish. 'I'm sorry, I shouldn't have suggested it,' he apologised.

She placed a hand on his arm. 'Not at all. It was an experience, if nothing else. And it was lovely to go out for the evening. Made a nice change.'

That pleased him – all wasn't lost. 'At least you enjoyed the meal.'

'Oh yes,' she enthused. 'I did indeed.'

'And so did I.' The truth was, he'd been so revelling in her company the food hadn't really registered with him.

'So thank you.'

He glanced around at the crowd streaming from the theatre, many of them looking for taxis, others hurrying off to catch public transport. If it had been earlier he'd have taken her for a drink somewhere, but it was past closing time for the pubs.

'Let's walk for a little bit if you don't mind,' he smiled. 'If we wait here for a taxi it could take us ages. I know of a rank that's not too far away, we'll get one there.'

He was thrilled when she slipped her arm through his. 'Lead on, *m'sieur*.'

Luckily it was a fine August night, the moon high in the sky, stars twinkling in abundance. As they walked she quizzed him about Aunt Cakey who'd given him money, and he asked for further details about her life in Montmartre.

As he'd predicted they found a taxi at the rank he took her to and Sandy gave the driver Sophie's address, explaining to her that he'd drop her off en route before continuing on to his own house.

'Here we are then,' he said as they drew up outside her close, hating the fact their evening was about to end. He'd have given anything for it to go on.

'I had a lovely time, Sandy. Thank you.'

'Maybe we can do it again sometime?' he queried hopefully.

'You mean Harry Lauder?' she teased.

'No no, something else. Just the meal perhaps.'

Her response surprised him, for he hadn't been expecting it. There was a quick kiss on his lips, then she was out of the taxi and hurrying into the tenement.

With a sigh he gave the driver his own address.

'I'll telephone when we arrive, just to let you know we arrived safely,' Cakey declared to Harriet.

'Thank you.'

Under Mathew's direction a porter had already loaded the luggage into their compartment. Normally he wouldn't have bothered coming but had seized the opportunity as it meant he could drive the Rolls.

'Be a good girl now, and do what Aunt Cakey tells you,' Harriet instructed a very excited Laura.

'I will, Ma. Promise.'

Further goodbyes were said, then Cakey and Laura climbed into the compartment, Mathew closing the door.

There were tears in Harriet's eyes as the train moved off. This was the first time Laura had been away from home. How she wished she was going with them instead of to Largs the following day.

'Come along, dear,' Mathew urged. 'No use hanging around.'

But Harriet made him wait until the train was out of the station and steaming southwards, an agitated Mathew desperate to get behind the wheel of the Rolls again.

For him the Rolls was a dream come true, even if it was only going to last a fortnight.

* * *

Thank God they'd finally gone, Sandy thought, going into his bedroom. What a fuss his mother had made, instructions to Morag, orders to Cook, all a repeat of what she'd already told them countless times up to his parents' departure.

It had been the same with him. Don't forget to switch off all the lights at night, make sure the front door was locked, curtains drawn, etc etc. The list had been endless. Honestly, you'd think he was a child or had a rotten memory.

But now they were gone, leaving him in peace to paint to his heart's content. And do what else he had a mind to without taking them into consideration.

He picked up a fresh canvas he'd prepared and placed it on his easel. He'd have started there and then except he still hadn't decided what pose he wanted Sophie in, nor the setting.

Crossing to his desk he opened a sketchpad and flicked through it, hoping for inspiration, but none came.

He toyed with the idea of pouring himself a drink, then decided against it. It was far too early in the day for that. He pushed the sketchpad aside and started leafing through another one.

The idea, when it hit him, was so startling it left him stunned for a few moments. Of course. Of course. Why not?

But would she do it, that was the thing? And more to the point perhaps, would he have the courage to ask her?

It was how she normally made her living after all, he reminded himself.

* * *

'I've been watching you since you arrived,' Sophie said, sitting beside Sandy. 'You haven't drawn a thing.'

'That's because I'm here to talk to you, not draw.'

'Oh?'

He took a deep breath, willing himself to go through with this. He couldn't help but feel it was a little obscene somehow, which was absolute nonsense if you thought about it. Nonetheless, deep down he couldn't help being the product of a Calvanistic upbringing.

'I have a proposition for you,' he stated quietly.

Sophie arched an eyebrow. 'Proposition?'

'Yes. How would you like to earn some extra money?'

She was gazing at him steadily, a quizzical expression on her face. 'I could certainly use some extra. Why, what do you have in mind, Sandy?'

He forced himself to match her gaze. 'I'm willing to pay whatever your going rate is, more even, if you'll pose for me.'

'I see.'

'A life pose, that is.'

Sophie couldn't help but smile at his seriousness. 'You mean nude?'

'As you do at the Art School, and for those painters in Montmartre. It wouldn't be any different.'

'No?'

'No, I swear.'

'No jiggery pokery?'

'My word of honour, Sophie, no jiggery pokery. I want to paint you nude. A sitting pose with you smoking.'

She thought of his drawings, all of which she genuinely liked. So what was the difference between Sandy and the other artists she posed for? None really. It was only a job of work.

There again, her artist friends were men of the world, professionals, whereas Sandy was, well whatever, not a man of the world, and not a professional but, rather, an enthusiastic amateur.

'Please?' he pleaded. 'I so desperately want to do this.'

'Do you have a studio?'

He shook his head. 'Not really. But I do have a sort of make-shift one in my bedroom.'

'Ah!' She smiled. 'Your bedroom.'

Sandy heard the scepticism in her voice. 'I meant what I said about no jiggery pokery, Sophie. Truly I did.'

'Have you ever painted a naked person before?' she teased, having already guessed the answer.

'No, I haven't wanted to before.'

'But you do now. And you want that person to be me?'

'I mean, who else can I ask? There's no one. And that's what you normally do for a living after all. What I'm suggesting is a straightforward business arrangement, no more.'

She was beginning to find this amusing, aware of the discomfort he was so obviously trying to hide. 'I thought you lived with your parents?' she queried.

'I do. But they've gone away on holiday for a fortnight which means I'm alone in the house. Well, at night anyway, the staff are there during the day.'

'So I would come at night, is that it?'

'By taxi, there and back which I'll pay for.'

'Hmm!' she murmured, eyes glinting with merriment. 'So let me see if I've got this right. I come to your house at night and then pose naked in your bedroom, *non*?'

He blushed. 'Sounds awful put like that, doesn't it?'

He was suddenly a little boy who'd been caught doing something naughty, she thought. She found it endearing. 'Awful,' she agreed, laughter in her voice.

'So you won't do it?'

'I didn't say that.'

'Then you will?' he queried hopefully.

'I haven't said that either.'

His face fell. 'So what is your answer?'

'That I'll think about it.'

That was disappointing, but at least he hadn't been turned down flat. 'Just don't take too long, Sophie, they are only away for a fortnight and I want to get as many sittings in as I can.'

'So you'll want me more than once?'

He didn't catch the inference in her tone. 'Oh yes. Once wouldn't be nearly enough. It would only give me a start.'

She'd already decided, but would keep him dangling in suspense a while longer, simply for the fun of it. 'I must get back now before I'm missed,' she declared.

'When will you let me know?'

'Perhaps tomorrow.'

'Only perhaps?'

'Only perhaps, Sandy.'

'I'll be here then.'

He didn't have to say that, she knew it anyway. She tapped him on the end of his nose before rising and walking away. She'd enjoyed their chat.

Immensely.

Laura had read about the British Empire Exhibition in the newspapers, but had never for one moment dreamt she'd be visiting it. And now, here she was sitting in a tented restaurant adjacent to the Burma Pavilion, which they'd just been to, taking tea and sandwiches with Aunt Cakey. The whole thing was thrilling in the extreme.

Cakey focused on Laura, and smiled. 'Tell me something about yourself? I know so little.'

Laura frowned, wondering how to answer that. 'There isn't much to tell, Auntie. I was born, I go to school, and that's about it. Nothing's happened, and I haven't done anything, yet. And that's about it.'

'Let's take school then, are you good at your lessons?'

Laura thought about that. 'Fairly average I suppose. I get on well with French, but not Latin, which is surprising.'

'Why so?'

'They're both languages. You'd think that if I could easily grasp hold of one then it would be the same with all of them. But in my case I'm a complete dunce at Latin.'

There was a certain logic in that, Cakey conceded. 'How about English?'

'So so. I get better marks in maths. My teacher for that is very pleased with me.'

Cakey suspected Laura was being modest, for she had struck her as an extremely intelligent child. There again, intelligence and school work didn't always equate. 'Have you any idea what you'd like to do when you leave school?'

'Do?' Laura laughed. 'I won't be *doing* anything. Pa wouldn't hear of it. He'd have a fit if I even suggested having a job.' She leant forward and lowered her voice. 'It would worry him that people thought we needed

162

the money, that he wasn't able to support his family. Pa's very old fashioned in that way.'

And very stupid, Cakey thought. But that was Mathew all over. 'Let's say you were allowed to have a job, what would interest you?'

'I don't know,' Laura mused. 'I've never really thought about it. But possibly a nurse.'

'A nurse!' Cakey exclaimed. 'Because your father's a doctor and Sandy will become one?'

Laura shook her head. 'Not really. I like the idea of helping people, that's all. To be a nurse must be a very rewarding and satisfying thing.'

'I see,' Cakey murmured.

'If not a nurse then something to do with helping people in other ways. That would also appeal.'

'I believe you'd make a splendid nurse,' Cakey acknowledged. 'As you say, it's a most worthwhile profession.'

Laura shrugged. 'But it'll never be. I'll stay at home till I, hopefully, get married some time and then it'll be husband and, again hopefully, family to look after and care for.'

'Nothing wrong with that,' Cakey declared. 'But it is nice to have done other things before that happens.'

'It would be,' Laura agreed wistfully.

Chapter 11

Sophie was late, Sandy fretted, glancing at the clock. More than half an hour so now. Where was she?

He moved away from the window, curtains wide open despite the late hour, and began to pace. Perhaps she'd changed her mind, or something had come up? He wished he'd thought to give her his telephone number, that way she could at least have got in touch to explain.

He considered nipping upstairs and having another whisky to calm himself down a little, then decided against it. He'd already had three, and didn't want to get drunk. He certainly couldn't paint decently if he was.

'Damn!' he muttered, filled with frustration. Returning to the window he looked out hoping to see the arrival of her taxi, but there was nothing, no sign at all.

Maybe she'd been making fun of him? Promising him she'd come with no intention of doing so. He shook his head. No, he couldn't believe she'd do that. Not Sophie.

Quarter to now, the clock steadily ticking the night away. He resumed pacing.

It was almost an hour past the time they'd agreed when he heard the sound of a motor car drawing up outside, and its engine starting to idle. She was here at long last!

'Sorry I'm late,' she apologised as he helped her out of the taxi onto the pavement.

'That's all right.'

He closed the cab door and paid the driver, giving the man a fairly generous tip, more through relief than anything else.

Sophie was staring up at the house as he lightly grasped her by the elbow. 'Shall we?'

She flashed him a broad smile as they went into the hallway. 'I've bought some wine and thought we might have a drink first. Or would you prefer just to get on with it?' he asked.

'A glass of wine would be lovely.'

He took her into their sitting room and indicated a chair. 'I don't know much about wine I'm afraid, but the licensed grocer who sold it to me said it's a good one.'

Sophie settled herself. 'I'm sure it will be.'

'The staff have gone, as I said, so we're quite alone.'

His nervousness wasn't lost on her, nor the fact she'd smelt alcohol on his breath as he'd escorted her inside. 'It's a very nice house,' she commented.

'Thank you.'

'Your father must be a very successful doctor.'

Sandy gave a small laugh. 'Not according to him. But there again, he has delusions of grandeur.'

That puzzled Sophie. 'I don't quite follow you?'

He handed her a glass of wine, having opened the bottle well before she'd arrived. 'It means he thinks he's far better off than he actually is.'

'Oh!' Sophie smiled, nodding. 'I understand now.'

'Pa wanted to be the top surgeon in Scotland, and very, very rich. Unfortunately he achieved neither.'

'Why not just a surgeon?'

Sandy sighed. 'The truth, though he'd deny it, is that he simply wasn't good enough to be one, far less the best in Scotland. That's why he has such high hopes for me. I'm supposed to achieve what he couldn't.'

'And will you?'

'Never in a million years,' Sandy admitted ruefully. 'In fact I'll be lucky, but I think I told you this before, if I ever manage to qualify at all. Whatever ability I may have certainly isn't in the medical field.'

Sophie tasted her wine.

'Well? I'm no judge in such matters,' Sandy asked.

'Excellent.' Typical of the wines served in Scotland, she thought. Poor in quality, and no doubt overpriced. Still, it wasn't that bad, she served a lot worse at the hotel.

'Good.' Sandy was pleased.

'Do you mind if I smoke?'

That alarmed him, he'd quite forgotten she smoked, a habit both his parents loathed. He'd have to ensure all smell of smoke had gone when they returned from Largs. 'I'll get an ashtray,' he declared, desperately wondering what he could use. He solved the problem by producing a little dish his mother called a 'cappy', whatever that was.

Sophie lit up. 'I'm ready to begin when you are,' she stated.

'You'd better finish your cigarette first.'

She noticed he was gulping his wine rather than sipping it, another sign of nervousness. She felt sorry for him and would do her best to put him at his ease.

They chatted another few minutes, then rose to go upstairs, Sandy asking if she'd mind bringing the cappy with her as he'd be carrying his glass and what remained of the wine. She was happy to oblige.

He inwardly cursed himself as they mounted the stairs. How could he possibly have forgotten she smoked when he'd specifically told her he wanted to paint her smoking. How stupid could you get! The reason was that his mind was in turmoil because of what lay ahead.

'Here we are then,' he declared, ushering her into his bedroom where he'd rearranged things so that his easel faced into the centre of the room instead of as it had been. He'd also borrowed a screen from his parents' bedroom for her to use.

Sophie glanced around, taking in the screen which she guessed had been placed there for the reason Sandy intended.

'It isn't much of a studio,' Sandy apologised. 'But I did warn you it was a make-shift one.'

'It'll do fine.'

'Would you like me to light the fire?'

'I don't think so,' she smiled. 'But I'll let you know if I get cold.' How considerate he was, she reflected. She liked that. So unlike many of the artists she'd posed for.

'Right,' Sandy declared, a sudden huskiness in his voice. 'We'd better get on with it.'

Sophie was finding this amusing. 'I'll get undressed then.'

'If you would. And I'll set up.'

He already was set up but needed something to do. The last thing he wanted was to just stand there.

He fussed around his easel and paints pretending to be busy, his heart pounding fit to burst and the palms of his hands sweating copiously. Every few seconds he wiped them on his trousers, still not believing the moment had finally arrived when he was going to see Sophie naked.

He must try to forget that, he told himself. Just concentrate on the painting. That was what mattered, the painting.

He paused to pour himself more wine, hardly tasting it as it slid down his throat, wishing it was whisky.

'So, how would you like me?' she asked on her reappearance.

His heart which had been pounding now seemed to jump into his mouth as he turned to face her. My God, he thought. My God. She was incredible, even more beautiful than when she was dressed. And that was saying something. He prayed that he didn't embarrass himself, and her, by getting obviously excited in the trouser department.

Sandy thought of the cadavers he'd seen in the hospital. Older women, and working class, raddled from life and childbirth. This was very, very different, as he'd known it would be.

A smile twitched the corners of Sophie's mouth,

for Sandy was staring at her goggle-eyed, his face ever so slightly flushed. She took his reaction as a compliment.

Sandy wrenched himself out of his stupified reverie. 'Eh . . . let me think,' he murmured. 'I was going to have you leaning against the mantelpiece, but I've changed my mind. Could you try lying on the bed for me?'

Sophie went over and stretched out.

'Up on one elbow, Sophie.'

She complied.

'And bring your hair sort of over your left shoulder please.'

She did that.

It was a vision of pure feminine gorgeousness, he thought.

'What about the smoking?'

He wasn't sure about that any more. 'Not for the moment. I'll see as we go along.'

Her hair wasn't exactly right, he decided. Going to it he arranged it just as he wanted. 'There,' he pronounced. 'That's better.'

Crossing back to his easel he set to work, thinking he was going to enjoy this more than any painting he'd done previously. Enjoy it far, far more.

He'd been painting for an hour, his expression one of twisted concentration, the pair of them having exchanged only a few words, before he thought about asking her if she'd like a break.

'Please. I have to go to the bathroom.'

'Oh dear!' That flustered him. 'You should have said.'

'I didn't want to interrupt you.'

He laid his brush aside. 'Come and I'll show you where it is.'

She followed him out of the bedroom and along the corridor to the relevant door. 'There you are.'

'*Merci.*'

Returning to his easel he peered at what he'd done, which was only really an outline so far. He'd been surprised by the size of her breasts which were larger than he'd imagined, and further surprised by the dark colouring of her nipples. He thought the breasts and nipples were delightful.

He suddenly realised that he too had to go to the toilet, and excused himself when Sophie returned. When he got back to the bedroom he found her sitting on the bed smoking and drinking her wine, which he noticed she'd topped up.

'Did you look?' he queried.

'*Naturellement.* You never said not to.'

'And?'

'Too soon to tell, Sandy.'

'Of course.'

He perched on the edge of his desk and glanced from his canvas to her, and back again, thinking line and colour and all manner of things he intended doing and how he was going to go about them. 'Still warm enough?' he asked.

'Still.'

'I had thought of painting you standing but somehow . . . when I saw you, that didn't seem right. I much prefer you on the bed. It's more . . . sensuous. More . . . erotic.'

'Is that how you see me, sensuous and erotic?' she teased.

'Very much so.'

'Then I'm flattered.'

He wagged a finger at her. 'You're making fun of me. You must have been told that many times in the past.'

'Perhaps,' she demurred.

'And certainly how beautiful you are. A Venus descended.'

Sophie laughed. 'Isn't that just a little pretentious, *cheri*?'

'I wouldn't say so.'

How very young he was, she thought. In mind and experience as well as years. For her anyway, it was a very attractive quality. But then, she'd thought that before.

'When do you have to leave?' he queried.

'I have work in the morning so I mustn't be too late. They get cross if I'm not there on time.'

'No cigarette,' he suddenly announced. 'I have been toying with the idea, but, in this instance, it would be quite wrong. I can see that now. So we can forget that.'

'As you wish.'

He was impatient to get painting again, inspiration, if that's indeed what it was, strong within him.

Sophie caught his mood, so ground out the remains of her Gitanes and drank off her wine.

Sandy had to rearrange her hair to get it exactly as it had been, before hurrying back to his easel. Within moments he was again completely engrossed.

Sandy hung up the telephone and turned to Sophie. 'A taxi will be here in ten minutes. Shall we wait in the sitting room?'

They went through and she resumed the seat she'd occupied earlier. Sandy cleared his throat. 'Now, I owe you money.'

'Please.'

'The workman is worthy of his hire,' he joked. 'And you were certainly that.'

'Thank you.'

He'd laid out the cash on the sideboard before she'd arrived which he now collected and handed her. 'That's your fee plus for the cab home. All right?'

'Fine.'

'Now,' he said, sudden eagerness in his voice. 'When can you come again?'

'The night after next?'

'Excellent. Same time?'

'And I'll try not to be late.'

He laughed. 'I'd appreciate that.' He hesitated, then said earnestly, 'Thank you for posing for me, Sophie. You've no idea how much it means to me.'

She didn't know what to reply to that, so didn't. 'Will you be at the hotel tomorrow?'

'No, I want to continue work on the painting. Do what I can even though you aren't there.'

To her surprise, she found that disappointing. She'd been enjoying his visits to sketch her, they made her shifts pass more quickly. Besides, he was good company when they had the chance to speak together.

'I wish you could have stayed longer,' Sandy said.

'Perhaps another night when I don't have to get up early the next morning.'

'That would be nice,' he beamed.

Neither knew exactly why, but it was suddenly awkward between them. Each was unsure of what to say next. So it was with something of a relief that they heard the taxi draw up.

'The night after next,' Sandy said when she was settled in the back seat.

'I look forward to it.'

'And so will I.'

As he returned indoors he felt as though he was walking on air. What an evening. What a fantastic evening! The best he'd ever had. Ever. No doubt about it.

For the umpteenth time Harriet wondered how long Mathew would be away for. He was off driving the Rolls as usual. Why, since their arrival in Largs he was never out of the damn thing!

Morning, noon and night, I think I'll just go for a little drive, dear. Would you like to come? To begin with she had accompanied him, but it was so boring just driving hither and yon with no proper objective in mind. Simply showing off. For that's what it boiled down to, showing off. Pure swank.

Harriet closed her eyes and leant back in her chair, thinking about her and Mathew. A holiday without the children had turned out just as she'd feared. They had nothing, or very little anyway, to say to one another. The house, his job, the children, all the props had been removed. And what remained? Nothing.

She'd hoped, stupidly of course, that the holiday might turn out to be a sort of second honeymoon. Well that certainly wasn't on Mathew's agenda, nor had he taken it on board when she'd hinted once or twice. All he cared about was that damned Rolls and being seen in it.

She thought back to what it had been like before they'd been married, and how different that was. He'd been caring then, loving, attentive. But now? Completely different.

He'd changed a great deal down through the years, as the bitterness about his profession bit deeper and deeper, to the point where he was nothing like the man she'd walked up the aisle with.

As for lovemaking, there had been lots of that at the beginning, every night to be exact. Well, more or less depending on circumstances. As it was she couldn't even remember the last time they'd made love. In fact, if she was being brutally honest she couldn't even recall the last time he'd shown her any special tenderness.

Was this how all marriages turned out? she wondered. Surely not, that couldn't be so. That would be far too cruel. It wasn't as if she was old; in your midforties was hardly old. All being well with their health there were years ahead of them yet. And with Sandy grown up, and Laura fast approaching that, these should be the best years, particularly after the children eventually left home.

Harriet sighed. What a misery she was today. An absolute misery. And filled with what, regret? Was that it, did she regret marrying Mathew?

It wasn't as if he'd been her only suitor. There had been James Ballantine, a dashing young man if ever there was. Certainly a kind man. But she'd chosen Mathew over James which had seemed the right decision at the time. Only now, with hindsight, she had to ask herself if it had been?

She didn't know what had become of James who'd been in the retail trade. He was no doubt married himself, probably with a family. She hoped he was happy, he deserved that.

How different would it have been if she'd married James? Would married life have been any different – or better?

How she envied Cakey and her marriage to Herbert. Theirs had been a real love match and they had idolised one another. Nor had Herbert been the rascal Mathew always insisted. He'd been an entrepreneur, that's all, an adventurer, someone who took chances, even outrageous ones at times. And just look how he and Cakey had ended up – rich as Croesus. And, more to the point, just as happy as they'd started out.

At least she had two lovely children to be thankful for, that was something Cakey had never been blessed with. How proud she was of them. All she could hope was that when it was their turn to marry they chose more wisely than she had done.

'Oh well!' she sighed, she'd made her bed and now had to lie on it. That's how it was.

But what might have been? That was a question she'd never have an answer to.

Laura emerged from the changing room in a fashionable Bond Street salon to parade herself before Cakey.

'Like it?' Cakey queried.

The lilac blue dress was made from all rayon canton crepe. It had tiered puff sleeves and an ankle-swirling, slim-fitting skirt cut on the bias. A black sash gave it a nipped waistline.

'Like it? I love it!' Laura enthused, eyes gleaming. 'It makes me look so grown up. Why, I could be taken for . . . twenty.'

The dress certainly complemented Laura's new bob hairstyle, Cakey reflected. As for twenty, that was a bit of an exaggeration. Eighteen perhaps, at a stretch.

'Shall we have it?'

'Oh, please, Aunt Cakey. Though it is—'

Cakey held up a hand, interrupting Laura. 'I don't want to be told again how expensive something is. I can afford it. OK?'

'OK,' Laura acknowledged, repeating her aunt's expression.

'A coat next I think,' Cakey mused. 'You definitely need a new one.'

'I believe we might have just the thing,' a hovering lady assistant twittered.

'Then bring it on. Let's have a look.'

Laura was beside herself with excitement and pleasure. Wait till she told Madeleine Abercrombie about all this and showed her what they'd bought. Madeleine would explode with jealousy.

And Sandy, she suddenly thought. She couldn't wait to show him either. He'd certainly view her in a new light now. A grown-up Laura McLean.

She shivered at the delicious prospect.

'Tell me more about Montmartre,' Sandy said. He was in the middle of the third session with Sophie and the painting was coming on.

'What would you like to know?'

'Everything! What's the favourite drink there, for example?'

'Ah!' she exhaled. 'It's very naughty. And banned, because it makes you go mad in the end.'

That startled him. 'Really?'

'Some people call it the green death.'

'Why green?'

'Because that's its colour, emerald green. To drink it you pour cold water over a perforated spoonful of sugar which turns the alcohol into a milky-white liquor that's very strong. Believe me, potent and habit-forming. It was the favourite drink of Van Gogh and Beaudelaire who believed, at least so I was told, that it stimulates creativity. It is also believed . . .' she paused to smile in a catlike way, 'to be an aphrodisiac.'

He wasn't sure whether or not she was teasing him. 'And is it?'

Sophie contemplated her answer. The truth? 'I find it so,' she replied slowly.

'You mean personally?'

'Yes.'

Sandy cleared his throat. 'I see.'

Sophie was amused to observe how discomfited he'd suddenly become. 'Do you disapprove?'

'No, of course not.'

'Montmartre is Montmartre, Sandy. It's very different to here.'

'I know, you've already said. It's quite accepted for models to live with artists and other artistic types. Right?'

She nodded.

'And what's the name of this demon potion?'

'Absinthe.'

'Absinthe,' he repeated. 'And it drives you mad?'

'Eventually, if you overindulge, which I try not to knowing what can happen if you do.'

'But you said it's habit-forming?'

'If you allow it to be. If you took it, say, every day.'

Sandy frowned. 'But hold on, how can you if it's banned?'

'Montmartre, Sandy, anything's available there if you know the right person and have the money to pay for it. Anything at all.'

Damn! he inwardly swore. His concentration had gone, he shouldn't have started this conversation in the first place. 'Shall we have a break?'

Sophie immediately came to a sitting position and reached for her cigarettes. Sandy watched her as she lit up, thinking how gloriously wanton she looked at that moment. Wanton and desirable.

He excused himself and went to the bathroom where he splashed cold water on his face to cool himself down a little.

He really needed to.

Sophie was restless, unable to sleep, and she knew exactly why. Perhaps it was the conversation she'd had with Sandy earlier at his house; whatever, she was missing a man in her life. No, to be absolutely honest, she was missing sex with one.

It had been months since Jack, and now there was a terrible need in her crying out to be satisfied. She wasn't one of those women who could put sex aside and forget about it, that wasn't her at all.

Sophie brushed a stray wisp of hair away from her face, her body craving what she could only temporarily substitute. A substitute she'd indulged in for a while but which was now not enough. She needed the real thing, and the sooner the better.

She felt no shame about any of this, why should

she? Sex was the most natural thing in the world, at least the world she came from where it was recognised as such. Also a commodity to be bought and sold, a practice she herself had often resorted to in the past when it was necessary, or the whim took her.

How Sandy would be shocked to know that, she thought. Such a naive young man, so utterly inexperienced in life. A virgin, that was obvious. And at his age too! That would never have been the case in Montmartre where life was very, very different, where morality was merely a word, a pretence, no more.

There could be no doubting how attracted he was to her; all she'd have to do was crook her finger and he'd come running.

She thought of Jack whom she'd genuinely loved, and who'd deserted her. She wasn't over him yet, but had finally, at long last, accepted he wasn't coming back, that he'd gone for ever.

'Jack,' she murmured aloud, a name at once both so dear to her and so hateful because of what he'd done to her.

Well, it was time to move on. She needed a man, and there was one readily available.

'It's finished,' Sandy announced. 'Come and tell me what you think?'

Sophie padded across the room to stand beside him. 'You work very quickly,' she commented.

'I always have when it comes to painting and drawing. I either get the subject right away or I never do. It's as simple as that.'

'It's good,' she declared after a few seconds' perusal.

'You like it then?'

'Very much so. And you have made my eyes the right colour.'

He laughed. 'Thank you.'

'And now my posing here is finished, *non*?'

'Christ,' he muttered, suddenly dejected, all elation at having finished leaving him. 'I suppose it is.'

She stared into his eyes, smiling at what she saw there. Something she'd seen in men's eyes many times before. Taking his hand she placed it on her crotch. 'I think we should celebrate you finishing, don't you?'

His entire body had gone rigid from shock. 'You mean . . . ?' he croaked.

'*Oui, chéri*. I mean just that.'

He followed her meekly to the bed where she began undressing him.

Chapter 12

'There we are, Margaret, the car keys,' Mathew declared, handing them to her, his smile so forced it was almost cracking his face.

'Why thank you, Mathew. I trust you found driving it a pleasant experience?' Cakey was laughing inside, well aware of how difficult this must be for her brother-in-law.

'Very,' he acknowledged.

'Who knows?' she teased. 'Perhaps one day you might acquire a vehicle of your own. A Rolls-Royce, that is.'

Harriet was highly amused by this interplay for the same reason as Cakey.

'It's wonderful to be home,' Harriet enthused, glancing round in appreciation.

'Didn't you enjoy yourself?' Cakey queried.

'Of course she did,' Mathew snapped. 'We both did.' He turned on Sandy who was also present. 'And you, Alexander, did you get lots of study done?'

'Lots, Pa,' Sandy lied.

Mathew nodded his satisfaction. 'Harriet, ring for tea. I think we could all use some. And where's Laura?'

'Upstairs,' Cakey explained. 'She wanted a bath after our journey.'

'Hmmh,' Mathew murmured.

'I want to hear all about London,' Harriet said to Cakey. 'But not now, later when we're alone and have the time to chat.'

Cakey rightly interpreted that as when Mathew wasn't there. 'And you can tell me all about Largs.'

Harriet sighed. 'Quiet really. A nice rest though.'

Cakey knew her sister well enough to realise that she meant bored stiff, which is exactly as she would have expected.

'How was the train journey, Aunt Cakey?' Sandy inquired politely, feeling he should contribute something to the conversation.

'Long, and tedious. But there you are, it's over now.'

Morag appeared in answer to Harriet's summons on the bell pull, and was despatched again to bring them tea.

A few moments later a smiling Laura appeared wearing one of the many new dresses Cakey had bought her. 'Hello, everyone. I thought I heard talking.' Going to Harriet she kissed her mother on the cheek. 'I've missed you.'

'What have you done to your hair?' Mathew's voice was an accusatory whiplash of disapproval.

'Had it cut and styled, Pa. Do you like it?'

His eyes had gone flinty hard. 'No I do not, it's far too old for a schoolgirl.'

Laura's face crumpled, while Cakey looked on in anger. Harriet stood quite stunned by this unexpected outburst.

'And that dress is ridiculous for the same reason,' Mathew continued coldly. 'Far too old.'

'Hold on, Pa, isn't that a bit harsh?' Sandy interjected before Mathew could go on.

The flinty eyes now blazed fury. 'I'll thank you to mind your own business, Alexander. It's got nothing to do with you. And I suggest you only speak when spoken to.'

Sandy was suddenly angry. Normally he wouldn't have stood up to his father, but he did now. 'May I remind you how old *I* am. I will not be treated like some infant.'

'As long as you're in my house, under my roof, and dependent on me for your welfare, you will do as I say. Understand?'

Sandy bit back a retort. What his father had said, if unfair, was nonetheless true. He was dependent on him.

'If there's a fault here it's mine,' Cakey stated quietly, but firmly. 'It was my suggestion Laura have her hair cut that way, and the clothes we bought had my approval.'

Laura was completely distraught. She'd been so proud of her new hairstyle and clothes, and now this! She'd thought her father might object a little, but had never anticipated a scene of such magnitude. It was awful, and completely humiliating.

'Oh, Ma!' she sobbed.

Harriet went to her and took her into her arms. 'There there,' she consoled.

Sandy had never felt like hitting his father before, but he did at that moment.

It was having to hand back the Rolls, Harriet realised. That's what this was really all about.

'Now go back upstairs this instant and change into what you would normally wear,' Mathew barked. 'We can't do anything about the hair except let it grow again. Which you will, my girl.'

Laura, face streaming with tears, tore herself away from Harriet, and fled.

There were a few minutes' silence, finally broken by a white-faced Harriet. 'Cakey, could you and Alexander please leave us for a while. I wish to speak privately to Mathew.'

'Of course,' Cakey muttered, still having trouble keeping control of herself.

Harriet watched them go, then turned to face a defiant-looking Mathew. In all the years of their marriage she'd been the perfect wife, bowing to his every wish and command, behaving as she believed a wife should. Well, in the light of what had just happened, which was totally unforgivable, that was now over.

She'd be a doormat no longer.

'Go away!' Laura sobbed into her pillow when there was a tap on her bedroom door.

'It's me, Sandy. Can I come in?'

'No.'

'Please? I'm on your side, remember.'

There was no reply.

'Sod it,' he muttered and opened the door anyway. Crossing to the bed he sat beside her.

'I don't blame you for being like this. Pa was pretty rotten downstairs,' he murmured, gently stroking her hair. 'And for the record, I think you look terrific.'

'Do you?' The voice was muffled by the pillow.

'Oh yes. Quite stunning actually.'

That mollified her a little. Changing position she came to rest in his arms. 'Thank you.'

'No need for that. It's absolutely true, I swear.'

'If I had the means I'd run away from home, Sandy,' she choked. 'I'm going to hate it here now.'

'No you won't. This will all blow over and soon be forgotten. You'll see.'

'No it won't.'

'Yes it will,' he insisted.

'We had such a lovely time in London too. This has just spoilt it.'

'It must have been wizard?'

She came out of his arms and sat up properly. 'Oh, it was, Sandy. I enjoyed it so much.'

'I'm glad to hear it.'

Laura snuggled even closer to him. 'We did all sorts of exciting things, including going to the Empire Exhibition. We spent an entire day there.'

'I say, how wonderful!' he enthused, groping in his pocket to produce a handkerchief. 'Here, let me. And don't worry, it's clean.'

She smiled as he wiped her tears away. 'I think it's lovely how close you and I have become of late. Ever since that first night I visited you in your bedroom. Remember?'

'Of course I do.'

'You were always a bit horrid to me before that.'

'Was I?' he asked in surprise.

Laura nodded. 'Quite sharp at times. And certainly not interested, which was such a shame for I was always interested in you and what you were up to.'

'Well well,' he murmured, not really knowing what to reply to that. 'But it's all right now, isn't it?'

'You know it is.'

On impulse, and in relief, he kissed her on the cheek.

'It feels so safe like this, being held by you,' she stated after a few seconds' silence. 'As if the rest of the world has been shut out, and there's just the two of us.'

'I wonder what Ma's saying to Pa?' he mused. 'She wasn't best pleased to say the least. None of us was.'

He stayed and chatted with Laura for well over an hour, and during the entire time she remained snuggled up in his arms. When he finally left she was more or less her old self again.

'What are you doing here?' Sophie appeared behind the bar to discover Sandy sitting at it.

'I couldn't wait till tonight. I had to see you now.'

'Is something wrong?'

Sandy shook his head. 'Nothing at all. I just wanted to see you.'

How sweet, she thought. How very sweet. 'Well now you're here you'd better have a drink.'

It should have been coffee at that time of the morning, but he wanted something stronger to calm him a little. Thinking about Sophie had filled him with a burning frustration at having to get through the entire day before their rendezvous at her place. 'A large whisky please.'

Sophie raised a well-plucked eyebrow, but didn't comment. '*Oui, m'sieur.*'

He was in love with her, Sophie realised, which pleased her to a certain extent. On the other hand it could complicate matters as she had no intention of falling in love with him. She liked him, yes. And was prepared to use him for sex, but that's as far as it went. Besides, she intended returning to Montmartre soon now she'd given up all hope of Jack coming back to her.

She took the money he handed over and rang it up on the till, acutely aware of his gaze following her every move.

'There you are,' she declared, laying his change beside the glass she'd already placed on the bar.

'You're lovely,' he whispered.

'Am I?'

'As if you didn't know.'

She smiled. 'And you're nice too. Now stop this as I'm working.'

'We're the only ones here.'

'Not for long, so stop it.'

She was flattered by this attention, and thoroughly enjoying herself. A shiver of anticipation ran through her at the prospect of what lay ahead that evening.

She began to ache most deliciously.

Sandy stared about him. This was the first time he'd been in Sophie's home. He was surprised at how untidy it was – and none too clean either if he'd looked closely enough – clearly housekeeping wasn't her forte.

Somehow there was a French, or at least foreign, feel about the place, though he couldn't have said why. Bohemian was the word that came to mind. He liked it. Yes, Bohemian.

She would make him wait, Sophie decided. Tease the occasion out before going through to the bedroom.

Make him suffer a little. That would amuse her, and heighten their pleasure when it finally occurred. At least it would hers and she didn't think Sandy would be disappointed either.

'I've seen and spoken to Conor again,' Madeleine Abercrombie announced to Laura.

'You have! Where?'

'I bumped into him, quite by chance, in Buchanan Street. He was going one way, me the other. We stopped and chatted for absolutely ages. But the best part is, wait for it! He's invited me to a dinner dance this Saturday at the Grosvenor.'

'Really?' Laura was thrilled for her friend.

'Really.'

'Will your parents let you go?'

'I've already asked. Pop said he thought I was too young for that sort of thing, but Ma talked him round. Bless her. I am sixteen now, after all, and leaving school next year. I'm sure it helped that Pop knows Conor's father.'

'Well, congratulations.'

An extremely excited Madeleine clapped her hands together. 'I can't wait for Saturday night. He's calling for me in his father's car. How about that!'

'I'm impressed.' Laura became suddenly serious. 'So what are you going to wear?'

They fell to discussing that.

Cakey popped her head round Sandy's open bedroom door. 'Can I have a word?'

'Of course, Aunt Cakey. Come in.'

She did, closing the door behind her. 'I was talking

to a Mr Moon who owns the Sauchiehall Street Gallery earlier today. You know the gallery, I take it?'

Sandy nodded. 'It has a good reputation. The best in Scotland and that includes the fancy Edinburgh ones.'

'Well, during our conversation I spoke to him about you and suggested you might be exhibited in the autumn when he's putting on an exhibition of young Scottish painters.'

Sandy was astounded. 'You're joking!'

'Not at all. I went in, introduced myself, and had a natter. Don't forget my husband Herbert was reasonably well known in the art world, so I was able to mention names and galleries that Mr Moon was aware of. Anyway, he hasn't promised anything, but has asked to see a selection of your work. What do you think?'

Sandy didn't know what to think, his mind was numb from shock. Him! Exhibited!

'Do you really believe I'm good enough?' he asked in a tremulous voice.

'I wouldn't have recommended you otherwise.'

'Christ,' he muttered, still not able to take this in. It was incredible. More than that, it was bloody fantastic!

'Don't forget he isn't promising anything. He might turn you down. But nothing ventured, nothing gained, eh?'

'True enough.'

'Now,' she declared, matter of factly. 'Let's get down to business. I'd like to see your work again and help you choose what to show him. If you don't mind, that is?'

'I don't mind at all. In fact, I'd be delighted for you to help.'

'Right then, anything new since I was in here last?'

Sophie, the painting of Sophie was new, but dare he show it to her? It was a nude after all and Cakey was his aunt which made it difficult, embarrassing even. He certainly wouldn't have dared show it to his mother or father, particularly the latter. He could well imagine Pa's reaction.

'There is a painting,' Sandy admitted slowly.

'Let's see it then.'

'It's, eh . . . eh . . . a nude, Aunt Cakey. Will that offend you?'

Cakey laughed. 'Don't be ridiculous, of course it won't. I'm not a prude you know.' A wicked glint came into her eyes. 'That's the last thing I am.'

Sandy pulled out the painting from those stacked against the wall. Picking it up he stood it on his desk. 'This is it.'

'Hmmh,' Cakey mused, eyeing it keenly. 'Is it a copy of someone else's work or did you do it yourself from real life?'

Sandy could feel himself squirm. 'Real life.'

'Interesting. She's certainly a pretty woman.'

'A professional model,' Sandy explained, thinking that sounded better. 'I hired her.'

'Did you now?'

'She usually models at the Art School, which is how I got to hear of her.'

'And where, if you don't mind me asking, did you execute the piece?'

Sandy blushed. 'In this room actually, while Ma and Pa were at Largs. Sophie, that's her name, came here. That's my bed she's lying on.'

He'd got the face just right, Cakey reflected, particularly the eyes which appeared to reflect the female's innermost being. Quite an achievement for someone so young and inexperienced. The skin tones were also excellent, as were the line and proportion. Overall it was a wonderful effort, certainly of professional standard in her opinion. She couldn't imagine Mr Moon not liking it.

'We'll take this,' she pronounced. 'Most definitely. Does it have a title, by the way?'

Sandy thought furiously, not having given that any consideration. 'How about "The French Woman"?'

Cakey nodded. 'That'll do. And is she?'

'French? Yes, from Montmartre in Paris. She's modelled, or posed, for all sorts of famous artists over there.'

'You must tell me more about her sometime. In the meanwhile, let's see what else there is.'

Eventually three of Sandy's oils were chosen and eight of his drawings, to be taken, in the Rolls, to be shown to Mr Moon the following week, as already arranged by Cakey.

The letter arrived during breakfast and was given to Sandy by Morag. His heart sank when he saw the franking on its front. The contents were his exam results.

'Is that what I think it is?' Mathew inquired.

'Yes, Pa.'

'Then hadn't you better open it?'

'Yes, Pa.'

Please God make them good, he prayed as he tore open the envelope. His hands were trembling when he extracted the single sheet of paper it contained.

If his heart had sunk on being given the letter, it

sunk even lower now. A quick perusal confirmed that his results were indeed awful, even worse than he'd expected.

'Well?' Mathew demanded.

Sandy swallowed hard, unable to meet his father's penetrating gaze. He wished he was anywhere but where he was.

Laura was staring at her plate. It wasn't difficult to see Sandy had done badly, his expression gave it away. She truly felt for him.

'Well?' Mathew repeated.

'I've got through,' Sandy repeated, trying to put a smile on his face and failing miserably.

'I should damn well hope so. But what are the marks?'

'I could have done better.'

'Stop prevaricating, boy!' Mathew said, raising his voice to almost a shout.

'Mathew,' Harriet admonished quietly. 'Please.'

'Please my foot. What are the marks?'

Sandy read them out one by one.

'Oh dear,' Harriet muttered. 'But at least he's through to next year. That's something.'

Mathew was fighting back his fury. 'Those marks are a disgrace. A damned disgrace,' he snarled.

Sandy felt himself shrinking into his chair, still not daring to look at his father.

'Language, Mathew,' Harriet chided. 'We are at the breakfast table.'

'What have you got between your ears, boy, porage? Or is it simply an empty space?'

This had gone far enough, Harriet decided. After the scene with Laura she'd promised she'd take a harder stand with Mathew in future, such as now. 'I don't understand how you can make remarks like that, Mathew. It wasn't that long ago I came across your marks when at Medical School. Those were none too clever either. According to them *you* also scraped through on several occasions.'

Mathew stared at his wife in disbelief. How dare she bring that up? How dare she!

'So you're hardly in a position to criticise, don't you think?'

'That's not the point,' he choked.

'But I believe it is. Isn't it a case of the pot calling the kettle black?'

Mathew came to his feet, face contorted with anger. 'I'm due at the surgery.'

'You hurry along, dear. You're already late,' Harriet urged.

Mathew swept from the room without saying another word.

'Thanks, Ma,' Sandy croaked.

Cakey, who'd listened to this interchange in silence, smiled into her napkin. Good for Harriet, she thought. The worm was turning at long last. And not before time, in her opinion.

Sandy collapsed in a heap beside Sophie, his entire body gloriously drained.

Sophie glanced knowingly at him. Under her expert tuition he was learning fast. Every time they went to bed she introduced him to another aspect of love-making, another little 'something' to be indulged in, and enjoyed.

But best of all, as far as she was concerned, and

which owed nothing to her tutelage, was that he had staying power. Once she'd coyly explained to him that he needn't be so fast or urgent, that it was better for her, for both of them, if he slowed down, the sex had improved dramatically.

She traced a finger along his thigh. 'Sandy?'

'Mmm?'

'Nothing. I just like saying your name.'

He came on to one elbow to stare at her, thinking how wondrously beautiful she was. Particularly in her present, satiated state, her breasts still flushed from their recent exertions. 'I want to paint you again, but can't at home. Can I do so here?'

She thought about that. 'I don't see why not.'

'Another nude.'

'If you wish.'

'In a different position this time.'

She laughed, slowly and wickedly. 'And what position would *m'sieur* care to have me in?'

He knew he was being teased. 'Every possible one there is. And maybe we can even invent a few that have never been thought of before.'

'Maybe,' she smiled.

He wanted to tell her he loved her, but some instinct warned him not to, that it was too early for that. Such a declaration might put her off, scare her away even.

Sophie closed her eyes, luxuriating in how she felt, the warmth and sense of satisfaction that encompassed her. She could easily have drifted off into sleep if she'd allowed herself to.

When she finally re-opened her eyes it was to find that it was Sandy who'd nodded off.

* * *

'Did he kiss you?'

Madeleine nodded. 'Before I got out of the car to go on in. It was ever so lovely.'

Laura was curious. 'Did you really mean it when you said you were going to marry him one day? Or was that just talk?'

A look of fierce determination came onto Madeleine's face. 'I meant it all right. Conor and I were made for one another, there's no doubt in my mind about that. I knew it the first time we met.'

'He's obviously keen otherwise he wouldn't have asked you out.'

'And he's done so again. He wants to take me to the pictures next Saturday.'

'You accepted, of course?'

'Of course, Laura!' Her eyes took on a dreamy look. 'He's such a dish. I noticed other girls at the dinner dance staring at me in envy. I couldn't have been more proud to be with him.'

How romantic, Laura thought. It was like something straight out of a storybook.

'There's something else,' Madeleine went on.

'What's that?'

'I explained to him that I want to be a typist when I leave school, and he's promised, once I'm trained that is, that he'll put in a good word for me at his firm and hopefully get me a job there. That means we'd be working together, or in the same building anyway. Isn't that spiffy?'

Laura couldn't help but be jealous. Not about Madeleine and Conor, but that Madeleine was going to be allowed to work. 'Have you spoken to your parents about getting a job?'

'Oh yes, some time ago actually. They don't have any objections. None at all. In fact Pop said it would be a good thing.'

Laura couldn't imagine her own father saying that in a million years. She was destined to stay at home until such time as she got married. If she ever did that is.

Madeleine's revelation about getting a job after school had suddenly depressed her, but she tried to hide her feelings as Madeleine went on about all that had happened during the evening with Conor.

Chapter 13

'Well, that was a success, don't you think?' Cakey smiled as she and Sandy drove away from the Sauchiehall Street Gallery and their meeting with Mr Moon.

'I should say so,' Sandy replied enthusiastically. Only one of his oils had been rejected, everything else was accepted.

'Pleased?' She knew that to be a rhetorical question, but just wanted to hear his answer.

'Delighted. Delirious. Beside myself.'

Cakey laughed. 'So it would seem.'

'Thank you for arranging it, Aunt Cakey. In fact I can't thank you enough.' He shook his head in wonder. 'I still can't believe I'm going to be exhibited.'

What Sandy would never know was that money had changed hands, and promises made about connections with Canadian galleries. Cakey had absolutely no intention of telling him. Let Sandy think his work had been accepted on merit, which, indeed, it had. Moon would never have agreed to show it if it hadn't been good enough. The money and promises were simply a way of oiling wheels.

'Are you going to tell your parents?' Cakey asked casually.

'Not on your life. Pa would have a fit. Especially if he came along and found out I'd done a nude. He'd expire on the spot.'

'Pity that.'

'I'm not sure about Ma's reaction, but I am about Pa's, so I shan't be saying anything.'

'I'll be sorry to miss it, but I'll have gone back by then. You must write and tell me how it went.'

'I will,' Sandy promised her.

'And if you sell, and if so which ones.'

Sell! Sandy positively glowed inside at the thought of that.

Cakey glanced sideways at him. 'When do you return to Medical School?'

His euphoria vanished in an instant. 'Next Monday.'

'So soon?'

''Fraid so.'

'I take it, judging from your tone, that you're not looking forward to it?'

'Not in the least.'

'Ah well,' she sighed. 'Things could always be worse.'

Not much, he thought bitterly, at the same time knowing full well that was an exaggeration on his part. He was simply feeling sorry for himself.

'If only . . .' he started to say, then trailed off. 'Nothing.'

Don't interfere, Cakey told herself. Don't interfere, though she dearly wanted to.

'Look what the cat dragged in!' Grant Bell exclaimed as Sandy joined him at the downstairs bar in The Clachan. 'I haven't seen you in ages.'

'I've been busy.'

'Oh?'

Sandy caught Myrtle's eye. 'A pint of heavy please, Myrtle, and a large dram.'

'Hello, stranger. What brings you back to this den of iniquity?'

'I missed you, darling,' he lied graciously to the old crone.

Myrtle cackled. 'That'll be the day.'

'So what have you been up to then?' Grant persisted. 'Found yourself a lassie, is that it?'

Sandy had already decided not to mention Sophie, he'd only be pressed for details if he did. Their relationship was strictly private and certainly not to be discussed in pubs. 'As if.'

Grant glanced around. 'Not much talent in here the night. A few hairies, that's all.' A hairy was the term for a common working-class girl. He sniffed. 'Not that I'm worried. I've already been seen to.'

Sandy's drinks were placed in front of him which he paid for. 'I take it that means Blythswood Square?'

'Every Friday night without fail. I've been seeing the same tart for a few weeks now and she really knows her stuff. Oh aye, she does that.'

'Good, eh?'

'Fantastic shag.'

Sandy couldn't help teasing him. 'And does this

one take her clothes off, or just her drawers?'

'Are you taking the piss?' Grant growled, eyes narrowing.

'Not in the least,' Sandy lied. 'Just curious, that's all.'

'Well, I'm not saying, so there.'

'Which means it's only her drawers.'

'It does not!' Grant retorted hotly.

Sandy decided to drop the subject, he wasn't really interested one way or the other. 'Martin Benson about?' he inquired.

'Not so far. But he tends to get in later.'

Sandy wondered if he should tell Martin about his exhibition, and decided it was better not to. That might result in jealousy which he could do without.

He hung around for just over an hour, wishing he could be with Sophie who, unfortunately, was working late at the hotel. Eventually he left and headed for home in Lilybank Gardens, bored with The Clachan and the people there.

It had been a rotten Friday night without Sophie. He missed her dreadfully.

Sophie came to the end of the letter that had arrived in that morning's post from her friend Regine in Montmartre. They corresponded regularly.

The letter was full of gossip and general tittle-tattle that made her homesick, wishing she was back among the streets, cafés and people she knew.

Soon, she promised herself. Soon. There was nothing keeping her here after all, except Sandy. She had more than enough money saved to pay for the journey and could actually go whenever she liked. She hadn't reapplied to the Art School to model as that would have meant she was obliged to stay for a full term at least. With the hotel job all she had to do was give a week's notice.

A glance out the window confirmed how much the weather was beginning to change; autumn held sway and, before long, winter.

She'd arrived in Glasgow at the end of the previous one, and had instantly hated the cold and damp, damp that seeped into your bones and made you feel old before your time. It was the abject greyness of that time of year in Scotland that had affected her more than anything. Everything grey, grey, and more grey. Even the faces you saw were grey. Grey, haggard and pinched.

She thought of Jack, and how much she'd loved him. Still did, if she was honest, but she was getting over him now. Was there a part of her that was still hoping he might reappear and take up where they'd left off? She didn't think so, but it was possible.

A few weeks more, she thought. Let Sandy finish the second painting he'd started, and then she'd leave.

Home to Montmartre where there was lots of colour and excitement. Where she belonged.

'I've booked my return passage and leave next week,' Cakey announced to Harriet.

'Next week!'

'The Wednesday afternoon. Embarking that morning.'

'Oh, Cakey,' a disappointed Harriet breathed. 'It's all gone by so quickly. It's as if you'd just arrived.'

Cakey went to her sister and put her arms round her. 'I'll miss you, Harriet, more than you'll know. Not to mention Laura and Sandy. I think them both delightful and a credit to you. Fine young people you should be proud of.'

'I am,' Harriet replied, smiling despite herself. It wasn't lost on her that Cakey hadn't mentioned Mathew, which she quite understood.

'Maybe you'll return the gesture and come to Canada one day?' Cakey suggested, already knowing the answer. Mathew would never agree to that.

'Maybe,' Harriet prevaricated. 'Possibly when the children are off our hands.'

Cakey released Harriet, and sighed. 'I think you and I should put our hats and coats on and go out. How about a tearoom where we can spoil ourselves by eating lots of yummy cakes?'

Harriet laughed. 'You and your cakes.'

'Nothing like 'em, kid. So what do you say?'

There were things Harriet had planned to do that afternoon, but nothing she couldn't put off till another time. 'Let's go.'

Later, Mathew smiled with satisfaction when he heard of Cakey's imminent departure. He only wished it had been sooner.

'I'll write the second I get home,' Cakey promised. She and Harriet were embracing on the quayside. None of the rest of the family had been able to accompany them. Mathew was at work, Sandy at Medical School, Laura at school. Laura and Sandy had said their fond, and heartfelt, farewells that morning after breakfast. As had Mathew, though there had been nothing fond or heartfelt about his. A cross Harriet had detected that in his tone which betrayed he was secretly delighted by Cakey's departure. Cakey hadn't mentioned it, but she'd detected it also. Not that she'd been upset in any way, it was nothing less than she'd expected.

'I'll be waiting for the letter. I just hope the crossing won't be too rough.'

'It won't bother me if it is,' Cakey smiled. 'I've got a cast-iron stomach. The ship can heave as much as it likes.'

They were both putting off the moment, and knew it. 'Thank you for everything,' Cakey went on. 'I appreciate it.'

'Nonsense. I'm only sorry you can't stay longer.'

Cakey kissed Harriet on the cheek, fighting back the tears that were threatening. 'I'll miss you.'

'And I'll miss you.'

'We had some good chats about the old days, didn't we?'

Harriet nodded.

'And I enjoyed my trips, especially the one to London. That was really something.'

'Laura had the time of her life. Thank you for taking her.'

'The pleasure was all mine, I assure you.'

Cakey glanced at the nearby gangway, her luggage already on board. 'Right, no use drawing this out,' she declared, coming to her full height. 'And your taxi's waiting.'

'Yes,' Harriet agreed.

'Take care, Harriet.'

'And you.'

Turning abruptly, about to lose her battle with the tears, Cakey hurried to the gangway and went up it, pausing briefly at the top for a last look at her sister, before vanishing from view.

A waving Harriet had a sudden premonition that

she'd never see Cakey again. Not in this world anyway.

Nonsense, she told herself, fumbling for a handkerchief. Scots who went abroad always wanted to come back, even if only to visit. The need to do so was in their blood.

She'd see Cakey again. Probably not for a few years, but Cakey would return. No doubt about it. She was just being fanciful to imagine otherwise. Overemotional, that's all.

'So why didn't you tell me about this exhibition of your paintings coming up?' Laura demanded of a startled Sandy.

'How . . . how did you find out about that?'

'So it *is* you and not another Alexander McLean!'

Luckily Mathew was out and Harriet somewhere else in the house, Sandy thought, then realised that was probably why Laura had confronted him here and now.

'It is me,' he confessed. 'And how *did* you find out?'

'My friend Madeleine told me. She was passing the gallery the other day and saw a poster in the window advertising a forthcoming exhibition of young Scottish painters and there was your name. She put two and two together, as she knows from me you like to paint and draw.'

Sandy swore under his breath. This was awful. 'Aunt Cakey arranged it,' he informed Laura. 'And I naturally jumped at the chance of my work being shown.'

'But why so secretive?'

He took a deep breath. 'Because of Ma and Pa. Mainly Pa. I don't want him to hear about it.'

Laura thought about that. 'I suppose he might disapprove, but surely no more than that?'

'He'd do more than disapprove, Laura, he'd have a bloody heart attack! One of the paintings is a nude, you see.'

She stared blankly at him. 'You mean someone naked?'

'A woman to be precise.'

For some reason she thought that was funny, unable to visualise her brother painting naked women. It just seemed ludicrous somehow. 'How naked is she?'

He frowned. 'Naked is naked. Nothing on at all. Bare skud.'

'What I mean is, how much do you see?'

'It's a front view, Laura, you see everything.'

Her eyebrows shot up. 'Everything!'

He mimed breasts. 'Those and . . . well everything. Tastefully done, of course.'

'Of course,' she replied sarcastically. Sandy was right, Pa *would* have a heart attack.

'She's lying down,' Sandy went on. 'Lying across my bed actually.'

'*Your* bed!'

'You wouldn't recognise it as such. But it is my bed.'

'My God,' she said softly. This just got worse and worse. 'And when did a naked woman lie across your bed for you to paint?'

'When the parents were in Largs, and you and Cakey were in London. She's a professional model whom I hired.'

'So she's not someone you know?'

'Well, I do now,' he prevaricated. 'I heard of her through a chap at the Art School where she also models.'

Laura was intrigued. 'What's her name?'

'Sophie Ducros. She's French.'

That intrigued Laura even further. 'Is she beautiful?'

Sandy detected a strange note in Laura's voice which puzzled him. Natural female curiosity about another woman, he decided. 'Very, in my opinion.'

'With a good figure?'

'What is this, the inquisition?' He frowned. 'Yes, it is a good figure. At least I think so.'

Laura glanced around. 'Is the painting here?'

'No, it's already at the gallery.'

That disappointed her. 'Well, you don't have to worry, I won't say anything to Ma or Pa. Your secret's safe with me. Though I just wonder if someone else might not see your name and mention it to them. It's possible.'

Damn! he thought in alarm. Damn and blast! 'I'll just have to keep my fingers crossed no one does.'

For the rest of that day Laura speculated on what Sophie looked like, and what she *was* like. It never crossed her mind that Sandy might be sleeping with Sophie.

'Of course I'll go with you, *chéri*. It will be fun.'

'That's settled then.' Sandy beamed. 'You must have been to lots of these things in the past?'

Sophie was impatient, wanting to get Sandy into bed. There was an urgency in her that night, though why she couldn't have said. The need was simply there, howling to be satisfied.

'Many,' she agreed, starting to strip.

Sandy watched in admiration. It never ceased to amaze him just how gorgeous she was. 'I'll get set up,' he declared, crossing to his easel where the second painting of her stood, half completed.

Sophie laughed, a deep husky sound filled with sultry promise. 'Later, darling. Right now I want you.'

He raised an eyebrow. It wasn't the first time this had happened, so he knew exactly what lay ahead. An interlude of raw passion with absolutely nothing subtle about it. Sheer, frenetic, animal coupling.

He started towards her.

'Are you nervous about tomorrow night?' Laura asked. It was the eve of the opening of the exhibition.

'Of course. Wouldn't you be?'

She smiled. 'Probably.'

He hadn't told her he was taking Sophie, and had no intention of doing so.

'It'll be all right,' Laura assured him. Then, teasing, 'Who knows? Maybe no one will turn up.'

'Not when there's going to be free wine,' Sandy laughed. 'This is Glasgow after all. Glaswegians like their drink, especially if it's not going to cost them anything.'

Laura knew that to be so. Glasgow's reputation for drunkenness was well and richly deserved. You would only have to be on the central city streets any Friday or Saturday night to witness that, she'd been told.

'Anyway, I wish you all the best and hope it goes well for you.'

He was touched. 'Thanks, sis.'

'And you've been lucky so far, Ma and Pa know nothing about the exhibition.'

'Let's just hope it stays that way.' Sandy nodded.

'Must get on then, bags of homework to do.' Laura went to Sandy and kissed him on the cheek. 'Good luck.'

'Thanks.'

'I'll be thinking of you.'

Laura waited till she'd left the room before allowing a smile to light up her face. Did she have a surprise for him!

Mr Dickie, the *Glasgow Herald*'s art critic, was a small, thin man with ferrety eyes and dreadful halitosis. He was one of the two critics who'd turned up, the other being a Mr McGregor from *The Scotsman*, Edinburgh's most prestigious newspaper, whom Sandy hadn't talked to yet.

Dickie blinked at Sandy, having already introduced himself. 'Of course I prefer the Victorian school of nudes myself,' he stated rather pompously. 'Are you familiar with them, Mr McLean?'

'Some.' Sandy smiled, desperately searching his memory to come up with names.

'Lawrence Alma-Tadema's "The Tepidarium" is my favourite. Closely followed by William Etty's "Andromeda and Perseus". Do you know either?'

'Both very fine works,' Sandy replied, trying to look knowledgeable. He'd only vaguely heard of Etty, while Lawrence whatsisname drew a complete blank.

Dickie grunted and turned his attention to Sophie. 'Someone mentioned that you'd modelled in Paris. Is that correct, Miss Ducros?'

'Yes it is. I normally live in Montmartre where I've either modelled for, or know, most of the current artists there.'

'Such as?'

'Juan Gris, Severini, Pascin, Van Dongen, Picasso. Many, *m'sieur*.'

'Too avante garde for my taste,' Dickie sniffed. 'But they have talent, no doubt about it.'

Sandy had a sip of wine and glanced around. It was a good turn out, fifty, maybe more, people present. The gallery was humming with laughter and conversation.

He spotted Mr Moon, the proprietor, speaking to one of the other painters on display, a man Sandy had met, and taken an instant dislike to, earlier.

'And what brought you to Glasgow, Miss, or should I say *Mademoiselle*, Ducros?'

Dickie was showing a very keen interest in Sophie, Sandy thought. Which was understandable enough, any red-blooded man would. Perhaps it might even work to his advantage, if he was lucky.

So far Dickie hadn't commented on what Sandy had on display. He didn't know whether or not that was a good sign.

It had alarmed Sandy when he'd been told on arrival that the press would be present, he hadn't expected that. The worst thing of all was that Mathew took the *Herald*, so if anything was written about him Pa was bound to read it. There again, maybe not. He couldn't imagine his father being overly interested in the arts column.

Dickie made a clumsy attempt to speak French, which Sophie verbally applauded, declaring his accent to be excellent. Dickie visibly preened at this praise.

Good lass, Sandy thought. That should, hopefully, earn him some brownie points when Dickie came to write his review.

Sophie was suddenly distracted, a frown creasing her forehead as she stared across the room. She let Dickie waffle on for a few more minutes before excusing herself, saying she'd noticed an old friend whom she just had to have a word with.

'A very pleasant woman,' Dickie said to Sandy.

'Beautiful too.'

'Hmmh,' Dickie agreed, a lecherous expression momentarily flitting across his face. Then he too excused himself, and moved off.

Sandy gazed across to where Sophie was deep in conversation with some man he'd never seen before. It appeared to him there was a bit of an argument going on.

He wondered if he should go over and join them, but decided not to. The conversation seemed a very private one. Neither Sophie, or the chap, would probably welcome his intrusion.

'Hello, Sandy. Guess who?'

He turned to stare in astonishment at Laura, who had Madeleine with her. 'What are you doing here?' he croaked.

'Come to have a look. Haven't we, Madeleine?'

Madeleine giggled, and nodded.

'We've already seen your stuff.' Laura lowered her voice, 'Including the nude.'

He found himself flushing slightly. 'Have you indeed.'

'It's very good. That right, Madeleine?'

Again Madeleine giggled, and nodded.

'That's her you were talking to, isn't it?'

'You mean Sophie. Yes, that's her.'

Laura glanced over at Sophie. 'I think you make her look prettier than she actually is.'

'Not so.'

Laura smiled mysteriously. 'Why is she here? She's only the model after all.'

'She's here at my invitation. I thought it might help her get more work.' The latter was a lie of course, but it was all he could think of off the cuff.

'Can I meet her?'

He groaned inwardly, he could do without this. 'I suppose so.' He couldn't see how he could avoid introducing them, for sure as eggs were eggs Laura would insist. 'Now go and look at the other paintings while I mingle. All right?'

'Come on, Madeleine. Let's get some more wine.'

When he looked again Sophie was still busy apparently arguing, though in a quiet, contained way, with the chap she'd gone to talk to.

'So who was he?' Sandy asked casually as he began escorting Sophie home.

Sophie knew instantly to whom Sandy was referring. 'A friend of Jack's. Another painter who'd dropped in to view the exhibition not realising I'd be there.'

'You appeared to be arguing.'

'Not really. I wanted to find out where Jack was and why he'd left so suddenly without any explanation. He had no idea.'

'The friend?'

'I thought he was lying which is why it might have looked as though we were arguing. But in the end I believed him.'

'I see,' Sandy murmured, inwardly seething with jealousy.

'I just wanted to know why,' Sophie explained. 'Surely you can understand that?'

'Of course.'

'Anyway,' Sophie said, changing the subject. 'I thought

the evening was a great success and your sister charming.'

'It certainly surprised me when she appeared. She never warned me.'

'I liked her. As I said, quite charming.'

'You obviously fascinated her. There again, she's never met a model before. And certainly not a genuine French one.'

His jealousy was slowly ebbing away now they'd stopped talking about bloody Jack. 'By the way, thank you for how you handled Dickie. I thought him a right little creep.'

Sophie laughed. 'I agree!'

'Susceptible to your charms though.'

'You think?'

'Don't play coy with me, Sophie Ducros. You know he was.'

'Let's just hope he writes something nice about you, eh, *chéri*?'

'Let's hope.'

They continued chatting till they reached Sophie's close, where she said she wouldn't invite him up as she wanted an early night.

They agreed a date and time for his next painting session before he left her.

Chapter 14

Mathew strode into the room with a thunderous expression on his face. Marching straight over to where Sandy was sitting he threw a folded newspaper onto Sandy's lap. 'I think you have some explaining to do, my lad,' he snarled.

'What on earth is going on?' a bewildered Harriet queried.

Sandy didn't have to look at the newspaper to know it was open at Dickie's review.

'Well?' Mathew snapped. 'I take it the Alexander McLean mentioned is you?'

Sandy nodded.

'Mathew?'

He rounded on his wife. 'Our son has done a painting of a naked woman, *naked* mind you, and had it put on display.'

Harriet gasped. 'Is this true, Alexander?'

'Yes, Ma. It is.'

'Goodness gracious!' she exclaimed.

Laura's eyes were flicking from one to the other. How was Sandy going to deal with this?

'It's a very favourable review,' Sandy said weakly. 'I got mentioned more than the others.'

Mathew snorted. 'Good, bad, indifferent, what's the difference? It's there in the paper for all to read. I'll be a laughing stock, a bloody laughing stock! How could you bring such shame on the family? Not only me, but your mother as well.'

'I don't see why there's any shame in it,' Sandy countered. 'I rather thought you might be proud.'

'Proud!' Mathew went purple in the face. 'That's the last thing I am.'

'Hold on here, let me get this straight,' Harriet interjected. 'Where exactly has the painting been put on display?'

'The Sauchiehall Street Gallery,' Sandy explained. 'It's an exhibition of young Scottish painters. I just happened to be lucky in being selected.' He wasn't going to mention Cakey unless he absolutely had to.

'But you're not a painter, you're a medical student,' Mathew barked.

'Amateur, Pa. There's nothing wrong in having a hobby.'

'Can I see that review?' Harriet requested, holding out a hand.

Sandy rose, went to her chair and gave it to her. He'd hoped against hope this wouldn't happen. But it had.

Harriet began quickly scanning the article, brow furrowed in concentration.

'Filth, that's what it is,' Mathew stormed. 'Disgusting, degenerate filth spawned by my own son.'

'Wait a minute, Pa,' Sandy protested. 'Some of the greatest paintings in history, executed by the greatest painters, have been of nudes. Michelangelo, for example, you can hardly call him disgusting and degenerate. And what about classical sculpture? Roman, Greek works of art.'

Mathew glared at Sandy, momentarily lost for words.

'I don't think this is so bad,' Harriet declared. 'The critic has nothing but praise for Alexander's work. Aren't you overreacting just a little, darling?'

An aghast Mathew stared at his wife. 'Are you saying you *approve*?'

'Not quite,' she replied soothingly. 'I have to admit it's a bit of a shock to find out Alexander's been painting nudes. But I'm sure it's been done tastefully.'

'It has,' Laura stated, speaking for the first time since the row flared up.

'What do you know about it, madam?' Mathew queried sharply.

'I went along on the exhibition's first night and thought the painting was excellent.'

'You went . . .' Mathew spluttered.

'No one there was in the least offended, I can assure you. It's a work of art, Pa, not what you're making it out to be.'

'There, see.' Harriet smiled.

'I heard Sandy congratulated by quite a few people, including the critic from *The Scotsman* who called the painting outstanding. His very word, right, Sandy?'

That was a lie, as Sandy well knew. 'Right,' he agreed.

'It's a plot, you're all in this together,' Mathew accused.

'We're nothing of the sort, dear,' Harriet confirmed. 'I knew nothing about any nude or exhibition till you brought it up just now.'

Matthew took a deep breath. 'And what about my reputation as an upstanding member of the community? It'll be in tatters after this. People sniggering and pointing their fingers at me behind my back. Particularly my patients.'

'That's ridiculous, Mathew. The sort of patients you have don't read either the *Herald* or *Scotsman*. Far too literate for them.'

That infuriated Mathew even further. 'Are you insinuating I only deal with peasants, the lower orders?'

Harriet savoured her reply. 'Don't you?'

Mathew couldn't believe she'd said that. It might well be the case but that was hardly his fault, and there was certainly no need for her to rub it in.

'Is she a pretty nude?' Harriet sweetly asked Laura, still shocked though not showing it.

'I would say so.'

'And young?'

'Twenties or thirties. Sandy?'

All eyes swivelled on him. For a moment he panicked, his mind racing. 'I'm not sure,' he replied. 'You see I made her up. She doesn't actually exist. She's a figment of my imagination. After all, where would I get a naked woman to paint?'

Laura smiled to herself, thinking that explanation was neatly done.

'I should hope you wouldn't,' Mathew growled. 'The very idea.'

'I have seen naked women at Medical School, don't forget,' Sandy went on. 'Cadavers, I mean. So the subject isn't an entire mystery. And of course there are plenty of nudes in art books.'

'Perhaps we should go along to this exhibition, Mathew?' Harriet suggested.

He was horrified. 'I shall do no such thing!'

Harriet decided she would, but not tell Mathew. What he didn't know wouldn't upset him. And, pragmatically, it would also save an argument.

'I still think it's disgusting,' Mathew declared stiffly. 'You won't get me changing my mind on that.' He focused on Sandy. 'And there will be no more nudes, understand? In fact I'd prefer it if you gave up this entire art nonsense altogether. It only deflects you from what's really important, which is your studying.'

'Talking of which,' Sandy said, coming to his feet, 'I'd better get back upstairs. I still have preparation to do for tomorrow.'

Mathew nodded his approval. Now the lad was talking. This was more like it. Nudes indeed. He considered women over a certain age quite repulsive when naked, especially those who'd been through childbirth or were obese, an admission he'd never made to a living soul, including Harriet. Not that he had any homosexual tendencies, the very thought made him go cold all over. Personally he would have had all such men castrated. It was simply that female flesh once past its prime was abhorrent to him. Ugly and, in some extreme cases, completely hideous.

The moment Sandy closed the door behind him he let out a huge sigh of relief.

'The man's an idiot, a total idiot. And a bully to boot,' Sandy declared to Laura a short time later when she joined him in his bedroom. He'd been attempting to study but, because of what had happened, just couldn't concentrate.

She didn't reply to that, though she quite agreed.

'Thanks for that lie on my behalf though.' He smiled at her.

'The least I could do.' She regarded him with amusement. 'A figment of your imagination, eh? You made her up? That was a laugh.'

'Well, I had to say something, somehow get myself off the hook. I mean, Pa was bad enough, but can you imagine what he'd have been like if I'd told him the truth?'

'Such as Sophie lying naked across *your* bed, in *his* house?'

Sandy shuddered. 'It doesn't bear thinking about. He'd probably have thrown me out on my ear.'

'Oh, he wouldn't have done that,' a grinning Laura replied. 'Ma wouldn't have let him.'

'Whatever, it certainly could have been a lot nastier.'

She was still regarding him with amusement. 'Now that you are off the hook, and with a little help from me, I think we should reward ourselves, don't you?'

He frowned. 'How so?'

'A whisky each sounds good to me.'

'Laura!'

'Oh come on,' she cajoled. 'Don't be an old spoilsport. I'm not suggesting we get drunk or anything.'

'I should hope not.' It was a good idea though, he decided.

While he was dealing with that Laura left the room, returning with the glass she'd used on previous occasions. 'How stingy,' she complained when he poured her a tiny one.

'That's enough at your age.'

'You're still stingy.'

The look in her eyes which, for some reason he couldn't have explained, made him relent. 'Oh, all right then,' he conceded, and poured her some more.

'That's better,' she beamed.

'But you put lemonade in it. I insist on that.'

'I was going to anyway. So there.'

Once the lemonade had been added she crossed to the bed and sat down. 'Can I ask a question?'

'Of course.'

She had a sip of her drink. 'What is it like painting a nude woman? I mean, having her naked in front of you?'

'What sort of question is that!' he protested.

'A reasonable one, I should say. You are a man after all, what was it like? Did you get excited?'

'Honest to God, Laura, some of the things you come out with at times!' He shook his head in bewilderment.

'Does that mean no, you didn't?'

'It means I'm not going to answer.'

She laughed. 'Embarrassed, are you?'

'Extremely.'

'Well, I'm not.'

'It's not you being asked the question,' he pointed out.

'True.'

She stared at him from under half-lowered lids, a strange feeling churning in her stomach. 'I think you must have been. Otherwise why would you be so evasive?'

Sandy sighed in exasperation. 'Well, if you have to know I was sort of to begin with, but only for a short

219

while. Once I really got down to painting it went away, she became a subject and nothing more.'

Laura ran a hand across the bed, trying to imagine a naked Sophie lying there, which wasn't too difficult as she'd seen the picture. 'Is she the first naked woman you've seen, apart from cadavers that is?'

'Yes.' He noticed, as did Laura, the croak that had suddenly crept into his voice.

'And weren't you tempted to do something about that?'

He swallowed his whisky, and poured himself another. There were occasions like this, when his sister could be an absolute nightmare. 'It was a business arrangement, Laura, that's all. She's a model, not a common prostitute.'

Laura shrugged. 'I never thought she was, which is not what I'm talking about.'

'Then what *are* you talking about?'

'What it's like to see a member of the opposite sex naked for the first time. And in Sophie's case, an extremely attractive one.'

He searched his mind for a suitable reply, wondering if he could find the right words to express what he'd felt. He thought it bizarre he was actually having this conversation with Laura, that things could be so free between them.

'I suppose my initial reaction was to be stunned,' he admitted.

'Stunned?'

'Well, yes. It's obviously something you think about over the years, speculate about. And then suddenly, there it is right in front of you. Your imagination come to life.'

Laura considered that, wondering if that would be her reaction the first time she saw a naked man. Probably, she concluded. Especially if he was excited. The vision that flashed through her mind caused her skin to erupt in goosebumps. 'How interesting,' she commented.

'It's very different from viewing a cadaver as you can imagine. A dead body is just that, but a living, breathing one another thing entirely.'

Laura sipped her whisky, eyes gleaming. She was enjoying this. 'Did you touch her at all?'

'No, I did not!' he exclaimed, which was a lie. Or partially one. Not the first session anyway.

'I suppose you wanted to?'

'Laura!'

'Well, it's only natural. I know I would. Touch, and have a right good look.'

'I think you're turning into some sort of sex maniac,' he admonished. 'What other sixteen-year-old girl would ask questions like these?'

'Plenty, if they had the courage to do so, and someone they could ask them of.'

He thought of Sophie and what she could be like in bed, which was demanding at times to say the least. Yes, Laura was right, though he didn't think it applied to all women. But certainly some it would appear.'

'Madeleine and I have discussed the matter and agree on it,' Laura continued. 'You should hear what she says about her chap Conor, the poor boy would probably run a mile if she ever told him half of what she's told me.'

'Like what?'

'Oh, all sorts. How she thinks he's got ever such a lovely bottom. She's "accidentally" touched it on several occasions without him being aware of what she was up to. She's actually touched his willy as well, though only once. She pretended to trip and fall off balance, which is how she managed to put her hand on it. Only for a second though. She said it felt sort of soft and squidgy.'

Sandy was appalled. 'Is this true?'

'Cross my heart and hope to die. She wishes he'd "accidentally" touch her, but he never has.'

'Probably because he's a gentleman,' Sandy declared.

'Now you sound pompous and pious like Pa. It doesn't suit you.'

It didn't either, Sandy reflected.

'Morag's had sex, you know.'

He gaped at her. 'The maid?'

'Uh-huh.'

'How do you know that?'

'She told me.'

'That I don't believe,' Sandy stated firmly. 'Why would she tell you such an intimate thing?'

'I wheedled it out of her. It was a while back that she said something which made me suspicious, so I eventually wheedled an admission out of her. She says it's great.'

Sandy turned away so Laura couldn't see the expression on his face. 'Does she indeed.'

'Her chap's called Rab, and he's a tram driver. They're saving up to get engaged.' Laura sighed. 'It's rather sad where they have it though. Very unromantic.'

'And where's that?'

'Well, they both live with their parents you see, so there's no chance of them doing anything there. Instead they do it up dark alleyways and in behind middens.'

'How nasty,' was all Sandy could think of to reply.

Laura pulled a face. 'Imagine doing it behind a smelly, old midden? That's awful.'

He couldn't have agreed more, and it made him realise how lucky he was that Sophie had her own place. 'Doesn't Morag worry about getting pregnant?'

'Oh no, they always use a French Letter, an F. L. she calls them, that makes it safe as houses she says.'

Which he didn't, Sandy mused. After they made love Sophie always absented herself for a short while, taking her mysterious little sponge bag with her. When he'd asked her what she did she'd always dismissed the question with a wave of her hand and changed the subject. It had to be some kind of contraception that he, so far, knew nothing about.

'I just hope it does,' he commented. 'They have been known to fail, you know.'

Laura frowned. 'How?'

'Come off or get torn. It does happen.'

Laura drained her glass and came to her feet. 'I'd better let you get on. You've studying to do.'

He barked out a laugh. 'I didn't feel up to it before you arrived, and this conversation certainly hasn't done anything to change that.'

Laura went to him and kissed him on the cheek. 'Try. And thanks for that whisky.'

Well, Sandy thought after she'd gone. What did he make of all that? First it was being with someone of the opposite sex who was naked, then Madeleine touching her boyfriend's bottom and willy, followed by Morag at it behind middens.

He laughed. What else could he do? And poured

himself more whisky, absentmindedly noting he'd have to buy another bottle.

What a night it had been. What a night!

Laura went straight to her own room and threw herself on the bed. She was angry, and for the life of her didn't know why. Oh, she'd enjoyed the chat, particularly shocking Sandy as she had, except the bits where Sophie had been mentioned. It was those that had upset her.

But why? Sophie was nothing to her, or she to Sophie. Was it because the French woman was so damned good looking? Could be. She'd lied on the opening night of the exhibition when she'd said to Sandy that he'd made Sophie more beautiful than she was. Sandy had captured Sophie perfectly.

Maybe it was because Sophie had such a ravishing figure and she didn't. The damned woman simply oozed voluptuousness, she a pale shadow by comparison.

Well, if she was angry and upset it was her own fault, she was the one who'd instigated the conversation about Sophie and nakedness. It was true she'd been genuinely curious, but deep down she suspected there was more to it than that.

The only trouble was, she didn't know what.

Sandy totted up his final figure, and grunted with satisfaction. He'd done well on his racing 'book' this week, his profit nearly three quid. He snapped the ledger shut and slipped it into one of the top drawers in his desk.

Mugs, he thought. That's what the students were at school who used his services. Absolute mugs. The only person who ever consistently won out of gambling was the bookie.

With a sigh of resignation he opened the medical tome in front of him and tried to concentrate.

Anoxia, occurring for instance in shock, leads to pulmonary oedema from damage to the lung capillaries and this oedema increases the anoxia as well as interfering with the escape of CO_2. A state of asphyxia therefore supervenes . . .

Sandy groaned. Boring, boring beyond belief. Mindstupefyingly boring.

He forced himself to carry on and try to assimilate what he was reading.

'I'm afraid that's already sold,' Mr Moon announced to Harriet who was staring at Sandy's painting of Sophie.

'Is that what the little red sticker means?'

Moon smiled. 'Precisely.'

'May I inquire how much it went for?'

'Forty pounds, madam.'

That surprised her. 'So much? I mean for a young artist, one I'm sure isn't well known.'

'It's a particularly fine work, madam, and shows great promise on behalf of the young man in question. A good investment I'd say.'

'Really?'

'Oh yes, madam. Are you a collector by any chance?'

Harriet laughed. 'No, not at all. To be honest I just came in out of curiosity.'

'Ah!'

Harriet continued staring at the painting, not knowing what to think. She found it hard to believe that her son had painted such a thing. There was so much sensuousness in it, so much . . . She took a deep breath, putting such thoughts from her mind.

'Perhaps madam would be interested in one of the artist's other oils or his drawings?' Moon queried.

'No thank you.'

'As I said, a potentially excellent investment in my view. This young man has the capabilities, given experience, of going far.'

'Let me think about it,' Harriet demurred. She had no intention whatsoever of buying anything in the gallery.

'Would you care to have our card? We are on the telephone.'

Harriet accepted the card pressed on her, then took her leave of Moon and the gallery.

Forty pounds! If nothing else that would have impressed Mathew. A great deal.

'My God, it just gets better every time,' Sandy declared, chest heaving slightly. Beside him a satiated Sophie was almost purring with contentment.

'We did have to celebrate your finishing the painting,' she smiled. Coming into a squatting position she reached for her cigarettes. 'Will you pour me another drink, *chéri*?'

'Of course.'

She watched him through slitted eyes. '*Merci*,' she breathed, accepting the glass he handed her. A wicked, knowing, smile crossed her face. 'Bottoms up!'

He laughed, well aware of what was in her mind. 'Slainthe,' he toasted in reply.

'This painting is better than the first,' she pronounced.

'You really think so?'

'Certainly.'

That pleased him enormously as he thought highly of her judgement on these matters.

Sophie swung her feet to the floor and stood up. Moments later she'd shrugged herself into a pale blue gossamer-thin wrap. 'Now we must talk, I'm afraid.'

He didn't like the ominous sound of that. 'About what?'

'Us, Sandy.'

He frowned, but didn't reply, waiting for her to go on.

'Do you remember when you walked me home the night of the opening to your exhibition you asked me who the man was I'd been talking to?'

'I remember. You said it was a friend of Jack's.'

Sophie had a swallow of brandy. She was hating this, but it had to be done. She knew only too well how much it was going to hurt Sandy.

'I lied. That was Jack himself.'

Sandy felt as though he'd been punched in the stomach. 'Oh?'

'It was true that he'd gone there to view the paintings and was as surprised to see me as I him.'

She paused for breath, and had another swallow of brandy. 'He asked me if I'd take him back. Pleaded with me.'

Sandy was suddenly filled with dread and felt sick. 'What did you say?'

'That I'd have to think about it. That I wanted to know precisely why he'd run off in the first place. So we agreed to meet.'

'And?' Sandy croaked.

'I won't go into his explanation, but I could understand it. What I also realised was that I still loved him. I'd pretended to myself that I didn't, not any more. But I still do.' She glanced away, unable to keep looking at the expression on Sandy's face. 'I'm sorry.'

'So that's it then?' He was trying to sound casual, offhand, and failing miserably.

Sophie nodded. 'I won't be seeing you again after tonight.'

'Have you slept with him since the exhibition?'

'Don't torture yourself, Sandy. Please.'

'Which means you have.'

She didn't answer that.

'And yet you slept with me tonight?'

Sophie took a deep breath. 'It was a sort of saying goodbye gift. I thought I owed it to you.'

Grown-up men don't cry, Sandy told himself. Not in front of someone else anyway. 'Is there anything I can say that might change your mind?'

'No.'

He knew from her tone she meant that.

In a complete daze Sandy laid his drink aside and began to get dressed. While he was doing this Sophie finished her cigarette and then immediately lit another.

'Please don't think badly of me,' she begged when he was fully dressed.

Sandy laughed bitterly. Feel badly? That was an understatement if ever there was.

Suddenly he wanted out of there, to be alone, and the sooner the better.

'Your things, the painting!' Sophie cried out to him as he stumbled towards the door.

He was too choked to reply, which was probably just as well as he could easily have told her to stick them up her beautiful, gorgeous arse.

He managed to make it to the street before the tears came.

Chapter 15

'Are you unwell, son?'

Sandy glanced across the breakfast table at his mother, only too aware of how ghastly he looked. He'd hardly had a wink of sleep the previous night.

'I think I may have a cold coming on,' he lied.

Harriet was immediately sympathetic. 'I'll give you something before you go off to lectures.'

The aroma of the untouched kipper in front of Sandy was making his stomach churn. Normally he liked kippers, but at that moment found its smell utterly revolting. 'I thought I might stay at home today,' he suggested.

Mathew's eyes swivelled onto Sandy. 'Is that necessary?'

'I am under the weather, Pa.'

'He is rather peaky,' Laura volunteered, trying to be helpful.

'No stamina or staying power the youngsters nowadays,' Mathew muttered. 'We weren't like that in my day. Different breed entirely.'

Sandy pushed his plate away. 'I'm sorry, Ma, but I can't.'

'Try a little toast then, dear. See if you can get that down.'

'Explain to Cook, Morag,' he said to the maid as she removed the offending item. 'Nothing wrong with it. It's me.'

'Yes, sir.'

Sandy thought of Sophie and the night before. What had been so marvellous one moment had turned into a nightmare the next. Damn her, damn her to hell!

'Toast, Sandy,' a smiling Harriet gently reminded him.

He wouldn't go to Medical School, Sandy decided. But he wouldn't stay at home either. A good long walk was what he needed, more time to reflect and attempt to put things in perspective. And a drink perhaps. Yes, that was the ticket. A decent drink to drown his sorrow and pain.

'Will you be back at the usual time, dear?' Harriet inquired of Mathew.

He grunted.

'Is that a yes or no, dear?'

'I've no idea, Harriet,' he replied, irritation in his voice as he was trying to concentrate on his newspaper.

'Very well, dear.'

'Have you moved your bowels recently, Alexander?' Mathew suddenly snapped at him.

Harriet winced; what a thing to ask at the table. There were occasions when she despaired of Mathew. For someone who took a great pride in manners he could be incredibly lax at times.

'Yes, Pa.'

'When?'

'Earlier.'

Mathew grunted again and returned to his news-paper where he was engrossed in an article about a new three-engined Handley Page Hampstead airliner recently delivered to Imperial Airways, which the makers claimed would ensure passengers greater safety.

Sandy managed a slice of thinly spread toast, having to force it down, which did at least satisfy his mother. When he excused himself she also rose declaring she'd get something for him from her medicine box.

When her attention was elsewhere Sandy slipped the two pills she gave him into a pocket and swallowed merely water.

He hadn't intended to go anywhere near the Station Hotel where Sophie worked but an hour later found himself wandering past its main entrance.

She'd be in there now, he thought miserably, prob-ably setting up behind the bar, preparing for when cus-tomers would arrive. He was tempted, oh so tempted, to go in and have another talk with her. Go down on his bended knees if necessary, if only she'd forget Jack and stay with him.

Don't be ridiculous, he chided himself. Nothing he did would alter her decision, he'd heard that in her voice the previous evening when she'd sprung her bombshell on him.

He'd lost her, and would have to come to terms with the fact, that was all. But Christ how he ached inside, ached with an intensity he'd never have believed pos-sible.

Just to hold her again, be with her, kiss her, take her to bed one more time.

'Sophie!' he whispered, the beginnings of tears wetting his eyes. 'Oh, Sophie.'

He hurried away from the hotel, and her. She was gone for ever out of his life. For ever.

He swore under his breath, wishing it was time for the pubs to open. He desperately needed that drink he'd promised himself, the way a man dying of thirst needs water.

Drink, and the oblivion that went with it.

Laura was passing Sandy's bedroom when she heard what sounded like a muffled sob.

'Sandy, are you in there?'

There was no reply.

She frowned. 'Sandy, are you all right?'

'Go away!'

The vehemence in his voice startled her. Something was wrong, no doubt about it. Should she continue on her way, or see if she could help? She opened the door and poked her head round.

Sandy was sitting on the bed, his face flushed, his expression one of extreme anguish. 'Go away, Laura, there's a good girl.'

She had no intention of doing that. Closing the door behind her she went and knelt in front of him. 'Are you ill?'

She had no sooner said that than she smelt it, the acrid reek of alcohol. 'My God, you're drunk,' she accused.

'As a fucking skunk. Now be a good lass and bugger off.'

'Not until I find out what the problem is,' she replied defiantly.

'You can't help, Laura. No one can,' he choked.

Suddenly he collapsed in on himself and began to cry, huge tears rolling down his cheeks, his body shaking with grief.

She sat alongside and put an arm round him. This was nothing to do with illness, that was obvious. But what?

'Oh, Laura,' he whispered. 'She's left me. Given me up for the chap she used to be with.'

'Who, Sandy?'

'Sophie. Gave me the heave last night. Told me it was over.'

Now Laura understood, cross with herself for not having realised before that something was going on between her brother and the French woman. Stupid of her.

'There there,' she crooned, trying to console him.

His body shook even more violently. 'I love her, Laura. I love her.'

She had no idea what to reply to that, so kept quiet. She now noted the empty bottle of whisky on his desk and wondered just how much he'd had. A lot by the looks of things. He certainly smelt that way.

'What am I to do?'

'I don't know,' she answered, holding him even tighter. 'But you go ahead and cry. Get it out of your system. That's best.'

'She's beautiful, Laura. I was besotted with her. Still am. I can't bear the thought of losing her or never going to bed with her again.'

That shook Laura. 'You mean you were actually having an *affair*?'

'Yes,' he whispered.

She swallowed hard; this put an entirely different complexion on things.

'She's wonderful in bed, Laura. Wild and wonderful. You can't begin to imagine.'

'That's enough,' she stated firmly. 'I don't want to hear the details.' Though, if she was honest, part of her did.

They sat in silence for a few seconds, Sandy's body continuing to shake. 'Why don't you start at the beginning and tell me all about it,' Laura eventually suggested.

This time, despite having said to the contrary – she was normally extremely inquisitive after all – she didn't stop him when he strayed into the nitty gritty.

Sandy woke with a start, sweat pouring off him and his clothes already saturated. He'd been dreaming about himself and Sophie, making love, a montage of sessions they'd had together.

He groaned when the pain in his head hit him, a monumental hangover had set in. He felt like death warmed up.

It was about half an hour later when the door opened and Laura came in carrying a tray. 'You're awake, I see,' she observed.

'I haven't been for long.'

'How do you feel?'

'Awful. Simply awful.'

'I've brought you something to eat. Ma was going to do it but I persuaded her to let me. They believe you're down with a stinking cold.'

'Thanks Laura,' he said huskily.

'I opened the window before I left earlier,' she informed him. 'It was like a distillery in here which would have been a dead giveaway if anyone else had come in.'

He eyed the food with distaste. 'I can't eat, Laura. I'd be sick.'

'There's tea here. How about that?'

'Please.'

She'd already placed the tray beside him. When he reached out for the cup his hands were trembling.

'You'll have to sit up first,' she told him. 'And I'd better help or you'll have that tea everywhere.'

He grimaced as he pulled himself into an upright position, his head thundering mightily. He'd never had such a bad hangover, and he'd had a few in his time.

'Better?' she asked when he'd taken a sip.

'A little.'

'Good. Have some more.'

When he'd done that he gestured to the poached egg on toast she'd brought. 'That looks disgusting,' he rasped.

'Well, you must eat something as I don't suppose you had any lunch?'

'Only in a glass.'

That was obvious, she thought. 'Now I've got to get you sorted out. Ma's coming in later so you'll have to be ready for her. That means getting into your pyjamas for a start. And I would suggest, no I *insist*, you also have a wash and clean your teeth, because you still stink of booze.'

He knew that made sense. 'I'll never reach the bathroom. I doubt my legs will take me that far.'

'Don't worry, I'll get you there. Even if I have to carry you.'

He gave her the weakest of smiles. 'You're terrific, sis. Thank you.'

'Forget it. I couldn't bear the scene that'll follow if Ma or Pa finds you like this.'

She waited patiently till his cup was empty. 'Now, out of bed and into your dressing gown. Come on.'

He was right about his legs, he nearly fell over when he tried to stand.

Laura steadied him. 'Off with those clothes which I'll fold away.'

He suddenly realised what she intended. 'I can't strip in front of you,' he protested.

'Why not? I'm a woman just like Sophie and you must have stripped in front of her.'

'That was different!'

'No doubt,' she commented drolly. 'I'll look the other way if you can do it by yourself.'

'I'll try.'

Laura moved off a few paces, quickly whirling round again when he crashed back onto the bed. 'Right then,' she declared firmly, and went to him.

'Like jelly. Just like bloody jelly,' he croaked. His head was now not only thumping but spinning round and round like some demented carousel.

Laura started with his shirt, and soon had that off. She then moved to his trousers, unbuttoning them and tugging them to the floor.

'Not my underpants,' he pleaded, holding fiercely onto the top of them.

It wasn't necessary to have those off, she decided, leaving him some modesty, and went for his socks instead.

When he was naked, apart from his underpants, she hauled him onto his feet again and into his dressing gown, all the while having to support him.

'Just lean on me,' she instructed, and together they stumbled towards the door.

Laura looked out first, checking the coast was clear, after which she guided Sandy to the bathroom. Once inside she had him hold onto the basin while she twisted the key in the lock.

She used his flannel, rinsed in hot water and well soaped, to wash him down. 'Here, you can do that for yourself,' she said, handing him his toothbrush.

When everything was to her satisfaction she took him back to his bedroom where he collapsed onto the bed. With a groan he grabbed his stomach.

'Are you going to throw up?' she demanded.

He thought about that for a second. 'No.'

'Good. Now try and eat a little of this egg.'

'I can't, Laura. I simply can't.'

'You must. I'll cut it up for you.'

He managed three mouthfuls before declaring emphatically that if he had anymore he actually would vomit.

Laura removed the tray to another spot and then looked out fresh pyjamas for him. When he was finally in those, after quite a struggle, she tied the waist cord.

'Ma sent up a couple of pills which you'd better have,' she stated. 'They might do something for that head of yours.'

'I think I'm going to die,' he moaned.

'I doubt you'll do that.'

He suddenly began crying again. 'Oh, Laura.'

She wrapped him in her arms, and hugged him tight, as he sobbed his heart out. Laura muttered words of consolation and assurance, telling him he'd get over it, that it was only a matter of time. Words that didn't seem to do any good whatsoever.

It was after ten o'clock the following morning when Harriet appeared in Sandy's bedroom. She noted with approval that his breakfast, brought up earlier by Morag, had been eaten.

'How are you now?' she asked, sitting on the bed beside him.

'A lot better, Ma.'

'Hopefully it's one of those colds that only lasts a couple of days.'

'I think it must be,' he lied. His head was still hurting, and he felt absolutely drained. Despite that, he was on the mend.

'Will you get up later?' she queried.

'Give me a little while longer and then I'll come downstairs.'

'Don't rush things, mind. That's never a good idea.'

'I won't. I promise.'

She smiled at him, seeing him again as a little boy, remembering childhood illnesses that had caused so much concern at the time. Particularly when he'd had whooping cough, that had been nasty.

'I went to the gallery and saw your work on display,' she informed him.

That was a shock. 'You did?'

'And very good it is too. I was most impressed. Mr Moon, the proprietor, had some lovely things to say about you.'

'Have you told Pa you went?'

Harriet laughed. 'Don't be daft. That would only cause a right old ruction, as you well know.'

He was quite touched. 'Thanks for going, Ma. I appreciate it.'

'Are you aware the nude painting has been sold?'

'Really!' he exclaimed in delight.

'For forty pounds apparently.'

He was about to say, bugger me! Then remembered it was his mother he was talking to. 'Well well,' he said instead.

The corners of Harriet's mouth twitched. 'I thought the young lady was a wonderful figment of your imagination.'

Christ, she's guessed! Sandy thought in alarm. 'You weren't offended, were you?'

Harriet considered that. 'I thought I might be, we are a pretty straitlaced family after all. But in the event I wasn't. I found it perfectly charming, not in the least offensive. It's the way God made us after all, why should we be ashamed? Though I would imagine your father would take a different view.'

'He's a prude,' Sandy commented. 'And a bigot. But I don't have to tell you that.'

Harriet glanced away. 'He does have his limitations, I must admit, and certain prejudices, but underneath he's a good man, Alexander. Never forget that.'

It was as though he was back at school and had just been ticked off by the teacher. 'Yes, Ma.'

'I was wondering . . .' She turned her attention to him again. 'Did Cakey have anything to do with you being exhibited?'

'Why do you ask that?' he prevaricated.

'I'm not a complete fool, Alexander, and I know my sister. I somehow detect her hand in this.'

'She was behind it, Ma,' he confessed.

'I thought so.'

'But Mr Moon wouldn't have exhibited me if he hadn't considered me good enough.'

She recalled her conversation with Moon who'd certainly been convinced Sandy had talent. Either that or Moon was a superb actor. 'I appreciate that. You got there on merit, and a little assistance, plus know-how, from Cakey. I shall write to her about it.'

'I already have, Ma.'

'Then I shall confirm what you undoubtedly said.'

Harriet came to her feet. 'I'll leave you now and look forward to seeing you downstairs later.'

'Thanks, Ma,' he smiled. 'For everything.'

'You're welcome, son.'

She paused at the door. 'By the way, I hope this won't happen again, Alexander?'

That puzzled him. 'What, Ma?'

'Cook made an interesting discovery in the bin this morning. An empty whisky bottle which Laura, covering for you no doubt, must have put there.'

Sandy's face flamed.

'Do I make myself clear?'

He swallowed hard. 'Absolutely, Ma.'

'And don't worry, I shan't be saying anything to your father. Heaven forbid I did. What he doesn't know won't harm him. Right, Alexander?'

'Right, Ma.'

A dumbfounded Sandy was left staring at the door as it clicked shut behind her.

* * *

Laura sighed; Madeleine was beginning to irritate her. Ever since they'd met up an hour previously it had been Conor this, and Conor that. What Conor said, what Conor thought, his views on marriage, politics, how much he adored Madeleine, et cetera, et cetera.

'So what do you say?' Madeleine suddenly demanded.

'Sounds interesting,' was the first thing Laura could think of to reply, not really having been listening properly.

'That's what I thought.'

Laura tried to change the subject, to no avail. Within moments Madeleine was back to harping on about Conor again.

'Did I mention he's asked me to his firm's Christmas party?' Madeleine said.

'I believe you have.' Only about a dozen times, Laura mentally groaned.

'I've spoken to Ma and she's agreed to buy me a new dress for the occasion. Isn't that exciting?'

'Very.' Laura thought of the beautiful clothes Aunt Cakey had bought her in London, and which she hadn't yet worn because of her father's objection. It really was ridiculous letting them go to waste, not to mention how good she looked in them.

'Have you been invited to any Christmas parties yet?' Madeleine asked sweetly, knowing full well Laura hadn't.

'Not so far.'

'Maybe you would have been by now if you had a boyfriend.'

Bitch! Laura mentally raged. She wasn't sure she liked the person Madeleine had become since meeting Conor. It had changed her.

'But I don't,' she smiled in reply.

'I can't imagine life without Conor now, he's become everything to me,' Madeleine went on. 'I just live for our meetings.'

'Is that so?' She tried not to sound too sarcastic.

'Just live for them.' Madeleine smiled smugly. 'I'm ever so lucky to have met him. I certainly landed on my feet there all right. Love at first sight, you could say.'

'Yes, you could.'

'I simply can't wait to get engaged. What a happy day that's going to be.'

'Yes,' Laura forced herself to agree.

'He just adores me, you know. Says he worships the ground I walk on.'

'How wonderful.'

Laura again tried to change the subject, again to no avail as they were soon back to Conor, Madeleine droning on about him.

Laura made her escape at the earliest opportunity, relieved to be parted from what had become a very boring friend.

Sandy wondered why Martin Benson was giving him such a strange look as he joined him and Grant Bell at the table they were already occupying. He soon found out.

'So how come you managed to get exhibited at the Sauchiehall Street Gallery?' Martin asked ominously. 'I never even knew you painted.'

'It just happened, that's all,' Sandy prevaricated, not liking Martin's tone one little bit.

'What's all this about?' Grant demanded.

Martin explained.

'Oh, that's great, so it is,' Grant enthused. 'Good for you, pal.' And having said that he smacked Sandy in a congratulatory way on the back.

Martin's expression became even blacker, his eyes brooding and sparking with anger. 'I had a looksee myself,' he stated.

'Oh?'

'How did you manage to get hold of Sophie to paint her?'

Grant frowned. 'Sophie who?'

'The French model,' Martin explained. 'Remember she came in here one night?'

'Her!' Grant exclaimed. 'You sly old dog, Sandy. You painted her?'

'A life pose,' Martin elaborated.

'You mean starkers?'

Martin nodded.

'Fucking hell!' Grant swore softly. 'I must go and have a gander at that.'

Sandy wished he hadn't come to The Clachan, the first time he'd done so since the exhibition opened.

'I submitted a few pieces for consideration,' Martin went on. 'They were rejected.'

'I'm sorry,' Sandy sympathised, and meant it.

'So how come a bloody amateur gets chosen over me? That's what I want to know,' Martin hissed.

This was getting ugly, Sandy thought, hoping it wasn't going to end up in a fight. 'Just luck I suppose,' he replied casually.

'Do you know that bastard Moon or something?'

Sandy shook his head. 'I do now obviously, but not before.'

'So how did you get chosen over me?'

'Hey, come on, lads,' a suddenly concerned Grant intervened. 'We don't want any bust-ups.'

Martin glared at him. 'Why don't you shut your cake-hole?'

Grant regarded Martin steadily, his previous jovial air having suddenly vanished. 'I'd watch my tongue if I were you, Martin. Otherwise we'll be discussing this outside.'

Martin immediately backed off, for Grant was broad and powerful, and would easily have made mincemeat of him. He turned his attention again to Sandy. 'Well?'

Sandy shrugged. 'As I said, just luck I suppose. Now, can we drop this? I came for a friendly pint, not an argument.'

Martin, well aware of Grant's presence, came to his feet. 'Let me just say your portrait of Sophie was shite anyway. Absolute shite.'

Sandy didn't reply, instead gazed into his glass hoping Martin would go away.

A few seconds ticked by, then Martin said, 'I'm going to another pub. This one stinks the night.'

'Jealousy,' Grant smiled at Sandy after Martin had left them. 'That's what that was.'

Sandy nodded his agreement, saddened that the scene had taken place. It would be a long while before he returned to The Clachan.

Sandy stared at his painting of Sophie, his mind filled with memories of their relationship, memories that had already brought a lump to his throat. Thankfully Moon wasn't present, and the assistant taking his place was deep in conversation with a couple of potential buyers.

You have to come to terms with this, he told himself. Accept what's happened. Put it behind you. But that was hard, oh so very, very hard.

One thing was certain, he'd never forget Sophie and their time together. Never.

Not till his dying day. Of that he was convinced.

Chapter 16

It was a bitter cold day, an icy wind blowing in off the Clyde. Harriet shivered; when she'd finished her shopping she'd treat herself to a nice cup of coffee and, she shouldn't really but would, a sticky bun or cake. She smiled to herself at the prospect.

The windows of Daly's department store sported a fine array of Christmas offerings, the holiday now only several weeks away. She still hadn't bought anything for any of the family, but there was plenty of time remaining. The trouble was, she couldn't think of what to get.

She was aware of a man standing beside her, he too gazing at the various displays. She presumed he was also speculating about what to buy for Christmas.

'Excuse me, are you Harriet Lawrie?'

The use of her maiden name startled her. Slowly she turned to face the chap beside her who'd spoken.

'I was, I'm Harriet McLean now.' He seemed vaguely familiar.

The man smiled. 'Thank goodness for that. I'd have felt a right idiot if it hadn't been you.' He took in her puzzled expression. 'Don't you recognise me?'

The penny suddenly dropped. 'James Ballantine!'

'How are you, Harriet? It's lovely to see you again.'

She removed a glove and shook hands with him. It was the moustache that had fooled her, that and age. 'How long has it been?' she asked.

'Too long. A lifetime.'

She nodded her agreement. 'You look well, James.'

'And you. As it's McLean I take it you're married now?'

'That's right. With two children. And yourself?'

He pulled up the collar of his coat. 'Listen, it's freezing out here and I was just about to go for lunch. Nothing special, a little café nearby, but the food's good. Would you care to join me and we can catch up with one another?'

She was about to refuse, then thought, why not? It would be interesting to find out what James had been up to all this long time.

'That would be nice. And I am somewhat peckish.'

He beamed. 'That's it then. Shall we?'

They fell into conversation as she walked alongside him. How exciting, and unexpected, this chance encounter was.

'Well well,' James declared after they'd ordered, fish for him, lamb cutlets for Harriet. 'You haven't changed a bit.'

Harriet smiled. That was a load of nonsense of

course, but it was gallant of him to say so. 'I only wish that was true.'

'But it is,' he protested. 'I swear.'

'I'm carrying more weight for a start.'

'I can't say I'd noticed.'

'And I have lines where there weren't any before.'

He leant forward slightly. 'If so then they're most becoming.'

James Ballantine, she marvelled. Her old suitor over whom she'd chosen Mathew. Only that summer, when in Largs, she'd wondered what had become of him. And now, here he was, sitting across the table from her. 'I like your moustache,' she said. 'It suits you.'

He stroked it. 'I've had this for so long I forget it's there half the time.'

'It lends you a sort of military bearing.'

James laughed. 'I'd never thought of that.'

'Well it does.'

He placed a hand over hers for a second. 'It really is wonderful bumping into you like this, Harriet. It brings back all sorts of memories.'

'Good ones, I hope?'

'Where you're concerned, always.'

She flushed a little. 'Let's start with you. Still in the retail trade?'

He nodded. 'I'm the general manager of Daly's. A post I only took up two months ago, and which brought me back to Glasgow.'

'Back?' she queried.

'I've lived in Nottingham for the past twenty-odd years. Down amongst the Sassenach.'

They both laughed. 'Was it nice?'

James considered that. 'There are worse places than

Nottingham. And as for living amongst the English, I've always got on well with them.'

She'd already noticed he wasn't wearing a wedding ring. 'And your wife, is she English?'

An odd expression came over his face. 'I never married, Harriet. I've remained a bachelor all this time.'

That surprised her, for he was a handsome man. And obviously successful in his job. 'I see,' she murmured.

'The right woman just never came along, I'm afraid. Oh there were several occasions when I considered taking the plunge, but in the end never did. I suppose it boiled down to the fact I didn't love them. Or at least, not enough to walk down the aisle.'

Harriet thought that extremely sad. What a waste, she reflected, sure he'd have made a wonderful husband and father. 'I'm sorry,' she mumbled.

James shrugged. 'I'm not. I'd rather be a bachelor than unhappily married. That must be awful.'

A shudder ran through her, for wasn't she just that? At least she had two children to be thankful for, and the reason she didn't completely regret marrying Mathew, for if she hadn't there would be no Alexander or Laura.

'So where are you living?' she asked.

'I have an apartment just off Charing Cross. Small, but comfortable. I don't need any more, and it's handy for work. Yourself?'

'Lilybank Gardens in Hillhead.' She went on to tell him about Mathew, Alexander and Laura, her voice filled with pride when she spoke of the latter two.

'That is what I do rue,' he replied. 'Not having any children. But there we are, it simply wasn't to be.'

'Are you enjoying being back in Glasgow?' she queried, changing the subject.

'Very much so. I was always a little bit homesick all the time I was away. But now I'm home it's for good, my present post will, hopefully, see me through to retirement. When that happens I'll buy a place in one of the Clyde resorts as I fancy being by the sea.'

'Sounds marvellous.' She smiled.

He smiled too, but didn't comment on that.

Their conversation was interrupted by the arrival of their food, a steaming plate laid in front of each of them.

'Simple fare, but delicious,' James stated. 'That's why I come here. It's a small family business so it's all home cooking.'

That simple statement somehow conveyed to Harriet how lonely his life really was. Her heart went out to him.

After James had paid the bill they went outside where snow had begun to fall. 'Thank you so much,' Harriet said. 'I really did enjoy that.'

'My main meal of the day,' James declared. 'I'll only have a snack later on.'

Once more it struck Harriet how lonely he was, a great yawning gap where a family, or at least a wife, should have been. 'Perhaps we'll bump into each other again one day?' she said.

'Perhaps,' he agreed. 'I don't see why not now that I'm back in Glasgow.' He hesitated, looking uncertain of himself. 'I, eh . . . well I come to this café Monday to Thursday, but every Friday I treat myself and have lunch at the Station Hotel where they have a wonderful grill room. I usually arrive at twelve-thirty and have a drink in the bar first before going on through at one. I was wondering if you'd care to join me there sometime?'

Harriet simply didn't know what to reply to that, she was a married woman after all. Bumping into James, especially after all these years, and having lunch was one thing; what he was proposing, an actual rendezvous, quite another.

'I'll fully understand if you feel it wouldn't be proper,' James went on. 'But the invitation is there should you ever want to take me up on it.'

'Then let's leave it at that,' she hedged.

'Of course.'

'Now I must hurry along.'

James glanced at his wristwatch. 'Me too. I have a mountain of paperwork to get through, and several meetings to sit in on.' He extended a hand. 'I can't tell you the pleasure it's been, Harriet. Quite made my day.'

When they parted she, intentionally, went in the opposite direction to him. The Grill Room at the Station Hotel! She knew it by reputation, but had never been there. It was far too pricey for Mathew's pocket, or so Mathew would have insisted. It was certainly a tempting offer but completely out of the question.

Or was it?

'You seem very cheery tonight, dear,' Mathew commented without lifting his eyes from the evening newspaper.

Harriet paused in what she was doing. 'Do I?'

'You've been smiling ever since I got in earlier, and

now you're humming away to yourself. Has something nice happened today?'

Instantly guilt gnawed at her. But why should she feel guilty? She hadn't done anything wrong, simply had lunch with an old friend after a chance meeting. For a brief moment she considered telling Mathew about James, then decided against it. The lunch would remain her secret.

'Not that I can think of,' she lied. 'Just a day like any other.'

Mathew's reply was a grunt.

She hated it when he grunted, it was so rude! She had mentioned it to him several times in the past, but the habit persisted. 'By the way,' she said sweetly, having been waiting for an opportunity to bring this up. 'I'm going to need some extra money from you. Quite a bit actually.'

Mathew glanced at her, his expression a combination of surprise and irritation. 'What for?'

She'd known the mention of parting with money would get his attention. 'New school clothes for Laura. What she has have not only worn out, they're long past their best anyway, but don't fit properly any more.'

Mathew frowned. 'Why don't they fit properly any more?'

'Because, in case you haven't noticed, she's grown a lot in the last year. Filled out considerably. She can't possibly go on the way she is, she'll be a laughing stock.'

'Well, we can't have that,' Mathew admitted grudgingly, thinking that would reflect on him.

'And then there are her other clothes, they need replacing as well for the same reasons.'

'Surely not all of them?' he protested. This was going to cost an absolute packet.

'Most of them, dear.'

Mathew digested that. 'What about the January sales coming up?'

Harriet was amazed he knew about those. 'School clothes won't be in the sales, dear. But I can try and get the other ones in them. Do my best anyway.'

Harriet waited a few seconds before adding, 'Seems a shame really.'

'Why's that?'

'Because she already has all those beautiful clothes upstairs that Cakey bought her in London. If she wore those it would save you absolute heaps.'

'But they're far too old for her,' he objected.

'No, they're not. She's not a little girl any more, Mathew, you'll have to accept that. Believe me, those clothes are ideal. I think the only reason you disliked them in the first place was because Cakey bought them which you somehow thought showed you up.'

'That's nonsense!' he exclaimed.

She gave him an enigmatic smile which clearly angered him.

'Well, it's up to you, dear,' Harriet went on. 'Entirely your decision to chuck money away when you needn't.'

Mathew blanched. He was the last one to do that. 'I'll think about it,' he mumbled.

'You do that, dear.'

Harriet went back to busying herself, almost certain she'd won. When it came to money Mathew was notoriously tight, which she'd always considered a not very endearing quality.

It was later when they were going to bed that he

remarked in an offhand way that it would be a pity to waste the clothes as Laura already had them.

A jubilant Harriet, keeping a straight face, didn't reply to that. She'd tell Laura the good news in the morning.

'Can I ask you a question?'

Sandy, who'd been about to go out, stopped to face his sister. 'What, Laura?'

'I noticed earlier when I was passing your bedroom, the door *was* wide open, that your easel and other painting things aren't there. Why's that?'

Sandy glanced down at the floor, not wanting Laura to see his expression. 'I've given up painting.'

She stared at him incredulously. 'But you love drawing and painting.'

'I did. Not any more. I just don't want to do it ever again. I'm finished with it.'

Laura placed a hand tenderly on his arm. 'Why, Sandy. Why?'

He shrugged, but said nothing.

It suddenly dawned on her what this was all about. 'It's Sophie, isn't it?'

'I don't really wish to talk about it, sis.'

'Oh, Sandy,' she breathed. 'This is a mistake, one you'll regret.'

'Maybe,' he muttered. 'It's just how it is, that's all. The very thought of picking up a paintbrush again makes me feel sick inside.'

That damned woman! Laura inwardly raged. This was what she'd done to her brother. If Sophie had been present she'd have scratched the bitch's eyes out.

'Now I must get on or I'll be late for my lecture,'

Sandy declared, and hurried away leaving a sad, and fuming, Laura behind.

She remained distressed for the rest of that day.

'Oh, dear,' Harriet muttered, her brow suddenly lined with concern. She was reading a letter which Morag had just brought her at the breakfast table.

'Bad news, Ma?' Sandy asked.

Harriet nodded. 'It's from your Aunt Cakey. She's been unwell recently and the doctors don't know what's wrong with her. She's to go into hospital for some tests. I must reply right away.'

'Does she say what the symptoms are?' Sandy asked, concerned.

'Loss of weight, headaches, shortness of breath, sudden stabbing pains.'

'Well, she could certainly do with losing weight,' Mathew commented sourly.

Harriet glared at him. 'That's an unkind, not to mention callous, thing to say.'

Mathew shrugged. 'True nonetheless. She could easily do with shedding a few stone.'

'I hope she'll be all right,' Laura declared, for she, like Sandy, had become extremely fond of their Aunt Cakey during her visit.

'What do you think, Pa?' Sandy inquired. 'You've heard the symptoms, any suggestions?'

'Could be almost anything,' Mathew replied casually. 'I could name half a dozen things, from cancer to liver dysfunction, which could fit the bill.'

'Cancer!' an aghast Harriet exclaimed. 'Oh, please God, not that.'

'It's probably something minor, Ma,' Sandy said,

trying to calm her fears. 'Nothing to get unduly upset about.'

'Then why is she going into hospital for tests?'

'As a precautionary measure, I'm sure,' Sandy went on. 'Wouldn't you agree, Pa?'

'Possibly,' Mathew mused. 'There again, it might well be an unscrupulous doctor, or doctors, wanting to make money out of her. She is extremely rich, don't forget.'

Sandy hadn't thought of that possibility.

'They wouldn't do such a thing, would they?' Harriet asked.

Mathew laughed, cynicism in his voice. 'Don't be naive, dear, of course they would. These foreign doctors get up to all sorts, I've heard. Quite disgraceful.'

'I doubt that's the case,' Sandy countered. 'Aunt Cakey's no fool. I can't believe she'd be taken in. No, if she's agreed to go into hospital for whatever then she thinks it's necessary.'

'You wouldn't do that, would you, Pa?' Laura asked mischievously.

'You mean continue treating a patient who doesn't need it?'

'That's right.'

'Of course not. As I said, it's unscrupulous.'

'Besides which, most of your father's patients are poor as church mice so the opportunity would never present itself,' Harriet pointed out, well aware that comment would annoy Mathew. How dare he make such a disparaging remark about Cakey's weight!

Mathew scowled at her, hating to be reminded of that fact. 'Morag, a fresh pot of coffee,' he snapped, the patiently attending Morag immediately picking up the present one and quickly scuttling from the room.

256

The subject of Cakey and her mystery illness wasn't mentioned again during the remainder of breakfast.

'I know what I want you to give me for Christmas,' Laura announced to Sandy.

'Do you now?'

'Oh yes.'

'I suppose it'll cost a fortune?'

'Not in the least.'

He noted the twinkle in her eye which told him there was some sort of catch here. 'Let me guess,' he mused, playing along. 'Scent?'

'No.'

'Something for the bathroom?'

'No.'

'A solid gold bracelet?'

She laughed. 'Don't be ridiculous. It's something far simpler than that. And I've already said it wouldn't cost a fortune so it's hardly a gold bracelet.'

Enough, he thought. 'All right, I give up. What is it?'

'I want you to take me to a pub.'

'Bloody hell!' he exclaimed. 'I can't do that. You're under age. And anyway, nice girls like you don't go into pubs. It just isn't done.'

'Female art and medical students do, you've told me that yourself.'

'They're different.'

'Why's that?'

'Well, for a start they're over eighteen. And secondly, that's the sort of thing they get up to. It's kind of accepted.'

'I can look eighteen if I want to,' Laura riposted. 'Honestly I can.'

Sandy's expression was one of scepticism. 'What I don't understand is why you want to go in the first place? They're horrible, smelly places, often filled with undesirables.'

'Sounds exciting. And I want to go because I've never been. I'm curious, surely there's nothing wrong with that?'

There wasn't, but he had no intention of admitting it. 'I don't think so, Laura. It's a bad idea.'

She changed tack, becoming winsome and coy. 'Please, Sandy. Pretty please?'

Could she look eighteen? he wondered.

'I'm allowed to wear the clothes Aunt Cakey bought me now,' Laura went on. 'They'll make all the difference, I promise you. That and a little make-up.'

'You have make-up?' he queried in surprise.

'Something else Aunt Cakey bought me which I haven't told either Ma or Pa about. I've been practising using it in my room and am getting quite good at putting it on.'

Sandy's objection began to waver. It might be fun after all. Bit of a laugh. Then he remembered how sympathetic Laura had been to him after Sophie, he owed her for that. 'It would have to be a night when Ma and Pa are out,' he said slowly. 'They mustn't see you.'

'They're playing cards next Wednesday,' Laura replied. 'They'll be gone for at least three or four hours. How about then?'

His resistance crumbled. 'On one condition though.'

'What's that?'

'If I don't think you can get away with the age thing then it's off. Agreed?'

'Agreed. And you won't object, I'll make sure of it.'

He certainly hoped so, already trying to think of what pub he'd take her to. Certainly not The Clachan, that was definitely out. Some place nice and quiet and, above all, respectable.

He'd have to give it some thought.

Harriet was standing in front of the full-length mirror she had in their bedroom, studying herself, face and figure. She was trying to recall exactly what she'd looked like when younger, particularly on her wedding day.

She'd put on weight, but that was only to be expected, most women her age did. The important thing was that she hadn't put on too much, just a pleasing voluptuous amount, she decided.

Her breasts had dropped, but there again, what else could you expect after having two children? And it wasn't as if they'd dropped disastrously, hardly that. She'd been lucky in that they hadn't been too large to begin with. But dropped they had, or maybe drooped was a better word, there was no denying it.

There were streaks of grey in her hair, but fortunately they hadn't increased over the past few years. In fact, they were rather attractive and lent her a mature, sophisticated mien.

As for her face, well there were lines there where before it had been smooth, but not seriously so. Character, she thought, that's what the lines did, gave her face character.

After a short period of brutal analysis she came to the conclusion she was still an attractive woman – and fervently hoped she wasn't deluding herself.

She thought of Mathew and his lack of sexual interest in her nowadays, and wondered if the fault was somehow hers? If it was, it wasn't because of how she looked. She was certain of that.

He'd never been a demonstrative man, the sort forever giving you kisses and cuddles, quite the contrary actually. But a compliment or two, from time to time, would have been nice. She couldn't remember the last occasion when that had happened. As for the little things, the cherishing gestures, a surprise bunch of flowers or present, he'd simply never gone in for those. She supposed that what she'd never had she shouldn't miss – except she did.

The hard fact of the matter was Mathew took her for granted, and probably, although she might not have been aware of it in the early years, always had.

Harriet sighed, and turned away from the mirror, thoroughly depressed. Life was so humdrum and boring it occasionally made her want to scream.

Oh well, she thought in resignation, all she could do was make the best of what she had. There was nothing else for it.

Sandy literally gaped when Laura presented herself to go to the pub. 'So, what do you think?' she demanded eagerly.

He wouldn't have recognised the person standing in front of him as his sister. She'd become an absolute stunner. 'Lovely,' he stammered.

'Not too much make-up?' she asked.

'No, just right.'

My God, he thought, she was beautiful. And she certainly looked over eighteen. If he hadn't known better he'd have judged her to be twenty, if not more.

The dress she had on was plum coloured, its bloused

bodice belted with a wide crushed girdle, the collar cut in a most flattering line. The embroidery on the jabot and the pipings were of a lighter shade. The overall effect was not only pleasing but, Sandy gulped, sexy in the extreme.

'Do I pass your test?' she demanded with a cheeky smile on her face.

He nodded.

'Are you sure?'

'Absolutely.'

That delighted her, but then she'd known she would. 'Not overdressed, am I?'

'Not at all, Laura. You look absolutely delightful. I shall feel proud to take you out.'

'Have you decided where we're going yet?'

'A little pub I know that's quiet and dimly lit. Not exactly your average boozer, but somewhat more genteel than that.'

Laura suddenly laughed. 'You should see your face. It's a picture.'

'I have to admit I am a bit suprised. I hadn't realised . . . well not to this extent anyway, just how grown up you've become. You're quite the young lady.'

'Good. For I shall be drinking alcohol, Sandy, let's be clear about that right now. All right?'

'All right,' came the bemused reply.

'Then shall we, brother dear?'

Several minutes later they were walking along the Byres Road looking for a taxi, Laura having taken Sandy's arm as if he was her beau.

Chapter 17

'I really did enjoy that, Sandy, thank you again,' Laura said as he helped her out of her coat.

Truth was, he too had thoroughly enjoyed himself. It hadn't been like going out with his sister at all. What fun she was, what a laugh. There had been points where she'd had him in stitches with stories about what went on amongst the girls at her school. Talk about a real eye opener! Whoever said 'sugar and spice' didn't know what they were talking about. My word, they didn't.

'Me too. We must do it again some night.'

She turned to face him. 'Do you mean that?'

'I wouldn't say it otherwise.'

Her eyes were sparkling, though that might have had something to do with the alcohol she'd consumed. 'Then I'll hold you to it.'

He too was a little drunk, Sandy realised. He hadn't

felt so when he left the pub so it must have been the cold night air that had brought it on.

'Ma and Pa won't be home for a good hour yet, so we're nice and early.' Laura smiled.

He nodded, having been watching the time ever since they left.

Laura suddenly giggled, then covered her mouth. 'I do believe I'm just a teensy bit tipsy,' she declared.

'You want to know something?'

'What?'

'So am I.'

Laura giggled again, interrupted by a solitary hiccup.

'You all right?'

'I think so.' She patted her chest. 'I don't know what brought that on.'

'Three Gins and It, I should imagine,' he replied drily.

'It's possible.'

'I'd say it's highly likely.'

Laura sighed. 'It's almost a shame to go to bed, but I am rather tired.'

'Me too.' He'd had more than three drinks, considerably more. Laura would have had too if he'd allowed her.

He guided her towards the stairs. 'Come on, Cinderella, the ball's over.'

She found that extremely funny, and laughed. 'Well, if I'm Cinderella then you must be Prince Charming?'

'Not Prince Charming, but the coachman escorting Cinders upstairs to her boudoir.'

'Cinderella never had a boudoir,' Laura protested. 'She was firmly in the kitchen with the pots and pans.'

'Whatever,' Sandy sighed; this was becoming silly now.

They stopped outside his bedroom door, Laura's frivolous mood disappearing to be replaced by a more serious one. 'Don't forget your promise that we'll do it again some night.'

'I won't.'

Her eyes looked deeply into his, the expression in them quizzical. 'Goodnight, Sandy,' she whispered.

'Night, sis.'

She made to kiss him on the cheek but because he moved his head slightly she ended up kissing him on a corner of his mouth.

'Ooops!' she muttered apologetically, before slipping into her room.

Minutes later there was a tap on Sandy's door. 'Come in.' What did she want now? he wondered.

'You're going to think me a right idiot,' she declared. 'But I can't undo the hooks at the back of my dress. Will you help me?'

'Of course.'

'I did them up myself,' she explained. 'But for some reason I can't *un*do them.'

He smiled wryly. She'd been sober when getting into the dress, not quite that in trying to get it off. It was perfectly understandable.

'Turn round then,' he instructed.

It only took him seconds and the upper part of the dress was suddenly open, to fall away. Laura, taken by surprise at the swiftness of it, failed to grab hold of the dress which slithered to the floor leaving her standing in her underthings.

The breath caught in Sandy's throat at the sight of her. The swell of her breasts, the delicious curve of her hips, the . . . Christ! he suddenly thought. This was his sister, he shouldn't be ogling her as he was.

Laura, face flushed, pulled the dress up to cover her front. 'I see you've had plenty of practice doing that,' she croaked, the first thing that came into her mind. She was thrown, confused, and highly embarrassed.

He knew she was referring to Sophie. 'A little,' he admitted, forcing himself to smile.

'See you in the morning then,' Laura mumbled.

'See you then.'

Well, if he'd needed any further confirmation that his young sister had turned into a woman, that had been it, he thought, after she was gone.

Quite an ending to the evening.

Harriet stopped outside Daly's Department Store to gaze into one of its many windows, this one featuring children's toys. Should she go in? she wondered. If she did she might bump into James again.

Highly unlikely, she told herself. He was bound to be in his office, not wandering around the shop's floors. Nor would he be in the café he'd taken her to, it was too late in the afternoon for that.

James, he'd hardly been out of her thoughts since their chance meeting, haunting her day and night. His face staring back at her whenever she closed her eyes.

He'd been such good company, she reflected, actually listening, not pretending to, when she spoke, paying attention to her, enjoying being with her.

What a change that had been after Mathew who did none of these things any more.

Harriet literally shook herself. This was ridiculous, of course she wouldn't be seeing James again, unless by accident. As for lunch one Friday at the Station Hotel, that would only make matters worse, leave her even more discontented.

She was a married woman, she reminded herself for what might have been the thousandth time. And had to behave like one. Certainly not rendezvousing with a man not her husband, no matter how innocent it might be.

There again, she would only be playing the good Samaritan, for wasn't James desperately lonely? That had been blatantly obvious. Seeing him again would be bringing a little friendship, and companionship, into his life. What was wrong with that?

Nothing, she told herself. Nothing at all. And where was the harm as long as Mathew never found out? It wouldn't be as if she'd be meeting James regularly, no no, she couldn't do that. But occasionally, once in a while. Every few months or so . . .

And let's face it, despite Mathew and the children, she was as lonely as James. In a different way, that's all.

It was a miserable February evening, the festivities long past, when Sandy had the idea of returning to Betty's Bar where he hadn't been for absolutely ages.

He pulled up the collar of his coat as he hurried along the Broomielaw, glancing over occasionally at the variety of ships, flying flags from all over the world, docked at the quayside. When he reached Betty's Bar he quickly slipped inside, instantly grateful for the heat that assailed him.

He smiled when he saw the look of surprise on Tommy, the barman's, face.

'Hello, stranger,' Tommy exclaimed. 'What's it to be?'

'A pint and a dram.'

'Coming right up, Rembrandt.'

That made Sandy laugh. Rembrandt indeed! If only . . . He noted his drawing of Archie was still on the wall, which he would have expected, but there was no sign of the old man or Mick.

'As it's Friday I thought Mick might be in tonight?' he said affably to Tommy, thinking the terrible scar on his face was just as hideous as he remembered.

Tommy's eyes flicked to Sandy, then away again. 'I doubt we'll be seeing him,' he replied casually.

'Oh, why's that? I thought he always came in Fridays.'

'Not recently.'

Sandy, disappointed to hear that, wondered why. He asked Tommy again, but for some reason the barman was evasive, moving on to another customer as soon as he'd rung up the till.

A few of the regulars were present, the fat woman whose face was raddled with old smallpox scars, and a couple more that he recognised. He decided to sit down rather than continue standing at the bar.

It was about ten minutes later when Bob, the owner, appeared and came over. 'Hello, son, I thought you'd forgotten your way here?'

'It's been a while,' Sandy acknowledged. 'Just one of these things.'

Bob sat facing Sandy. 'Tommy tells me you were asking about Mick Gallagher?'

'That's right. I thought he might be in.'

Bob slowly nodded, as if confirming something to himself. 'I take it you don't know then?'

Sandy frowned. 'Know what?'

'Mick's in prison.'

That stunned Sandy. 'In prison!' he exclaimed quietly. 'What did he do?'

'Nearly killed a chap, that's what. He's lucky he's not up on a murder charge, so he is.'

This was dreadful news. 'How did it happen, Bob?'

'Here's the story. Mick had an accident at work one day, a hook slipped and badly gashed his side. He was told by the gaffer to take the rest of the day off and go to the infirmary to get it stitched, which Mick did. When he got home, hours before he normally would have done, he found Beryl in bed with a next-door neighbour, the pair of them stark bollock naked with the chap giving Beryl a right seeing to.'

'Bloody hell!' Sandy swore.

'As you might expect,' Bob went on, 'Mick went berserk, dragged the chap off a shrieking Beryl and proceeded to beat the shite out of him. It wouldn't have been too bad if it had stopped there, but it didn't. Mick threw the bastard clean through the window.'

'Dear God,' an appalled Sandy whispered.

'Not that terrible in itself except Mick lives three storeys up! The chap was more dead than alive when the polis and ambulance arrived. Mick was carted off to jail in a Black Maria; the squaddie, he's the next-door neighbour's son home on leave, to hospital. I'm surprised you didn't read about it in the papers.'

Sandy shook his head. 'I don't always get a chance to read them, so I must have missed it.'

'It was touch and go with the squaddie, only eighteen by the way, nothing more than a wee boy when Mick and Beryl moved in, but he pulled through in the end. A helluva mess, mind. Two broken legs, broken arm, broken collar bone, smashed pelvis plus serious internal injuries. It's possible he'll never walk again.'

Sandy recalled that night with Mick and Beryl, when she'd confided in him, and how she'd made it plain she was available if he was interested. Well, it seems the squaddie had taken up her offer, with such tragic consequences. 'What about Beryl?' he queried.

If Bob's expression had been grim before, now it became truly so. 'Mick had no sooner been taken away than she packed a suitcase and disappeared, no one knows where. Just as well really, Mick's pals, and there are plenty of those, would have been having a heavy word with her if she hadn't. She'd probably have been badly cut for what she did.'

'You mean razored?'

'Aye, son, that's precisely what I mean. She'd have been given a few stripes for her troubles. No more pretty face then.'

Sandy swallowed hard, knowing Bob wouldn't be exaggerating. The Glasgow working class had a very strong sense of right and wrong, and rough justice, or their version of it, could be summarily dished out. Beryl had been smart in doing a runner.

'So there you have it,' Bob declared. 'That's why Mick won't be in tonight.'

'I had no idea,' Sandy murmured, shaking his head in disbelief. 'How long did he get?'

'That hasn't been decided yet. His trial has been going on for the past couple of weeks, and he's due to be sentenced on Monday. Then he'll know the worst. And worst it will be, for that old bastard Judge Cameron is presiding. Ever heard of him?'

Sandy thought for a moment. 'Can't say I have.'

'Well, they call him the hanging judge, and it's a name well deserved. If Mick had killed the squaddie, despite the extenuating circumstances, he'd have swung for sure with Cameron on the case. That man has hanged more men than any other judge in the history of Scotland. He's renowned for it. There's never any leniency where Cameron is concerned. May he roast in hell when his time comes!'

Bob leant across the table. 'Myself and some others will be there on Monday when Mick is sentenced. Do you want to join us?'

Sandy was about to say he couldn't, that he had lectures scheduled all day Monday, then thought the better of it. The least he could do was show up and give Mick an extra bit of support. 'What time?'

'Ten o'clock at the High Court, court number one.'

'I'll be there,' Sandy promised.

Bob nodded his approval. 'I'll leave you to it then. I've got a job to do.'

'Thanks for the explanation. It's something of a shock.'

'Not as much as it was for Mick when he walked into that bedroom and saw what was going on.' Bob hesitated, then added in a gentle, sympathetic tone, 'The really sad thing is he loved that bitch. Poor bloody sod.'

It was a chastened group of Betty's Bar regulars, including Sandy, who left the High Court that Monday morning, emerging into swirling snow which had blown up since they'd gone in.

'Fuckin' bastard,' Archie muttered. 'Rotten fuckin' bastard.' He was referring to Judge Cameron.

Tommy was there, with his wife Kathleen, Mick's

sister, who was in tears. 'Eighteen years,' she choked. 'It's not fair so it isn't. It's just not bloody fair.'

'I'd like to meet Cameron on his own up a dark alley one night,' Archie said, clenching his hands into fists. 'I'd mollicate him, the evil swine.'

Sandy closed his eyes for a brief second, recalling the look on Mick's face as he'd been sentenced. He'd never seen such agony, or total despair, in his life.

'We'll go back to the pub and have a drink on me,' a white-faced Bob announced. Even he hadn't dreamt Cameron would be that severe.

'I won't if you don't mind,' Sandy said to him. 'I've got to get on to my lectures.'

Bob stuck out a hand. 'Thanks for coming, son. Mick will have appreciated it.'

Not that his attendance had done Mick any good, Sandy thought. But at least he'd been there.

'And don't be such a stranger to the pub in future. You're always welcome, don't forget.'

Sandy said his goodbyes, then walked away from the little group. Eighteen years, was all he could think. At Mick's age that was a lifetime. He'd be an old man when he finally got out. If he ever did.

James Ballantine's face lit up with pleasure. 'Harriet! You've managed at last.' He was instantly on his feet and helping Harriet out of her coat.

'You did say any Friday.'

'I did indeed. It's wonderful to see you again.' He beamed. 'It truly is.'

'Now what would you like to drink?' he asked when she'd sat down.

'A medium sherry would be nice.'

'Then that's what you'll have.' Leaving her, he went up to the bar.

Well, she'd done it, a bemused Harriet reflected. Right up until the last moment she hadn't thought she'd have the courage to go through with it, but she had. And now here she was in the Station Hotel, at James's long-standing invitation, to have lunch with him.

Out of curiosity she glanced around her, taking in the décor and general feel of the place. Plush, was how she would describe it, if somewhat faded. Well worn were other words that came to mind. And comfortable, the chair she was sitting in was definitely that. Yes, she decided, she approved of the Station Hotel, or this part of it at least.

'So,' James declared on returning with her sherry, 'how have you been?'

She noted the genuine interest in his voice, which was most gratifying. The question hadn't been a rhetorical one. 'Fine. Glad Christmas and Hogmanay are over. I always find them such a trial.' The expression that briefly flashed across his face told her she didn't find it nearly as big a trial as he did.

'Did you have guests on Hogmanay?' he asked.

'No. Not even a first foot. I'm afraid it was quite quiet.' Courtesy made her ask in reply, 'And you?'

'The same,' he answered enigmatically.

She knew what that meant, he'd spent both on his own. Difficult time for single people, she realised, never having previously thought about it. He'd probably stayed home alone on both occasions, for newly back in Glasgow after so many years she doubted he had any friends to invite him anywhere.

'The shop was busy,' he declared, slightly changing

the subject. 'Sales were excellent, considerably up on the previous year.'

They sat chatting for a short while, and then it was time to go through to the grill room. As they passed the bar Harriet noticed the woman serving behind it, and frowned. The woman's face somehow familiar, though for the life of her she couldn't place it.

'Well,' Harriet declared as they left the hotel. 'I thoroughly enjoyed that. The grill room certainly lived up to its reputation.'

'As I told you before,' James smiled, 'it's my weekly treat to myself.'

It had been so expensive, she thought, having managed a sneaky peek at the bill. Mathew would have been horrified to be asked to pay such an amount for two meals and a bottle of wine.

'I hope you'll come again,' James said, suddenly serious. 'That this wasn't just a one-off.'

For a moment or two she didn't know what to reply to that, not wishing to commit herself as she still wasn't sure about the arrangement. 'Hopefully I can,' she prevaricated.

'Just hopefully?'

How vulnerable he suddenly looked, she thought. It was almost as if he was pleading with her. 'Let's leave it at that, shall we. Please?'

He nodded. 'I understand.'

'Thank you, James.'

'Goodbye for now then.'

'Goodbye.'

He extended a hand, and they shook. Harriet smiled, then turned round and hurried away.

She hadn't gone far when, out of the blue, it dawned on her who the woman behind the bar was. The female in Sandy's picture, the one he'd painted nude. Now she'd recognised it the face was unmistakable.

'Good God,' she whispered, wondering how on earth Sandy knew her. For it was the same woman without a doubt.

'Laura, wait for me. Wait for me!'

Laura groaned inwardly, she'd thought she'd dodged Madeleine for the walk home from school, something she'd been doing more and more of late.

'I must have missed you again at the gate,' Madeleine said breathlessly, arriving beside Laura.

'I promised Ma I'd be in early as possible,' Laura lied. 'She's got things for me to do apparently.'

'Oh! Like what?'

Laura shrugged. 'No idea until I get there.'

How long before Madeleine started on about Conor? Laura wondered, for it was certain she would.

In the event it took less than two minutes, much to Laura's annoyance. She was sick to death of hearing about Conor and Madeleine.

As usual, of late, she thought about other matters as Madeleine burbled on about her precious boyfriend.

Sandy was having trouble getting off to sleep, the image of Mick Gallagher after sentence in the High Court haunting his mind, as it had been doing so ever since.

Poor Mick, by Beryl's betrayal and the harsh sentence he'd been reduced to a broken man. No, worse than that, a man smashed to bits, his life blown to smithereens.

How he felt for Mick, ached for him. Eighteen years didn't bear thinking about, especially if spent in Barlinne, Glasgow's notorious prison, known commonly as the Bar-L.

Mick didn't deserve that. Punishment yes, for he had done a terrible thing, but the provocation had been extreme. As Bob had said, Mick had desperately loved his wife, and maybe, inside all that anguish, still did.

Sandy knew then what he had to do, and there was no time like the present. With a sigh he got out of bed, switched on the light, and shrugged himself into his dressing gown.

Although he'd left all his painting materials at Sophie's house, he still had paper, pencils and charcoal sticks in his room.

Within minutes he was sitting at his desk drawing Mick in the dock.

Harriet glanced over at the ticking clock on the mantelpiece from which was coming the only sound in the room, and that's how it had been for the past hour.

Mathew sat slouched opposite her, his attention riveted to the medical journal he was engrossed in. She too had been reading but had long since given up.

Tick tock.

Tick tock.

A whole hour without any conversation, nothing said at all. How many nights had there been like that? She hated to think. Nights without number. Or nights where, if they did speak, it was cursory. Would you like some coffee, dear? Is your newspaper interesting, darling? Those sort of tedious, mundane, monotonous, uninteresting, boring boring boring things.

Suddenly the telephone rang out in the hallway causing Mathew to grunt with annoyance at having to put his journal aside. 'I'll get it,' he said. 'It's no doubt for me.'

No doubt, she thought. It nearly always was at that time of night, way past when any friends, such as they had, might ring.

Harriet wondered what James was doing as Mathew left the room, probably by himself, lonely as she was. She smiled, recalling the wonderful time she'd had at lunch with him. There had been no dearth of conversation then, it had flowed freely. Not only flowed but it had been interspersed with lots of laughter.

What would it have been like if she'd married James all those years ago instead of Mathew? Would their marriage have reached this stale state? Somehow she didn't think so. James was such a different type of person to Mathew, he'd never have allowed it to happen. Or perhaps it wouldn't have been the case of his not allowing, but it simply not occurring in the first place.

'I've got to go out on a call. I could be a while,' Mathew announced on his return.

'Shall I wait up, dear?'

He didn't even think about that. 'No, don't bother.'

Abruptly he left the room again to collect his things, and a few minutes later the front door clicked shut.

Not even a peck on the cheek, Harriet thought bitterly. Far less a civil goodbye.

She bit her lip in anger. Anger at him, anger at herself, anger at the whole situation.

The mantelpiece clock ticked on.

The barman wasn't one Sandy recognised. 'Is Bob around?' he queried.

'Aye, who shall I say wants him?'

'Sandy McLean.'

'Just haud on a moment, chief.'

Sandy stood his drawing on the bar and undid the brown paper he'd wrapped it in. He'd just finished doing that when Bob appeared.

'Hello there, son. What can I do for you?'

Sandy indicated the drawing which he'd had framed. 'I thought you might like this for the pub. Something to remember Mick by.'

Bob stared at the drawing which depicted Mick in a happy mood, the way he might have been lounging at the bar having a pint and a laugh.

'It's Mick to a T,' he said slowly.

Sandy had done several of Mick in the dock as he'd originally intended, but decided they weren't suitable to be hung in the pub. He wanted people to remember the real Mick. 'Thank you.'

'His friends will appreciate it, including me. It's awfy good of you, son. I'll have a whip round . . .'

'No whip round,' Sandy interjected quickly. 'I didn't do it for that.'

Bob sucked in a deep breath. 'But you won't refuse a drink on the house, I hope?'

Sandy smiled. 'No, I won't.'

'Well, we'll have that and then you can help me hang it. Deal?'

'Deal,' Sandy agreed.

He glanced again at the drawing thinking it one of the best he'd ever done. He was well pleased with it. And, as Bob had said, the gesture would be appreciated.

It was something he'd felt he had to do.

Chapter 18

Tears sprang into Harriet's eyes as she read the latest letter to arrive from her sister. Mathew continued with his breakfast while both Sandy and Laura stared at their mother in concern.

'Ma?' Sandy queried.

Harriet allowed the hand holding the letter to drop, her face now contorted. 'Cakey's only got weeks to live,' she choked.

That shook Sandy, as it did Laura. 'Have they diagnosed what's wrong with her yet?' he asked quietly.

Harriet nodded. 'A tumour on the brain. The doctors say it's inoperable.'

Mathew laid down his knife and fork; it would be unthinkable for even him to go on eating after that bombshell. 'Are they absolutely certain?' he demanded.

'Apparently. She doesn't go into any of the details,

just says what it is and the fact she's only got a short while left.'

Laura got up from her chair and went to her mother to put her arms round Harriet. 'Oh, Ma,' she whispered.

Harriet placed the letter on the table. 'I wouldn't have recognised the handwriting as Cakey's. It's degenerated into a sort of spidery scrawl.'

'Well, let's look on the positive side,' Mathew declared, thinking to be helpful. 'With her money she'll get the very best of care and attention. That's something.'

Harriet glared at him through her tears. Trust Mathew to come out with a statement like that. Even if it was true.

Mathew's mind had slipped into overdrive as he thought about the ramifications of this news. Harriet was Margaret's next of kin, and, as such, bound to inherit, Cakey not having any family of her own. That meant Harriet, and he as her husband, were about to become stinking rich. He fought to keep the exultation from his face at the prospect of all his dreams being about to become reality.

'It's a tragedy,' Mathew declared solemnly.

None of them had really expected this, Sandy thought. Aunt Cakey had written saying she was ill and the doctors were having trouble diagnosing what the problem was, but they'd never, at least not him, had thought the problem to be life threatening.

Laura, distressed by her mother's state, and also because she had a great affection for Cakey, burst into tears as well. She and her mother, both sobbing, clung to one another.

Oh for Pete's sake! Mathew felt like exclaiming, but

wisely didn't. 'Perhaps you should have a lie down, Harriet?' he suggested instead. A quick glance at the clock told him he had to watch the time otherwise he'd be late for surgery. Not that it had ever bothered him in the past.

'I think that's a good idea, Ma,' Sandy added.

Mathew rose from the table. 'I'll get you a sedative before I go,' he declared to Harriet, and hurried off.

Sandy didn't know what to do. Just sit there, or what? He himself was severely shocked by the contents of Cakey's letter, he'd become very fond of his aunt during her stay with them. And now this.

'I'm all right,' Harriet said, having stopped sobbing. She dabbed at her eyes with a napkin.

Laura also got control of herself. 'Shall I help you upstairs, Ma?'

'In a moment, Laura.' She picked up the letter again and re-read it.

When Mathew returned he was carrying his bag plus a glass of water. Setting both down he opened the bag and rummaged amongst its contents.

'Can I stay home today, Ma? I don't want to go to school now.'

'Of course you can darling.'

'What about me, Ma,' Sandy queried. 'Would you like me to stay home as well?'

'I don't think that will be necessary,' Mathew stated coldly. 'You mustn't miss your studies with the exams coming up. Besides, anything your mother might need either Laura or Morag can attend to.'

Mathew poured a powder into the glass, stirred it, and then went to Harriet. 'Here, swallow this. It'll help calm you down.'

Harriet meekly did as ordered.

'It'll take about five minutes to have an effect,' Mathew explained. 'In the meantime why don't you take your mother off to bed, Laura.'

Sandy couldn't help but think his father should have done that himself, but clearly Mathew didn't see the necessity. Typical of him, Sandy reflected.

Harriet started to get up, then suddenly, without warning, fainted, Laura unable to stop her crashing to the floor.

Mathew swore.

Mathew was cock-a-hoop as he drove to the surgery. Of course he was sorry about Margaret; even if he'd disliked her, he certainly hadn't wished her dead, but that's what was on the cards.

How much would Harriet inherit? he wondered, excitement bubbling within him. Certainly enough for a house in Kelvinside, one of the really big ones, with more than enough left over for him to either open, or buy into, a far better practice.

It was the life of Riley from here on, he mused. Nothing but the best for him and Harriet; they'd be able to have whatever they wanted. For Margaret, from what he understood, hadn't only been rich, but filthy rich. Rolling in the damned stuff.

Thank God she hadn't had children of her own to pass her money on to. Nor did Herbert, he knew this for fact, have any surviving relatives, which left only Harriet.

A broad smile creased his face at the prospect of what lay ahead. Happy days indeed. He felt like singing.

What he mustn't do was let on to Harriet what his

real feelings were, he must go through all the motions of being sympathetic and so on. And act surprised, as if he hadn't thought about it, when the subject of Margaret's will came up, as it had to eventually.

How long would it take them to hear from the lawyers in Canada? he mused. Whatever, it didn't really matter. All that did was that they would. Had to.

And then . . . The world was his oyster. Finally, at long last, he was going to be somebody. Move in the circles he deserved to move in. Be a man of importance and substance.

His mouth almost watered at the thought.

'What an awful day,' Laura said later to Sandy whom she'd come to visit in his bedroom. He was at his desk where he'd been trying to study, but now was only too happy for the interruption.

Sandy nodded. 'There were no signs of Aunt Cakey being unwell when she was here. She looked fit as the proverbial fiddle to me.'

'Poor Ma,' Laura sighed. 'This has hit her hard. She and Cakey, despite the distance separating them, were very close.'

'Nasty business a brain tumour,' Sandy grimaced. 'I don't know too much about them except that they're nasty. Not a very nice, or easy, way to go.'

Laura glanced over at the new easel standing where the old one had been. She also noted the brand-new brushes and paints that were in evidence. 'I hadn't realised you'd started painting again?'

He shrugged. 'I haven't yet. I can't come up with a subject that interests me. But I will. It's only a matter of time.'

'Does this mean you're over Sophie?' she asked softly.

Sandy thought about that. 'I wouldn't say "over" exactly, perhaps have come to terms with the situation is more appropriate.'

'That's good. I'm pleased, for your sake. You've too much talent to throw it away because of her.'

Sandy thought of Mick Gallagher, the real reason why he'd started again. Mick's face in the dock had compelled him to put pencil to paper. He considered telling Laura about Mick, then decided against it. Some other time perhaps, but not now.

'Ma's gone back to bed,' Laura informed him. 'She's written to Aunt Cakey and the letter's been posted. Pa's given her another sedative.'

'She frightened me when she fainted this morning,' Sandy confessed. 'For one horrible moment I thought her heart had given out on account of the news.'

'It was scary,' Laura admitted. 'The whole thing was an absolute nightmare.'

Sandy ran a hand over his forehead; he had the beginnings of a headache, and felt completely drained. Hardly surprising, he supposed, after the day's goings on. He decided he'd done enough studying for one night. 'Fancy a drink?' he asked.

Laura's face lit up. 'I'll get that glass from the bathroom.'

It was a new bottle which Sandy opened. He poured himself a hefty measure, then added a generous amount of lemonade.

'Here we are,' Laura declared, placing her glass on his desk. 'I certainly can use this.'

'Me too,' Sandy agreed.

It was while he was topping up her drink with

lemonade that Laura had a sudden idea. 'I've just thought of a subject for your next painting,' she announced.

'What?'

'Well, we both know how good you are at portraits, so why don't you do one, from memory, of Aunt Cakey and give it to Ma when it's finished? She'd love that.'

'My God, it's brilliant!' Sandy exclaimed in delight. 'Ma truly would love that. And I'd enjoy doing it.'

'There we are then,' Laura beamed. 'Aren't I clever?'

Sandy laughed. 'You certainly are.' Adding sarcastically, 'And modest with it.'

'None of your cheek now,' she pouted.

'None intended,' he lied.

This time they both laughed.

'I'm off out now,' Sandy declared, popping his head round the door of the sitting room, which Mathew on occasion would refer to as the parlour.

Mathew immediately frowned. 'Again? That's the second time this week. Where are you going?'

'Just out, Pa. I need to clear my head.'

Mathew glanced at the clock. 'It's early yet, you should still be studying. Don't forget the exams are coming up.'

Sandy sighed; as if he could forget. 'Don't worry, I'll be ready for them when they happen.'

Mathew glared. 'I hope so. I'm expecting better results than last year's lot. They were a travesty.'

'Don't go on, dear,' Harriet chided him. 'Sandy is old enough to know what he's doing.'

'I sometimes wonder,' Mathew grumbled.

'Shan't be late,' Sandy said cheerily, and promptly left them to it.

Bloody exams, Sandy fumed as he strode down the street towards a local pub he sometimes frequented. Why oh why did he find it so hard to retain the information he studied? The answer was simple really, it was because he wasn't that interested.

In fact he wasn't the least bit interested in medicine if he was honest.

'Would you like me to make you some coffee, darling?' Mathew asked Harriet after Sandy had gone.

Harriet stared at her husband in astonishment. In all their years of marriage he'd never ever made her a cup of tea or coffee, or anything else come to that. This was unheard of. 'Why, thank you. That would be lovely.'

'And a few chocolate biscuits I think, don't you?'

Harriet couldn't believe her ears, this was incredible. What on earth had come over Mathew? And then it dawned on her, he was being this way because of Cakey. It was his way of being nice and giving her support.

'Back in a tick,' Mathew declared, and headed off to the kitchen.

Harriet was touched by this gesture. How kind, she thought. How very kind of him. She could only hope this change of attitude would continue.

Mathew gave a sigh of relief as he locked the surgery door from the inside. All morning he'd been champing at the bit, waiting to be rid of his final patient.

Returning swiftly to his consulting room he opened

a drawer and took out the large brown envelope that had arrived at the surgery earlier, the contents of which he now intended to read.

Inside were the details of three houses currently for sale in Kelvinside, all at a price that would previously have been unthinkable for him. But with Cakey's demise imminent that wouldn't be the case for long.

Too soon to make a bid on any of them of course, but that didn't stop him seeing what was on offer, something that would give him enormous pleasure.

He carefully laid out the three sets of details, then picked up one and began reading through it.

When he'd read all three thoroughly, he started back on the first one and started reading it all over again.

He couldn't wait for Harriet's legacy to come through. The sooner the better as far as he was concerned. Then it was goodbye to Lilybank Gardens and hello to Kelvinside and a house of his dreams.

Laura arrived in from school to find that the news they'd all been dreading had finally come from Canada. Aunt Cakey had passed away.

'Your mother's in bed,' Morag informed her. 'And your father's with her.'

'Do you think I should go on up?'

'I don't know. You must do what you think best.'

Although they'd all been expecting this it was still something of a shock. She could just imagine the state her mother must be in. Poor Ma.

Later, when Sandy got home, a quivering-lipped Laura told him what had happened, he then holding her as she finally broke down and wept.

For days afterwards a dark depressing gloom hung

over the house, while Harriet was rarely seen down-stairs, keeping mainly to her bedroom and bed.

As Sandy commented, it was a very sad time.

Thank God for that, Sandy thought as he left the lecture hall, the first day of his exams was over.

He considered he'd done well which had surprised him, the questions easier than he'd expected. At least he'd had answers for all of them.

He prayed they were the right ones.

Mathew stopped outside the Rolls-Royce showroom to admire the gleaming Silver Ghost on display. He wondered if he dared go in and inquire about it.

Why not? he thought. Harriet hadn't yet heard about Margaret's will, but surely she must soon.

'Can I help you, sir?' the assistant inquired when Mathew went inside.

Mathew spent half an hour there, asking about, and going over, the car in detail. If money had been available he'd have bought it there and then.

When he eventually left he vowed he'd return. And when he did the Silver Ghost would be his.

Harriet was irritating Mathew and had been all evening. Everything, including the tone of her voice, was getting under his skin. Couldn't she see he just wanted some peace and quiet to read his newspaper? He'd have thought it was obvious from his manner and curt replies when asked something directly.

'Oh for God's sake, woman, do shut up!' he exclaimed, his patience finally snapping. 'You've been going on and on for absolutely ages about nothing at all, repeating yourself over and over again. You're beginning to sound like a cracked gramophone record.'

'Dad!' Laura admonished. 'Don't be horrible.'

Sandy decided to say nothing.

'Mind your own business, young lady,' Mathew retorted, his voice a whiplash.

Harriet's expression reflected how hurt she was by Mathew's outburst. Going on and on, sounding like a cracked gramophone record! Where was the nice Mathew of late? The one who'd been so kind and considerate after Cakey's death? Gone it would seem.

Laura glanced at Sandy, who shook his head. Best for her not to interfere further when their father was like this.

Harriet rose from her chair in as dignified a manner as she could. 'I'm off to bed,' she announced.

Mathew looked at the clock, then her. 'This early! It's not even nine o'clock yet.'

'I don't care what the time is, I'm going to bed.' And without a further word Harriet left the room.

'Me too,' Laura declared, and followed her mother.

Mathew rounded on Sandy. 'And what about you, boy?'

'I'm twenty-five years old, Pa, I'm hardly a boy,' Sandy replied softly.

'It's an expression, nothing more.'

'Well, it's one I don't care for. At my age it's not only demeaning, it's insulting.'

Mathew was taken aback by this, it wasn't often Sandy stood up to him. 'Well, don't expect an apology, for you won't get one.'

'I wouldn't expect one. Not from you anyway.'

'That's impertinent,' Mathew snarled.

Sandy didn't reply, merely got to his feet and followed his mother and Laura out the door.

Mathew shook his head, angry with himself for having lost his temper with Harriet, knowing he shouldn't have done so. The reason he was out of sorts had nothing whatsoever to do with her, but because he'd learnt that afternoon a house in Kelvinside he'd set his heart on had been sold.

When, oh when, were they going to hear from the lawyers in Canada? It was months now, they surely should have had some sort of word.

He decided the best thing would be to go upstairs and make it up, or try to anyway with Harriet. Best keep her sweet, after all.

He was actually in the hallway when the telephone rang summoning him out on a call.

In the event, an apology was never made.

'What's bothering you Harriet?' James Ballantine asked. 'You seem distracted.'

She gazed down at her lunch, not in the least hungry even though it looked delicious. 'My sister died recently,' she explained quietly. 'I suppose it's that.'

'I am sorry,' he sympathised. Reaching across the table he placed a hand over hers. 'You were close I take it?'

'Very, despite the fact she's lived in Canada for years. She paid us a visit not that long ago, and she appeared fine at the time, and now she's dead. It was quite unexpected.'

'Can I ask what she died from, or don't you want to talk about it?'

'A brain tumour. She didn't last long after it had been

diagnosed. She managed to write twice before the end, which was something. It would have been worse to get a letter out of the blue saying she'd passed over. At least I was prepared for it when word finally did come.' Harriet smiled wryly. 'I say prepared, but it was still a body blow. I just can't believe I'll never see her again.'

James stared at Harriet, thinking how lovely she looked in her grief, even more lovely than she normally did. 'Is there anything I can do?'

Harriet shook her head.

'Are you sure?'

'Yes, James, and thank you for offering.'

'Anything for you, Harriet. Absolutely anything at all.'

She knew from his tone he meant that, which touched her deeply. 'I would like to talk if you don't mind.' She hesitated. 'It can be difficult with Mathew who's not the best listener in the world. He has tried over this, but . . .' She broke off and shrugged. 'That's just the way he is.'

James told himself he mustn't criticise, it wasn't his place to do so. 'Some men are like that,' he commented instead.

'But not you.'

'I take that as a compliment.'

'It's meant as one.'

'Thank you.'

For the rest of their meal Harriet spoke about Cakey, reminiscing about their childhood, relating all manner of things about her and the bond they'd had between them.

When Harriet finally parted from James she felt strangely elated, as if a great burden had been lifted from her shoulders. She was extremely grateful to him for that, all the more since Mathew had been so rude to her the other evening. It underlined the contrasts between the two men.

'Haven't you finished Aunt Cakey's portrait yet?' Laura asked Sandy. They were alone in his room.

'I haven't been able to get it quite right, and I'm not handing it over until I do. Then there were the exams, I had to stop work on it while I was concentrating on those. But now they're finished I'll get back to it.'

Laura nodded that she understood. 'How do you think they went? The exams, that is.'

'So so. Good in parts, not so in others. Overall I was quite pleased.'

'Well, I hope you get a decent result. I had my fingers crossed for you while they were on.'

He smiled at her. 'Thanks, sis.'

He watched Laura walk out, thinking he must paint her some day. Her face had changed considerably over the past year, there was now a very clear definition about it that hadn't been there before. And the character it had lacked was certainly now present, very much so. Character and a sense of strength.

Yes indeed, some day. Perhaps even some day soon. Possibly during the summer holidays which were looming.

He might even tease her and ask her to do it nude. There again, that could be a bad idea. She might not realise it was a tease and clout him one.

'No post this morning, Morag?' Mathew frowned at the maid.

'No, sir, there isn't.'

Damn! Mathew swore inwardly. When *were* they going to hear about Cakey's will? This waiting was never ending, not to mention bloody infuriating.

'Are you expecting something special, dear?' Harriet inquired politely.

'No, no, nothing special. I just wondered if there was post, that's all,' he lied.

There was something going on, Harriet thought to herself. This wasn't the first time recently that Mathew had shown interest in the mail, there had to be a reason, though he obviously wasn't saying.

How curious.

Harriet's eyes widened in surprise and delight when Sandy removed the cloth covering the painting.

'It was Laura's idea,' Sandy explained, giving credit where it was due. 'We both thought you'd like it.'

'Well?' Laura prompted.

Harriet came closer, all the while staring at Cakey's portrait. 'I'm lost for words,' she managed at last.

'*Do* you like it?' Sandy queried.

'I think it's wonderful. Absolutely wonderful. Mathew?'

'A fair likeness,' he grudgingly admitted.

'It's a lot more than that,' Harriet declared. 'I'm half expecting it to open its mouth and speak.'

That pleased Sandy enormously.

'We thought it might hang above the fireplace?' Laura suggested.

'Ideal,' Harriet nodded, voice clogged with emotion. 'That's exactly where we'll put it.'

'I'm rather chuffed with it myself,' Sandy said proudly.

'I found it tricky to do, it was just so difficult to catch the essential Aunt Cakey, reflect her spirit. But in the end I thought I'd managed it.'

'You certainly have,' Harriet enthused. 'I shall treasure it always.'

Mathew was about to make a criticism, then thought the better of it. He was furious with Sandy for painting the portrait; the last thing he wanted was Margaret's image staring at him day in, day out. But, in the circumstances, he could hardly object to it being hung where Laura had suggested.

'I can't thank you enough, son,' Harriet said to Sandy, eyes now glistening.

'That's all right, Ma.'

Going to him, she kissed his cheek. 'I know Cakey would have loved it too. God rest her soul.'

'Do you really think so?'

'I know so.'

Laura, standing beside Sandy, reached out and squeezed his hand.

Chapter 19

Sandy stared at the official-looking envelope Morag had just handed him, wondering who on earth it was from. He glanced over at Laura who'd received a similar envelope. Laura shrugged, at a loss as he was.

Sandy ripped his envelope open and pulled out the single sheet of typewritten letter it contained. He frowned as he read.

'Who's yours from?' he queried.

'A firm of lawyers called Boyd and Semple. Yours?'

'The same.'

A suddenly very attentive Mathew was watching them both. 'What do they say?' he asked casually.

'They want me to get in touch and make an appointment to see them at my convenience,' Sandy replied.

'Me too,' Laura added. 'Only I've to bring a parent along.'

Had to be connected with Margaret's will, Mathew

deduced. In which case, why wasn't there a similar letter for Harriet? That must be coming separately, he decided. As for Sandy and Laura, it would seem they were to receive a small legacy of some sort. The bulk would be going to Harriet.

'I don't know what to make of this,' Sandy mused. 'I mean, why would a firm of lawyers want to see me?'

'And Laura,' Harriet stated, bemused by this turn of events. How very mysterious.

'Only one way to find out, Alexander. You'd better telephone them,' Mathew declared. 'You can do so on behalf of yourself and Laura. Make these appointments they've requested.'

'I'll do it after breakfast,' Sandy replied, thinking he could go along any time as the Medical School had closed for the summer break. It was the same with Laura whose school had also shut for the same reason.

'Have you any idea what this is about, Mathew?' Harriet asked.

He, playing the innocent, shook his head. 'None at all.' He was surprised that none of them had put two and two together. It seemed obvious enough to him.

'I wonder . . .' Harriet murmured.

'What, dear?'

'Is it possible these letters have something to do with Cakey's death?'

At last the penny had dropped, an amused Mathew thought. 'Could be the case,' he nodded in reply. 'Perhaps she made provision to leave them each a little minding in her will.'

That startled Sandy. 'You mean money?'

'I would imagine so.'

'That would be just like Cakey,' Harriet smiled. 'I

know she certainly took a huge shine to the pair of you when she was here. She mentioned it on a number of occasions.'

'If it is money I wonder how much?' Laura mused, thinking this terribly exciting.

'Lots and lots I hope,' Sandy said, half joking, half serious. Surely it wouldn't be less than what she'd given him while visiting? And that had been a tidy sum.

'Well, one thing's for certain,' Sandy declared. 'The sooner we get to speak to these people the better.'

Laura laid her letter aside and readdressed the boiled egg she'd been eating. She hadn't been particularly hungry before, but she was now.

Quite ravenous, in fact.

'I've had my interview and been accepted. I'm starting college this September,' Madeleine Abercrombie announced to Laura that afternoon, having called in at the house.

'But you've still got another year to go at school,' Laura pointed out.

'I don't have to do it, I'm old enough to leave whenever I wish. Which is precisely what I'm doing. The college are perfectly happy with the academic standards I've already achieved.'

'This is because of Conor I take it?' Laura queried drily.

'Of course. The swifter I can get through college the sooner I can join his firm and be with him every day. Isn't that wonderful?'

'If it's what you want.'

'I most certainly do,' Madeleine enthused. 'He says I'm guaranteed a job once I have the necessary training behind me. He's spoken to his father about it and it's been agreed.'

How she envied Madeleine, Laura thought. Not Conor, but the prospect of a job, going out to work. Something she'd never be allowed to do. 'You didn't mention that you intended applying to this college when we broke up from school?'

Madeleine shrugged. 'I didn't mention it in case they turned me down. I didn't wish to risk the embarrassment.'

'I see.' Well, that was understandable, Laura thought.

'Aren't you pleased for me?'

'Of course I am, Madeleine.' Laura smiled. 'And I wish you all the luck in the world with your course.' She briefly toyed with the idea of telling Madeleine her own news, then decided against it for the same reason Madeleine hadn't let on about applying for college. It would be embarrassing to say she was about to come into some money, only for it not to happen. It was mere supposition on their part after all that that's what the summons from the lawers was all about.

'Now as I haven't seen you for a while let me bring you up to date on Conor and myself,' Madeleine beamed.

Laura inwardly groaned.

Mr Boyd, the senior partner at Boyd and Semple, was an old man with a decidedly Victorian air about him. He welcomed Harriet, Laura and Sandy into his office and invited them, after the ritual of shaking hands, to sit.

Mathew had considered being the one to go along with Laura, then thought it better that Harriet did as the dual appointment had been made for a time right smack in the middle of his morning surgery. He would hear what took place later in the day.

Mr Boyd sat behind his desk and opened a manila folder lying there. 'We were contacted several weeks ago, recommended to them apparently, by a firm of Canadian solicitors acting on behalf of . . .'

Sandy froze in total shock when, after much pre-amble, and legal jargon, Boyd finally got round to the actual amount that Cakey had left him. According to Boyd, after various donations to charities, etc., etc., he'd been left half of her remaining capital, plus a sub-stantial number of Canadian and American stocks, their name for shares, with half the value of Cakey's house, now in the process of being sold, on top of that.

'Dear God,' Sandy managed to whisper at last. This was incredible! The capital amount, by itself, was an absolute fortune. He was suddenly rich beyond his wildest dreams.

Sandy had received half, Laura was to receive the corresponding half. A thousand pounds was to be released to her now, the rest held in trust until she reached her majority.

An open-mouthed Laura was gaping at Boyd as she tried to take in what he'd just said. She glanced at Sandy whose expression was as stupified as she guessed her own to be.

'So there we have it,' Boyd said quietly. 'Are there any questions you'd like to ask me, Mr McLean?'

It took Sandy a moment or two to realise it was he who was being addressed. He slowly shook his head. If there were questions they'd come later when he'd had time to think, but not yet.

'It will take a further short while for the transfer of

capital to be made. In the meantime, Mr McLean, I'll require your bank details.'

'Certainly,' Sandy mumbled.

Boyd droned on for another few minutes before declaring he thought their business concluded for the present. His office would be in touch again in the near future.

Sandy's mind was whirling.

The colour completely drained from Mathew's face. 'Everything?' he croaked in disbelief. 'Margaret left *everything* to Alexander and Laura?'

Harriet nodded.

'But what about you? You're her sister, and as such should be the main beneficiary.'

'Clearly Cakey didn't see it that way. I wasn't left anything, nor did I expect to be. Such a thing happening simply never crossed my mind.'

'But she must have left you something!' Mathew suddenly exploded in fury. 'What about her jewellery? There must have been lots of that.'

'It was never mentioned.'

'Never . . .' He trailed off, and knotted his hands.

'A thousand pounds is to be released to Laura, the rest held in trust until she reaches twenty-one,' Harriet further explained.

'A thousand . . .' Mathew staggered to the nearest chair and slumped into it. This was . . . a disaster. 'There's some mistake,' he said feebly. 'Has to be.'

'There's no mistake, Mathew. It's all legal and above board. What Mr Boyd told us was in accordance with Cakey's will.'

Mathew closed his eyes. 'There's a lovely house in

Kelvinside for sale,' he babbled. 'I've already viewed it.'

Harriet stared at her husband, now realising why he'd recently been so interested in the post. He'd already thought about Cakey's will and been expecting her to receive a letter, not Sandy and Laura, as the main beneficiary. That all Cakey's money would be coming to *her*, as she'd already said, had never crossed her mind.

She also now knew why Cakey had done as she had. If Cakey had left her the money then Mathew would have had access to it, total access in fact. That was something Cakey hadn't wanted.

'I take it you intended buying this house in Kelvinside with the money left to me?' she accused.

Mathew opened his eyes again and glared at her. 'Damn right I did. You know I've always wanted to live there. This was going to be my opportunity to be somebody, for us to move in the circles we should be moving in.'

She regarded him with contempt. Any feeling that had remained in her towards Mathew now disappeared. 'When did you first think of the will? Answer me that.'

He didn't reply.

'Probably the day I received the letter from Cakey saying she was dying. While I was grief stricken all you could think of was her money and what you were going to do with it. Isn't that right, Mathew?'

Again he didn't reply.

'So it's been in your mind all along, and you never mentioned a word. Tell me, what else did you intend buying?'

'Nothing,' he mumbled.

'You're lying. I can see it in your face.'

He was incredulous that Harriet would speak to him like this. 'Don't call me a liar,' he snapped.

'Why not, you obviously are.' Then she made an inspirational guess. 'And a Rolls-Royce too no doubt. You've always coveted one of those. I remember how loathe you were to give Cakey her car keys back when we returned from Largs, and how you were hardly out of the blessed thing when we were there. Driving all over as if you were Lord Muck. You were going to buy one, weren't you?'

He nodded. 'Where would have been the harm? We'd have been able to afford it.' His eyes suddenly narrowed. 'You haven't yet said how much she actually did leave?'

Harriet considered the pros and cons of telling him. 'I don't think it's any of your business so I'm not about to say. Enough, that's all you need to know. Enough.'

And having said that Harriet swept from the room. Out in the hallway she discovered herself to be shaking, partly with anger, but more so from having confronted Mathew as she'd done. Something she never really had done before. Well, certainly not to that extent.

Despicable, she thought. That's what Mathew was. Utterly despicable.

'This alters absolutely everything where we're concerned,' Laura stated to Sandy, having come to his bedroom.

He nodded. 'Life will never be the same.'

'It's hard to take on board, isn't it?'

He laughed softly. 'You can say that again. Talk about a bolt out the blue! That was one, and no mistake.'

Laura smiled in memory. 'Dear Aunt Cakey. Who'd have thought she'd do such a thing?'

'Not me.'

'Me neither.'

The pair of them sat brooding in silence for a few moments. 'It's going to take some getting used to,' Sandy finally said.

'Any idea what you'll do with yours?'

'None at all, Laura. It's far too early for that. I'm still trying to believe that what happened today was real and that I'm not dreaming it.'

'I know what you mean.'

'I was aware Aunt Cakey was rich, but not that rich. Christ, we're set for life, you know that?'

'I suppose so,' she mused.

'There's no supposing about it, it's true. As for you, every eligible bachelor in Glasgow is going to be after you once this gets out, so you're going to have to be careful. As will I where women are concerned.'

He laughed. 'That could be fun though.'

'As it could be with me and men.'

He gave her a warning look. 'That's not exactly what I meant. I was referring to something else.'

'Sex,' she stated bluntly.

He found himself blushing. 'Well, yes actually.'

She regarded him thoughtfully. 'Would you really take advantage like that?'

'If they're silly enough to throw themselves at me for my money, then why not if they're willing?'

Laura didn't think she approved of that. In fact she was certain she didn't.

Sandy gazed into the window of what was considered to be the most expensive jeweller's shop in Glasgow. Gold watches, rings, cufflinks, diamonds, pearls, rubies, jade. Nothing was priced, the reason, he believed, being that those who frequented the establishment didn't have to worry about cost.

He shook his head in amazement to think that he too was now numbered amongst people like that. If the fancy had taken him he could have had any item on display.

Well, not today, thank you very much. He wasn't about to go daft with his inheritance by spending it on silly things, certainly not horrendously expensive ones. But still, he reflected, it was nice to know he could have done had he wanted to.

So what did he want, now that virtually everything he might want was available to him? The answer, for the moment anyway, was nothing at all.

He was turning away from the window, thinking he might have a lunchtime pint, when he spotted her across the street. Sophie, arm in arm, with a chap he presumed to be Jack.

A wave of jealousy swept over him as he watched them, Sophie as beautiful as ever. Jack, in his opinion, was something of a scruff.

He suddenly smiled, wondering how she'd react if he was to go over and tell her about the wealth he'd come into, that he was now an extremely rich man? That on giving him up she'd lost out on being treated like a princess.

Perhaps he was being cynical, but he'd realised how practical women could be where money was concerned, especially in a relationship. Would Jack have survived the news? He wouldn't have bet on it. Sophie might have insisted she loved Jack, but would that love have endured in the face of the sort of temptations he could now offer?

The question was, did he want her back? A few months previously he would have jumped at the chance. But now? Did he want a woman who was only with him because of the size of his wallet?

The answer was no. With other women, perhaps. But not Sophie, she'd meant too much to him. Far too much. Better to let things remain as they were, she with Jack and he on the loose.

Of course he could've gone over and told her out of sheer spite, a sort of revenge, but that wasn't him at all. He might have many faults, but spite and malice weren't included.

Watching her disappear up the street it came to him; seeing her again had suddenly given him the idea, that there *was* something he wanted.

The more he thought about it the more the idea excited him.

'A holiday in Paris!' Mathew exclaimed in astonishment. 'Why in God's name would you want to go there?'

'For the experience,' Sandy explained simply.

Mathew snorted. 'I won't hear of it. Filthy place, I understand, as are the French. They eat unspeakable things while their toilet habits are positively disgusting.'

'Ma?'

Harriet considered her reply. 'It might do you a lot of good to widen your horizons by travelling to a foreign country. I know I've often wished I'd done that.' Her eyes took on a wistful look. 'Sadly, it was never to be. I never had the opportunity.'

'Well, I'm against it,' Mathew declared somewhat pompously. 'Who knows what might happen to you?'

Sandy smiled, who knew indeed? 'I'm sorry to hear

you say that, Pa. Paris is a great favourite amongst the aristocracy, by all accounts.'

That immediately caught Mathew's interest as Sandy had guessed it would. 'It is?'

'So I believe. The aristocracy and gentry. Paris, Rome, Venice, all great favourites, but especially Paris. Even royalty visits on a regular basis.'

'Royalty?' Now he was really impressed. 'Is that a fact?'

'I assure you it is, Pa. The Prince of Wales and his entourage are forever popping across. I read it in an article recently that he loves it there.'

'Hmmh,' Mathew mused. That made things different.

Sandy glanced over at Laura who winked at him. She already knew about his proposed trip, and it had been her suggestion that he adopt this tactic to win his father's approval. As she'd put it, Mathew was an out-and-out snob, talk about hob-nobbing it with the upper classes and he'd be all for it.

Then Mathew had a sudden thought. 'How are you going to pay for this proposed trip when your capital hasn't come through yet? Don't look to me, I can't help you there.' He could, but had no intention of doing so.

The simple answer was that Sandy had enough left from what Cakey had given him when she'd arrived, plus a considerable amount saved from his gambling activities, neither of which his parents were aware of. 'I thought I might speak to Mr Boyd and ask for an arrangement to be made,' he lied. 'I can't see him refusing me in the circumstances.'

Mathew slowly nodded; that seemed a fair possibility.

'When would you go, son?' Harriet queried.

'As soon as I can organise it.'

'You'd have to be back before Medical School re-opens of course,' Mathew stated sharply. 'Can't have you gallivanting off and falling behind in your studies as a result.'

'I'll be back in plenty of time, Pa, I promise.'

'Paris,' Laura mused. 'It's supposed to be ever so romantic there. Just think, Sandy, you might meet, and fall in love with, some titled lady or other, and she with you.' Again this was a tactic on her part to make Mathew agree.

A titled lady as a daughter-in-law? Mathew thought. Now that would be something.

'Will you be all right travelling on your own?' Harriet asked.

'I'll be fine, Ma. It's only Paris after all, not the far ends of the globe. I'll be perfectly safe, I assure you.'

'Then I hope you enjoy yourself,' Mathew declared. 'I shall look forward to hearing all about it on your return.'

There it was, permission granted, Sandy thought in relief. Now all he had to do was make the arrangements.

'I'll expect you to bring me back a present,' Laura smiled.

'You have my word on that. Something special too. My word on it.'

Paris! But more specifically Montmartre where he intended staying. He couldn't wait.

James Ballantine listened grimly as Harriet described the confrontation she'd had with Mathew over Cakey's will, and heard how deeply it had upset her. Also that

Mathew had been far more concerned about the money she might get than Cakey's imminent death or her grief on learning about it.

James was appalled by the story, and Mathew's attitude. How callous of him, how downright mercenary. James may never have met Mathew but he knew, with certainty, that he wouldn't have liked him if he had, that they'd have absolutely nothing in common. Except Harriet, that is.

'Tell me something,' James said quietly after Harriet had finally stopped speaking. 'Have you ever considered leaving him?'

Harriet frowned. 'You mean leave Mathew?'

'Yes, I do.'

She stared at James in consternation. 'That's impossible.'

'Why is it?'

Harriet struggled to find the words. 'People in our position just don't separate, or divorce. It simply isn't done. Then there are the children, what would they think?'

'Sandy is a grown man, soon to make his own way in the world, while Laura is surely old enough to cope and understand.'

'But it just isn't done, James. There would be a scandal.'

'Would that bother you?'

'Yes it would,' she declared firmly. 'I'd never hold my head up again.'

He had to be very careful how he put this, James warned himself. He didn't want to frighten her off. 'If the thought of scandal bothered you then you could move elsewhere, another city perhaps, and start a whole new life there.'

This was getting ridiculous, Harriet thought. 'And live on what? I don't have any money of my own, and Mathew certainly wouldn't give me any.'

'Money wouldn't be a problem if you divorced and re-married again.'

Harriet felt like laughing. 'At my age? Having already been married and had children. Who would want me?'

'I would,' he stated, staring directly into her eyes.

'You . . .' She trailed off, completely dumbstruck.

'There's something I have to confess, Harriet. May I?' She nodded.

'The reason I never married, the real reason that is, was because I was still in love with someone from my past and didn't want to settle for second best. And I'm still in love with her to this day.'

Harriet didn't have to ask the question to know the answer, it was blatantly obvious from his expression. But still she asked, 'Do I know this woman?'

He smiled. 'Oh yes. It's you.'

Harriet, blushing slightly, looked away. Her heart had started thumping wildly. 'You shouldn't have said that, James,' she whispered in a tremulous voice.

'Why not?'

'You just shouldn't have.'

'But it's true.'

'That may be but . . .' She trailed off. This was the last thing she'd expected when presenting herself for lunch.

Of course it was flattering, very much so. Not only that he loved her but the fact he had carried a torch down through all those years. 'I had no idea,' she said at last.

'It was because of you I left Glasgow and went to

England. It would have been too painful to stay and run the risk of bumping into you from time to time. The centre of Glasgow is quite small after all, it would have been bound to happen.'

'Harriet?' he queried when she didn't reply.

'I simply don't know what to say.'

'Then don't, only promise me you'll think about what I just said?'

Again she didn't reply.

'Promise me?' James urged.

She stared at him, as if seeing his face for the first time ever. 'You really have gone on loving me all this time?'

He nodded.

'And that's why you never married?'

'Yes.'

'And you left Glasgow because of me?'

'I did.'

'Oh, James,' she whispered. 'That's so sad.'

'And yet it could still all have a happy ending. If you'll let it.'

Could it? she wondered. 'And you'd marry me after I was divorced?'

'In a flash, and thank God for the opportunity. One other thing I must mention, you wouldn't have to worry about money throughout everything. I earn a considerable salary and have a substantial amount in the bank.' He smiled wryly. 'Being a bachelor I never had much cause to spend most of what I earned. So will you promise me you'll at least think about it?'

'Yes.'

Harriet couldn't believe she'd just said that, but she had.

Chapter 20

Grant Bell greeted Sandy like a long-lost brother when Sandy appeared in the downstairs bar of The Clachan. 'Where the hell have you been?' he demanded. 'Haven't seen you in ages.'

'Busy, Grant.'

'Doing what? Your exams are well over.'

'We had a death in the family,' Sandy replied, which was as good an explanation as any.

'Oh! Sorry. Was it someone close?'

Sandy nodded. 'Now, if you don't mind, I don't want to talk about it.'

'Aye, fine. I understand.'

Sandy glanced around, looking for Martin Benson, not having forgotten their last meeting and the jealousy on Martin's part. 'Is Martin here tonight?' he inquired casually.

'Naw. It's the vac, don't forget. He's probably gone

somewhere until Art School starts up again. He's another one who hasn't been in.'

That suited Sandy admirably. It was because of Martin that he'd made himself scarce, not wanting a repeat of the previous unpleasantness. 'Been to Blythswood Square earlier?' he teased.

'I have. It's a regular thing with me every Friday night. Why don't you come with me some time?'

Sandy shook his head. 'I told you once before, that sort of thing just isn't for me.'

'Well, it's your loss, pal, believe me. Worth every penny.'

'Are you still seeing the same one?'

'More or less. It depends. Occasionally she isn't there like and I don't want to hang around waiting for her to be free again.'

How sordid, Sandy thought. Then he remembered what he'd said to Laura about women chasing him for his money which made him wonder if he wasn't being hypocritical. Maybe he was.

'No talent tonight,' Grant commented. 'The vac again, I suppose.' He hesitated, then went on. 'I dropped by that gallery after the last time you were here and had a look at the picture you did of the French bird. What a cracker, eh? What a bloody cracker, you jammy sod. I envy you having seen it in the flesh.'

Sandy closed his eyes for a moment, remembering Sophie and their times together. It wasn't that long ago but already she'd receded in his memory. He hardly ever thought about her at all nowadays, and every time he did the pain was less than before. One thing Grant was right about, she did have a gorgeous body. And what's more, knew how to use it. By God and she did.

He changed the subject.

Sandy had been doing some late shopping for his trip to Paris, during which he'd bumped into a friend from Medical School. A drink had been suggested, and of course one had led to two and so on, the time, as it always did in these situations, simply flying by unnoticed.

As it was such a lovely evening, well night actually, he'd decided to walk home for the exercise. He also planned to stop at various pubs he knew en route for a quickie before moving on. Ma wasn't going to be pleased when he got home as he'd already missed dinner, but he'd deal with that problem when he came to it. In the meantime, slightly drunk, though only that, he was thoroughly enjoying himself, his mind filled with thoughts of his forthcoming trip.

It suddenly dawned on him that the route he was taking passed close to Blythswood Square and, on a whim, he decided to cut through it to take a look at the whores Grant Bell talked about. He'd been through Blythswood Square a number of times in the past but never at night when the whores plied their trade. He thought it might be amusing to see what went on.

Sure enough, when he reached the square there were female figures casually walking up and down, others standing either alone, or huddled in groups.

'Have you got the time, mister?'

Sandy hadn't noticed the figure that had materialised out of the shadows alongside him. He knew from hearsay that he wasn't being asked for the time at all, but if he was interested in 'business'.

He turned to face the speaker. 'I'm sorry but . . .'

Beryl Gallagher stared at him in horror. 'Holy shite, it's you!'

So this was what Mick's wife had been reduced to, Sandy thought grimly. A common prostitute. 'Hello, Beryl,' he said, voice cold as ice.

She grabbed his arm. 'You'll no tell anyone at Betty's that you've seen me here? They'll do for me so they will if they find out where I am.'

He gazed at her in distaste, her fear almost palpable, remembering Mick's face as he'd been sent down. 'Mick got eighteen years, did you know that?' he asked quietly.

Beryl nodded, biting her lip as she did.

'Eighteen years, a lifetime for someone his age.'

'I know,' she croaked. 'It was far more than I thought he'd get. Poor bastard.'

'I think the most awful thing about it all was that he loved you. Might still for all I know. And you had to do that to him.'

'Don't,' Beryl pleaded. 'I feel bad enough as it is.'

'In the married bed too. No wonder he went berserk.'

Beryl started to cry. 'If only he hadn't thrown Dennis out the window the polis would never have been called and it would all have blown over so it would. He shouldn't have done that.'

'But he did, Beryl. Think what it must have been like for him to come home and find you as you were. No wonder his mind snapped, the woman he idolised, being shagged by another, younger, man.'

The tears were now streaming down Beryl's face. 'You don't understand how hard it was for me after Mick had his accident, the first one that is. Try as he

313

would he couldn't get it up any more, leaving me high and dry every time.'

'You were his wife.'

'That might be, but I also have needs, Sandy. Desperate ones at times. It's just the way I'm made. I couldn't face a life without shagging, I just couldn't. It would have driven me mad eventually.'

For the first time he experienced some sympathy for her. She did have a point. 'But why not be discreet if you were going to be unfaithful? Surely you could have managed that.'

Beryl began to sob, her shoulders gently heaving. 'It's not so easy living round there. Everyone watches you all the time. They're all so fucking nosy. Christ, if you farted in the street it would be all round Betty's Bar that night. You get ma meanin'?'

'But in the man's own bed, Beryl. That's unforgivable.'

'I'd do anythin' to turn back the clock, Sandy. Anythin' at all. But I can't. And I had to get out of there once it happened. You don't know those people, his friends, they'd bloody do for me.'

Sandy recalled his conversation with Bob, the owner of Betty's Bar, she was right about that.

'They might even kill me,' she added, and shivered.

He doubted they'd go that far, but wouldn't have liked to put a bet on it. A razoring, Bob had said, the most likely revenge. 'I have to go,' he declared, and made to move away.

Beryl grabbed him again, this time violently. 'Swear you won't let on where I am? For Christ's sake, swear to me.'

Sandy shrugged himself free. He had no intention

314

of telling Bob, or any of the others in Betty's Bar, of her whereabouts. He didn't want the consequences on his conscience. But he wouldn't tell her that, let her suffer the fear of possible retribution, let her worry herself sick about it. That was a small repayment for what she'd done to Mick.

Beryl suddenly changed tack, becoming all coy and winsome. 'I'll give you a free one if that'll help keep your mouth shut. What do you say? Anything you like, whatever. Understand?'

Sandy couldn't believe she was actually offering herself to him. He was outraged. 'Piss off!' he snarled.

'I can be a helluva good fuck, Sandy. And it'll be free.'

Words failed him. He strode off into the night feeling sick to the pit of his stomach. He was glad Beryl didn't try to come after him. He might have hit her if she had.

Laura was intrigued. Sandy had whispered in her ear to come up to his room in a few minutes as he had a surprise for her. What sort of surprise? she wondered, enjoying the anticipation.

'Champagne!' he announced when she joined him. 'I assume you'll have a glass with me?'

'Oh yes, please. I've never had champagne before. It's supposed to be wonderful.'

'You'll soon find out.'

Laura barely suppressed a squeal as he popped the cork and frothing wine bubbled into the glasses he'd set on his desk. 'Why are we having it?' she asked, eyes wide.

'To celebrate the fact I'm off in the morning.'

'To Paris!'

'For a whole two weeks.' He handed her a now-brimming glass. 'Sorry it isn't chilled, and that these aren't the proper glasses, but it was the best I could do.'

She waited for him to pick up his glass before raising hers. 'To your trip, Sandy. I hope you enjoy every moment of it.'

'I'm sure I shall.

'Well?' he demanded after she'd had a sip.

'I like it,' she pronounced.

'Well, that's a relief,' he commented sarcastically.

Laura laughed. 'I like it a lot. Better?'

'Much.'

She had another sip, and giggled. 'It's true what they say, it actually does get up your nose.'

Sandy sighed, his eyes taking on a faraway look. 'This time tomorrow I'll be well on my way.'

'Excited?'

'Of course I am. In fact I'm more than excited, I'm euphoric.'

How happy he was, Laura reflected. Which made her happy also. 'I wish I was coming with you.'

'Do you?'

'Oh yes,' she breathed. 'I enjoyed London with Aunt Cakey, but I'm sure I'd enjoy Paris even more.'

'At least you've been to London. I've never been anywhere outside Scotland. This is a first for me.'

Laura crossed over and sat on his bed. 'I'll be thinking about you all the time you're away. Wondering what you're doing, what you're getting up to. Wondering, and imagining, all sorts.'

Now it was his turn to laugh. 'I'll tell you when I get back.'

'Everything?' she teased, a twinkle in her eyes.

'Naturally.'

'Even about the ladies you might meet?'

'Especially about those.'

She wagged a finger at him. 'Try to remember what they're wearing, the styles, the fashions. That's what I want to hear about most of all.'

'I'll try.'

'You'd better.'

'Anything else?'

'A souvenir or two. Nothing expensive, but something specifically French.'

'Like French knickers?' he teased in return.

'Yes please,' she enthused. 'I've heard about those. Very daring I'm told.'

'Then that's what you shall have. My word on it.'

'Really?'

He made a sign across his chest. 'Cross my heart and hope to die.'

'Ma will be scandalised. As for Pa, he'll go through the roof. He'll think them obscene.'

'And degenerate,' Sandy added with a grin. 'But then Pa need never know about them as I'm sure he's hardly familiar with any of your knickers. Is he?'

'Certainly not!' an indignant Laura retorted.

Sandy finished off what was in his glass. 'More?'

'The merrier.'

'I take it that's a yes.'

'What do you think?'

'I'll miss you while you're away,' Laura confessed after he'd refilled her glass.

'Will you?'

'Well, I'm used to having you around. Will you miss me?'

'To be honest, I hadn't thought about it.'

'Then think about it now.'

What an odd question, he reflected. But yes, he probably would miss her for the same reason she'd miss him. He nodded. 'I imagine so.'

That pleased her. 'Cream or blue,' she stated.

Sandy frowned. 'Cream or blue what?'

'French knickers, daftie. Either colour would suit.'

'Then either colour is what I'll get.'

Laura stared pensively into her glass. 'Can I ask you something?'

'Go ahead.'

'Have you noticed anything different about Ma recently?'

'Different? How different?'

'She seems a lot quieter than usual. Moody almost, which is quite unlike her.'

Had he noticed that? He didn't think so. 'Perhaps she's got a lot on her mind?' he suggested.

'You don't think . . .' Laura trailed off, finding this difficult to articulate. 'She's upset because Aunt Cakey left all her money to us and nothing to her?'

Sandy considered that. 'She hasn't said anything.'

'Well, she wouldn't, would she?'

'I suppose not,' he mused.

'Maybe I'll ask her while you're away. I'd hate to think she was upset.'

'Me too,' Sandy agreed. 'If you do ask let me know what she said when I get back.'

'All right.'

Sandy took a deep breath, his thoughts returning to Paris, and Montmartre in particular. As he'd told Laura, he wasn't merely excited at the prospect, he was euphoric.

He simply couldn't wait.

* * *

Mathew had fallen asleep in the chair, his head lolling to one side, a fine trickle of spit dribbling from the side of his mouth.

Not a very edifying sight, Harriet thought, sitting opposite and staring at him. She just hoped he didn't start to snore, she got enough of that during the night.

Strange, she reflected. She didn't even like Mathew any more. Forget about love, she didn't even like him. What's more, he got on her nerves for all sorts of reasons.

She was still angry with him about Cakey's will, knowing she'd never forgive him for that. Not in a million years.

She began thinking about James and his proposition, which she'd been doing a lot of lately. Leave Mathew, was it really inconceivable she might do so? A life with James, who was kind and considerate, not to mention in love with her, had a lot more to offer than her current situation.

She smiled, imagining what it might be like, so very different to what she had now. She could well believe it would be a joy to be with James who would surely look after her in a way Mathew hadn't in years.

The question was, or one of them anyway, did she have the courage to walk out on Mathew, to pack her things and go? He'd be horrified of course, no doubt lose his temper to scream and shout. But what would he be more concerned about, losing her or the ensuing scandal? She had the suspicion it would be the latter.

Then there were the children to think about. How would they react? Badly she supposed. That was bound to be the case. And she had to remember that the ensuing scandal would reflect on them as well. Unfair perhaps, but that's what would happen.

Oh, but it was a lovely dream though, a blissful one. The very thought of it made her feel all warm and glowing inside.

It wasn't something she'd have admitted to anyone, it being so unladylike, but she missed regular love-making. In truth, she missed it enormously as it had more or less ceased between her and Mathew. She couldn't even remember the last time they'd done it. A year, more? Had to be.

What would it be like to go to bed with James? she wondered, having only ever been to bed with one man in her entire life, her husband. Certainly different, bound to be. It was an intriguing thought.

Would she be shy initially? No doubt about it. Shy and, well, reserved. But willing, if she should make that choice then she'd be willing all right. The change would just take some getting used to, that's all.

Mathew snorted, mumbled incoherently, and shifted position. Without waking he reached up and scratched his nose. A nose, Harriet observed, that could do with a hair trim. It was as if little bushes were sprouting from both nostrils. She made a mental note to mention it to him later.

James Ballantine, *Mrs* James Ballantine. She continued to wonder and speculate.

Sandy stared out of the taxicab's window, drinking in the sights. How exotically foreign everything was, even the air smelled differently, filled with scents and odours he'd never encountered before.

He was staying at the Hotel Rembrandt in the rue

Berthe, having chosen that particular hotel because he couldn't resist the name.

Paris, he was actually here. His great adventure had well and truly begun. Once he'd booked in he intended not bothering with unpacking, that could be done later, but going straight out again for a wander round, and perhaps something to eat as it was nearing lunchtime. He was hoping his school French was good enough to get by with.

And then he saw it, a sign declaring they were now entering Montmartre. His smile broadened as the taxicab chugged on its way.

Laura had purposely waited to get Harriet on her own, when her father was out at the surgery. 'Ma, can we have a chat?'

Harriet glanced at Laura in surprise, this being a rare request. 'Is something wrong?'

'I don't know. That's what I want to find out.'

Harriet had been about to consult with Cook over the following week's menus, but that could easily wait for a little while.

Harriet sat, and indicated Laura do the same. 'So, what's this all about?' she queried.

'You've seemed different recently, Ma, and I was wondering what's up?'

Harriet was immediately on the defensive. 'Have I?'

Laura nodded. 'I've noticed. Moody at times, withdrawn on others.'

Because of James's proposition, Harriet thought grimly, annoyed with herself for having shown outward signs of what was concerning her. 'Well, I can't say there's anything bothering me,' she lied.

'I wondered if you weren't feeling very well?'

Harriet forced a laugh. 'I'm on top of the world, I assure you.'

'Hmmh,' Laura murmured.

'In fact your father commented only the other day how healthy I was looking,' she further lied. Mathew had done no such thing.

'Then . . .' Laura hesitated, finding this difficult, dreading to get the answer she didn't want. 'Are you upset with Sandy and myself over Aunt Cakey's will?'

Harriet stared at her in astonishment. 'Why ever would that upset me?'

'Because she left us all her money and you nothing.'

'Ah!' Harriet smiled, now understanding Laura's anxiety.

'Well, are you?'

'Not in the least. Though your father is, as you've probably been aware. In fact he was quite beside himself when I told him.'

'But you're not?'

'As I said, not in the least. Please believe me.'

Laura digested that. 'Why did Aunt Cakey do what she did, Ma? That's what's puzzling me. I can understand her leaving us something, but why everything and nothing for you? I thought, I certainly got the impression, you and Aunt Cakey were close.'

'We were,' Harriet nodded. 'Extremely.'

'Then why, Ma?'

Tell the truth or not? After a few moments considering that she decided she would. 'The reason is quite simple really. Money coming to me would also belong to your father and Cakey didn't want him to get his hands on it. Not a penny piece obviously.'

'I see,' Laura murmured. 'She and Pa didn't get on, did they?'

'Not at all. Cakey disliked Mathew, and he was jealous of her wealth. Very jealous. As you know your father has rather grandiose ideas about living in Kelvinside and all manner of things, which is where the money would have gone. In other words, it would have been spent on what he wanted with little, or no, reference to me.'

'But it needn't have been that way,' Laura pointed out. 'You're perfectly entitled to have a bank account in your own right nowadays. That's the law.'

Harriet arched an eyebrow. 'And how do you know about such things?'

Laura had no intention of telling her mother about the literature from the Marie Stopes Clinic she'd read. 'I just do,' she prevaricated.

Harriet glanced away, her heart suddenly heavy. 'Let me put it this way then. Ever since I married your father he's taken care of me, fed and clothed me, put a roof over my head, and done the same for you and Sandy when the pair of you happened along. That being so, I couldn't exclude him from an inheritance that came my way. It wouldn't be right. Can you understand that?'

'Of course I can, Ma. But from what you said Pa would have been in total control of the money without you having a say, which *isn't* right.'

'Your father can be rather old fashioned at times, Laura, he does things as his own father did before him. Besides, Cakey understood that I'm perfectly happy in Lilybank Gardens and with our life as it is.' Not quite true, she instantly thought. There was the small matter of James Ballantine to contradict that. 'I have no desire to live in a grand house and mix with the sort of nobs your father wishes to. It just doesn't attract me at all. So, in my opinion, Cakey was very wise and acting with my best interests at heart in bequeathing everything to you and Sandy.'

'So much money though,' Laura mused. 'It's a fortune.'

'Most of which should be invested. But the bank will advise you on that when the time comes. Just as it will advise Sandy.'

'It still isn't all quite real to me yet,' Laura confessed.

'It will be soon enough. I promise you.'

Harriet came to her feet. 'Now we've got that out of the way I must get on. I need to have a word with Cook.'

She left Laura brooding over their conversation.

The Place du Tertre was exactly as Sophie had described it, artists, some sitting, others standing, busily painting and displaying their wares. Several of them closest to Sandy were cartoonists, doing quite fine sketches of any member of the public wishing to have one done.

Sandy strolled amongst the artists and tourists, stopping every so often to study a particular piece of work, some of which he liked, others he didn't.

Some of the styles were bizarre to say the least. Fascinating in a way, but nothing to do with art as he understood it. These were the modernists, experimenting with light, shade and colour, not to mention perception of the subject. Sandy knew he could never have painted like that, preferring the traditional approach himself. When he painted a woman, say, he wanted it to be lifelike, a true reflection of the subject, not some goggle-eyed monster bearing, in his opinion, no resemblance to the female in question.

One group of painters particularly caught his eye. They were using some sort of paint he'd never come across before, the result a glistening metallic look that seemed to shimmer on the canvas. He found their work relatively pleasing, yet disturbing at the same time.

In one corner of the square he came across pottery for sale, bowls, cups, dishes, pots, a whole medley and assortment of articles, some plain, others delicately hand painted. It crossed his mind he might take one of the pots home as a present for his mother. Something she could put flowers in, he decided. She loved flowers and had them in the house whenever possible.

Further along was a woman making, and selling, cheap silver jewellery. He watched in admiration as she expertly fashioned strands of silver wire into a necklace, finishing it off by attaching a clasp.

The woman smiled at him, and he smiled back. She then rattled something off in French which he could make neither head nor tail of.

'Sorry,' he apologised, and shrugged.

'No Englis,' the female replied, and shrugged also. A very Gallic shrug that reminded him of Sophie who'd done it exactly the same way.

A little later he paused to sniff the smell of food being cooked. He had no idea what sort of food, but it smelled absolutely delicious and made his mouth water.

Everywhere was chatter, mainly French, but also a number of other languages. He heard German, that was easy to distinguish, but others were a complete mystery to him. A middle-aged couple strolled by speaking what could only have been American, and he remembered Sophie had once told him a lot of Americans came to Paris, which had surprised him at the time. For some reason he didn't associate Americans with Paris, probably because America was so far away. Well, the middle-aged couple were proof they did make the journey.

After a while he decided it was time for a beer and something to eat.

Chapter 21

Sandy sighed in exasperation; he was certain the bill he'd been presented with for lunch was far too much, but try as he might he couldn't seem to make the waitress understand his complaint.

He was about to try again when a young man sitting at the next table leant over. 'Excuse me, I couldn't help but overhear your problem. Would you like me to explain for you?'

'Please,' a relieved Sandy agreed.

The young man took the bill and glanced through it. 'What exactly did you have?' he asked.

Sandy recounted every item.

'Well, you're right, you have been overcharged. It's something they often try with tourists.'

The waitress was now looking decidedly annoyed, and looked even more so after the young man had addressed her in fluent French.

There was a waving of hands, an uttering of expletives, and the bill was snatched from the young man's hand. There was one final comment and then the waitress flounced away.

'She doesn't seem very pleased,' Sandy commented wryly.

'No, she doesn't.'

The young man now smiling at Sandy had extremely blond hair, with blond eyebrows and a slightly florid complexion. From what Sandy could see he was built like the proverbial barn door.

'New to Paris?' the young man queried.

Sandy nodded. 'First day. I'm over on holiday.'

'And unless I'm mistaken you're Scottish?'

'I am indeed.'

'We don't get all that many Scottish people here, though many English.'

Sandy was trying to place the young man's accent which certainly wasn't French. It had a curious lilt to it, almost a sing-song quality. 'Are you also on holiday?' he asked.

'No, I live here. Have done for five years.'

'You work in Paris then?'

An amused twinkle came into the young man's eyes. 'In a manner of speaking. But you could say that.'

Well dressed, Sandy observed, with the air of a gentleman about him. 'Thank you for helping. It was kind of you.'

'I adore France and the French,' the young man replied. 'But sadly they will try to take advantage of foreigners, especially those who don't speak the language. It's a habit of theirs I disapprove of.'

'I'll keep that in mind,' Sandy acknowledged. 'Thanks for the tip.'

They chatted for a few minutes more and then the waitress returned with the amended bill which was considerably less than previously. Thrusting it at Sandy she then held out her hand.

'She is bad tempered,' Sandy murmured to his new-found friend, who smiled. 'Do you want to check this again?'

'I shouldn't think that's necessary. It'll be correct this time.'

Give the woman a gratuity or not? Sandy wondered, and decided not. Why should he when she'd tried to cheat him. He counted out the precise money and laid it on the table.

'I was about to have a cognac. Will you join me?' the young man asked.

'That would be grand. Thank you.'

The young man placed his order and then watched in appreciation as the waitress walked away. 'Very nice *derrière*, wouldn't you say?'

Sandy had to agree, it was.

'By the way, my name is Harald Haraldson,' the young man said, holding out a hand.

Sandy shook it. 'And I'm Sandy McLean.'

'Pleased to meet you, Sandy. I hope you have a wonderful holiday.'

'Thank you, Harald. And I'm pleased to meet you.' Sandy thought about the young man's name. 'Are you Swedish?' That would fit in with the accent and colouring.

Harald laughed. 'Close. I'm Icelandic from Reykjavic.'

'Really!' Sandy exclaimed. That was interesting.

'Who has no intention of ever returning home because it's so boring there. Not to mention cold. I much prefer Paris which I think must be the most exciting place on Earth.'

Icelandic, Sandy mused. Well well well. 'I wonder if you could help me further?' he requested.

'If I can.'

'Where would you recommend I go in the evening for entertainment? I was considering the Moulin Rouge, which I've read a great deal about. But outside of that I've no idea.'

Harald shook his head. 'Go there by all means, but it's not what it used to be twenty or thirty years ago. At least so I'm told. Now it's commercialised and full of tourists, which is fine if that's what you want.'

That disappointed Sandy. 'Not really.'

'But there are still plenty of places that reflect the real Montmartre,' Harald went on. 'If I was you I'd start with the Lapin Agile.'

'Lapin Agile?' Sandy repeated. 'What does it mean?'

The amused twinkle was back in Harald's eyes. 'The jumping rabbit. Originally it was called the Cabaret des Assassins, but at some point the caricaturist Gill painted a sign of a rabbit jumping into a cooking pot and called it the Lapin Agile, which was also a pun on the artist's name. You should find it fairly lively there.'

'Sounds wonderful,' Sandy enthused.

'And don't bother getting too dressed up. It's very informal to say the least.'

'Then that's where I'll go tonight.'

They stopped talking when the waitress returned with their cognac. Harald exchanged a few words with her which made her laugh, and her attitude completely changed. Sandy watched fascinated as Harald clearly flirted with her.

'You seem to have a way with women,' Sandy commented when the waitress was gone.

Harald smiled broadly. 'So I've been told. It just comes naturally to me, for which I'm most grateful. But that aside, I shall also be at the Lapin Agile tonight. We can meet up if you like, and maybe I'll be able to introduce you to a few more foreigners, now locals like myself. They're an interesting lot.'

'That would be wonderful.'

'Good. I shall look forward to seeing you there. It's on the rue Saint-Vincent. Can you remember that?'

Sandy nodded. 'I shan't forget.'

They talked for a little while longer, enjoying their cognac, before Harald excused himself, saying he had an appointment with a lady. That statement was accompanied with a knowing wink.

How lucky to have met up with Harald Haraldson, Sandy reflected when the Icelander had left. He wondered what Harald did for a living? That hadn't been mentioned. There again, he hadn't mentioned he was a medical student.

'The Cabaret des Assassins and Lapin Agile,' Sandy murmured aloud, and laughed.

How exotically French. At least, he thought so.

Sandy hadn't known what to expect, which was just as well, for the Lapin Agile was unlike any place he'd ever been before. Shabby was a word that sprang to mind, Bohemian another. The walls were hung with a variety of paintings, all different styles and subjects, the furniture plain, badly scuffed and scarred wood. As for the clientele, they were generally bizarre in appearance, of both genders and all ages. The smell of unwashed bodies was sickly sweet in the nostrils.

Harald spotted Sandy looking around uncertainly, and waved him over. 'Take a seat and have a drink,' Harald slurred when Sandy joined him. Picking up a bottle of red wine Harald slopped some into a glass that had already been used and pushed it in Sandy's direction.

'So what do you think?' Harald demanded.

Sandy considered that, not wishing to be offensive. 'Definitely unusual. We don't have anything like it in Glasgow, that's for sure.'

Harald laughed. 'This is the real Montmartre, believe me. The haunt of painters, sculptors, writers, poets and dancers. They all come here to talk, drink, exchange ideas and be rude about one another. I love it.'

Sandy had a sip of the wine which was rough and clearly cheap. Strangely, he found it enjoyable.

'How did your appointment with the lady go?' Sandy asked, making conversation.

The twinkle was back in Harald's eyes. 'Very satisfactory. At least, she found it so which is all that matters.'

'Oh?'

'Of course. What else? Satisfactory, as in satisfaction, is what they all want.'

Sandy didn't understand that. 'I'm not quite with you, Harald?'

'Ah! Rocky!' Harald suddenly exclaimed, and waved at a man who'd just entered. To Sandy he said, 'You'll like Rocky. He's an American over here to write the great novel. He started it two years ago and still hasn't finished.'

Sandy judged Rocky to be in his late thirties or early forties. He was small and had, in Sandy's estimation, shifty eyes. He was as bald as a coot. Rocky plonked himself down next to Sandy and the introductions were made.

'Have a drink,' Harald said to Rocky, gesturing at the bottle. 'I suppose you're broke as usual?'

Rocky reached for the wine. 'We can't all make as much money as you, dear Harald. With me, it comes in occasionally, and then goes out very quickly.' He shrugged. 'What's money anyway?'

'Important when you don't have any. Especially for someone with a thirst like yours.'

Rocky grinned ruefully. 'True. Very true.'

Harald waved a hand in the air, and a few moments later a waitress arrived at their table. Sandy went goggle-eyed when he saw her for she was naked to the waist.

Harald played with her breasts while he ordered, she apparently enjoying the attention, and then she disappeared again.

Dear God! an appalled Sandy thought. Naked like that in public! His mind was reeling.

Rocky pulled out a packet of Gitanes and lit up. Almost instantly he was racked with a fit of coughing.

'You smoke too much,' Harald commented.

'Psshh!' Rocky replied when he'd caught his breath again. 'Who cares?'

'Does the waitress always serve like that?' Sandy quietly asked Harald.

'Always. They all do. Why, don't you approve?' The latter was said in a teasing tone.

'Very much so. It just took me a bit by surprise, that's all.'

'You can give them a feel when she gets back,' Harald declared nonchalantly. 'It's allowed.'

Sandy didn't think he'd dare. Not with everyone watching. He'd be far too embarrassed.

'Tourist, eh?' Rocky said.

Sandy nodded.

'What do you do?'

'I'm a medical student.'

'Lots of work for a decent doctor round here,' Rocky replied. 'Especially if he's good with the clap. That right, Harald?'

'I'm afraid so.' He pointed at several gaudily and scantily dressed females at the other side of the room. 'They're all tarts,' he explained to Sandy. 'Here hoping to pick up business, which they invariably do. But they're cheap, street walkers really. If you want a whore for the night I can make a recommendation. Expensive, but guaranteed clean.'

'No thank you,' Sandy gulped.

'Suit yourself. But the offer's there if you change your mind.'

'You never pay for it, do you, Harald?' Rocky jibed with a wicked, razored smile.

'On the contrary,' Harald replied. 'The boot's on the other foot, as you well know.'

Sandy was mystified. 'How can that be?' he ventured to ask.

The twinkle returned again. 'I entertain well-bred ladies for gain. In other words *they* pay *me* for my services.'

'He's a male tart,' Rocky explained, and laughed. 'Damn good at it too from what I hear.'

'The best in Paris.' Harald smiled. 'And I prefer to be called a gigolo. Amongst friends that is.'

Sandy was gaping at him. 'You . . . for money?'

'And gifts. There are often lots of those.'

'He only goes with rich bitches,' Rocky declared. 'He makes a fortune.'

'Shocked?' Harald queried with a frown when he saw Sandy's expression.

Sandy thought about that. 'Yes, I suppose I am. I've never met a gigolo before.'

'Well, you have now. Do you disapprove?'

Rocky emptied the remains of the bottle into his glass. 'Where's the waitress, we need more wine,' he grumbled.

'To be honest, I'm not sure,' Sandy replied to Harald. 'I don't think so. Women do that sort of thing after all, so why not men?'

'Quite right,' Harald nodded. 'And there's a need for such in Paris, believe me. You'd be surprised.'

Sandy didn't think he would, not any more. 'Have you . . .' He took a deep breath. 'Have you always been that?'

'No, I was a would-be painter when I first arrived here. But I soon came to realise I wasn't very good. In fact, I was downright awful. The most untalented painter around. I became what I am to stop myself starving, which I very nearly did, and now make a most comfortable living at it.'

The waitress appeared out of nowhere with two opened bottles of wine which she placed before them. 'Don't forget you can feel her tits if you want,' Harald said to Sandy as he gave her money.

And lovely they were too, Sandy noted. Full and heavy which contrasted delightfully with her slight frame. 'No thanks,' he stuttered in reply.

Rocky chuckled, finding that funny.

'Where do you meet these women who pay you?' an intrigued Sandy asked Harald after the waitress had moved away.

'It was difficult to begin with, but gradually, over the years, I've built up a succession of contacts. I'm invited to parties, functions, that sort of thing, where the great and good are present. It sort of goes from there.'

'You also have a reputation,' Rocky commented drily, attacking one of the new bottles.

'That's true,' Harald agreed. 'Ladies talk amongst themselves you see,' he explained to Sandy. 'And I'm considered to be particularly good in bed. Quite brilliant actually, as I've been told many times.'

'His modesty is overwhelming.' Rocky grinned.

'It's simply a job at which I'm an expert,' Harald declared. 'Thankfully I've been blessed in the sexual department, for which I'm eternally grateful.'

'He means he's got a big one,' Rocky elaborated.

'That isn't everything, Rocky, as I've told you before. There's far more to it than merely being well endowed. I've made it my business to learn about women and their needs, which can be different to what your average man might think. When I go to bed with a woman I pride myself in playing her like a virtuoso does a violin.'

Sandy was fascinated, there was obviously a lot more to the sexual act than he so far understood, or what Sophie had taught him.

Their conversation was interrupted when Sandy spotted two figures who'd just come into the club. It took a moment or two for the penny to drop, but when it did his mouth fell open in astonishment.

The two figures wore smartly tailored suits, collar

and ties, with fedora hats on their heads. The startling thing to Sandy was that they were women.

'Bloody hell!' he muttered.

'What is it?' Harald asked with a frown.

'Those two,' Sandy replied, nodding in their direction.

'What about them?'

'They're women dressed in men's suits.'

Harald and Rocky both laughed, finding Sandy's reaction incredibly funny. 'So what?' Harald queried, shoulders heaving.

'Are they what I think?'

'And what do you think?' Rocky teased.

Sandy lowered his voice to almost a whisper. 'Lesbians.'

'Really!' Rocky mocked.

Sandy nodded, well aware he was the butt of their humour.

'Of course they are,' Harald said. 'There are lots in Paris, though they don't all dress up like that. They usually frequent their own clubs, but not always, as you can see tonight.'

'Nor do they always dress up like men,' Rocky added. 'Just some, the more masculine variety.'

Sodom and Gomorrah, Sandy thought. That's what he'd come to, Sodom and Gomorrah. 'Do you know them?' he asked Harald.

'Why, would you like to be introduced?'

'No!' Sandy exclaimed in alarm, which set Harald and Rocky off again.

'I'm afraid not,' Harald replied eventually. 'But I think you're beginning to understand why I consider Paris to be the most exciting place in the world.'

Sandy reached for the nearest bottle. He needed a drink.

A slightly drunk Sandy later stood at his bedroom window staring out over the lights of Paris spread below. As Montmartre was on a hill he was able to see for miles.

What a night, he reflected, going over the events in his mind. His first visit to the Lapin Agile was certainly one he'd never forget. Not for as long as he lived.

He thought of Glasgow and tried to find a comparison between the two cities. There just wasn't any. One was dull and, seemingly, forever grey, the other vibrant with life and colour, a cornucopia of experiences and adventures that were forever changing, he presumed, like a child's kaleidoscope. He already knew that when it was time for him to go home again he'd do so with the heaviest of hearts.

His face suddenly clouded over as he thought about the year of study that lay ahead. 'Damn!' he muttered. But the bright side was it was still a few weeks away and in the meantime he had a whole fortnight in Harald's beloved Paris, and what a fortnight it promised to be.

Just wonderful.

'Now that your aunt's money has come through I want to make something absolutely crystal clear,' Mathew announced pompously. 'The thousand pounds available to you will only be released in small quantities, and with my approval. Do you understand?'

'Yes, Pa.'

'I don't want you frittering it away on fripperies and the like. That wouldn't do at all.'

'But you won't be too harsh on her, dear, will you?' Harriet interrupted. 'She should have some enjoyment out of it, after all. I'm sure that's what Cakey would have wanted.'

Mathew glared at her, still chafing from the fact that the entire bequest hadn't gone to Harriet, and therefore him. 'And what would you call enjoyment, dear?'

She had to tread warily here, Harriet warned herself. She could do more harm than good. 'Clothes, for example.'

Mathew snorted.

'After all, Mathew, that would stop you having to pay out for them,' she pointed out.

'Functional clothes if she wishes, but nothing fancy or expensive. Fancy and expensive would only be a waste.'

'In your opinion, dear,' Harriet chided softly.

'What sort of things *can* I take money out the bank for, Pa?' Laura asked.

'That depends. I would review each case on its merits,' he snapped in reply.

In other words, Laura thought bitterly, she wasn't going to see much of her thousand pounds until her majority when the full amount of what she'd been left was released to her.

Harriet shot Laura a sympathetic look. She would have a word later with Mathew about this, but knowing him, doubted she'd be able to change his mind on the matter. It wasn't that she disagreed with what he intended, simply the way he was going about it. She couldn't imagine James Ballantine being so belligerent in his approach.

Laura sighed. 'Is there anything else, Pa?'

He considered that. 'No, there isn't. So you can run along if you wish.'

She'd had enough of this. 'I'm not a child to run along, Pa. I'm a young woman, which you seem to forget.'

'Don't be impertinent, Laura!'

'I'm not being impertinent. Merely reminding you how old I am.' And having said that she walked from the room.

Harriet turned away from Mathew, not wishing him to see her expression. Fool, she thought. That's what he was. A fool!

Sandy squinted in concentration as he drew a scene from the Chat Noir, a club he and Harald had spent the previous evening at. He was sitting outside a café bar in the Place du Tertre where he'd taken refuge under an umbrella as the weather was so incredibly hot.

'Ah, there you are!' Harald said, and flopped onto the chair opposite. They'd arranged to meet for lunch.

'Your last day, eh?' Harald smiled sympathetically.

Sandy laid down his sketch pad and pencil. 'I'm afraid so.' He shook his head in amazement. 'The time has simply flown by. It seems as if I arrived only yesterday.'

'Have you enjoyed yourself?'

'Of course I have. I've loved every minute. Now it's the train later on this afternoon followed by a night-time crossing on the boat.'

Harald was regarding him keenly. 'You'll be back, Sandy. I'll put money on it. Once Paris ensnares you she never lets go.'

Sandy shrugged. 'Hopefully next year. In the mean-time there's the dreaded Medical School to be getting on with, which I'm not looking forward to.'

'You don't like it there?'

'Not really. But you have to do something in life, and medicine is my chosen profession.'

Harald beckoned a waiter across and they placed their orders, both going for something light on account of the heat.

'May I?' Harald requested, pointing at Sandy's sketch pad.

'If you wish.'

Harald picked up the pad and flicked it open. 'I didn't know you drew?'

'And paint. But only in an amateur way.'

Harald carefully studied page after page. 'You have talent,' he pronounced eventually. 'It's still raw, but definitely there.'

Sandy was both delighted and embarrassed to hear that. 'Do you really think so?'

'I wouldn't say it if I didn't believe it. And don't forget, I have some little knowledge of the subject having been an artist myself, albeit a terrible one.'

'Then thank you,' Sandy replied quietly.

Harald glanced through the drawings a second time, smiling in places where he recognised someone or something. 'If I'd been as good as this, by which I mean having as much potential, I wouldn't be doing what I do today.'

Harald placed the sketch pad back in front of Sandy. 'What a dark horse you've turned out to be. Hiding your light under a bushel as you English say.'

'Scots,' Sandy corrected him. 'I'm Scots, not English.'

'Sorry, I forgot for the moment. No slight intended.'

'And none taken.'

'Good.'

The waiter returned with a bottle of wine Harald had ordered, and poured out two full glasses. 'We must have a toast,' Harald declared. 'That's only right and proper.'

Sandy picked up his glass. 'What shall we toast then?'

'Why you, of course. And your return to Paris, whenever that may be.'

'Soon I hope.'

'Indeed. And when you do return you must look me up. I shall give you my card before we leave here.'

Return to Paris? Sandy thought as he sipped his wine. He would too, wild horses wouldn't keep him away.

'Morag, pass Alexander that letter on the mantelpiece,' Mathew instructed. The family, including a very tired Sandy who'd arrived home late the night before, were gathered round the breakfast table.

Sandy knew as soon as Morag handed him the letter that it contained the results of his exams. He was horribly aware of his father's gaze boring into him.

'When did it come?' he asked, momentarily putting off the inevitable.

'Last week,' Laura replied.

Mathew shifted impatiently in his chair, waiting for Sandy to get on with it.

It was with a horrible sinking feeling in the pit of his stomach that Sandy began opening the envelope. He'd thought he'd done well, he reminded himself. Certainly far better than the previous year. He prayed that was the case.

His fingers were trembling slightly as he unfolded the single sheet of paper the envelope contained.

Chapter 22

'Go away!'
      Laura ignored that, and went into Sandy's bedroom anyway where she found him sitting behind his desk with a face like thunder. Despite the earliness of the hour he had a glass of whisky in front of him.

'That was unforgivable on Pa's part,' she stated quietly, her expression one of sympathy.

'I want to be alone, Laura.'

Laura shook her head, recalling the terrible scene that had taken place over breakfast, culminating in Mathew slamming the door behind him as he left for the surgery.

'Is there anything I can do?' she asked, wanting to go and put a comforting arm round him, but sensing that would be the wrong thing to do.

Sandy had a swig of whisky. 'No,' he hissed.

'Well, don't get cross with me. I'm on your side, remember,' she admonished.

He was instantly contrite. 'Sorry.'

'Ma's in a right old state. At one point down there I actually thought she was going to hit Pa.'

'He was lucky I didn't after talking and shouting at me like that. The irony is, I actually thought my results would be better than last year's.'

If anything they'd been worse, Laura thought grimly. When Mathew had read them he'd exploded with rage and fury.

Sandy took a deep breath, and then another. 'What am I to do, sis?' he queried in a choked voice. 'Try as I might I just can't seem to do well at the exams. I'm a bloody failure, that's what. A bloody failure.'

'You're nothing of the sort, Sandy McLean,' she retorted sharply. 'The trouble is, despite Pa wanting it so badly, you're just not cut out for medicine. Your heart simply isn't in it.'

How very true, he reflected sadly.

Laura crossed over and sat on the bed from where she studied him speculatively. 'Can I make a suggestion?'

He shrugged. 'Go ahead.'

'I don't think you've really taken on board yet what Aunt Cakey's inheritance means to you.'

He frowned. 'Go on.'

'You're not reliant on Pa for board and lodging any more. You're rich, Sandy. Stinking rich. And as such you can do whatever you want with your life now. If you had a mind to you wouldn't even have to work at all if you chose not to.'

Sandy hadn't thought of it that way. Laura was right, he hadn't really taken the full import of Aunt Cakey's inheritance on board yet.

'For example,' Laura went on. 'You don't have to live here any more.'

That startled him. 'Not live here?'

'You could easily buy a house of your own, and employ staff to look after you. A housekeeper, cook and maid say. That way you'd be fully independent and free of father.' A look of determination came across her face. 'It's certainly what I'll do when I get my money. I've already made up my mind on that.'

A house of his own? a bemused Sandy reflected. It was certainly an attractive proposition. One that very much appealed.

Laura suddenly laughed. 'You could buy a house in Kelvinside. That would drive Pa wild with jealousy.'

Sandy smiled. He could just imagine Mathew's reaction to his doing that. He'd go pea green with envy.

'What about Ma though?' Sandy countered. 'She wouldn't be happy if I left home.'

'She'd understand, I'm sure of it. And she could visit you whenever she wished.'

Sandy's mind raced back to the earlier part of their conversation. He wouldn't have to work if he chose not to. In other words, he could give up Medical School and any career as a doctor. Suddenly his pulse was throbbing.

'Well?' Laura demanded.

'It's definitely an idea. But one I'll have to think about. I don't want to rush into things and perhaps regret it later.'

'You wouldn't regret it,' Laura insisted. 'Certainly not leaving here. Now you're a man of means it's the most natural thing in the world for you to do.'

Sandy's eyes were gleaming. 'God, you're a genius,' he declared. 'An absolute genius.'

Laura preened. 'I wouldn't go that far.'

'Well, I would.' He was already imagining a life free of his father. Free of Mathew's whims and tantrums. Free of feeling it was his duty to fall in with his father's wishes. Free to do whatever he himself wanted, whenever he wanted.

They continued discussing the possibility for quite some time, Sandy becoming keener and keener with every passing minute.

'He was absolutely beside himself,' Harriet related to an attentive James Ballantine, having joined him for lunch in the café he used. 'I actually thought he was going to have a heart attack, it was so bad. Poor Sandy, I truly felt for him.'

James reached across and squeezed her hand. 'It sounds horrendous.'

'It was, James. I was still shaking hours after he'd gone off to the surgery.'

'And how's Sandy?'

'Withdrawn, as you might expect. He and Mathew haven't exchanged a single word since.'

'I'm not surprised,' James mused.

'The trouble is, Mathew has such high expectations of Sandy, wanting Sandy to achieve what he never did which it now appears Sandy is incapable of.'

'Disappointment is one thing, but to fly off the handle like that quite another.' James hesitated. 'Has he ever hit you when in one of these rages?'

Harriet shook her head. 'Never.'

'Do you think he's capable?'

Harriet considered that. 'I wouldn't have thought so

before the other morning. But now . : .' She trailed off and shrugged. 'I can only say it might be possible.'

How wonderful he always felt when in her presence, James reflected, wishing with all his heart she'd married him and not Mathew all those years ago.

'Have you thought any more about separation and divorce?' James asked quietly.

Harriet bit her lip. 'It would be such a momentous step. I just don't know if I could.'

'A new beginning, Harriet, for the pair of us,' he went on. 'And don't forget what I said. I love you and always have. Surely that must come into the equation?'

She didn't reply, instead stared down into her coffee cup. 'I need time,' she whispered. 'Please don't try to rush me.'

'Take all the time you want, Harriet,' he replied, disappointed. 'Just tell me what your decision is when you make up your mind.'

'I promise,' she whispered again.

'Good.'

She smiled in appreciation when he again squeezed her hand.

Sandy was pleased with himself as he left the bank having had a long chat with the manager. Everything to do with his account had been discussed and agreed. A sizeable chunk of capital would be available to him at all times, while another chunk was to be invested in a variety of ways. As far as he was concerned everything was now nicely arranged and squared away.

He was walking down the street when he spotted a familiar face coming towards him, Tommy from Betty's Bar who was married to Mick's sister.

Tommy halted when he recognised Sandy. 'Hello, how's it gaun?' Tommy asked.

'Fine. Yourself?'

'Oh aye, never better. Still at Betty's as you might expect.'

'And Bob?'

'The same. He never changes, that one.'

'Any news of Mick? Is he coping?'

Tommy pulled out a packet of cigarettes and lit up. 'I've been to see him several times, me and the wife like. He found it hard to start with but is settling down.' Tommy gave a hollow laugh. 'There's nothin' else he can do, is there?'

'Will you give him my regards next time you visit?'

'Oh aye, consider it done.' Tommy looked away. 'They found that bitch Beryl, you know.'

Oh Christ! Sandy thought. 'Did they?'

'Whooring it in Blythswood Square, of all things. Nane of us will tell Mick that though. Best he disnae ken.'

Sandy nodded his agreement.

'Well, she got her comeuppance after all. A couple of the lads surprised her one night and striped her good and proper. She'll no be so pretty from here on in.'

Sandy had gone cold all over. 'They razored her face?'

'Three slashes on either side apparently. Deep ones too frae what I wuz telt. Left her lying there bleedin' like a stuck pig. They'll no be many blokes interested in her now.' Tommy spat on the pavement. 'Serves her right for what she done. Serves her bloody right.'

Sandy felt sorry for Beryl when he finally left Tommy.

With good behaviour Mick might be out in ten or twelve years, whereas Beryl would be hideously scarred for the rest of her life.

Sandy gazed around the downstairs bar of The Clachan, thinking what a boring place it was, even more so after Montmartre. He couldn't help but smile remembering the Lapin Agile, not to mention the other clubs he'd been to. Now *they* had been exciting, some of them seedy perhaps, but exciting nonetheless.

He then recalled his last conversation with Harald Haraldson, going over it in his mind. Talented, Harald had said, raw but talented.

Suddenly, in that instant, he knew precisely what he was going to do. The obvious really, except he hadn't thought of it until now. It was as if an enormous weight had been lifted from his shoulders.

He decided he'd make all the necessary arrangements before telling his parents.

Mathew was aghast, absolutely thunderstruck. 'Paris!' he exclaimed, eyes bulging.

'That's what I said, Pa. I'm going to live there and be a painter.'

'Oh, son!' Harriet whispered, this bombshell coming completely out of the blue. She'd had no idea, not an inkling, that Sandy was considering moving away, far less to another country.

'But what about Medical School?' Mathew protested.

'I'm not going back, Pa. I'm finished with medicine. I'll never be any good at it anyway so why persist. From now on I'm going to do what makes me happy, and that's paint.'

A stunned Laura was staring at Sandy in disbelief. Why hadn't he confided in her? That was the least he could have done. She now bitterly regretted having suggested he buy a house of his own for that was obviously where this extention of the idea had sprung from. She'd never dreamt he'd leave Glasgow.

'It's preposterous,' Mathew spluttered. 'I forbid it, you hear? I forbid it.'

Sandy realised he wasn't scared of his father any more, that his newly acquired independence was more than mere money, though the money was certainly the catalyst. In a funny way he felt as if he'd just grown up. 'You can't forbid me, Pa. It's as simple as that.'

'You'll damn well do as I say!' Mathew thundered.

'No, I won't. And I suggest you quieten down as you're frightening Ma.'

Mathew went puce. 'Are you telling me what to do in my own house?'

'I'm thinking of Ma.'

'And how do you think she's going to feel with you throwing your future away and gallivanting off like this?'

Sandy turned to face Harriet. 'I'm sorry, Ma, but I have to go. I hate medicine, truly hate it. Please say you understand?'

Harriet, emotions in a turmoil, took her time in replying. 'I can't say I understand, Sandy, because I don't. But according to you leaving will make you happy and, in the end, that's all that matters. All that really counts.'

Sandy smiled. 'Thanks, Ma.'

'I still think it's preposterous,' Mathew went on. 'Who in their right mind would want to live amongst the French? They're a disgusting people. Not to be trusted.'

'I like them, Pa.'

'Then more fool you.' Mathew slammed a fist into the palm of his other hand. 'Margaret's to blame for all this nonsense. She should never have left you all that money in the first place. It should have rightfully gone to your mother as her next of kin.'

'But Aunt Cakey didn't,' Sandy stated quietly. 'And I'm sure she had her reasons.'

'When will you leave?' Harriet asked, a choke in her voice.

'Monday morning. It's all arranged.'

'Mon—' Harriet took a deep breath to stop herself sobbing. 'So soon?'

'I'm afraid so.'

'To be a painter.'

'To try anyway. Even if I don't succeed I'll enjoy what I'm doing. And again, if I don't succeed I'll hardly starve.' He smiled wryly. 'Will I?'

Harriet could see the humour in that. 'No,' she agreed. 'You won't.'

'Dissolute and decadent, that's what you'll become,' Mathew declared disapprovingly.

Sandy couldn't help himself. 'Who knows? Maybe you're right, Pa. An unwashed, unshaven, alcoholic Bohemian living in a cesspool of vice and sin.'

'You wouldn't dare!'

'No?' Sandy teased.

'If that happens then you'll no longer be my son. I'll disown you.'

Harriet's hand flew to her mouth. On seeing that Sandy decided enough was enough, he didn't want to distress her further. 'I doubt it'll come to that,' he laughed, making it obvious he'd been joking.

Going to Harriet he kissed her on the cheek. 'I'd never let you down, Ma. Never in a million years. You have my word.'

Tears sprang into Harriet's eyes. 'I believe you, son.'

'Do, because I won't.'

Harriet rounded on Mathew the moment they were alone. 'This is all your fault, you know.'

'Mine?'

'Push, push, pushing him into medicine, trying to make up for your own failure and inadequacy.'

Mathew was outraged. 'Inade—'

'Inadequacy,' Harriet interrupted. 'And as for what happened the other morning when he got his exam results, that was appalling. I was mortally ashamed of you.'

Mathew almost staggered where he stood, unable to believe Harriet was actually speaking to him like this.

'It was probably that which finally drove him into leaving home,' Harriet went on mercilessly. 'If you'd been more reasonable, more understanding, this might never have happened.'

'Don't try and blame me,' Mathew snapped in reply. 'I'm not having any of that.'

'You're a bully, Mathew McLean,' Harriet accused. 'An out and out bully who thinks he's always right and never wrong. Well, let me tell you you're often wrong. So put that in your pipe and smoke it!'

Mathew felt as if his whole world was crumbling around him. Bully? Him? A load of nonsense. 'Control yourself, woman,' he hissed. 'You're becoming hysterical.' He paused, and sniffed, 'Typical female, I suppose.'

That enraged her. 'Being a female has nothing to do with it. You hear? *Nothing.*'

'Of course it has,' he replied dismissively.

'It hasn't!' Harriet shouted.

Mathew blinked in disbelief. Harriet was actually shouting at *him*. 'Don't dare speak to me like that,' he snarled.

'Why not? It's how you often speak to us. Have a taste of your own medicine and see how you like it.'

'Get a grip, Harriet.'

'No, it's you should get a grip before you drive Laura away as well. Or me for that matter.'

He laughed, thinking that funny. Harriet walking out on him? Cows would fly first.

Harriet stared at Mathew, naked contempt in her eyes. 'And it is on account of you that Alexander's leaving. Nor can I blame him. Now he's got money he can be his own man, which he's clearly set on being. I only wish he was staying in Glasgow and not going abroad, that's all.'

'You don't know what you're saying, woman.'

'Oh yes I do. I should have stood up to you a long time ago. Really stood up that is instead of letting you have things all your own way. And Sandy leaving is the result.'

Mathew was shaken to the very core. The evening was rapidly turning into a nightmare. First Sandy's announcement, and now Harriet behaving as she was. Accusing him of God knows.

'I'm going out for a walk,' he declared stiffly. 'Maybe that'll give you time to cool down and come to your senses.'

Harriet had the last word. 'Bully!' she repeated as he was going through the doorway.

While all this was going on Laura was upstairs with Sandy. 'I wish you'd told me before springing it on us like that,' she complained.

'Sorry. I did mean to but just never got round to it.'

That mollified her a little. 'I'm going to miss you, Sandy. Dreadfully.'

'And I'll miss you too. You know I will.'

'The house will seem so empty. Lonely too without you to talk to.'

'You'll soon get used to it,' he replied, trying to re-assure her.

'Probably. But things just won't be the same.'

He glanced away, unable to stand her accusing stare. 'I thought you might be pleased for me.'

'I am, I suppose.'

'Only suppose?'

Laura shrugged. 'When I was babbling on about you buying your own house it never crossed my mind that house might not be in Glasgow. If it had I'd never have mentioned it.'

Sandy smiled, realising for the first time just how much he *was* going to miss his sister. Over the past few years they'd become extremely close. 'It was that conversation which did get me thinking,' he confessed. 'That and another one I had with a friend in Montmartre.'

'This Harald you've mentioned?'

'That's right. He told me I had talent as an artist and he's someone, even though I've only known him a short while, whose judgement I trust.'

'Then good luck to you, Sandy. And I mean that.'

'Thanks, sis. Anyway, it's not as if you can't come over and visit sometime once I'm settled.'

Laura shook her head. 'I doubt Pa would agree to that, so I wouldn't have the money to make the trip.'

'I could always send you what's required. How would that do?'

'Even though, he'd never let me go. A single girl travelling on her own? Now can you just imagine what Pa would say. And I have to admit I don't think Ma would be too keen either.'

Sandy knew she was right. 'Oh well,' he murmured. 'It was just an idea.'

'And a lovely one, Sandy.'

'I'm bound to come back from time to time, don't forget. To see Ma and you if nothing else.'

'If nothing else,' she repeated with a smile.

'You know what I mean.'

'Of course I do. I'm only teasing.'

Laura fell silent for a few moments. 'Monday is only three days away,' she stated.

'I thought it best if it was done quickly. Once my mind was made up I didn't want to hang around.'

She nodded that she understood.

'It would only have made the parting worse somehow,' he added lamely.

'Yes.'

'This way it's a clean, sharp break.'

Laura turned away so he couldn't see her expression. She was desperately trying not to cry.

'Don't make it harder for me, Laura. Please? I feel bad enough as it is. Not bad about going, but leaving you and Ma behind.'

'Sorry,' Laura whispered.

'So buck up. There's a good lass.'

She faced him again when she'd brought herself back under control, and even managed a smile. 'You will write regularly, won't you?'

'I promise.'

'I mean it, Sandy, regularly.'

'I said I promise. Once a week, faithfully. How's that?'

'Perfect.'

'Good. And you'll reply?'

'To every letter I get. And that too is a promise.'

'Right then. It's agreed.'

Going to him she kissed him tenderly on the cheek. Not trusting herself to speak again less she lost her composure she left him to it.

Harriet was sitting in the darkness of their bedroom lost in thought. Mathew still hadn't come home from his walk which suited her fine. The longer he stayed out the better as far as she was concerned.

How things had changed between them over the past years, she reflected. What had once seemed a nice, comfortable marriage had degenerated into a mess. At least she wasn't allowing herself to be walked all over any more, of which she was proud. Extremely so, and only wished she'd defied him long before she had.

Her defiance had began with little things, like calling Sandy that, instead of Alexander, while in Mathew's presence. The funny thing was Mathew had never noticed, or if he had hadn't commented on the fact.

What was the expression? From little acorns . . .

And now there was James and his proposition to consider. A proposition looking more and more tempting the more she thought about it.

But had she the courage to actually walk out on Mathew, and all that entailed?

That was the question.

'Sandy!'

Having just tipped the porter who'd carried his suitcase and loaded it aboard the train compartment, Sandy turned in surprise at hearing his name called out. He was further surprised to see Laura hurrying along the platform.

'What are you doing here?' he demanded when she reached him. 'You're supposed to be in school.'

'I complained of being unwell and was allowed to go home,' she explained rather breathlessly.

'And are you?'

'Don't be silly. I'm absolutely fine. I simply couldn't let you go off without someone there to wave goodbye.'

Sandy was touched by that. Mathew was at work, while Harriet had said she couldn't bear coming to the station as that would be too much for her. Her farewell had been a tearful one.

'That's kind of you,' Sandy acknowledged with a smile. 'But naughty all the same.'

Laura shrugged. 'I wanted to be here, and so here I am. I thought it the least I could do. After all, it isn't every day your brother leaves home to go abroad and stay there. It's a big occasion. And . . .' She hesitated. 'A sad one.'

'Yes,' he agreed. 'It is. But what I'm doing is right, Laura. I know that.'

'I'm sure it is.'

'I hated medicine, don't forget. This way I'll be doing what I truly want to do. What I'm good at. So from that point of view it isn't sad at all. But joyous, I suppose.'

'You won't forget to write now?'

'No, I won't.'

'I'll be looking forward to that first letter. I want to hear about everything.' Then, remembering a previous conversation they'd had, 'Well, almost everything.'

He laughed. 'And so you shall.'

They stared at each other intently for a few seconds, then Sandy said, 'I'd better get aboard.'

'Yes, you'd better.'

Suddenly she was in his arms, he hugging her tight, the smell of her strong and wild in his nostrils.

'There there,' he said, releasing her. Further down the platform he spotted the guard preparing to wave his green flag.

Sandy climbed into the compartment and closed the door behind him, the window sliding open when he released the strap.

'Good luck!' Laura, now misty eyed, said as the train juddered, then moved off.

'You take care of yourself now, sis.'

'And you.'

She waved and waved till he was finally lost to sight. Slumping, she turned and began wearily trudging back along the platform.

She'd never felt so lonely, or desolate, in her entire life. A life she knew would never be the same again now that Sandy, her beloved brother, had gone out of it.

Chapter 23

'It must be easier for you to make a decision now your son has left home,' James Ballantine said to Harriet, as the pair of them lunched in the Station Hotel.

Harriet moved a piece of fish around her plate as she considered her reply. 'Well it is, and it isn't,' she declared at last.

'How so?'

'There's still Laura to think about. What would happen to her? I mean, I can't leave her with Mathew. That simply wouldn't be fair on her.'

'Then she would come with you.'

Harriet sighed. 'It's not as easy as that, James. She's still at school, don't forget.'

'But in her last year according to you.'

'True,' Harriet admitted. 'But I have to also take her feelings into account. She'd be horrified, and deeply hurt, if I left Mathew. She'd be part of the scandal that would ensue, which would be awful for her. She'd be so ashamed, of me most of all.'

James had a sip of wine, studying Harriet over the rim of his glass. Damn these complications, he inwardly raged. Why did it all have to be so difficult?

'Would she?'

'Of course she would, James. I'm her mother, and children see their parents in a certain light. I just couldn't bear it if I lost her respect. It would break my heart.'

'Does that mean you're turning me down?'

Harriet shook her head. 'It means I'm asking you to give me more time. Not that you haven't been patient as it is, you have. And I appreciate that.'

He smiled wryly. 'After all these lost years what does a few more months matter? I'm willing to wait for as long as it takes.'

Harriet's eyes filled with gratitude. 'Thank you.'

'Just don't forget I love you, Harriet. And always have.'

The sincerity in his voice made her tingle inside. What a good man he was. And how understanding.

He decided to change the subject, lighten things up a little. 'Now, what are you going to have for dessert? And don't say you don't want one. I know you have a sweet tooth.'

Harriet laughed. 'I've got my figure to think about.'

'Let me think about it. Which I do all the time. Night and day. Awake and asleep.'

Harriet coloured. 'You've made me all embarrassed now.'

'Have I?' he teased.

She coloured even further. To her surprise what he'd said had excited her. 'Yes,' she whispered.

'Well I do, Harriet. Night and day.'

'The gateau,' was all she could think of to reply. 'I'll have that for dessert.'

James just smiled.

'He's broken it off!' Madeleine Abercrombie wailed, and burst out crying.

Laura hadn't seen Madeleine for months until she'd turned up at the house a few minutes previously saying she had to speak to her. And now this!

'Conor, I take it?'

Madeleine nodded, quite beside herself. 'Oh, Laura, what am I to do?'

Laura had absolutely no idea. 'When did this happen?'

'Last night. We went out for a drink. He told me outside my house after he'd taken me home.'

'Poor Maddy,' Laura murmured sympathetically, and put a comforting arm round Madeleine's shaking shoulders. 'Did he say why?'

'That's the awful part,' Madeleine sobbed. 'He's met someone else.'

Worse and worse, Laura thought. 'Can I get you anything?' She was horribly aware she wasn't handling this very well. The truth was, she and Madeleine had grown apart since Madeleine had met Conor and become quite irritating, if not downright boring, with her Conor this, and Conor that. She felt for Madeleine nonetheless.

'I came to you because you're my best friend,' Madeleine, now red eyed, sobbed.

'Maybe you should sit down.'

'I don't want to sit down. I want to die.'

A bit melodramatic, Laura thought. Though there was no denying Madeleine was in a terrible state.

'And I want him back,' Madeleine added. 'I love him so much and thought he loved me. He said he did. Swore he did. Now he's met someone else and I'm to be cast aside like an old shoe.'

'I don't know what to say or advise,' Laura confessed. 'It must be terrible for you.'

'You can't imagine. It's tearing me apart inside. I feel as if I'm going to explode. All I want to do is lie down somewhere and die.'

Laura desperately wished Harriet was at home to help her out, but her parents had gone off to play cards and wouldn't be back for hours yet, so she would have to handle this on her own.

'There there, you mustn't say things like that,' she gently chided. 'You don't mean it.'

'But I do!' Madeleine howled. 'I really do.'

Laura racked her brains, trying to think of something, anything, to calm Madeleine down. 'Perhaps it's just as well this has happened,' she said hopefully. 'He may have sworn he loved you but clearly didn't. If that's the case then you're probably well rid of him.'

Madeleine stared at Laura in horror. 'But I love him, and always will. You don't understand what that feels like.'

Laura couldn't think of a reply to that.

'I just can't . . .' Madeleine broke off and shuddered. 'Imagine him being with another girl, doing the things we did together.'

'You haven't . . . You know?'

Madeleine frowned. 'What?'

'Had, eh . . . the full thing?'

Madeleine shook her head. 'We never went that far. Almost, but not that far.'

That was a relief, Laura thought. It seemed to her it would have complicated matters even further if they had.

'I was saving myself for my wedding night,' Madeleine explained. 'We both agreed that was the right thing to do. And now . . . and now . . .'

Madeleine sort of collapsed in on herself, her entire body shaking with grief.

Laura coped as best she could.

Laura sat on her bed having just seen Madeleine off. She didn't know if she'd been any help, but at least she'd tried. In the end she'd been quite hard on Madeleine, trying to snap her out of the hysterical fit her visit had degenerated into. After a while it had appeared to work and Madeleine had regained a semblance of composure.

Laura took a deep breath, then another, glad that was all over. She could only hope that Madeleine came to terms with the situation before too long, for Madeleine certainly couldn't go on like this. To take her mind off Madeleine's distressing visit Laura picked up Sandy's latest letter, which had arrived that morning, and started to re-read it.

He was well, over the cold he'd had a few weeks previously, and painting like a maniac. The use of that latter word caused Laura to smile. How could you possibly paint like a maniac? But she got the gist.

His hectic social life continued on apace, out most nights at various clubs and bars, sometimes with his friend Harald and a writer called Rocky, other times on his own.

She reflected that so far there had been no reference

to any women and could only wonder if he was simply neglecting to mention them.

Sandy had rented a house which he'd shortly be moving into. A huge place on the rue Gabrielle, wherever that was, which sounded wonderful from his description. He'd already selected a room with good light to be his studio, and wished she was with him to help choose furniture and so on.

She would have loved that, Laura mused. It would have been enormous fun, especially as money wouldn't have been any object or barrier. Sandy could more or less afford whatever took his fancy.

She briefly wondered what this Harald, whom Sandy was forever alluding to, did for a living? Or was he a gentleman of leisure who didn't require to work? She made a mental note to ask Sandy in her reply.

As always he said how much he missed her and Ma, often thinking about the pair of them, wondering how they were and what they were up to. In her case not much, she thought. School was about it. Very dreary.

As she read on she forgot all about Madeleine and Madeleine's problems.

'Ah, Sandy, there's someone here I'd like you to meet.'

Sandy paused in his sketching to glance up at Harald Haraldson standing before his table. With Harald was an elegantly dressed older woman who was smiling at him. He immediately came to his feet.

'Lady Barbara, this is Sandy McLean the artist I was telling you about. Sandy, I'd like to introduce Lady Barbara Vaughan-Thomas, a friend of mine.'

Not unattractive, Sandy thought as they shook hands.

He rightly guessed Lady Barbara to be one of Harald's 'clients'.

Pleasantries were exchanged, then Sandy asked if they'd care to join him, which they did. Harald was politeness itself as he assisted Lady Barbara to a chair.

'Harald has told me you're an excellent artist,' Lady Barbara declared, arching an eyebrow.

Harald was looking round, trying to catch the attention of a waiter or waitress.

'That's very kind of him,' Sandy murmured.

'Yes, he has nothing but praise for your talent.'

Harald grinned at Sandy.

Sandy didn't know what to reply to that, so kept quiet.

'I saw you sketching as we came over,' Lady Barbara went on. 'May I?'

'Of course.' Sandy handed her his pad which she placed in front of her before opening it.

She had a good bone structure, Sandy noted, studying her face. He then noticed the many rings flashing and sparkling on her hands, including a wedding band. She was married then, or perhaps a widow.

Harald had a word with the waiter now in attendance, ordering champagne, the best in the house. That and three glasses.

'I thought I'd find you here,' Harald said to Sandy when the waiter had gone. 'Le Bar Americain has become quite a haunt of yours lately.'

Sandy shrugged. 'I like it. And most people speak English which helps.'

Harald laughed. 'You really must try to learn the local lingo, old boy. It's not that difficult.'

'It is for me,' Sandy replied ruefully. 'I've always been rotten at languages. Just not my forte, I'm afraid.'

'Nonetheless, you must persevere. You should find picking it up easier when you're hearing it on a daily basis.'

'Time will tell.' Sandy smiled.

Lady Barbara glanced over at him. 'Harald is right, you are good judging from these sketches. Are you as good in oils though?'

'That's not for me to say,' Sandy answered modestly.

'He is,' Harald stated bluntly.

'Indeed,' Lady Barbara purred. 'That's interesting. Now why don't you tell me about yourself, Mr McLean. I'm interested.'

'Sandy, please.'

She nodded. 'Then tell me about yourself, Sandy. I'm all ears.'

She was just being polite, making conversation, he thought as he began recounting what she'd asked to hear.

Harald looked on approvingly.

'Is something bothering you?' Harriet asked Laura. 'You seem very introspective.'

'I'm feeling somewhat guilty,' Laura confessed.

That surprised Harriet. 'About what?'

'Madeleine Abercrombie. I feel I should go round to see her but keep putting it off as I don't want to go through all that again.'

'Go through what, dear?' Harriet queried patiently. 'I've absolutely no idea what you're talking about.'

'Sorry,' Laura apologised. 'I haven't mentioned.' She then told the story of Madeleine's visit and how distraught Madeleine had been.

'But you *must* go and see her,' Harriet insisted when she'd finished. 'You owe that to her as a friend.'

'I suppose so,' Laura sighed. 'It's not that I don't care. I do. It's just . . .' She trailed off.

'Just what?' Harriet prompted.

'It'll be such a pain.'

'Don't you think that's rather callous and cold-hearted of you?' Harriet reproved. 'And even if it will be a pain it'll be nothing like the pain that girl is currently experiencing.'

Laura knew that to be true enough. 'You're right, Ma. I'll go soon.'

'I hope you do. It's at times like these you need your friends most. Even if it is a pain, as you call it, to see them.'

Laura thought of Madeleine wailing and blubbering and how ghastly it had all been. Perhaps she'd have been more understanding if she hadn't already been sick to the back teeth of hearing about Conor. But she had tried to help, she reminded herself. She'd certainly done that, which was something.

'Lady Barbara wants me to paint her?' Sandy exclaimed.

Harald nodded. 'Thanks to me suggesting you.'

'Well,' a bemused Sandy murmured, unable to believe his luck.

'There is one further thing,' Harald went on, eyes twinkling with amusement.

'Go on.'

'She wants to be painted wearing only a *chemise de nuit*, that's a nightdress to you.'

That totally bemused Sandy. 'Really?'

'*Really.*'

Sandy shook his head. 'I don't know what to say.'

'No doubt she'll pay handsomely, she certainly does me for my services. So are you interested?'

'Of course,' Sandy replied quickly. 'It'll be my first commission since coming to Paris.'

'I thought you'd be pleased,' Harald commented drily. 'Did she happen to mention why a nightdress?'

'No. I didn't ask and she didn't volunteer the information. But that's what she wants. If you're agreeable she'll present herself here on Tuesday afternoon after lunch so you can make a start.'

'That's fine with me,' Sandy agreed.

'One final item.'

'Which is?'

'My percentage.'

Sandy hadn't expected that. But then he hadn't expected any of this. 'And why should I give you one?'

'Because I introduced you, and recommended you for the job. Something I may also be able to do in the future with other clients and friends of mine. Look on it as a business arrangement.' Harald shrugged. 'From my point of view it's all part and parcel of earning a living. I thought twenty-five per cent would be about right.'

'Twenty-five per cent! That's daylight robbery.'

'Take it or leave it. That's up to you.'

Sandy was beginning to find all this extremely funny. 'All right. It's a deal.'

'Good. And I'll trust you to give me the proper amount and not cheat me. Besides, I'll probably find out if you did and then that would be the end of that.'

'I won't cheat you.' Sandy smiled. 'You have my word.'

'Which I accept. Now, how about we go out and celebrate with a cognac or two?'

'Sounds great to me. I've stopped painting for the day anyway.'

There was a little bar only a few minutes walk away and that's where they went.

Laura turned away from the door in relief, Madeleine's mother having just informed her that Madeleine wasn't home, and wouldn't be for another couple of hours yet so there had been no point in waiting.

Well, at least she'd attempted to speak to Madeleine, Laura told herself, so she could now stop feeling quite so guilty. She'd try again in a couple of days' time she promised herself.

Yes, that's what she'd do.

'I'm afraid I've only recently moved in and haven't quite got things sorted yet,' Sandy apologised.

Lady Barbara glanced about her, nodding approval. 'It's very nice. Is the whole house yours?'

Sandy nodded. 'Yes, it is.'

'Then you must be a most successful artist to be able to afford such a grand place.'

'I only rent,' Sandy explained. 'And it's not as expensive as you might think.'

Knowing Parisien rents, even in Montmartre, Lady Barbara doubted that, but didn't comment further.

Sandy was nervous and hoped it didn't show. She would be wearing a nightdress, he reminded himself. She wasn't going to be naked or anything like that. Perhaps it was the fact that Lady Barbara was older and titled that was unnerving him.

'Would you care to have some coffee or a glass of wine before we begin?' he queried.

'No thank you. I've just taken luncheon.'

'Then we'd better get on with it.'

As Sandy had written to Laura, his new studio received a great deal of light and was an ideal room in which to paint. There were two large windows which weren't overlooked thus giving the room privacy.

Sandy had already taken Lady Barbara's coat and hung it in the hall. He now gestured to a patterned screen he'd set up, behind which was a chair. 'If you'd like to use that I'll get ready.'

'Thank you.'

'The robe is a brand new one,' Sandy called out as Lady Barbara disappeared behind the screen. 'So it hasn't been worn before,' he added rather unnecessarily.

As there was no reply he started fiddling with his brushes and paints, waiting for her reappearance.

When a smiling Lady Barbara did reappear she was wearing a stunning rose-coloured silk negligée that was simply the most gorgeous, and somehow erotic, Sandy had ever seen. It had wide lapels falling to the waist where there was a tie, these lapels heavily embroidered at the edges in intricate patterns, the embroidery of the same rose colour. The sleeves were slashed at the elbows, and also embroidered at the edges. The entire garment ended at mid-calf.

'Approve?' she queried, eyes crinkling with laughter to see his expression.

'Very much so.' Damn she was sexy, he thought. Even if she was an older woman. He cleared his throat. 'Any preference for a pose? Or will you leave that to me?'

'Actually, I do have a preference. I'd like to be seated facing the artist straight on. Is that all right?'

'Very much so.' Well why not! He didn't mind. It was all the same to him.

'Seated on a chair. The one behind the screen will be perfect.'

Sandy fetched the chair and placed it about a dozen feet from his easel. He couldn't help but think that even in her night attire there was an air of elegance and breeding about the woman. Fully dressed, or like this, she certainly had class.

'How's that?' she queried when she'd sat.

'Excellent.'

'Good.'

How businesslike she was, Sandy reflected, without a trace of shyness or embarrassment. She'd acted as if he'd seen her in a negligée a hundred times before when she'd stepped out from behind the screen.

'Have you wondered why I want the painting done?' she asked as he selected a brush.

'It has crossed my mind I must admit.' He laughed. 'I can't imagine it'll be hung in the family drawing room.'

Lady Barbara found that amusing. 'Hardly. It's to be a gift for a very special friend of mine back in England.'

Obviously a lover, Sandy assumed.

And instantly fell to work.

'So how did it go?' Harald asked Sandy, joining him in Le Bar Americain.

'Fine.'

'No problems then?'

'None at all.'

Harald nodded his approval. 'There's one thing I must warn you about though.'

'What's that?'

371

'How shall I put this?' Harald mused, eyes twinkling. 'She's a very amorous lady, constantly in need of attention, if you get my meaning?'

Sandy stared at the Icelander. 'Are you saying she's a nymphomaniac?

Harald laughed. 'No, she's not that bad. But she does like sex, and lots of it. That's why she comes to Paris every year. Over here she can indulge herself as much as she wishes without having to worry about a husband lurking in the background.'

'Are you suggesting she might, eh . . . ?'

'Precisely,' Harald nodded. 'You're a good-looking young man which would make you fair game as far as she's concerned. There again, you might not be her type. The point is you should consider the possibility of her making an advance towards you in case she does. Yes or no, so to speak.'

'I see,' Sandy murmured.

'Any thoughts on the matter?'

'How old is she?' Sandy asked cautiously.

Harald laughed again. 'I have no idea. But if I was to guess I'd say late forties, or thereabouts. I know she has two children, but not much more.'

'The husband?'

'A bore from all accounts who's not very good in bed. She did let that slip once.'

Sandy was fascinated. 'Is he aware of what she gets up to?'

Harald shrugged. 'Possibly. It might even be that he's doing the same thing elsewhere. The English aristocracy are a strange lot. Quite bizarre in my opinion.'

'I don't have any experience of them,' Sandy confessed.

'Strange and bizarre,' Harald repeated, and signalled to a passing waiter.

Yes or no? Sandy wondered. He'd have to think about that.

It was Sandy's fourth session with Lady Barbara and it wasn't proving successful due to her constant fidgeting. He'd done everything he could think of to try to relax her to no avail. Finally, with an exasperated sigh he laid his brush aside.

'We'll call it a day,' he announced.

'But I've only been here an hour!' she protested.

'I simply can't concentrate with you continually squirming around like that. I'm sorry.'

'No, I'm the one who should apologise.' A wicked grin curled her mouth upwards. 'If I had any on I'd say I had ants in my pants.'

Sandy found that amusing.

'Have you any wine in the house?' she asked.

'Of course.'

'Can I have a glass?'

'Red or white?'

'Red would be preferable right now.'

Sandy came out from behind his easel. 'It's in the kitchen. I'll fetch some.'

When he returned with a bottle and two glasses he found the studio empty. Perhaps she'd gone to the toilet, he thought. Setting the glasses down he began to pour.

'Sandy!'

That was odd, her voice had come from upstairs. 'Lady Barbara?'

'I'm in what appears to be your bedroom. Will you join me?'

Well, she didn't want him up there to discuss the weather, he thought, still not having made up his mind whether it would be yes or no.

It had been a long while since Sophie, he reflected for the umpteenth time. And, despite her age, Lady Barbara was still an attractive woman.

He picked up the glasses again and headed for the door. The answer was yes.

'Good God!' Mathew exclaimed in surprise. He was glancing through the newspaper while having breakfast.

'What is it, dear?' Harriet inquired.

'There's a new story here that a Madeleine Abercrombie, aged seventeen, has been found dead floating in the River Kelvin. Foul play isn't suspected.'

Laura, who'd been listening, suddenly went cold all over and felt sick to the very pit of her stomach.

'Do you think it's your friend?' Mathew asked.

Laura took a long time in replying. 'Yes,' she finally whispered.

Chapter 24

Harriet found her gaze returning time and time again to Madeleine's parents sitting on the pew in front and to the side of her, their profiles quite visible. Beside her Laura was ashen and stony faced as the minister droned on.

What indescribable pain the Abercrombies must be experiencing, Harriet reflected. It simply didn't bear thinking about. All the more awful for them as Madeleine had been an only child.

What if she was ever to lose Sandy or Laura? She shuddered at the thought. Either lose them or . . . their respect. Would the latter happen if she went off with James Ballantine? There was a strong possibility that it might.

Laura was numb with guilt and self remorse. All she could think was this might never have happened if she'd been more of a friend to Madeleine, gone again to the house as she'd promised herself she would, and never had. How she bitterly regretted that now.

Selfish, that's what she'd been. Bloody selfish. Uncaring. Not there for Madeleine when she was needed. If only she could turn back the clock how different things might be. But she couldn't. That was impossible.

She'd been selfish, uncaring, and now Madeleine was dead and about to be buried. Madeleine, whom she'd gone all through school with, shared so much with in the past.

A hymn was announced and the congregation, Mr Abercrombie having to hold, and support, Mrs Abercrombie by the elbow, rose to its feet.

When Laura tried to sing she found she couldn't. The words just wouldn't come.

'Can I ask a question?'

'Go ahead,' Harald replied. They were having coffee and a cognac in a little café bar they sometimes frequented.

'Does Lady Barbara still use your services now that she and I . . . Well you know?'

Harald smiled. 'She does indeed. Every single day, in fact.'

Christ! Sandy thought. The woman was insatiable.

'Why, does that bother you?' Harald queried.

Sandy shook his head. 'I just wondered, that's all.'

'I did warn you that she's extremely amorous.'

'Yes, you did.'

Harald glanced at his watch. 'Actually I'm due to meet up with her in about an hour and a half to give her yet another damned good servicing.'

Sandy winced. Servicing! What a horrible way of putting it. So cold and clinical. It's not a word he would ever use in that context.

'How's the painting coming along by the way?' Harald inquired.

'It's nearly finished.'

'Are you pleased with it? Or more importantly, is she?'

'Lady Barbara hasn't seen it yet. I insisted on that. And yes, I think I'm pleased. Or as pleased as I am with anything I paint.'

'Well, I'd like to see it, if you'd allow that.'

'Really?'

'Yes. I'm curious, knowing her as intimately as I do.' He laughed. 'I'll correct that, as we *both* do.'

'Come round later then, after you've been with her.'

Sandy hoped Harald would approve. He'd learned enough of the Icelander by now to know that even if Harald was a rotten painter himself he was an excellent judge of other people's work.

'It's good,' Harald declared. 'Very good indeed.'

That pleased Sandy enormously. 'Thank you.'

'If not quite a true representation in places.'

Sandy shrugged. 'She asked me to be kind and so I have. I didn't see anything wrong with that, especially as she's the client.'

Harald moved across to where other paintings were stacked, these completed. 'May I?'

Sandy made a gesture indicating go ahead.

A thoughtful Harald studied each in turn. 'I think I know where I can sell a couple of these for you.'

'Oh?'

'A gallery owned by a friend of mine in Montparnasse. I do believe he might be interested.'

'Then take them with you by all means.'

'It'll be the usual commission, of course, if they sell.'

'Of course,' Sandy replied drily. 'I'd expect nothing else from you.'

When Harald left he was carrying two of the paintings that he'd chosen.

'Come on, Laura, it's high time you bucked up,' Harriet chided. 'You can't go on like this for ever.'

Laura shrugged, and didn't reply.

'Laura?'

'You know what's bothering me, Ma.'

'Of course I do. But you can't keep on blaming yourself. Madeleine might well have killed herself no matter how many times you'd seen and talked to her.'

'Possibly,' Laura admitted. 'But on the other hand she might not. At least my conscience would have been clear if I'd put myself out more.'

Harriet was becoming really worried about her daughter who'd sunk into a fit of depression since news of Madeleine's unfortunate suicide.

'She was my friend and I let her down,' Laura stated morosely. 'How do you think that leaves me feeling?'

'Pretty bad,' Harriet acknowledged.

'She actually spoke of killing herself and I didn't believe her, didn't take her seriously, when I should have.'

'It's over and done with, but life goes on. You'll just have to come to terms with what's happened, that's all.'

Laura glanced at Harriet through anguished eyes. 'That's easy enough for you to say.'

'No, it's not,' Harriet snapped, getting angry now.

'Don't think I haven't made decisions which I've come to regret. It's all part and parcel of being grown up.' One of the decisions she was thinking about was marrying Mathew instead of James.

'But nobody has died as a result, have they?'

Harriet changed tack. 'Perhaps your father can prescribe something to help. A tonic maybe.'

'A tonic won't do any good,' Laura replied scornfully. 'There's nothing wrong with me physically. I'm not run down or anything. I'm just . . .' She broke off and burst into tears, hiding her face in her hands.

Harriet was instantly by her side, putting her arms round Laura. 'There there,' she crooned. 'There there.'

'Oh, Ma!'

'I know, dear. I know.'

Laura continued to cry while Harriet gently rocked her to and fro.

'There you are,' Sandy declared, handing Harald a sheaf of notes. 'Twenty-five per cent as agreed.'

Harald's eyebrows slowly rose in surprise as he counted the cash. It was considerably more than he'd expected. 'She really did like it, didn't she?'

'I didn't put a price on the painting, simply asked her to give me what she thought was right. I have to admit she was generous.'

Harald tucked the money away. 'I have someone else who might be interested in having you paint her. But it's not certain yet, we'll have to wait and see.'

'Young or old?' Sandy queried.

'Twenties, and plain as a pikestaff. This one isn't titled, though filthy rich. Her father's a highly successful exporter.'

'Just let me know and I'll meet with her. All right?'

'Fine. By the way I have some news for you.'

'Oh?'

'One of the two canvases I took to my friend in Montparnasse has been sold. I haven't collected on it yet but will next time I'm down there.'

Another painting sold! Now he truly was beginning to feel like a professional. He liked it. A lot.

'You know all this has given me an idea,' Harald said. 'One I've been thinking about.'

'What's that then?'

'I might just become a full-time artists' agent.'

Now it was Sandy's turn to be surprised. 'Really?'

'Of course I'd have to build it up as a going concern, which could take a while. But the prospect does excite me.'

'Does that mean you'd give up being a gigolo?'

Harald shrugged. 'I can't keep on being one for ever. Nor do I want to. The time will come when I may wish to get married and have a family.'

Sandy gaped at his friend who was looking sheepish. 'You!'

'Why not? The last thing I want is to end up as some horrible old roué. That's not for me, thank you very much.'

Sandy grinned as a vision of that popped into his mind. 'Indeed,' he agreed.

'Besides, what I do now isn't as attractive as you and others might think,' Harald went on. 'I just happen to be good at it, that's all. But what about when my looks fade, or if my ability dwindles, what then? No, it's better I plan for the future before I suddenly find it might be too late.'

Sandy raised his glass of beer. 'Then all I can do is wish you luck. And you can handle all my work for as long as you like. How's that?'

A look of genuine appreciation came over Harald's face. 'Thank you, Sandy. I'm touched by that.'

An artists' agent, Sandy mused. Well well well.

It was Madeleine's death that caused Harriet to make up her mind. That, and Laura's reaction to it. There were more ways to lose a child than through death; she just couldn't take the risk for she loved her children dearly.

Another factor had been recalling her marriage vows. For better or worse, richer or poorer . . . She didn't love Mathew any more, but was that reason enough to leave him for another? He could be a pain, certainly a martinet, but he'd never mistreated her. She could never claim that. He'd always provided for her and the children, quite well really. All right, he could be a bully, Victorian in outlook, but then so were many men of his age and generation. It was the way they'd been brought up.

Selfish was a word Laura had used over and over following the funeral. Wasn't that exactly what she'd be if she left? Of course it would.

She was an honourable woman, she reminded herself. One who tried to do the right thing at all times. She couldn't suddenly change now. And wouldn't, despite the temptations.

No, the dream was over. And that's what it would remain, a dream that never became reality.

Poor James, she thought. Having lost her once he was now about to lose her a second time.

Truly, life could be cruel.

* * *

'I thought I might find the pair of you here amongst the rest of the low life,' an already drunken Rocky exclaimed, joining Sandy and Harald in the Lapin Agile. He flopped onto a chair at their table. 'Guess what, *mes amis*?'

'What?' a bemused Harald asked.

'I've finished my goddamn book. And now I want to celebrate.'

'Congratulations.' Sandy smiled. 'It looks as though you've already started.'

'Goddamn right I have.' He waved an arm to attract a waitress.

'Now all you have to do is sell it,' Harald commented wryly.

'I'll sell it OK. Don't you worry your sweet ass about that. I have every confidence.'

A waitress appeared, topless as was obligatory, and Rocky ordered wine and cognacs. He beamed at Sandy and Harald as he lit a cigarette. 'It took a while to get there, but I did in the end. Fucking ace!'

'Does this mean you'll be returning to America?' Sandy asked.

Rocky shook his head. 'Naw. I'm staying put. America is crap compared to here. Absolute crap.'

Sandy was about to take a sip of wine when he spotted her across the rim of his glass. For a moment he thought he was mistaken, but he wasn't. Sophie Ducros was sitting with another woman on the other side of the room. He hadn't noticed her come in so perhaps she'd already been here when they'd arrived. Whatever, she was here now.

What should he do? he wondered. Ignore her, or go over? And how did he feel about seeing her again? He wasn't at all sure about the latter.

He waited for about fifteen minutes in case Jack, the boyfriend, showed up, but when Jack didn't he decided to go across. If she was back in Montmartre he was bound to bump into her again anyway.

'Excuse me, chaps, I've just seen an old friend. I won't be long,' he declared.

'From Scotland?' Harald queried as Sandy had said *old* friend.

'Uh-huh, by way of Montmartre. I'll explain later.'

As he made his way over Sandy recalled how deeply she'd hurt him. But that was in the past, he reminded himself. He'd got over it. At least he believed he had. He was about to find out whether or not that was so.

'Hello, Sophie.' He smiled as he halted at her table. 'How are things?'

'Sandy!' she exclaimed in utter astonishment. '*Merde!* What are you doing here?'

'I live in Montmartre now. Have done for a while.'

'You live . . .' She broke off to stare at him, only tearing her gaze away when her companion muttered something in French. 'Excuse me, let me introduce you. Sandy, this is my friend Angelique. Angelique, Sandy.'

They shook hands, after which Angelique and Sophie had a brief conversation.

'Nice to meet you, Sandy.' And with that Angelique moved away to another table where women were sitting.

'I asked her to leave us alone for a while,' Sophie explained. 'Sit, sit. I want to hear everything.'

He'd forgotten just how green her eyes were, he realised, as he slid onto a chair. Or how beautiful she was. 'You're looking terrific,' he stated honestly.

'Thank you.'

'Is Jack around?'

Her expression hardened. 'He did it again. I went home one day to find he'd left, and again without a word or note. That was when I decided it was time to return to Montmartre. And so here I am.' She laughed. 'And here you are. The last person I expected to see.'

So Jack had done another bunk, Sandy thought. That should have pleased him, but strangely it didn't. He was quite unaffected by her news.

'Now, why are you here?' she demanded.

She lit a Gitanes as he spoke, her eyes never leaving his. Was it his imagination or had a certain calculating glint crept into them? The one thing he didn't tell her was about his inheritance.

'I see,' she murmured when he finished. 'How wonderful for you. And you're selling?'

'Beginning to. I think I'll be able to, with a bit of luck, get by.'

Sophie glanced down into her glass, making it obvious that it was empty. Sandy immediately hailed a passing waitress.

'Where are you living?' Sophie asked after the waitress had taken their order.

'The rue Gabrielle.'

'I know it well.'

'And you?'

Sophie gave one of her very Gallic shrugs. 'With Angelique at the moment until I can find work. Then I'll get my own place.'

'What sort of work?'

'Modelling, I suppose. It's what I used to do as you know.' Her face lit up. 'Are you in need of a model, Sandy? I could use the money.'

384

For an instant, just an instant, he was tempted. 'I'm sorry, Sophie, but I don't. However, I will keep you in mind.' The latter was a lie; he had no intention of ever employing her. That was a road he wasn't about to travel twice.

'Oh! Too bad.' Her face had fallen on hearing that.

Their wine arrived and Sandy sat back in his chair as the waitress poured for them, deliberately admiring her breasts, and letting Sophie see him do so, a mean sort of revenge on his part. He then paid for the wine including a sizable tip, something that didn't go unnoticed by Sophie.

'*Merci, m'sieur.*' The waitress beamed and walked provocatively away.

'I can't say I know many other painters who might need a model, but I have a friend who does. I'll speak to him on your behalf.'

She acknowledged that with a small nod. The stub of a pencil was produced and a scrap of paper which she scribbled on. 'My address,' she declared, passing it over.

Sandy didn't recognise the street and guessed it to be one of the more obscure, rather rough ones of which there were many in Montmartre.

'To your new career!' Sophie toasted, raising her glass.

Sandy raised his and they both drank.

'Can I . . .' She broke off in apparent confusion. 'This is terribly embarrassing.'

Sandy didn't reply, merely waited for her to go on. He was fairly certain he knew what was coming next.

'Could you lend me a few francs, Sandy? I promise to pay you back as soon as I can.'

He'd been right. He also knew it would be the last

he'd see of any cash he handed over. She had no intention of repaying it.

Suddenly he felt incredibly sad to think of what he'd once felt for Sophie, the esteem he'd held her in. The love he'd had for her. The creature in front of him might still be beautiful, but underneath she was just pathetic.

'Of course,' he smiled, again reaching for his wallet. He was aware of her watching him like a hawk as he counted out some notes.

'Will that do?' he queried, giving them to her.

'*Mais oui*. Thank you, Sandy.'

'My pleasure at being able to help.'

He rose to his feet. 'I'd better get back to my friends. It was lovely speaking to you, Sophie. I wish you well in the future.'

She frowned slightly. 'And you, Sandy.'

'Take care.'

And with that he left her.

Sandy stood staring out of his bedroom window over the lights of Paris spread below. He hadn't stayed long at the Lapin Agile after rejoining Harald and Rocky, excusing himself by pleading a bad headache. The night had gone flat for him after his encounter with Sophie.

His emotions were mixed, but one was stronger than all the other. That of relief. The question of Sophie had been well and truly answered. She meant nothing to him any more. Nothing at all. He hadn't been deluding himself in believing he was over her. He truly was.

He smiled in memory, recalling some of the good times they'd had together. The sex, the laughs, the just being together. All now in the past. In another world almost.

With a sigh he turned away from the window with the intention of re-reading Laura's latest letter which had arrived that morning. He hadn't heard from her for weeks and had begun worrying about her, wondering if she was ill.

The letter, an account of Madeleine's suicide, had explained everything, including what Laura believed to be her complicity in the matter, and how depressed she'd become because of it.

He'd reply right away he decided, though he wasn't quite sure what he was going to say. The least he could do was try to cheer her up with tales of his doings in Montmartre.

He briefly wondered if he should tell her about Lady Barbara, but decided it was a bad idea. About Lady Barbara yes, and the commission, but not that he'd been sleeping with her. Though he had to admit, under different circumstances he might have done, he and Laura having become that close he felt he could tell her everything. But not at the moment, he just didn't think it would be right somehow.

Retrieving her letter from where he'd placed it earlier he sat on the edge of his bed and began to read.

Dear Laura. Dear, darling Laura, how he missed her, he thought, as his eyes scanned the first page.

He missed her enormously, he realised with a jolt.

'I won't be staying for lunch,' Harriet announced to James as she joined him in the lounge of the Station Hotel.

His face fell in disappointment. 'I'm sorry to hear that. Something important?'

Harriet wasn't looking forward to this at all, and had

been dreading the moment since getting up that morning. It wasn't in her nature to hurt people.

'But let me get you a drink first,' James added before she could reply.

'No, don't bother. I'll only be here a few minutes.' And terrible ones they were going to be too.

Harriet took a deep breath, steeling herself to say what she had to. 'I've made my decision and won't be taking you up on your proposal, James. I really am sorry.'

Under different circumstances his expression could have been quite comical as the full import of those words sank home. 'Are you sure?' he croaked.

'Absolutely.'

Now it was his turn to take a deep breath. 'Can I ask exactly why?'

She'd come prepared for that, it was his due after all. Slowly, and methodically, she went over all the reasons while he listened attentively.

'An honourable woman?' he mused when she'd finally finished.

Harriet coloured slightly. 'I know it sounds daft, old fashioned, pretentious even, but nonetheless that's what I've always tried to be.'

'No no, I admire you for it. Truly I do.' He suddenly smiled, the sort of smile that could break your heart, Harriet thought. 'Looking on the other side of the coin I suppose that makes me dishonourable for trying to entice you away from your husband.'

'I didn't mean that,' Harriet replied quickly. 'Please don't think that's what I was trying to infer.'

The bitter smile stretched even further. 'Of course I don't. I was simply playing with words, that's all.'

'No, you weren't. I know you.'

'Do you, Harriet?' he gently mocked.

'Oh, James,' she whispered. 'I feel awful. I hope you don't think I've been stringing you along?'

He shook his head.

'I'm flattered by your proposal, and gave it very serious consideration, I assure you.'

'Will I see you again?'

Harriet glanced away, unable to stand the look in his eyes. 'It's a small city,' she whispered.

'That's not what I meant.'

'Then the answer is no. That wouldn't be fair, on either of us.'

'I suppose you're right,' he conceded after a few moments' silence. He'd already made up his mind what he was going to do. Same as last time, leave Glasgow. The job at Daly's was an excellent one, and extremely well paid, but no matter. He'd somehow find another.

He decided to have one last stab. 'Are you certain there's nothing I can say or do that will change your mind?'

Harriet shook her head.

'So this is it?'

'Yes, James.'

'Will you think of me from time to time? For I'll be thinking of you.'

God, this was proving even worse than she'd anticipated. 'Of course I will.'

'That's not so bad then.'

She had to get out of here, Harriet told herself. And fast. 'Goodbye, James,' she said, coming to her feet.

He also rose and moved to stand beside her.

'Goodbye, Harriet. Just remember I meant it when I said I love you. I do, and always will.'

Luckily they were the only people in the room so their conversation wasn't being overheard.

Harriet didn't know what to reply to that, so didn't. She was about to turn round when he placed a hand on her shoulder, drew her to him and kissed her on the mouth.

Then she was hurrying away, her heart beating nineteen to the dozen, her eyes misting over.

She'd done the right thing, she reassured herself when she reached the street. She'd done the right thing.

Chapter 25

'What!' Laura stopped in her tracks. She had just been about to enter the sitting room when she'd heard her father's explosion of anger. What was going on?

'Calm down, dear, there's no need to fly off the handle,' Harriet replied placatingly.

Suddenly Morag's voice burst out sobbing, and from the sound of things Laura guessed she was also crying.

'You tell me the maid's pregnant and ask if she can move in and expect me to take it quietly,' Mathew thundered on. 'Don't be so soft, woman.'

'Oh please, Dr McLean, please, I've nowhere else to go,' Morag blubbered.

'That's hardly my fault.'

'Show a little compassion, dear,' Harriet pleaded.

Pregnant! My God, Laura thought, remembering all too clearly about the lovemaking sessions Morag had once told her about. Well, it seemed she'd come well and truly unstuck.

'Your parents have thrown you out on your ear, you say?' Mathew repeated.

'That's right, Dr McLean.'

'And so they should. You're a bloody disgrace, Morag, that's what, a bloody disgrace.'

Morag began to wail, a wail that instantly made Laura go cold all over as it reminded her only too clearly of the last time she'd spoken to Madeleine before her friend had killed herself.

'And what about the father? Can't he help you?' Mathew went relentlessly on. Then, in a vicious tone, 'Or perhaps you don't know who the father is?'

The wailing intensified.

'That's quite unjustified, Mathew. Morag has been seeing the same young chap for years now and they were saving up to get married,' Harriet coldly declared, a trace of anger in her voice that Mathew should make such a nasty inference.

'Then let the scoundrel deal with the matter,' Mathew replied waspishly.

'I'm afraid that's not possible,' Harriet continued. 'He seems to have disappeared.'

Mathew laughed. 'After being told the good news I suppose?'

Harriet didn't reply to that, and Morag was obviously incapable because of the state she was in.

'Disappeared where?' Mathew demanded.

'Nobody knows, which is why I said he's disappeared. Even his parents have no idea. Or if they do they wouldn't tell poor Morag here.'

'Poor, my backside!' Mathew scorned. 'She's old

enough, and stupid enough, to be aware of the risks they were taking. She and this chap that is. What's his name by the way?'

'Rab. He's a train driver apparently.'

'Why in God's name didn't they use something?' Mathew declared vehemently. 'That's the trouble with the working classes, they're not only ignorant but feckless to boot. Few of them have any real sense of responsibility, in my opinion, and this business only proves the point.'

'Aren't you being just a little harsh, dear?' Harriet riposted reprovingly.

'Harsh! The slut standing beside you has brought disgrace and shame on her family by getting pregnant outside wedlock. I hardly think harsh is too strong a condemnation to describe that.'

'Surely we can allow her to stay here for a little while,' Harriet further pleaded. 'Just until she can get something sorted out.'

'And bring that shame and disgrace into my home?' Mathew snarled. 'Not on your life. She goes just as soon as she can pull herself together. I'll pay what's owed, and not a penny more. And don't you dare slip her any cash, Harriet. Don't you dare.'

'Mathew . . .'

'I'll not change my mind, and that's that. Hasn't she got friends or relatives who'll take her in?'

'She does have relatives, she says, but they won't have anything to do with her now. As for friends, well none of them are in the position to help.'

Mathew snorted. 'Well, that's her hard luck. Now get her to stop blubbering and out the door with her. And once out she never comes back in again. Is that clear?'

Again Harriet didn't reply.

Laura heard her father's footsteps and guessed he was heading for the hallway. Turning, she fled back the way she'd come, not wanting him to know she'd overheard.

'Morag, wait up!'

The maid, her face still red and puffy from crying, halted as Laura hurried towards her.

'Oh, Miss Laura,' she cried when Laura came alongside. 'What am I to do?'

'Have you any plans at all?'

Morag shook her head.

'Well, I have.' She reached for the pitifully small suitcase Morag was carrying which contained everything Morag owned in the world. 'Let me carry that.'

Morag hung onto the case. 'No, you mustn't, Miss Laura. It wouldn't be right. I'm the servant, don't forget.'

Laura wrestled the case from her. 'Not any more, you've been sacked which means you're now you're own woman entirely. Equal with anyone else.'

Morag sniffed. 'You're very kind.'

'What my father did was brutal and unforgivable. But then that's him all over.'

'Where are we going, miss?' Morag asked as they continued down the street.

'To catch a tram. And then to a place you've been before.'

Laura explained as they continued walking.

Mrs Mitchell listened sympathetically as Morag recounted her tale of woe, interrupting every so often when she wanted a point elaborated on.

'Can you help her?' Laura asked hopefully when Morag finally fell silent.

Mrs Mitchell sighed. 'We at the Marie Stopes Clinic don't deal with matters like this, I'm afraid,' she replied. Then, seeing Morag and Laura's crestfallen looks, added quickly, 'But we have contacts who do.'

'What sort of contacts?' Laura queried.

'Homes for women who're homeless, destitute, alcoholic, or in the family way who require assistance because of their situation. I can usually sort something out. It'll just take a few telephone calls, that's all.'

Mrs Mitchell beckoned over a young woman who'd been attending to some paper work. 'In the meantime I think a cup of tea is in order, don't you agree?'

Morag actually smiled. 'Oh yes, please. I could just do with a good strong cup.'

Inquiries were made about sugar and milk, then the young woman, whom Mrs Mitchell referred to as Kitty, went off into the rear of the premises.

'Excuse me for a couple of moments,' Mrs Mitchell said, and took herself over to another desk which had a telephone on it, her own not having one.

'Have you any idea where Rab might have gone?' Laura quietly asked Morag.

The maid shook her head. 'None at all. He might even have left Glasgow for all I know. Being an engine driver that would be easy for him.'

'I see,' Laura murmured.

'I just can't believe he's done this,' Morag said, lower lip trembling. 'We've been together for so long and he swore he loved me. I certainly love him.'

Laura thought Morag was going to start crying again, but Morag didn't.

'How did he take the news when you told him?' Laura queried.

'He went all funny and quiet like. Then he said it was terrific and he'd make the arrangements for us to get married as soon as possible. Inquiries at the factor's office about a house and that kind of thing.'

'And you never saw him again?'

'No,' Morag said sadly. 'We were supposed to meet up in a few nights' time, but he never showed. I went round to his place but his parents had no idea where he was. He'd simply gone without leaving a forwarding address.'

Sod, Laura thought.

'I put off telling my own folks for as long as I could,' Morag went on. 'But eventually I had to as it was becoming obvious. My da literally threw me down the stairs. I was still sitting there when Ma brought me this suitcase containing my bits and pieces. She called me a stupid bitch and said she wanted nothing more to do with me.' Morag paused to gulp down a breath. 'Them doing that really hurt, Miss Laura. It really did.'

Laura could well imagine, and could only wonder if her father would throw her out if she came home pregnant? Surely Ma would somehow stop him if he tried. Whatever, it wasn't going to happen. She'd make sure of that.

Laura patted Morag on the hand. 'I'm so sorry. All I can think is if your Rab has deserted you like he has, then maybe, love or not, you're well rid of him.'

Mrs Mitchell returned with a triumphant expression on her face. 'It's all fixed. An ambulance will be here in about half an hour to take Morag to the Downside Home, which is one of the best. She's lucky to get in there.'

'Thank you, Mrs Mitchell. I can't tell you how much I appreciate what you've done,' Morag replied.

And with that the tea arrived.

'Do you ever miss Glasgow?' Harald asked, as he and Sandy sat outside a little café bar just off the Place du Tertre drinking coffee.

Sandy smiled. 'Sometimes. Though it's my mother and sister I miss most. I'm very close to both of them.'

'What's your sister like?'

Sandy wagged a finger at him. 'Not your type, that's for certain. She's far too nice for the likes of you.'

'How protective,' Harald teased. 'I was only inquiring, that's all.'

'I know about your "inquiring" when it comes to women. You've got one thing, and one thing only, in mind.'

Harald laughed, finding that funny. 'Am I really so unscrupulous?'

'When it comes to women, yes. Most definitely.'

'Then I'd better not ask about your mother or you'd really get upset,' Harald further teased.

Sandy pretended to glare at him. 'I should hope not.'

'Ah well,' Harald sighed. 'I was only making conversation.'

It was a beautiful summer's day, sunshine streaming down. Sandy flicked an imaginary fleck of dust off the leg of the cream linen suit he was wearing. A suit he'd recently bought and was well pleased with.

'Laura has just left school actually,' he stated.

'Really?'

'She won't be going to work though, our father won't allow it.' Sandy smiled ruefully. 'He thinks it would reflect badly on him if she did. That it would appear he couldn't support her.'

'You father is rich then?'

'He's a doctor, Harald, and a very ordinary one at that. Do you know the word snob?'

Harald nodded.

'That describes him to a T. A snob who's got old-fashioned ideas. I hate to admit it, but he's not someone I admire, or respect, all that much.' He paused, then added, 'Sad to say that about your own father, but it's true.'

'What about your mother?'

'A lovely woman. You couldn't ask for better.'

'And Laura?'

'She's smashing, and rapidly developing into something of a looker. She was quite plain when younger, but that's changing as she gets older. We write to each other every week.'

Harald studied Sandy shrewdly. 'You're very fond of her, aren't you?'

'Very. I miss her a lot.'

'She sounds nice.'

'She is, believe me. At least I think so.'

Sandy lapsed into a brooding silence, and when he spoke again he changed the subject.

Laura laid aside the book she was reading, and sighed. She was bored witless.

She could go for a walk, she thought. But she was fed up with that as well. If only she could get a job, but there was fat chance of that. Pa would go through the roof if she even dared suggest it.

Was this to be her life until she met someone and

settled down? It seemed like it. Dreary days, months, years stretching endlessly ahead.

She was due to go to a summer garden party that coming weekend, which was at least something to look forward to, the party being given by friends of her parents. And then there was a dance to celebrate the eighteenth birthday of an old schoolfriend the weekend after that, which should be fun. And who knows who she might meet there? So life wasn't all doom and gloom.

She was reaching again for her book when the idea came to her, causing her to stop in mid-stretch to think about it.

'Of course I remember you, Miss McLean.' Mrs Mitchell smiled. 'What can I do for you? But please, have a seat first.'

Laura sat on the wooden chair in front of Mrs Mitchell's desk. 'Do you take on volunteers to help you here?' she asked.

Mrs Mitchell studied Laura. 'Yes we do,' she replied slowly. 'Who do you have in mind?'

'Me.'

'I see,' Mrs Mitchell murmured, looking at Laura in a new light.

'When I say volunteer I mean just that. I wouldn't expect to be paid. That's not necessary.'

'How old are you, Miss McLean?'

Laura told her.

'Just left school?'

'That's right.'

'May I ask which one?'

'Laurel Bank.'

Mrs Mitchell nodded approval. 'An excellent school.' She paused for a few moments, then said, 'Perhaps you'd like to tell me something about yourself. Your background, that sort of thing.'

Mrs Mitchell listened intently as Laura spoke, making the occasional note on a pad in front of her.

'You are rather young for this type of work,' she stated after Laura had finished. 'Some of it might shock you. And we do deal with rather rough types. Salt of the earth mainly, but rough nonetheless. Could you cope with that?'

'I believe so.'

'Hmmh,' Mrs Mitchell murmured. 'You do appreciate what it is we do here? Contraception, and sexual advice, for both men and women.'

'I have read some of your literature in the past,' Laura told her. 'And found it most informative.'

'You do agree with contraception for women, I presume?'

'I do indeed, and think it a great pity there aren't more clinics like yours.'

'Given time.' Mrs Mitchell smiled. 'Given time. We're a relatively new organisation but, despite public condemnation, from men of course, not women, we're rapidly expanding.'

'That's good,' Laura said, matching Mrs Mitchell's smile.

'Would it bother you handling contraceptive devices such as the "cap"?'

Laura had already considered that. 'I don't think so.'

'Or being present on the instruction of the fitting of such caps?'

That Laura hadn't thought about. 'To be honest, I

simply don't know,' she answered truthfully. 'But I'm sure I'd soon get used to it.'

'How about handing out sheaths to men?'

Laura swallowed hard.

'Would you find that embarrassing? You see, if we're embarrassed that makes it even more difficult for the man. Embarrass him and he might never come back again.'

'I can understand that.'

'So, would you be embarrassed?'

Laura dropped her gaze. What had started off promisingly had suddenly begun to hit difficulties.

'Well, Miss McLean?'

'Let me remind you my father's a doctor so I'm used to medical matters,' she replied, prevaricating slightly. 'I'd just have to accept, and deal with the situation, that's all.'

They were short handed, Mrs Mitchell mused. And Laura did show promise, no doubt about it. She made her decision.

'How about part-time to begin with? And then we'll see how you go from there.'

'Oh yes, please,' Laura enthused.

'Fine. Now when can you start?'

'Whenever you like.'

'Monday? Nine o'clock sharp?'

'I'll be here.'

Mrs Mitchell came to her feet and Laura did the same. 'I'll see you then, Miss McLean.'

When she was outside on the street Laura heaved a great sigh of relief. She'd got a job. Hooray!

The question remaining was, what did she tell Harriet? The truth, or a lie? Or a combination of both?

* * *

'Charity work!' Harriet exclaimed, raising an eyebrow in surprise.

'That's right, Ma. Part-time.'

The reason Laura was telling Harriet was because sooner or later her mother was going to ask where she kept disappearing off to. Harriet was home a great deal and bound to notice. Her father, on the other hand, was out a lot and needn't know as he wouldn't be aware of her disappearing act.

'What sort of charity work?'

'With orphaned children,' Laura lied smoothly. 'I shall be playing with them, reading them stories, that sort of thing. I need something to occupy my mind, Ma, and this would suit me down to the ground. It's also unpaid, voluntary, so it can't be classed as going out to work. Can it?'

'I suppose not,' Harriet mused, quite taken aback by this news.

'So is that all right with you, then?'

Harriet frowned. 'I suppose so. I can't think of any reason against it.'

'I start Monday.'

'So soon?'

'No time like the present, is there? And I am getting terribly bored having nothing to do all day long. This will give me an interest, and it will be in a worthwhile cause.'

Harriet certainly couldn't disagree with the latter. And in truth, it would benefit her as well, Laura having been getting under her feet since finishing school. Nice as it was having her around, it was somewhat restricting at times. 'Then I wish you luck,' she declared. 'And good for you in coming up with the idea.'

This was the tricky part, Laura thought apprehensively. 'I was wondering if we could keep it from Pa? You know what an old stick-in-the-mud he is, he might just object. I can't imagine why he should, but you never know. And this is something I really would like to do. It should be fun apart from anything else.'

Laura was right, Harriet decided. Mathew could be difficult when there was no need for him to be, as she'd found out to her cost on many an occasion.

'It won't be a lie,' Laura pointed out. 'We'll simply omit to tell him, that's all.'

'I can't say I take that view, there are many ways of telling a lie, and witholding information is arguably one of them. But, nonetheless, that's what we'll do. It'll make things easier that way.'

Relief surged through Laura. Going to Harriet she kissed her on the cheek. 'Thanks, Ma. You're a pal.'

Harriet looked Laura straight in the face, and winked. 'Besides, it's only a little lie and we women often have to tell them to get what we want, or for a man's own good.'

Laura laughed, thinking it wonderful her mother had said that.

Laura slipped the letter back into its envelope and laid that beside her breakfast plate.

'Anything interesting?' Harriet asked.

'It's from Morag. She's settled in a home for unmarried mothers and will be staying till the baby's born, after which it's to be offered up for adoption.'

'Is she happy there?'

'Apparently. She says everyone's really nice.'

'See, I told you she'd be all right!' Mathew declared rather pompously.

Harriet shot him a withering look which, perhaps for the best, he didn't catch.

'How would you like to come to a buffet lunch with me at the Canadian Embassy?' Harald asked Sandy.

'The Canadian Embassy?'

'That's what I said.'

It always amazed Sandy how Harald managed to get the invitations to posh events that he did. Contacts and friends, was what Harald had replied when he'd once asked him.

'When?'

'Tomorrow.'

Sandy thought about that. 'Any special reason why I should go?'

'It's high time you met people, the sort who might want to commission you. Look on it as business as well as pleasure.'

'Is this you doing your job as my agent?' Sandy teased.

'Indeed it is. I'm hoping you'll come with me so I can introduce you to lots of interesting people. And some of them can be most interesting, believe me.'

Sandy smiled. 'You wouldn't happen to be talking about women, would you?'

The familiar amused glint appeared in the Icelander's eyes. 'It's how I make my living, don't forget. I have a steady turnover of clients, so I have to keep replacing them. And events like this are prime situations in which to do so.'

Harald paused, his expression becoming thoughtful. 'Besides, I also have an ulterior motive for asking you.'

'Oh?'

'You're beginning to worry me.'

Sandy, who was painting, began to mix together two colours on his palette to come up with the shade he wanted. 'Why's that?'

'Apart from Lady Barbara you've never had a girl-friend since coming here. That isn't healthy.'

'Lady Barbara was hardly a girlfriend!' Sandy protested. 'Not in the proper sense of the word anyway.'

'Is there a reason for this lack in your life?'

Sandy shrugged. 'I simply haven't met anyone special. That's all there is to it, I suppose.'

'Fussy, eh?' Harald mocked.

'A lot more than some I could name.'

Harald laughed. 'Touché!'

Sandy laid his palette down, and yawned. He'd been at it for hours and needed a break. In a moment he'd suggest he and Harald go out for coffee and a bite to eat.

'No one at all has appealed?' Harald queried.

'No one.'

'And you don't feel the need to . . . you know?'

'The society I was brought up in teaches restraint, Harald. We're not as free and easy as you.'

'How very sad,' Harald commented drily. 'And so unnecessary, especially here in Paris. So will you come?'

'For business or the ladies?'

'Both. Why not?'

Why not indeed, Sandy thought. 'All right. But don't start trying to push anyone onto me. Got that?'

'Got it,' Harald nodded, tongue firmly in cheek.

In the event Sandy found a minor Belgian diplomat keen to have his portrait done. Arrangements were made for the man to come round and inspect his work.

And he left as he arrived, with Harald. Just the pair of them.

This was it, Laura thought, her first day at the clinic. She was both excited and apprehensive.

Taking a deep breath she went inside.

Chapter 26

'I want a word with you, young lady,' Mathew declared sharply, his face dark with anger, having just returned from the surgery.

Oh oh! Laura thought, wondering what this was all about. Whatever, it was clear he was cross with her.

'Is something wrong, dear?' Harriet inquired politely, coming up to them.

'I should say so,' he snapped in reply. 'I think it best you also attend.' And with that he swung on his heel and strode into the sitting room.

Harriet and Laura exchanged glances, Laura shrugging when Harriet raised an enquiring eyebrow.

Mathew made for the fireplace to stand with his back to it, hands clasped behind him.

'Shall I sit or stand?' Laura asked in a small, rather frightened, voice. This was obviously serious.

'I think you'd better stand,' he answered gruffly, after which he cleared his throat.

'I learnt some interesting information from a patient earlier today,' he stated, glaring at Laura. He paused to take a deep breath before going on. 'The woman in question was full of praise for you, saying what wonderful advice you'd given her and how easy you were to deal with in what, for her, was a rather embarrassing situation.'

Laura's heart sank. The cat was out of the proverbial bag. Her father knew about the Clinic and her work there. It took all her willpower to continue staring him straight in the eye. 'I see,' she mumbled.

'I should imagine you do!' he barked.

'Will someone please explain to me what we're talking about here?' Harriet pleaded.

Mathew snorted. 'It would seem our daughter has been giving the use of her time and services to . . .' He struggled to actually articulate what came next. 'The Marie Stopes Clinic. What do you make of that?'

Harriet shook her head, never having heard of the Clinic. 'Is it part of your charity work, Laura?' she queried.

Laura nodded.

'So what's wrong with her doing charity work, Mathew? Surely you can't object to that? Admirable in my opinion.'

Mathew's eyes bulged. 'The Marie Stopes Clinic deals for the most part in matters of contraception. Mainly female contraception, I may add.'

Harriet caught her breath, shooting Laura an accusatory glance for having lied to her. 'Dear me,' she murmured.

He swung his attention back to Laura. 'How on earth

could you do such a thing knowing my feelings on the matter? That I am totally against contraception of any kind. That I consider it obscene, blasphemous even.'

Laura quailed under the lash of his tongue, aware that tears weren't very far away.

'As for women to even discuss these things, far less practise them, is beyond me. I believe you give advice to men as well, isn't that so?'

Laura nodded.

'Speak up, girl! Admit your guilt.'

'Yes, Pa,' she replied quietly, wishing the floor would open up and swallow her. How embarrassing to be having this discussion, one-sided as it was so far, with her parents.

'Whatever possessed you, Laura?' Harriet demanded, shocked at this revelation.

Laura didn't reply.

'Answer your mother, girl! Don't add impertinence to your other sins.'

'I thought I was doing some good,' Laura whispered.

'Good!' Mathew threw back his head and laughed. 'What do you know about good, particularly in this connection, at your age? All you've succeeded in doing is humiliating me. Do you hear? Humiliate me.'

'Not every doctor thinks as you do, Pa,' Laura replied, finding the courage to do so. 'Many are in favour of what Marie Stopes is trying to achieve.'

Mathew knew that to be correct. 'Well, I'm not one of them!'

'And you're not a mother with too many children and not enough money to feed and clothe them because your husband is either out of work or drinks his pay packet every week,' Laura retorted firmly. 'Men who continually demand their conjugal rights without any thought to the possible consequence. Those are the sort of women we're trying to help and protect.'

If Harriet had been shocked before she was even more so now at the mention of conjugal rights coming from her daughter's lips.

'Self-control, that's what these people need. A little bit of self-control,' Mathew declared somewhat pompously.

'But many men simply haven't got that,' Laura riposted quickly. 'They're ill-educated, coming from backgrounds where their fathers did what they are now doing. They live for the day, not the next. That's all they know. They certainly know nothing about self-constraint. And if their wives try to object it's a beating more often than not followed by the men forcing themselves upon them. It's a whole cycle that has to be changed, starting with contraceptive education.'

'By God!' Mathew exploded. 'You sound like a socialist. Or worse still, some kind of revolutionary.'

'I'm neither of those things, Pa.'

'I'm glad to hear it!'

Harriet didn't know what to make of all this, she needed more information. But not now. This was hardly the time, not with Mathew in his present mood.

'You will cease working there forthwith,' Mathew informed Laura in an imperious voice. 'I absolutely forbid you to step over the doorway of that iniquitous place ever again.'

'But, Pa . . .'

'No buts about it,' he interjected. 'I shall have no daughter of mine involved in such an organisation. Do you hear me?'

Tears were back threatening her again. Dumbly she nodded.

'Would you like a glass of whisky, dear?' Harriet asked Mathew sweetly in an attempt to defuse the situation. 'Just the thing to calm you down.'

'Please.'

She hurried to pour him one.

'I can't tell you how deeply wounded I am that you went behind my back,' Mathew declared to Laura. 'Especially about such a contentious issue. Surely you were aware of my stance on this?'

Laura swallowed hard, wishing she'd been offered whisky. She could certainly have used a drop.

'Well?'

'Yes, Pa.'

'And still you did what you did. That was absolutely disgraceful, Laura, and utterly unforgivable. And for me to be informed of what you were doing by one of my own patients!' He shook his head, incensed.

'There you are, Mathew,' Harriet said, thrusting a glass into his hand. 'Have some of that.'

He had a large swallow, instantly followed by another. He was beside himself with anger.

'Better?' Harriet smiled hopefully.

He grunted in the affirmative.

A hint of irritation flashed across Harriet's face, she hated it when he grunted like that instead of actually speaking.

Laura's instinct was to get out of there as soon as possible and now that her father had fallen quiet seemed like an excellent opportunity. But something compelled her to stay.

Mathew finished off his whisky and thrust the glass

at Harriet. 'I'll have another,' he stated. That was most unlike him, as he was fairly abstemious with alcohol. It was also unlike him to drink so quickly.

'Yes, dear.' Harriet scuttled off to obey.

'Don't you think you might just be wrong in your attitude to contraception,' Laura found herself saying.

'Wrong? Don't be ridiculous,' he replied viciously. 'It's well known in the medical profession that contraception leads to a mania in women often resulting in suicide. As for men using . . .' He couldn't bring himself to use the word 'sheath' in front of his wife and daughter. 'It's documented fact that it causes mental decay, loss of memory, again mania and other conditions which lead to suicide. Well known.'

What claptrap, Laura thought. What absolute claptrap. She'd been at the Clinic long enough to know contraception led to no such thing. Her father was talking as if it was the Middle Ages and not the twentieth century.

'So you don't think it's a good idea for families to be limited then?' she persisted.

'Nature already takes care of that,' he replied.

'By so many children dying, you mean?'

Mathew shrugged.

'In the meantime the women carrying those babies have had to go through labour and giving birth to them often suffering terrible physical damage and repercussions as a result,' Laura went on.

'It's Nature's way.'

Laura was appalled. 'By the same line of reasoning if someone contracts a disease, which you could cure, you should just let them go ahead and die, for isn't that also Nature at work?'

Mathew accepted his refilled glass from Harriet,

amazed that he was actually debating this with a chit of a lassie. A lassie who, probably for the first time in his life, he realised had a brain in her head.

'That's different,' he muttered.

'Why so?'

'It just is,' he prevaricated. 'A doctor is there to save life, not take it, which is what contraception is all about.'

'It prevents conception, Pa. It doesn't destroy it.'

'Don't bandy words with me, young lady!' he snarled. 'It's the same thing in this instance.'

'I disagree.' Laura was astounded by her new-found boldness, so unlike how she'd been when her father had first confronted her.

'Disagree all you like. You're wrong.'

'Am I, Pa? And even if I am, surely it must be a good thing to relieve the suffering of those already alive, in this case the mothers, than increase that suffering, both physically and mentally, of women who simply can't cope any more. Who've long since been at the end of their tether? Women whose lives have been reduced to an absolute misery thanks to not having any control over their own bodies?'

'My, my, haven't you suddenly become the expert on medical matters,' Mathew sneered. 'And you hardly more than a child yourself.'

'That's unfair, Pa. My age has nothing to do with what I'm saying.'

'Hasn't it now?'

'No, it hasn't.'

Harriet, despite her anxiety, was fascinated by the conversation, never having really considered the subject before. If anything, she agreed with Laura, but wouldn't have dreamt of admitting it. At least not to Mathew.

'I've had enough of this nonsense,' Mathew declared. 'I think you should go to your room and remain there, young lady.'

Laura's gaze flew to the clock on top of the mantelpiece. 'At this hour?'

'At this hour,' Mathew confirmed.

'Pa, I'm seventeen. Not seven.'

He shrugged. 'That's got nothing to do with it. While you're in my house you'll obey my rules which you've broken by going behind my back and lying by omission. Can you deny that?'

Laura couldn't.

'Now get out of my sight.'

'Mathew?' Harriet pleaded. 'You are being just a teensy bit unfair.'

'You be quiet, Harriet. She'll do as I say and that's that.'

Without uttering a further word, a defiant Laura swept from the room.

Laura looked up when the door opened and Harriet slipped quietly into her bedroom.

'I've brought you a wee something to eat,' Harriet winked. 'Your father goes too far at times. Not that he didn't have provocation, mind.'

'Thanks, Ma. I am a bit peckish, to say the least.'

Harriet laid the plate of sandwiches beside Laura and joined her in sitting on the bed.

'Are you angry with me as well?' Laura asked, smiling in gratitude for the food.

'Well, I can't say I'm happy that you lied to me. The truth would have been better. It always is.'

'Then I'm sorry. I wanted so badly to do that job

and didn't think you'd allow me. I knew Pa certainly wouldn't.'

Harriet sighed. 'A man with very definite and set ideas, your father. Not all of which are right, I have to admit.'

'No,' Laura agreed.

Harriet eyed her daughter speculatively. 'Well, one thing's for certain.'

'What's that?'

'The little chat I was going to have with you before your wedding day, whenever that might be, won't be required now. I wouldn't be at all surprised, after listening to you downstairs, if you didn't know more about . . . well, you know what, than I do.'

'Physical relationships?' Laura gently teased.

'Exactly.'

Laura considered that, eventually deciding she probably did. Harriet was a woman of her time and class after all, of a society in which such things were hardly ever mentioned, far less discussed at length.

'You must have been taken aback?'

Harriet gave a low laugh. 'I most certainly was. Shocked more like. As was your father.'

'He is wrong you know, Ma,' Laura said earnestly. 'His ideas are old fashioned and well out of date. There again, he's a man and doesn't have to suffer the consequences as women do.'

Harriet was puzzled. 'How did you get involved with this clinic in the first place. That's what's intriguing me.'

Laura, feeling quite relaxed with her mother who was now treating her like another adult, started at the beginning with the literature Madeleine had originally come up with, and how she'd thought of the Marie

Stopes Clinic when poor Morag had got herself pregnant. Harriet listened attentively.

How little you knew of your own children, Harriet mused while Laura spoke. What secrets they had which you never even suspected.

'And you enjoy working at this clinic?' she asked eventually.

'Oh yes, Ma, I feel that what I'm doing is so useful.'

'You don't find it . . . well, embarrassing?'

'I did to begin with. Natural I suppose. But you soon get used to it. It's certainly rewarding work; so many of the women who come to see us are grateful beyond belief. I don't think I'm going too far in saying in many cases we completely alter their lives for them.'

'I see,' Harriet murmured.

'Would you like to hear some of the details?'

Harriet wasn't at all sure about that. 'All right,' she reluctantly agreed. Her eyes opened wide when Laura blithely talked about Dutch caps, pessaries, and other devices used in contraception.

'Dear me,' she muttered. 'And you actually show them how to fit these things?'

Laura nodded.

Harriet simply couldn't imagine letting anyone be so intimate with her. It made her go cold just to think about it.

'We have quite a laugh at times, Ma,' Laura went on.

'How so?'

'Some of the misconceptions these people have is beyond belief, which is why they desperately need educating in that department. We had a woman in last week who wanted to know if we could tell her why she wasn't getting pregnant despite persistently trying. Well, and this is where the ignorance comes in, we sat her down and quizzed her about how she and her husband went about having relations. The answer was an eye opener.'

Despite herself Harriet was intrigued. 'And?'

'The man had been rubbing his, you know, in her belly button for the six years they'd been married, which is how they thought babies were made. We soon put her right.'

Harriet felt herself redden.

'Isn't that hysterical?'

Harriet didn't know what to reply, so said nothing. In her heart of hearts she did think it funny. Casting her mind back, however, how little had she known when she'd married Mathew? It had been up to him to explain to her what was what.

'Ma?'

Harriet glanced away and nodded.

Laura wondered if she'd gone too far in telling her mother that story, Harriet was her *mother* after all. 'I'm going to miss the Clinic dreadfully,' she said. 'If Pa had his way I'd be sitting at home all day knitting and sewing, waiting for Prince Charming to happen along. That would be excruciatingly boring.'

'It's been my lot in life,' Harriet reminded her gently.

'But at least you have the house to oversee and run. That keeps you reasonably busy.'

True, Harriet reflected. 'Then perhaps you'd care to help me in that?' she smiled wryly. 'It would mean less knitting and sewing.'

'I suppose I'll have to,' Laura sighed bitterly. If only that damned patient of her father's had kept her big mouth shut it might never have come to this.

'I must say I was impressed by how you stood up

to your father. That took courage. He's a formidable person to cross.'

'Not after I come into my inheritance. I shall be moving out then, just as Sandy has done.'

'Oh, Laura,' Harriet whispered. 'Would you really?'

'A small house somewhere.' Then teasing, 'Possibly in Kelvinside which would really upset Pa.'

Harriet laughed. 'It undoubtedly would. He'd be pea green with jealousy.'

'Serve him right,' Laura declared, the bitterness back in her voice. 'I'll be free there, to do as I choose and not what he dictates. If I'm still unmarried I shall return to the Clinic, if they'll have me. If for no other reason I'd do it out of sheer spite.'

It was clear to Harriet how much this job meant to Laura, and what a blow it was to be forced to give it up. Was it possible she could do something about that? As she thought about it the germ of an idea crept into her mind.

Harriet came to her feet. 'I'd better get back downstairs, your father will be wondering where I am.'

'Thanks for the sandwiches, Ma. I appreciate you bringing them.'

'As I said, your father can go too far at times. And let's just leave it at that.'

At the door she paused. 'I enjoyed our little chat, Laura. It was most informative.'

'I enjoyed it too, Ma.'

'We must talk more often.'

'I'd like that.'

'So would I.'

Chat as grown-ups, Laura reflected after Harriet had gone. She felt as if she'd reached a milestone in her life. She'd been accepted, by her mother at least, as an adult.

It gave her a lovely warm glow inside.

Harriet was sitting brushing her hair, preparing to go to bed, while Mathew was struggling into his pyjamas. It was four days since his confrontation with Laura, time enough, Harriet had decided, for him to calm down.

'You know what's wrong with Laura, don't you?' Harriet said casually.

'What?' asked Mathew, tying the cord of his bottoms.

'She's so much like you. A chip off the old block, so to speak.'

Mathew frowned. 'Do you really think so?'

'Oh yes, without a doubt. That's what this business with the Clinic is really all about.'

His frown became puzzled. 'I don't follow?'

'Deep down she really wants to be a doctor the same as you. I would have thought that was obvious.'

'I don't hold with female doctors,' Mathew replied tersely. 'Nurses are one thing, doctors quite another. A ridiculous idea. They're simply not cut out for it.'

'I quite agree, dear,' Harriet lied smoothly. 'Not cut out for it at all. Don't have the authority for one thing, and then all their own female business would be bound to get in the way. Stands to reason when you think about it. But nonetheless, deep down, I'm certain that's what Laura would like to be. Probably inspired by your example.'

He brightened. 'That is possible I suppose.'

Vanity, vanity, Harriet smiled to herself.

'She's never said anything?'

'Well, she wouldn't knowing you'd be completely against it. As indeed would I.'

Mathew thought about that. 'So how do you know that's what she'd like to be. Has she said something to you?'

'Not directly,' Harriet replied. 'But there have been hints over the years, insinuations.'

'Well, well,' Mathew murmured, secretly pleased.

'She is your child after all, darling, half of her is you. And that half obviously includes the medical thing. I think you should be flattered.'

'Do you?'

'Oh yes. I mean, I can appreciate why you were angry the other night. She did go behind your back. That was unforgivable and not at all how we brought her up.'

He nodded. 'Quite so.'

'Not at all,' Harriet repeated.

'I'll be humiliated amongst my colleagues if it ever got out she worked at the Marie Stopes Clinic,' Mathew declared. 'A laughing stock.'

'I don't suppose it will, Mathew. She's only been there a relatively short while after all. And you did put your foot down once you found out.'

'Instantly.'

'That's one of the things I like about you, darling, and always have. You're such a manly man, so decisive.'

He visibly swelled to hear that. 'I don't stand for any nonsense.'

'No you don't, dear. A most admirable quality. A very . . . virile one.'

Mathew was now positively beaming at this praise.

'On the other hand, in a way it's a pity you feel the way you do about this clinic, which I'm sure can't be all that bad.' This was getting dangerous, she warned herself, be careful.

Mathew was back to frowning. 'Of course it's all bad. And un-Christian, don't forget. Man shan't cast his seed upon the ground. Remember?'

'Of course I do. I know my bible, as you're well aware. But I would have thought that was more of a Catholic ethic than a Protestant one.'

'Catholic?' he repeated. He loathed Catholics.

'Indeed. They're very strict and harsh, unlike our more enlightened Protestant religion.'

'Hmmh,' he grunted, which so irritated Harriet.

'Don't you agree?'

He was forced to admit that he did.

'Catholics certainly condemn contraception, and presumably always will.'

He eyed her beadily. 'Are you saying Protestants don't?'

'They're more liberal in their attitude, don't you think? Anyway, does it really matter if it became common knowledge that Laura worked at the clinic? It's not as if you condoned it. People would understand, surely?'

'But she lives under my roof, Harriet, and while she does that she obeys my rules.'

'Of course, of course. Though it is sad to think she won't be living under your roof for too much longer.'

That rocked him. 'What are you talking about?'

'She informed me only the other day that she intends moving out, if she isn't already married that is, as soon as she comes into her inheritance. Mentioned something about buying a house in Kelvinside.'

'Kelvin . . . !' he spluttered.

'A smallish one where she'll live by herself. Seemed quite set on the idea. She also mentioned she'd rejoin the clinic once she's settled in.'

Mathew was appalled. 'But what will people think? A single girl leaving her parents to set up on her own, and in the same city. It just isn't done.'

'It won't reflect too well on us, I suppose,' Harriet sighed.

'You mean *me*!'

Harriet refrained from answering that.

'Dear God!' Mathew whispered. 'She's intent on humiliating me.'

'Strong minded, Mathew, same as yourself. It's obvious where she gets it from.'

'And Kelvinside too.' That prospect filled him with envy.

'If only she wasn't coming into all that money, but she is. It'll make her quite independent.'

Mathew's mind was whirling. This was awful. Worse, a catastrophe.

'Of course Sandy leaving was totally different,' Harriet went on. 'Especially as he's gone to Paris to become a painter. But what Laura plans is something different entirely. Bound to cause speculation and idle chit-chat.'

Mathew positively cringed.

'If things had been different, who knows? Perhaps Laura would have bought a house for all of us in Kelvinside? That might have been a possibility. But not now I'm afraid. Pity.'

'And all because of me forbidding her to work at the Clinic?'

'But you were right about that, darling, completely. Although . . .'

He swallowed hard. 'Although what?'

'If you had allowed her I imagine you'd be seen as something of a progressive, at the vanguard of your profession. A lot of people would admire you for that. Especially the ladies, many of whom I would think sympathise with the contraceptive issue. You'd be quite a hero to them.'

'A hero?'

'Without a doubt. I can just hear them talking amongst themselves about that dashing Dr McLean, the one with such forward-thinking ideas. A man with his own beliefs who's not afraid to stand up and be counted. Oh, you'd be a hero with the ladies all right. Someone of standing and importance, someone to be admired and looked up to.'

Enough for now, Harriet told herself. The bait had been well and truly laid. It was only a matter of time before she reeled in the fish.

She pretended to yawn. 'But enough chatter for one night, darling. I simply must get some sleep.'

Mathew, mind still whirling, knew it would now be ages before he managed to sleep on account of their conversation.

A progressive! A hero! Someone of standing and importance! He liked the sound of that.

Oh yes, very much so.

Chapter 27

'Laura, isn't it?'

She snapped out of her reverie and turned to find a tall, somewhat gangly young man smiling at her whose face was vaguely familiar. 'Yes, that's right.'

He took in her puzzled expression. 'I'm Craig Abercrombie, Madeleine's cousin. We spoke briefly at the funeral.'

She remembered him now. 'Of course. How are you?'

'Fine.' He looked down at Madeleine's grave, and shook his head in sadness. 'What a shame. What a waste,' he stated quietly.

Laura sighed. 'Yes,' she agreed.

'I see you brought fresh flowers.' She had neatly arranged these in a pot placed there for that purpose.

'I do every time I come.'

He shrugged. 'I never thought. I should have done.'

Laura didn't comment on that. 'Were the pair of you close?'

'Not particularly. But I was fond of her. She was always a good laugh.'

Laura briefly closed her eyes, conjuring up an image of Madeleine. 'We were best friends, you know. Went all through school together. I miss her so much.'

Craig, whom Laura judged to be about twenty-six or so, extended a hand. 'It's nice to see you again.'

They shook. 'And you.'

He produced a packet of cigarettes. 'Do you think it would be irreverent if I lit up?'

'Not in the least.'

He offered the packet. 'Do you?'

Laura shook her head.

A match flared, and then he inhaled deeply. 'That's better.'

Not exactly handsome, Laura reflected. Though hardly ugly. Sort of . . . ordinary, yes that was it, ordinary. Certainly personable enough.

'I visit every few months or so,' Laura declared, but didn't mention that that was largely due to the guilt she still felt. 'How about you?'

'This is only my second time. I don't know why but I've been thinking about Madeleine all week, so decided to come today.' He glanced skywards. 'Though perhaps that was a mistake as it looks like rain.'

Laura also glanced skywards, noting the black clouds rolling in their direction. 'I believe you're right.'

He shivered. 'And it's got colder as well.'

Laura wondered how tall he was. Six foot one, two? Something like that. Tall for a Glaswegian. They tended to be on the short side.

'Don't you find cemeteries spooky places?' he asked.

'Not really. Though I wouldn't like to be in one when it's dark.'

Craig laughed. 'Me neither. If I so much as heard a twig break I'd probably jump right out of my skin.'

'You're not afraid of ghosts, are you?' Laura teased.

'To be honest, I don't know. There are accounts of them all through history of course, right back to ancient times. So perhaps there is something in it.'

'Oh dear!' Laura exclaimed when there was a sudden jagged lightning flash, followed almost instantly by a peal of thunder. 'Here it comes.'

Craig flicked the remains of his cigarette away. 'Tell you what, there's a little tea shop not far from here that sells the most wonderful scones and home-made jam. Shall we take shelter from the rain there? It's bound to be open.'

Laura couldn't see why not. It was harmless enough after all. And it wasn't as if she was accepting an invitation from an absolute stranger; Craig was Madeleine's cousin. 'That's a good idea.'

'Then shall we?'

Laura paused for a moment to have one last look at the grave, then turned away. 'I hope we get there before we're drenched.'

In the event, they were just entering the tea shop when the heavens opened and rain began bucketing down.

Laura was dog tired. It had been an even busier day than usual at the Clinic where she was now working a full five days a week. She still had no idea what had caused her father to change his mind on that subject,

426

but, amazingly, he had. And with reasonable good grace too! Wonders would never cease, she told herself as she hurried on her way home.

Harriet entered the room where Laura was reading a book. It was nighttime and Mathew was out on a call. 'The telephone's for you,' she announced.

'For me!' That was a surprise. No one ever rang her, not even the Clinic.

'A man.'

Laura digested that. 'Did he give a name?'

'Craig Abercrombie. He said he was Madeleine's cousin.'

Laura coloured slightly. 'Oh yes, I met him at the cemetery when I visited Madeleine's grave last weekend.'

'You never mentioned.'

'I didn't consider it important.'

Laura went out into the hall where she picked up the receiver. 'Hello, Laura speaking.'

'Laura, it's Craig. How are you?'

'Fine. And yourself?'

'Fine also.'

A few seconds ticked by during which Laura wondered what this was all about.

'There's a dinner dance at the Palm Court Hotel next Saturday,' Craig declared eventually. 'Do you know the place? It's at Charing Cross.'

'I know it.' Well, she'd passed it often enough, but had never been inside. It was considered to be 'posh'.

'I thought, if you were free, you might like to go with me? The food is excellent, I'm told.'

He was asking her out!

'Laura?'

'I'm still here.'

He didn't find her tone at all encouraging. 'Perhaps you're busy then. No matter.'

'I'm not busy, Craig,' she replied hesitantly. 'I just, eh . . . hadn't been expecting this, that's all.'

'If you like I could pick you up at seven?'

She made a decision. There was no reason why she shouldn't go. It might even be fun! 'I'll be ready, Craig.'

'That's wonderful,' he enthused.

'Till then.'

'I'm looking forward to it enormously.'

He certainly seemed keen, she thought as she cradled the receiver. Now what should she wear?

Harriet eyed Laura speculatively when she re-entered the room, dying to know what the telephone call had been about.

'I've been asked to go to a dinner dance at the Palm Court Hotel on Saturday night and have accepted,' Laura declared casually as if this sort of invitation was an everyday occurrence.

'Have you indeed?'

'Is that all right?'

'I suppose so,' Harriet mused. 'But it might have been polite to ask your father's permission first.'

'I've turned eighteen now, Ma. Surely I'm past having to ask permission?'

'Your father might see things differently,' Harriet answered truthfully. 'However, as you've already said yes then I suppose that's that.'

Laura slumped back into the chair she'd recently vacated, mentally going through her wardrobe.

'So tell me about this Craig?' Harriet inquired, affecting as casual a tone as Laura had adopted.

'As you know, he's Madeleine's cousin.'

'And?'

'He's a schoolteacher. History is his main subject.'

'Which school is that?'

Laura named it. 'He went to university here in Glasgow before taking up the job.'

'I see,' Harriet murmured. 'And did you learn all this at the cemetery?'

Laura blushed, having detected the faint sarcasm in her mother's voice. 'It started to rain while we were there so Craig suggested we take refuge in a tea shop, which we did. We had quite a chat while there.'

'Is he nice?'

Laura regarded Harriet scornfully. 'I wouldn't have agreed to go out with him if he wasn't.'

Harriet was well aware of how discomfited Laura was by this turn of events. Embarrassed you could say. 'Well, I'm sure you'll enjoy yourself. I hear the Palm Court is a lovely hotel, though I've never been there myself. Far too expensive for your father's pocket.'

Laura thought about that, and wondered how a schoolteacher could afford to take her there? Perhaps the family had money.

'What does he took like?' Again the question was asked casually.

'Tall, gangly, easy going. Very pleasant really. At least I thought so.'

The start of a romance? Harriet wondered. Time would tell. Before she could inquire any further Laura returned to reading her book. Harriet got the message; the subject was closed unless she pushed it.

She decided not to. For the moment anyway.

* * *

'There, that's done,' Craig declared as the waiter left them with their order.

Laura gazed about her. She hadn't known what to expect, but not the rather faded glory that comprised the décor and furnishings. She doubted anything had been done to the dining room since the turn of the century. Maybe even further back than that.

Craig pulled out his cigarettes. 'Do you mind?'

'Not at all.'

She watched him light up, horribly aware of how nervous she was, and desperately hoping the dress she'd chosen — a simple knee-length French crepe garment with a V-neck and pinched waist — met with his approval. Some of the other dresses on view were quite stunning by comparison. She'd wanted to go into town that morning and buy something new but her father had vetoed the idea, saying there was no need and what she already possessed was more than adequate. Even Harriet hadn't been able to make him change his mind.

'So tell me more about yourself?' Craig asked. 'You have a brother, I seem to remember.'

'Yes, Sandy. He lives in Paris nowadays where he's an artist.'

'An artist! A proper painter-type artist?'

Laura laughed at his expression of incredulity. 'That's right.'

'Does he make a living at it?'

'I believe so.'

'Then good for him. Though that sort of life wouldn't suit me at all.'

'Why, because you're not artistic?'

'No, because I'd find it far too precarious. I prefer

430

a job that's nice and secure where your pay packet is guaranteed. That's the sort of chap I am.'

For some reason that disappointed Laura. 'You're not a risk-taker then?'

'Only if I absolutely have to. I prefer to sleep soundly in my bed at nights rather than lie awake worrying. Always been like that and no doubt always will.'

'Sandy is just the opposite. I admire him for that. I think what he's done, and is doing, is quite wonderful. I envy him no end.'

'We are how we are I suppose,' Craig said slowly. 'I value security and knowing, more or less, what every day is going to bring.'

How deadly dull, Laura thought, but of course was far too polite to say so.

'Even what you do, at this Clinic,' Craig went on, 'seems most . . .' He struggled for an appropriate phrase. 'Unconventional to me.'

'And you prefer the conventional?' Laura teased.

'Every time.'

'So you don't approve of what I do?'

Craig screwed up his face. 'It is a rather delicate area you work in, wouldn't you agree?'

'That's not what I asked.'

He took a puff on his cigarette while regarding her thoughtfully. 'It's not my place to either approve or disapprove.'

'Very tactful,' Laura smiled.

'But if you were my wife, for example, I would have a very definite view.'

'Which would be?' As if she hadn't already guessed.

'I don't think it's a job a well-brought-up, and refined, young lady should be involved with.'

As his wife! That was jumping the gun somewhat considering this was their first time out together. 'And what would you expect of your wife, Craig?'

'Oh that's easy. I wouldn't wish her to be working for a start. She would remain at home to look after the house and family.'

'*Her* place in other words,' Laura replied. 'He completely missed the sarcasm in her tone.

'Exactly.'

Laura slowly nodded while she thought about that.

'Conventional again,' Craig mused.

Their conversation was interrupted at that point by the arrival of their first course, cream of watercress soup for Laura, prawn cocktail for Craig.

'I just adore prawn cocktail,' Craig commented, reaching for a spoon. 'I always have it if it's on the menu.'

Now there was a surprise, Laura reflected. The same thing over and over again. No sense of adventure whatsoever. But then that was precisely how he'd been describing himself.

Would he or wouldn't he kiss her? Laura wondered when they reached her door. If she was to make a guess it would be not.

'Thank you for a terrific evening,' she said.

'I can assure you, the pleasure was all mine.'

'I thoroughly enjoyed myself.'

'Did you?'

'Of course.' That was a lie, but only a white one.

'I did too. The food was delicious I thought. Most appetising.'

'Most,' she agreed.

'Can I ring you again some time?'

'If you'd like to.'

'I would, very much so.'

His eyes bored into hers. 'You're extremely pretty, you know.'

'Am I?'

'Oh, yes. You were by far the prettiest lady there tonight.'

'How flattering.'

'No, really, I mean it.'

He did too, she could see that. Well, at last a little romance was beginning to creep in. 'Thank you, kind sir.'

He paused awkwardly, then moved fractionally towards her. She'd been wrong, she thought, preparing herself to be kissed. He was going to.

'I'll ring soon. Goodnight, Laura.'

She managed a weak smile. 'Goodnight, Craig.'

He gave a little nod of his head before turning and striding away.

Not wrong, but right she reflected, reaching for the door handle. Now she would have to face the grilling from her parents that was bound to be waiting for her.

She was right about that as well.

Laura let herself into the room at the rear of the Clinic where the staff went for their breaks. She poured herself a cup of tea from the pot already made.

She'd purposely timed her break hoping to have it on her own as she wanted to read the letter from Sandy which had arrived in that morning's post. She hadn't wanted to read it at the breakfast table, preferring to save it until now when, hopefully, she'd be alone.

Once she was ensconced in one of the easy chairs that were available she eagerly tore open the envelope and extracted the four sheets of paper it contained. Good, she thought gleefully, a really long letter.

Sandy had much to tell her, making his life in Paris sound almost magical. He'd met this person, been to that party, had got uproariously drunk on another occasion with his friend Harald. But best of all he was painting well and selling. In short, life couldn't have been better.

Laura finished the letter with a heartfelt sigh, wishing she was in Paris with him, wishing she was doing all the exciting and glorious things he was.

How she envied him. But in the nicest possible way. She missed him too, dreadfully. Her own life quite simply lacked colour since Sandy had gone out of it.

One day she'd visit him, a promise she'd made herself not long after his departure and one she fully intended keeping.

One day, when she'd come into her inheritance and was no longer reliant on her father for money.

'Shall we sit?' Craig suggested, indicating a bench by the side of the path they were strolling along.

'Madeleine and I used to come to this park quite often on a Sunday afternoon,' Laura informed him once they were seated. 'It's a favourite of ours.' Then, remembering Madeleine was dead, 'Or was of hers, anyway.'

Craig reached into a coat pocket to pull out a pipe and black leather pouch.

'I didn't know you smoked one of those?' Laura said in surprise.

'Prefer it to cigarettes actually. But cigarettes are more convenient at times so I smoke both.'

Laura watched as he carefully packed the bowl with tobacco, and lit up. 'Hmmh,' he murmured, exhaling a long stream of smoke, his eyes taking on a distant, far-away look.

How much older the pipe made him appear, Laura mused. It somehow added years to him. Why, sitting there puffing contentedly away, he might have been middle-aged.

'Being a teacher, you must like children,' Laura commented, making idle conversation.

He exhaled another stream of smoke. 'Not particularly.'

That surprised her. 'No?'

Craig shrugged. 'I don't dislike them, but I don't particularly care for them either.'

'And what about your own when you have some? Which presumably you will one day.'

Craig considered that. 'I've no idea really, being honest about it. I suppose that'll be different.'

'Will you be the sort of father who gives them lots of hugs and kisses?' She was curious.

'Good God, no!' he exclaimed. 'I'd never be so demonstrative with them. Most inappropriate for a man to do that kind of thing. My own father certainly never did with me.'

Neither had hers, Laura reflected ruefully. Mathew wasn't a demonstrative man either. In fact, he could be quite cold at times. With her mother as well, she'd noticed over the years.

'So why become a schoolteacher if that's your attitude to children?' she queried.

'I love history, that's my passion, you see. I'm hoping my job will be a stepping stone to other things.'

Laura frowned. 'What other things?'

'My ambition is to be an academic with some institution or other. That would be sheer bliss.' He turned to face her. 'Scottish history is my subject, you know. I find it fascinating.'

Laura recalled only too well how boring her history lessons had been at school. A total yawn. It was beyond her how anyone could be fascinated by it.

'For example,' Craig went on, 'Robert the Bruce has always been hailed as a great Scottish leader and king. Right?'

She nodded.

'But he wasn't a true Scot. Not even a Celt. The family name was originally de Brus and they came over with William the Conqueror in 1066. His ancestors were actually Norman French.'

'Well well,' Laura commented, not knowing what else to say.

'Another misconception is that the Norman French were French, but they were no such thing. Norman is a contraction of the word Northman, or Viking. They invaded, and settled in, what is now Normandy, the land of the Northmen, but were no more French than I'm Chinese.' He laughed. 'I suppose a certain amount of interbreeding with the indigenous people went on, but you take my point?'

She nodded.

'Oh yes,' he breathed. 'Fascinating.'

'What exactly would you do as an academic?' she asked.

'Read mainly. Old books, some would be centuries old. Perhaps even write a few myself.'

'Old books,' she repeated. 'All day long?'

His eyes gleamed. 'Precisely.'

An appalled Laura was simply lost for words.

'Can I ask you something, Kitty?'

Kitty, who worked with Laura at the Clinic, and who'd originally shown her the ropes, nodded. 'Go ahead.' They were on a tea break together, alone in the room.

'What does it feel like when you kiss your chap?'

The question took Kitty slightly aback. 'I don't know really,' she mused. 'All sort of tingly inside I suppose. It's certainly nice.'

'So you *do* feel something?'

'Not half!' Kitty enthused. 'Kissing my Gavin is almost as good as eating chocolate.'

Laura laughed.

'We get quite worked up kissing sometimes. Both of us, that is. I become like putty in his arms.'

'You do?'

Kitty leant a little towards Laura and dropped her voice to a whisper. 'Don't think me a shameless hussy for admitting this, but I can't wait for us to get married so we can go the whole way. That must be fantastic with someone you love.'

Tingly inside. Almost as good as eating chocolate. Desperate to get married and go the whole way! She felt none of these things with Craig. Kissing him was like . . . well, like something was missing. Certainly not exciting. A let-down in fact, to what she'd expected.

There again, Kitty had surely hit the nail on the head by mentioning love.

Yes, she thought ruefully. Love didn't enter into it in her case. She'd kissed Craig a number of times now and hadn't tingled once. Not even the beginnings of a tingle.

It was always a . . . disappointment.

'A penny for them?' Harriet asked quietly of Laura who was lost in deep thought.

Laura brought herself out of her reverie. 'Pardon, Ma?'

'I said a penny for them.'

Laura smiled. 'I was just thinking, that's all.'

'I could see that,' Harriet replied a trifle waspishly. 'About what?'

Laura shrugged. 'This and that. Nothing important.'

A few seconds ticked by while Harriet regarded Laura shrewdly. 'How's the romance going?'

Laura coloured; how had her mother guessed she'd been thinking about herself and Craig? 'Fine,' she prevaricated.

'Are you sure? You don't seem too certain about that.'

'We're fine, Ma. I promise.'

Harriet got the message, it was none of her business. She shut up.

Laura was puzzled. More and more of late Craig was reminding her of someone, but she couldn't put her finger on who. It was most annoying.

'Would you like a cup of tea, dear?'

Laura shook her head. 'Not for me thanks.'

'There's coffee if you'd care for that.'

'No, honestly. Maybe later.'

'Then I'll wait as well.'

Laura settled herself back into her chair. Who on earth was it Craig reminded her of? The fact she was failing to make the connection was beginning to anger her.

And then, like a bolt out of the blue, she had it. Dear God! she thought, horror struck. Of course! Craig reminded her of her father. A younger version, of course, but her father nonetheless.

That scared her. Terrified her even. What was she doing going out with someone like Mathew. With all due respect, he was her father after all, but a truly awful man whom she was certain her ma, who'd naturally never said, had long since regretted marrying. She must be mad!

In those few moments Craig's fate was sealed. Laura wanted nothing more to do with him.

Telephone him now or tell him when they met up again that Friday night? Face to face, she decided. That was the decent thing to do. Nor would she change her mind, which was quite set on what had to be done.

Her father. Dear God Almighty! She was just amazed she hadn't seen the similarity before.

Chapter 28

L aura ran to the door of the Clinic and out into the street where she hurriedly looked first one way, then the other. 'Damn!' she swore softly. There was no sign of Mrs McLatchie who'd left her purse behind after a consultation.

Oh well, Laura thought, returning to her desk. The woman would no doubt be back later in the day when she realised what she'd done.

Laura had been at the Clinic for four years now, and during that time had risen to a position of some responsibility, a fact she was proud of.

A few months previously she'd had her twenty-first birthday and with her majority the right to solely manage her inheritance, which meant she could now use her money as, and when, she saw fit. A fact the still jealous Mathew hadn't liked, but had been powerless to do anything about. She'd celebrated the occasion by taking Harriet out for a very expensive lunch.

The purse, which she'd put safely in a drawer, went out of Laura's mind until almost five o'clock. Surely Mrs McLatchie had realised she'd forgotten the purse? Or could it be she thought she'd lost it elsewhere and not associated that loss with the Clinic?

Taking the purse from the drawer Laura opened it. Inside was some loose change, a folded rent book and five single pound notes, a great deal of cash for a working-class woman. She must be beside herself and desperate to get it back.

The address on the rent book was nearby, only a few streets away. Normally Laura would never have considered turning up at a client's house, as their visits were strictly confidential, but in this case surely it was right to make an exception?

Laura thought about that until it was time to go home, finally deciding she would visit the McLatchie house. The tenement she arrived at was typical of the area, soot-engrimed grey, the close stinking of old boiled vegetables, stale sweat overlaid with the faint sweet smell of human excrement. The stone stairs she mounted were worn concave in the middle from years of use.

She'd been hoping it was Mrs McLatchie herself who'd answer her knock, but it was Mr McLatchie. At least that's who she presumed he was, a surly, unshaven brute, red eyed and smelling strongly of drink.

'Aye, whit dae ye want?' he demanded suspiciously.

'I'm a friend of your wife's. Is she home?'

'Whit if she is?'

'Could I have a word with her?'

'A word? Whit kinda word?'

'I have something of hers that I wish to return.'

'Is that you, Miss McLean?' came a feeble voice, a

441

voice that seemed to be pleading for help. It was followed by a pitiful groan.

Something was wrong here, Laura just knew it. Brushing past Mr McLatchie she went into the kitchen where the sight that greeted her made her gasp.

Mrs McLatchie was sitting on the linoleum floor, with her back to a chipped and scarred tallboy. Her face was a mass of blood, one eye swollen and closed from having been punched, and there were hanks of hair lying about that had clearly been ripped from her head.

A baby, wrapped in a dirty old blanket, was crying from the inside of a wooden orange box that was its bed. Grouped round the box were three other small children, not one, Laura guessed, over the age of seven. These children were silent, eyes staring, faces white from fear.

'Dear God,' Laura breathed and hurried to Mrs McLatchie, kneeling beside her. There was no need to ask what had happened, it was blindingly obvious. Laura was dimly aware of the door to the house being snicked shut.

'He's mental. I tell you he's mental,' Mrs McLatchie whispered. 'Gone off his heid because I lost my purse with the rent money in it. He's never bashed me as bad as this before.'

'I have your purse here intact,' Laura replied, fumbling for it. 'You left it at the Clinic.'

'And just whit clinic is that?' McLatchie demanded, voice now slurred. He was swaying on the spot.

'The Marie Stopes Clinic,' Laura answered.

McLatchie let out a roar of rage. 'That Marie Stopes, is it! Goin' there behin' ma back, you fuckin' bitch.'

And with that he rushed forward and kicked Mrs McLatchie in the ribs. 'You're no gettin' me wearin' johnnies. You're a rotten enough shag as it is without yon bloody things.'

'She didn't come in for sheaths,' a terrified Laura protested. 'She got a cap. I showed her how to fit it myself.'

'Who the fuck asked you?' McLatchie roared again, and kicked his wife a second time. He then lurched over to an almost empty whisky bottle and threw what remained down his throat.

'You've got my purse?' Mrs McLatchie croaked, face now screwed up in pain.

'Here it is.' Laura pressed the purse into Mrs McLatchie's shaking hand.

'Thank you, Miss McLean. Oh, thank you.'

'You'll be able to pay the rent now. But first I've got to get you to hospital. You need attention.'

'Forget the fuckin' hospital,' McLatchie said, jabbing a finger at Laura. 'There's nae need for that.'

Laura rounded defiantly on him. 'Yes there is. You've half killed her.'

'Hauf kilt her!' He threw back his head and bellowed with laughter. 'Don't talk daft, woman. I've done nae such thing.'

'The police might take a different view.'

That stopped his laughter. 'The polis! Are you threatenin' me wi' ra polis?'

'I most certainly am.'

'Oh Christ!' Mrs McLatchie whispered. 'Now you've gone and done it, hen.'

McLatchie went berserk. 'Come intae ma hoose and threaten me wi' the polis, will ye?'

'Let's see if I can get you up into a chair, Mrs McLatchie,' Laura murmured.

Next thing she knew McLatchie had grabbed hold of her shoulders and hauled her to her feet where he began violently shaking her. To say she was petrified would have been an understatement.

McLatchie's face had gone purple, spit dribbling from one side of his mouth. 'I'll gie ye somethin' to go to ra polis about, by God and I wull.'

He slapped Laura hard, across first one cheek and then the other. 'You meddlin' fuckin' bitch. I'll gie you somethin' all right.'

He punched Laura viciously between the breasts which caused the breath to whoosh out of her. Using a foot he tripped her so that she fell to the floor where he pounced.

'Don't, Aly! Please don't!' Mrs McLatchie pleaded in vain on Laura's behalf.

He muttered something unintelligible in reply as his hand yanked Laura's skirt up over her waist. The same hand began ripping at her underthings.

Realising with horror what he intended, Laura started to struggle which earned her a clout on the jaw that knocked her senseless for a few moments.

When she came to again his foetid breath was strong in her face and he was forcing her legs apart.

Oh God, not like this! she mentally screamed. Please, not like this. But there was no stopping him, McLatchie having already, while she was briefly unconscious, unbuttoned his flies and exposed himself.

He grunted as he thrust into her, and then rapidly began to heave and buck.

If there had been any pain in losing her virginity,

Laura hadn't felt it, but she was horribly aware of the male flesh violating her.

Unable to look at the leering face gazing down at her she twisted her head to one side, to find herself staring at the three children, still silent, watching what was happening. In the background Mrs McLatchie was whimpering like a whipped dog.

'How does that feel, Miss High an' Mighty Marie Stopes Clinic?' McLatchie taunted. 'Are ye enjoyin' it?'

Hurry up, hurry up and get it over with, was all she could think, tears leaking from both eyes as he went on humping.

McLatchie grunted, and suddenly went still. 'There, ye bitch, take that,' he spat, and pulled himself free.

Laura sobbed, thankful beyond belief he'd finished. She was filled with a terrible sense of shame and degradation, and already knew that this act would haunt her for the rest of her life. A life that would never be the same again.

McLatchie stood up and began buttoning his flies. 'Now get the fuck out of here and don't come back,' he snarled, tapping the prostrate Laura with a foot.

Somehow she managed to turn over and come onto her hands and knees, her mind in a state of shock. The shaking and vomiting would come later.

'Do as he says,' Mrs McLatchie urged. 'Get the hell away before the swine does it again. He's quite capable.'

That galvanised Laura into action. Grasping hold of the kitchen table she pulled herself aloft, her skirt falling into place. Her underthings were in tatters but hadn't fallen off. Lurching, as though drunk, she headed for the outside door, and the safety, she hoped, beyond.

'I'm sorry, miss. I'm so awfy sorry, miss,' Mrs McLatchie called out as Laura reached the door.

Laura didn't hear her.

Back in the street she became aware of a wetness running down the inside of her leg. Realising what it was caused her to bend over and throw up into the gutter. While this was happening she started to shake from head to toe.

'Are you awright, missus?'

The speaker was a girl about twelve or thirteen who was staring at Laura in concern. 'Is there anythin' I can do?'

Laura was about to reply, call the police, then thought the better of it, a picture of her father's face having suddenly flashed before her. The police were the last thing she wanted.

'No, but thank you for asking,' she eventually managed to answer when the vomiting stopped.

'Are ye no well?'

'That's right. Now run along. I'll be fine.'

Fine! She'd never be fine again. Never in a million years. She desperately willed the shaking to stop, but it didn't.

Must find a taxi, she told herself. Must find a taxi.

It took her ages, she was in the wrong part of the city for taxis, but eventually she did.

'What's happened, miss?' an anxious Nettie asked. She was Morag's replacement as maid, and an exceptionally ugly woman. Mathew had chosen her because of that thinking that because of her ugliness there was little likelihood of her following in Morag's footsteps.

Laura knew she looked a right state. 'I think I'm coming down with something,' she lied. 'Would you run me a bath and then tell Cook I shan't be having dinner this evening.'

'Yes, miss.'

'Is my mother home?'

'Not yet, miss.'

Good, Laura thought. Her father wouldn't be either, he'd still be at the surgery.

Once in her bedroom she immediately stripped naked, exclaiming when she saw the bruises that were already starting to show on her thighs and lower abdomen. She also ached abominably between her legs.

It had been a nightmare, she thought, and an ongoing nightmare at that. What she wanted most of all now was a bath to scrub off the stink of him, which still lingered on her. Her stomach heaved when she caught a whiff of it.

'Dear God,' she whispered in revulsion. She felt dirty; defiled to the very core of her being.

The bath was at the temperature she usually had, but now that wasn't hot enough for her needs. The shaking returned as she turned on the appropriate tap.

What if she became pregnant? she suddenly thought as she was about to get in. What if that happened? Once was all it took, after all, she knew that only too well from her work at the Clinic.

Sliding into the steaming water she attacked herself with soap and flannel, scrubbing as hard as she could. When she'd covered every square inch of herself, she began all over again.

Somewhere in the middle of all this the dam burst

and she began to cry, tears splashing into the suds as she hung her head in shame.

At one point she felt sick again, but, thankfully, that passed.

Please God, she wasn't pregnant. Please, please God.

There was a tentative knock on Laura's door later that night. 'Can I come in, dear?' Harriet asked.

Laura had been lying staring blankly at the ceiling, her mind alternately numb and racing. Despite herself she kept visualising, again and again, everything that had taken place at the McLatchies'. She'd even been able to view the incident as though through the eyes of an onlooker, as if she'd been one of the silent, staring children.

The door opened and Harriet stuck her head round. 'I saw your light was on and presumed you must be awake.'

Laura tried to smile, but couldn't.

'Nettie said you're coming down with something. Would you like your father to see you?'

'No, there's no need,' Laura hastily replied. 'I'm not that bad. Honestly I'm not.'

Harriet came and sat on the edge of the bed. Reaching out she felt Laura's forehead. 'I think you might have a bit of a temperature.'

'It's my period, that's all. It's particularly heavy and painful this time round,' Laura lied.

Harriet was immediately sympathetic. 'Oh, darling, I am sorry. Is there anything I can get you?'

'Nothing, Ma.'

'How about a hot water bottle to put on your tummy? I find that sometimes helps.'

Laura smiled wanly, wondering what her mother would have said if she'd come out with the truth. It didn't bear thinking about. As for her father . . . She shuddered inwardly at the thought. 'I've tried that in the past and it doesn't do any good,' she said. In fact, she was one of those fortunate women who never had trouble in that department.

'Cook prepared a tray for you downstairs before she left. Would you like me to bring it up later?'

'No, Ma, all I need is sleep.'

Harriet nodded. 'Then I'll leave you alone.'

'Thanks, Ma.'

Harriet ran a hand gently over Laura's cheek, then lightly kissed it. 'I'll see you in the morning. Goodnight.'

'Goodnight, Ma.'

Now why had she used a period as an excuse? Laura wondered after Harriet had gone. Probably because that's what she was so worried about, not having the next one, that is.

How long was it till she was due to come on? A quick mental calculation told her ten or eleven days. Perhaps twelve at the most.

Those were days that were to prove a living hell for Laura.

The following evening Laura waited till her parents had left to play cards with friends, before returning to her bedroom. Secreted there was a bottle of gin, which she'd bought earlier.

She'd decided that if she was pregnant the best thing to do was to try to end it early on, and gin was the only method she could think of.

She had no idea whether or not it worked, or was

simply an old wives' tale, but she'd had clients at the Clinic in the past who'd sworn that it did.

Taking the gin from its hiding place she put it on her chest of drawers, then proceeded to strip. When she was naked she slipped on her dressing gown, picked up the bottle and went through to the bathroom where she began running a bath even hotter than the one she'd had the day before.

She'd considered bringing a glass with her, then decided against it. Surely, when in a bath, it was easier to drink straight from the bottle than fiddle around with a glass. At least so it seemed to her.

When the bath was ready she threw her dressing gown aside and tentatively, because of the temperature, got in. It felt as though she was being boiled alive but, gritting her teeth, she stayed put.

The gin tasted awful without tonic water, and horribly strong, though she couldn't see why it could be any stronger than whisky.

Laura had a good swallow, then another. Her plan, if she could manage it, was to drink the entire bottle.

She came to in a panic, thinking she was drowning, which indeed she would have done. Flailing around she grabbed hold of the edge of the large cast-iron tub and hauled her upper half out of the water to gulp in breath after breath.

She must have passed out, she realised. Passed out and slid under. Her chest heaved in fright thinking of how close she'd come to dying.

'Bloody hell!' she swore. If she hadn't come round when she had . . .

The bottle was in the bath where it had ended up

on slipping from her hand. As it was now full of bath water there was no telling how much she'd actually drunk, nor could she remember. Everything was hazy.

Then the humour of the situation struck her, making her laugh, albeit a laugh that was slightly hysterical. Well, it was funny when you thought about it. Inadvertently almost drowning herself while trying to effect an abortion. How stupid could you be!

It must have been the mental state she was in, for going from finding it merely funny she progressed to finding it hilariously so. She laughed so long and hard her sides began to hurt.

The laughter finally hiccupped to a stop when she noticed there was nothing in the water to indicate that she'd succeeded in what she'd been trying to do.

If she had indeed been pregnant when she'd got into the bath, then she still was.

'Leaving us!' Mrs Mitchell exclaimed. 'But why?'

Laura was nervous at being back in the Clinic, and it had taken all her willpower to come. She'd forever associate it with McLatchie and her rape. 'Personal reasons,' she replied evasively.

Mrs Mitchell frowned. 'Is it something to do with us?'

'No, no, as I said, personal reasons. I just won't have the time available to work here from now on,' Laura lied.

'You're leaving immediately then?'

Laura nodded. 'I'm sorry.'

'Not half as much as I am, Laura. You've been an excellent colleague to have. We're all going to miss you dreadfully.'

An embarrassed Laura lowered her gaze. The only reason she'd returned and not telephoned to tell Mrs Mitchell her decision was because she wanted to clear out her desk. 'Thank you,' she mumbled.

Kitty, who'd originally taught Laura the ropes, came over. 'Oh, Laura, I couldn't help but overhear. This is terrible news. As Mrs Mitchell just said, we're all going to miss you.'

'And I'll miss you, Kitty, as I'll miss everybody. But it just can't be helped.'

Ten minutes later she was back out in the street thinking that was the end of an era. Certainly a worthwhile part of her life, and one she'd thoroughly enjoyed. But it was over, finished. McLatchie had seen to that. McLatchie who she hoped would one day roast in everlasting hell.

'What's wrong with Laura? She's looking terrible lately,' Mathew said to Harriet. 'Why just this morning I noticed black rings under her eyes while her face has become positively strained, if not gaunt. When I mentioned it to her she insisted it was nothing and she was right as rain.'

'It's her monthlies, Mathew. Though I'd have thought she'd be over that by now.'

An embarrassed Mathew quickly glanced away. Even though he was a doctor he found the mention of such matters both distasteful and repugnant. 'Oh,' he muttered.

Harriet wondered if the problem was that Laura had become anaemic? Perhaps temporarily so, for hadn't she confided that her period was unusually heavy on this occasion?

That could well be it, Harriet decided. She'd have a word with Cook and change the evening meal to one of liver and bacon. That might help.

'Packed in your job at the Clinic?' Harriet frowned. 'Why on earth have you done that?'

Laura shrugged. 'I lost interest, that's all.'

'But you enjoyed it so much. You've often told me that.'

Laura was becoming irritated by this line of questioning, but she'd had to explain why she wasn't going to work any more and hanging round the house all day instead. The reason for the latter was that it made her extremely nervous just to go out the door now, especially on her own. She was well aware that the condition was a repercussion of the rape.

There was no logic to it of course, McLatchie was hardly likely to suddenly spring from nowhere and jump on her! But, illogical or not, that was how she felt.

'Perhaps you simply need a break from it for a while and you'll go back to it when you're ready?' Harriet suggested.

'Perhaps,' Laura replied unconvincingly.

Harriet studied Laura shrewdly for a moment or two. 'Is everything all right, dear. Is there anything else you want to tell me?' she asked casually.

'Stop fussing, Ma!' Laura snapped. 'I'm perfectly fine.'

And having said that Laura hurried from the room wishing to escape any further questioning. She knew Harriet was only concerned for her well-being, but she did wish her mother would mind her own bloody business!

* * *

Three days to go, Laura reflected, agitatedly biting a thumbnail. This was a new habit she'd acquired since McLatchie had raped her.

The passing days, the hours, even the minutes all seemed an eternity long. It was as though time itself had slowed down to torture her. And torture her it did, excruciatingly.

One thing was certain, pregnant or not, her parents must never find out what had happened. The shame and humiliation would be too great. She knew in her heart of hearts that Mathew would somehow blame her, albeit she was entirely blameless. And should it ever become public knowledge, which it probably would if she'd gone to the police, then that would be an utter disaster.

If only Sandy was at home to confide in, he would help in some way, know the right thing to do. She could trust him with her secret and have a shoulder to cry on.

But Sandy was in Paris with still no word of him coming back for a visit which she'd been hoping for for some time now. Dear Sandy, how she missed him and looked forward to his letters.

According to those he was becoming more and more successful, selling regularly and for good prices too, having cornered, as he put it, something of a niche market as a society painter.

'Oh, Sandy,' she whispered. She'd have given anything for him to have been there at that moment. Absolutely anything.

Except he wasn't, and her problem remained hers to deal with. What if she was pregnant? What then? An abortion was the only solution, but how, where, and who? Despite her work at the Clinic she had no leads in that direction. None at all. And yet, if she was pregnant then she'd have to come up with something, for having a baby was entirely out the question. Quite impossible.

She caught her breath as the answer came to her. Sandy, of course. If what she'd heard about Paris was true then that's where she'd find the ways and means. There and then she decided that no matter what the outcome of all this she was going to Paris, at least for a while. It would do her the world of good to get away from Glasgow, whose streets she was now too frightened to walk along.

Yes, that was it. No matter the outcome, Paris – and Sandy.

Laura sobbed with relief, for at last her period had arrived. She wasn't pregnant!

'Thank you, God, thank you,' she whispered in the privacy of the locked bathroom. He'd heard and answered her prayers. Everything was going to be all right.

She wasn't pregnant!

Later that evening she announced her plans for visiting Sandy in Paris, having written to him that afternoon.

Chapter 29

Laura was beside herself with excitement as the train arrived at the Gare du Nord where Sandy, as agreed by letter, should be waiting to meet her. The moment the train stopped she flung open the carriage door and stepped down onto the platform.

Sandy's face blazed with sheer pleasure when he spotted her, his immediate reaction being amazement at how changed she was. A few minutes later he'd swept her into his arms and was hugging her tight.

'Oh, Laura, it's so good to see you,' he choked, his voice thick with emotion.

'And you, Sandy.' She was almost tearful from the thrill of their reunion. At last, at long, long last they were together again.

'Christ, but you're a sight for sore eyes,' he declared, holding her at arms' length.

'So are you.'

'How was the journey?'

'Choppy in the Channel, but fun really. I thoroughly enjoyed the crossing.'

He shook his head in wonder. 'I can't believe how grown up you are.'

'It's been four years,' she reminded him. 'What did you expect?'

He laughed. 'And me, what about me?'

She traced an imaginary line across his cheek. 'You've put on weight. It suits you.'

'That's the French cuisine. Wait till you taste it, Laura, it's simply out of this world.'

'Sounds really yummy.'

'No more mince and tatties for you for a while, eh?' he joked. That was often called the true Scottish national dish.

'I should hope not. But I won't eat snails, you hear?' She pulled a face. 'The very thought gives me the dry boak.'

Her using that expression, which meant the dry heaves, amused Sandy no end. It was pure Glasgow. 'Now then, where's your luggage?'

'There's only one small suitcase,' she informed him. 'We should be able to manage that ourselves. By which I mean you.'

He dived into the carriage, where she had been the sole occupant, to re-emerge with the suitcase in question. 'Why are you travelling so light, sis?'

'This is Paris, isn't it? I shall be in the shops as soon as possible to see for myself if it's true what I've heard about French chic.'

'Oh, it is,' he assured her. 'Take my word for it. Now, shall we go and find a taxi?'

She hooked an arm through his free one as they made their way along the platform, questions and answers tripping from their mouths. They might have been long-lost lovers who'd found one another again.

'It's beautiful!' Laura exclaimed, gazing round Sandy's salon. 'Such wonderful taste.'

'I liked the house the moment I stepped into it. I felt a sort of affinity with the place. As if it was saying, come and live here, Sandy. Come and live here.'

Laura laughed. 'Dope. Houses don't talk.'

'Oh, you'd be surprised,' he teased. 'I'm sure this one did to me. Now come and view my studio, that's the most important room as far as I'm concerned.'

The studio, just as Laura had expected, was in a right old clutter, but she instantly understood what he'd written about it getting the light which was positively streaming in. The room was perfect for a painter's purposes.

He took her to the window and gestured. 'All of Paris at your feet. How about that, eh?'

Laura had to agree, it was an incredible sight.

'At night Paris is like a sparkling jewel, or a scattering, a myriad, of jewels to be more precise,' he boasted. 'It's quite breathtaking to stand here and stare out over it.'

Laura could well imagine that to be so. Leaving the window she crossed to his easel on which was the half-painted portrait of a woman nearing middle age. 'Who's this?' she asked.

'Madame Feneon, the wife of a rich Parisian banker. Her first name, believe it or not, is Divine. It's a commission.'

A finished painting leaning against a wall caught Laura's attention. It was of a naked female standing beside an unmade bed clutching a white piece of cloth that may, or may not, have been a chemise. 'And this?'

Sandy smiled. 'A model I hired called Yvette. Like it?'

The painting had a quality, a certain female mystique, about it which Laura found fascinating. 'It's very good,' she declared solemnly. 'You've improved a lot since leaving home. Judging by this one they're somehow more mature, have more depth to them.'

Her praise pleased Sandy enormously. 'I'm getting better all the time, at least so Harald says.'

'Well, he's right. I'm looking forward to meeting him, by the way. You've written a great deal about him in your letters.'

'He's a good friend, and my agent now, which he's being very successful at. You'll meet him later on.'

Sandy took Laura to the kitchen next where, she quickly realised, very little cooking took place. 'Ah!' Sandy smiled when she asked him about it. 'That's because I eat out most of the time. It's easier that way. And if I want to eat at home I have an arrangement with Madame Sagot who lives nearby and does for me.'

'Does for you?'

'She cleans, changes the bed linen, takes my dirty laundry off to be washed and ironed, then brings it back again. If I want to eat at home any night I simply leave a plate on the kitchen table during the day. This tells her my intention, as she often turns up while I'm working and has strict instructions not to disturb me, and then that evening at eight o'clock sharp she appears with a cooked meal. She won't use this kitchen as she says she prefers her own.'

'So she's a sort of general factotum?'

'That's right. Couldn't do without her, she's a real treasure.'

'Does she speak English?'

'Not a word, and my French is still extremely limited. But we get by somehow. If I have any difficulty I have Harald translate.'

'Old?'

'Ancient. At least she looks ancient. But there's nothing senile about her, not in the least. We get on together like a house on fire. She calls me her "*petit Écossais*", which means little Scotsman. Though why little, I've no idea.'

Laura's bedroom was next, with the luxury of an ensuite bathroom leading off. A bathroom stacked with towels and everything else she might need.

'Well?' Sandy demanded.

'Oh, it's perfect. Just perfect. And a double bed too! I'll enjoy that.'

'Nothing but the best for you, sis. Now, what would you care for first. Coffee or a bath?'

'Oh, a bath please. I'm feeling all grimy after the journey.'

'That's what I thought. Well, help yourself, the water's hot. Join me in the studio when you're ready and we'll go from there.'

She went to him and kissed him on the cheek. 'Thanks, Sandy. I'm really pleased to be here.'

'Good,' he smiled. 'I've been looking forward to it ever since your letter arrived telling me you were coming. We'll have a wonderful time together.'

Laura just knew they would.

* * *

Sandy and Laura had already been to the luxurious Scheherazade where they'd eaten grilled *mutton à la cosaque* and now they were in the Lapin Agile where they'd been joined by Harald, Rocky and a new American girlfriend of his called Alice Ginn, another writer. Alice was very loud and brash, though not unlikeable.

Laura's eyes went wide. 'I can see two men kissing over there,' she whispered to Sandy, who was sitting next to her.

When she nodded he looked in that direction. Sure enough, two young men were entwined in each other's arms. 'You'll come across lots of that sort of thing in Montmartre,' he whispered back. 'Anything goes round here.' He glanced at her in amusement. 'Shocked?'

She was, but not about to admit it. 'Not really.'

'We can leave if you like. Go somewhere else not quite so Bohemian.'

'No, no, I'm fine here,' she protested. 'It's just . . .' She thought for a few seconds. 'So unlike Glasgow I suppose.'

'Oh, it is that,' Sandy agreed, laughter in his voice. 'But you'll soon get used to it. I know I did.'

'I need more wine, hon!' Alice announced loudly to Rocky who'd been chatting with Harald.

Rocky's book, having been turned down by American and British publishers because of the explicit material it contained – sheer pornography was how several had described it – had finally been bought by a small avante garde French house. Its reception had been mixed in what reviews he'd had, though, according to Rocky, it was selling well. To his delight copies were being smuggled into both the States and Britain where, apparently, they were changing hands for large sums of money.

All very hush hush and under the counter of course.

A waitress was summoned, who took their order, Laura glancing away in embarrassment at the sight of the woman's naked breasts. She was horrified when Rocky reached up and fondled them. In front of his girlfriend too! What a den of iniquity Montmartre was turning out to be! A modern day Sodom and Gomorrah. Though, if she was honest with herself, she wasn't that offended. And it *was* exciting. Very much so.

'What are your plans while here?' Harald leant across the table and asked her.

'I don't know. But one thing I want to do is go shopping. I can't wait for that!'

He smiled his understanding, thinking how typical that was of a woman. He hadn't known what to expect of Sandy's sister, and the reality had been pleasantly surprising. She had a trim figure, he'd noted, and a charming personality. Facially he couldn't see a resemblance at all between them, though in other ways, gestures, vocal inflections, a similarity was more noticeable.

'Not tomorrow I'm afraid,' Sandy apologised to her. 'We can do some locally in the morning if you like. But I have Madame Feneon coming early in the afternoon for a sitting. I can't get out of it, I'm afraid.'

Harald saw the look of disappointment that flashed across Laura's face. 'Can I suggest something?'

'What's that?' Sandy asked.

'I'm free all day tomorrow. Why don't I escort Laura wherever she'd like to go?'

'What a brilliant idea,' Sandy enthused. Then to Laura, 'Harald knows Paris like the back of his hand. And not only that he speaks the language fluently.'

'Laura?' Harald queried with a smile.

'Why doesn't Sandy show me Montmartre in the morning, and then you take me shopping in the afternoon. Is that possible?'

'That's OK by me.' The use of the word OK was something he'd picked up from Rocky.

'Then it's agreed,' Sandy nodded.

Laura was suddenly horribly aware that Rocky was fumbling under Alice's skirt which immediately brought back memories of McLatchie. She knew without a doubt she'd have bad dreams again that night because of it.

'Whisky or cognac? I always have a nightcap before I go to bed.'

Laura considered. 'Whisky please.' She suddenly smiled. 'Remember how I used to come to your bedroom and drink whisky there from your secret stash?'

'How could I forget?' Sandy replied with a grin. 'We had a few laughs in that bedroom over whisky. I'll certainly never forget you asking me about the facts of life. A right forward little hussy you were.'

Laura accepted the whisky he handed her. 'It's been quite a day,' she acknowledged.

'First impressions?'

'What do you think! Bare-breasted waitresses, men kissing men in public.' She pulled a face. 'That was horrible. And what about your friend Rocky and that Alice. At one point he had his hand right up her skirt. I hate to think what he was doing.'

Sandy slumped into a chair, exhausted after their night out. He hadn't slept well the night before having been excited by Laura's imminent arrival. 'You'll see that sort of thing all the time around here. People are quite blatant about sex. It's part and parcel of the way they live.'

Laura sat facing him. 'Are *you* so bold in public?'

'No I am not!' he protested. 'But then I have the benefit of a good Presbyterian upbringing, if you want to call it a benefit, which instils inhibitions I'm afraid I'll never overcome.'

'And what about in private?' she teased gently.

Sandy shrugged. 'That's different, I suppose.'

Laura suddenly giggled.

'Why are you doing that?'

'Can you imagine if Pa had been with us tonight? He'd have had a coronary.'

Sandy laughed. 'Or Ma.'

Laura had a sip of her drink. 'You've never mentioned girlfriends in your letters. Why's that?'

Sandy took his time in replying. 'There have been some, but nothing serious which is probably why I never mentioned them.'

Laura nodded that she understood.

'So what about you and boyfriends?'

'Same as you. A few, but no one special. None of them particularly interested me.'

'Me too. With women that is.'

They both sat in brooding silence, finally broken when Laura said, 'Can I stay here with you as long as I like? Or would you prefer it to be a relatively short visit? I mean, I'd perfectly understand if you did.'

That surprised him. 'Of course you can stay as long as you wish.'

'I won't be in the way of your work?'

'I shouldn't think so. Besides, I'll enjoy the company.

It gets kind of lonely sometimes in this huge house all by myself.'

Relief pulsed through her. 'Thank you, Sandy.'

'There's nothing to thank. In a way you'll be doing me the favour.' He hesitated, then said, 'I really have missed you, sis. I didn't realise how much until you wrote that you were coming over. It's . . . well just wonderful having you around again, having you to talk to and be with.'

She knew exactly what he meant by that, feeling the same way about him.

He came to his feet. 'How about another dram? I don't want to go to bed just yet.'

'Neither do I,' she confessed.

'We'll sit and chat a while longer, eh?'

A burst of sheer pleasure welled through her, that and something else. Something she couldn't quite put a name to.

Harald watched in expectation as Laura tasted her first sip of onion soup. He'd brought her the following lunchtime to Les Halles which was famous for the dish.

'Oh my, it's delicious!' Laura exclaimed in delight.

'I was hoping you'd say that.'

She shook her head in wonder. 'Sandy wasn't exaggerating when he told me how good the French cuisine was. Everything I've had so far has been superb.'

'I'm gratified you approve,' Harald said. 'And when we've finished here we'll go shopping.' He paused. 'Just so I don't waste your time by taking you places that are far too expensive for your pocket, are you on a limited budget?'

Laura dropped her gaze, always wary of disclosing

how well off she now was. Did Harald know about Sandy's and her inheritance? She didn't think so, otherwise he wouldn't have asked the question.

'That depends,' she hedged. 'Let's just wait and see, shall we?'

In the event she bought a few clothes, enough for her present needs as she hadn't brought much with her. And nothing outrageously expensive.

She found Harald attentive and fun to be with. He made her laugh a lot.

'So what do you think of Harald now you've spent some time with him?' Sandy asked casually. Laura had just returned from her shopping expedition. Harald had had a quick coffee with them before he left.

'He's very nice. I like him.'

'Women usually do. He has a way with them,' Sandy commented drily.

'Perhaps that's because he shows interest and actually listens to what you have to say. A lot of men don't.'

'Am I included in that number?'

Laura smiled. 'You're better than many. But you don't always listen. If I was giving marks I'd give you seven out of ten.'

Sandy laughed, finding that amusing.

'But tell me, does he make a good living out of being an artists' agent? Or does he do something else as well?'

Oh dear, Sandy thought. Should he tell her the truth or what? He mused on that for a few moments, then decided he would. Harald didn't exactly keep it a secret, and chances were she'd find out sooner or later anyway.

'Being an agent is only a sideline, something he started with me. Eventually he hopes to build it into a full-time career, but that may take some time, as you may appreciate.'

'So he does do something else?' she persisted.

'Yes,' Sandy admitted. 'He's a gigolo.'

Laura frowned, sure she hadn't heard properly. 'A what?'

'A gigolo, Laura. He sleeps with women for money and presents. From all accounts he's rather good at it.'

Laura was astounded. 'Bloody hell!' she muttered. 'I have heard of such men but never thought I'd actually meet one. He's a male prostitute, in other words?'

Sandy shrugged. 'Well, it's not *quite* the same as being a common prostitute. He only deals with wealthy, and often aristocratic, ladies, also often foreigners, who've come to Paris especially to . . . let off steam, shall I say.'

Laura shook her head in wonder. 'I'd never have guessed. That explains why he's so easy to be with, it's his job!'

'But one he'd like to leave, hence becoming an agent.'

Laura poured herself more coffee from the pot.

'Do you disapprove?' Sandy asked.

'I'm not sure whether I do or not. It *is* different!'

Sandy laughed. 'It's certainly that.'

How amazing, Laura thought. Paris was certainly proving to be full of surprises . . . Harald a gigolo.

Bloody hell!

Laura had been in Paris for almost three weeks when Sandy woke late one night knowing something was wrong. He lay in bed listening, but heard nothing untoward. But something was wrong all right, he just knew it. An intruder perhaps? He decided the first thing to do was check on Laura.

Getting out of bed he slipped on his dressing gown, then padded along the corridor to stand outside her bedroom from where he could distinctly hear crying. 'Laura?' he called out softly.

There was no reply, but the crying stopped.

He opened the door and went in, snapping on the light. Laura was sitting up in bed, her face puffed and red, tears streaming down her face.

'Oh, Sandy,' she choked.

He went straight to her, sat alongside and took her into his arms. 'What's wrong? Have you had a nightmare?'

'The same one,' she sobbed in reply. 'Always the same one. I'm sorry.'

'There there,' he consoled. 'There's nothing to be sorry about. Can I get you anything?'

'No, just stay here with me.'

He gently rocked her to and fro for a few moments, wondering what this nightmare was that she was on about.

'Want to talk about it?' he prompted.

Laura took a deep breath, and tried to control herself. She'd been in that kitchen again with McLatchie, he pounding into her while the three silent children watched. The sheer horror of the experience had been as real in her nightmare, as it always was, as when the rape had actually happened.

'Laura?'

'I've never told anyone. Not a single soul,' she confessed, her voice shaking. 'But I want to tell you. And I would have done if you'd been at home in Lilybank Gardens.'

'Well, I'm here now, and listening.'

'Oh, Sandy, it's awful. Truly it is.'

'I'm still listening.'

'It wasn't my fault. I swear.'

He began stroking her hair, waiting for her to go on, thinking it must be pretty bad for her to get into a state like this.

'Ma and Pa must never find out. This is just between you and me. Promise that, Sandy. Promise?'

'You have my word of honour, sis.'

She shuddered, then took an extra deep breath. Slowly, falteringly, she recounted the story of why she'd gone to the McLatchie house, and what had happened there.

'Jesus Christ,' Sandy whispered when she was finally done. 'You poor, poor thing.'

'For weeks afterwards I was terrified I might be pregnant, but luckily I wasn't.'

Sandy shook his head in disbelief. 'Why didn't you go to the police? Surely that was the obvious thing to do.'

'I couldn't, Sandy,' she wailed. 'If I'd done that it would have gone public and my name might have got out. Can you imagine if that happened? Even though it wasn't my fault Pa would have been humiliated beyond belief, and I know, just know, that in his heart of hearts he would have thought I was somehow to blame. Men think like that, Sandy, believe me.'

'Jesus Christ,' he repeated, quite stunned, and horrified by all she had told him.

'I would be damaged goods, Sandy. Who would marry me then? No one. Except possibly for my money which is the last thing I want. And Ma, she'd have been beside herself. Who knows? It might even have killed her. No, by keeping my mouth shut I let McLatchie off the hook but I also kept my reputation which is more important to me.'

She buried a tear-stained face in his shoulder, just as she'd wanted to do since the rape. 'Afterwards I was scared to walk the streets alone, which is why I had to get away from Glasgow. I kept seeing McLatchie lurking behind every lamppost and hedge. My nerves were ragged by the time I finally left.'

Sandy wasn't a violent man by nature, but at that moment he would cheerfully have strangled McLatchie. That, or stuck a knife in the bastard.

'You're the only one I can confide in, Sandy. The only one,' she went on.

'You're safe with me now, sis. I'll look after and care for you.'

'The nightmare is always the same, I go through the whole thing again and again. Sometimes, even though I'm asleep, I can even smell his stinking breath.'

He understood now why she'd asked if she could stay as long as she liked. And stay she would, for ever if she wanted.

'I wasn't to blame in any way, Sandy. Please believe that.'

'I do,' he crooned. 'I do.'

'Do you think any less of me now?'

'Why should I do that? You're still the same Laura to me. And always will be.'

'I just couldn't take the risk of going to the authorities, the repercussions might have been horrendous. People sniggering behind my back if it got out, pointing their fingers at me, whispering.'

'Oh, lassie,' Sandy croaked, almost on the verge of tears himself. 'Oh, lassie, lassie.'

'If only I could turn back the clock, but I can't. And will never be able to.'

'Shoosh!' he crooned, a lump coming into his throat as her body pressed against his for comfort and consolation. 'You should have told me sooner about this.'

'I kept meaning to, but it was so hard. I had to wait for the right moment.'

'Well, now I know. We'll talk about it any time you want, or not if you choose.'

They were silent for a few seconds, each lost in their own thoughts. Then she said, 'Harald accidentally touched my hand earlier when we were shopping and I recoiled as if bitten by a deadly snake. He must think . . . God knows what.'

'Don't you worry about Harald. If he mentions it I'll explain it away somehow.'

'But you won't tell him?'

'Not him or anyone else. This is our secret, Laura. And that's how it'll stay, little sister.'

They continued talking, and gradually Laura calmed down to the point where Sandy thought it was safe to leave her.

'Don't go,' she pleaded when he offered to tuck her in. 'I don't want to be alone. Stay with me for the rest of the night.'

'Laura . . .'

'Please?'

He turned off the light before getting into bed alongside her. 'Like the lost babes in the wood,' she muttered as she was drifting off.

Sandy's last thought was, strangely, that it seemed the most natural thing in the world to sleep cuddled up to his beloved sister.

Chapter 30

Betty's Bar was exactly as Sandy remembered it. Even Tommy was still behind the bar.

'Hello, Rembrandt,' Tommy called in greeting, the hideous scar running from eye to mouth as vivid, and ugly, as ever. 'It's been a long time.'

''Fraid so.'

'Been busy?'

'Very.'

'Good for you, son.' Tommy nodded. 'A pint of heavy?'

'Please.'

Sandy glanced around as Tommy poured. There on the wall was the drawing he'd done of Archie, and a little further along the one of Mick Gallagher.

'How's Mick?' he asked as Tommy placed the pint in front of him.

'No' too bad, considerin'. He's resigned to the long haul, I suppose.'

Sandy shook his head in sympathy. 'Do you still visit?'

'Oh aye, me and the wife regular.'

'Will you give him my regards next time you go?'

Tommy accepted Sandy's money. 'I will indeed. He's aye pleased to know he's no' forgotten like.'

Sandy had a sip of beer, thoroughly enjoying it. It was great to have a decent pint after all this time. 'And what about Beryl? What's happened to her?'

Tommy's face clouded over. 'Nobody's seen hide nor hair of her since she got marked. Seems to have vanished into thin air.'

Probably just as well, Sandy reflected. 'Is Bob around? I'd like a word.'

'He's just gone out, but he'll be back in a few minutes. I think he went to buy a paper.'

'I'll wait then.'

'Aye, right.'

Sandy took himself over to the table furthest away from the bar not wanting Tommy, or anyone else, overhearing what he had to say to Bob.

Sure enough, as Tommy had promised, Bob soon returned to the pub. Sandy came to his feet as Bob breezed in through the door. 'Can I speak to you, Bob?'

The owner marched straight over and shook his hand. 'It's good to see you again. How's it gaun?'

'Fine. Yourself?'

'Mustn't grumble. Can I get you a dram?'

'No please, let me. It's my shout.'

Bob sat as Sandy returned to the bar and ordered two large whiskies, adding a splash of soda to his. 'There you are,' he said to Bob on rejoining him at the table.

'Slainthe!' Bob toasted.

'Slainthe.'

Bob cleared his throat. 'You said you wanted to speak to me?'

'I need a favour.'

'Oh aye?'

'For which I'm willing to pay handsomely. And I mean just that.'

Bob's eyes narrowed. 'Go on.'

'But before I tell you *what*, I'm going to explain *why*. That way you'll understand.'

'Sounds serious,' Bob mused, having noted the sudden steel that had entered Sandy's voice.

'It is, which is why I've come all the way back from Paris where I now live.'

'Do you indeed!'

Sandy suddenly grinned. 'I live and work there as a professional painter. Making a decent living at it too.'

That pleased Bob enormously. 'Good for you, lad. I'm delighted to hear it. But what happened to the medical studies?'

Sandy decided to be honest. 'I was never really all that keen, and then I came into some money which gave me the opportunity to do as I wished. So I went to Paris to see if I could make a go of it, and have. I couldn't be happier.'

'And where do I fit into all this?'

The steel was back in Sandy's voice. 'It seems to me you'd have the contacts to have more or less anything done in this city.'

Bob eyed him shrewdly. 'Depends what it is, like.'

'Some while ago a bastard named McLatchie raped my sister. That's the *why*.'

Bob's expression became grim. 'And now you want him given a seeing to. Right?'

'Right.'

'Striped or killed?'

'Neither. I want him castrated. His balls cut off.'

Bob pursed his lips and silently whistled. 'Poetic,' he declared at last. 'Very poetic.'

'I want to make sure he'll never do to another woman what he did to my sister. Can you arrange it?'

'Oh aye, it won't be too difficult, for the right money, that is.'

Sandy took out his wallet and extracted twenty crisp new white five-pound notes. 'That's a hundred quid. Is it enough?'

Bob laughed. 'Enough! I could have the bloody Pope murdered for that. It's more than enough.'

'Whatever, just as long as it's done.'

Bob accepted the cash which quickly disappeared into an inside jacket pocket. He then held out a hand for them to shake on the deal. 'Leave it with me.'

'Thanks, Bob.'

'But I'll need some information, you understand.'

Sandy produced a small notepad and pencil. 'That's the address,' he murmured, writing it down. He then described McLatchie to Bob as Laura had described McLatchie to him.

'And how do I let you know it's been carried out?'

Sandy wrote his own address on a separate sheet of paper. 'Drop me a line there. All right?'

'All right.'

Sandy suddenly felt as if a great weight had been lifted from his shoulders. He felt no guilt or remorse whatsoever about what he'd just set in motion. As far as he was concerned, McLatchie well and truly deserved what was now coming to him.

'You surprise me, son,' Bob said slowly.

'Why's that?'

'I wouldn't have figured you for the type to go in for this sort of thing.'

Sandy stared him straight in the eye. 'It wasn't your sister who got raped.'

Bob had no reply to that.

'I wish you were staying longer. One night is hardly enough after all the time you've been away,' Harriet fussed.

'I did warn you on the telephone it was only a flying visit, Ma.'

'Even so, surely you can manage two nights at least.' Her expression softened, and she added quietly, 'Please?'

How could he refuse? 'Two nights then, Ma, but no more. I have a lot of work waiting for me back in Paris.'

Mathew sniffed. 'Are you really selling or is that just a story?'

'Mathew McLean!' Harriet admonished sharply. 'How could you say such a thing? It's tantamount to calling your own son a liar.'

'That's all right, Ma,' Sandy intervened. He was furious but did his best not to show it. He rounded on his father. 'It's not a story. I *am* selling well. Extremely well to be precise. And for good prices too.' He'd forgotten how much he disliked Mathew, now he realised it had possibly gone even further than that.

Mathew didn't reply, but his expression said he remained unconvinced. It just didn't seem possible to him that Sandy could be successful as a painter.

'Now what about Laura,' Harriet asked. 'Why isn't she with you?'

'Because she's enjoying herself too much where she is, Ma. She's having a whale of a time.'

'So when is she coming back?'

He'd been prepared for this, having discussed it with Laura before he left. 'I believe she's considering living in Paris more or less permanently,' he replied.

Harriet was aghast.

'She can't do that,' Mathew growled.

'Why not, Pa?'

'Her place is here, with us. You tell her that now.'

'Her place is wherever she wants it to be, Pa. She's over twenty-one, don't forget, and a woman of means in her own right. If she wishes to live in Paris then that's her decision and no one else's.'

'I don't think I like your tone, Alexander!' Mathew snapped.

'And what tone is that?'

'An impertinent one, which I won't stand for. You hear?'

Sandy bit his lip. If he wasn't careful this could escalate into a full-blown row which was the last thing he wanted. He had his mother to think about, if nothing else.

'Then I apologise. No impertinence was intended.' The latter was true enough.

Mathew grunted.

'Does that mean my apology is accepted?'

'You've become awful high and mighty since coming into all that money,' Mathew accused. 'It doesn't suit you. Not one little bit.'

So that was what was really behind all this, Sandy thought. The inheritance. He should have guessed. 'Have I?' he replied drily.

'Indeed you have.'

'Mathew, will you stop it!' a distraught Harriet pleaded.

'I didn't start anything.'

'Oh yes you did. Alexander is hardly in the house and you're having a go at him.'

'Nonsense.'

'Forget it, Ma.' Sandy smiled at her.

'Anyway, that money was rightfully yours as Margaret's next of kin,' Mathew couldn't help adding.

'Except she chose not to leave it to me. And we all know why.'

Mathew blinked at her. 'Are you suggesting it was because of *me*?'

'Why else? She didn't want you getting your hands on it. That's blindingly obvious.'

Mathew was outraged, for he knew that to be true. 'Well, a lot of good it's done your children. Alexander gave up his studies on account of it, and now Laura has moved away as well as him. Not only moved away but to another country into the bargain.'

This had gone far enough, Sandy decided. He wasn't going to let his father speak to his mother like this. 'Cut it out, Pa,' he said, steel in his voice, as when he'd spoken with Bob in Betty's Bar.

Mathew stared at him in disbelief. 'Are you telling me what to do in my own home?'

'You're behaving childishly.'

'Childishly!' Mathew spluttered. 'More damned impertinence!'

Sandy crossed over to where the whisky was kept and, without asking, poured himself one which he swallowed in a single gulp. He then poured another.

'Feel free,' Mathew taunted waspishly.

Sandy ignored that. 'Would you care for something, Ma?'

'A sherry, please,' she said with a defiant glance at Mathew.

He poured that as well and handed it to her. 'It's good to see you again, Ma.'

She attempted a smile. 'And you, Sandy. You don't know how much.'

'Laura sends her love and says she'll write soon.'

'Will she be living with you in Paris?'

'No reason for her not to. I have a large house so there's plenty of room to spare. We rub along very nicely together anyway.'

'I'm pleased about that.'

'She really does love it there, Ma. Taken to it, and the way of living, like a duck to water. We have some great times.'

'Do I get offered any of my own whisky?' Mathew queried peevishly from his chair.

Sandy bit back the urge to tell him to damn well get it himself. 'Of course, Pa.'

'She will come and visit regularly, won't she?' Harriet asked anxiously as Sandy attended to his father's drink.

'I'm sure she will,' he lied. Though it wasn't out of the question she might occasionally, very occasionally, visit, especially after he told her about McLatchie and what he'd arranged.

'Oh, I hope she does.'

Sandy felt sorry for his mother, but couldn't explain to her the reason Laura would be reluctant to return to Glasgow, even for a short visit.

'So if you're not here to see *us*, why are you here?' Mathew asked as Sandy gave him his drink.

'I had business with the bank that had to be dealt with personally,' Sandy lied smoothly. That was the excuse he'd concocted.

'Oh?'

'To do with investments,' he added.

A look of pure jealousy flashed across Mathew's face. 'I suppose it's all right for some,' he muttered.

Sandy ignored that. If it wasn't for his mother he'd have left and booked into an hotel.

'Are your investments doing well?' Harriet asked ingenuously.

'Very. They're all highly profitable.'

'Well, you know what they say, money goes to money,' Mathew commented somewhat nastily.

Sandy couldn't resist it. He'd had a bellyfull of his father. 'Well, you had your chance to make your pile.'

Mathew frowned. 'How so?'

'If you'd been good enough to be a specialist instead of a mere doctor,' he replied, sliding the knife home.

Mathew went very still, his eyes blazing. For a moment or two he simply couldn't speak. The great failure of his life, which he regretted every single day, had just been thrown in his face. 'How dare you!' he hissed.

'It's true though, isn't it, Pa? You always wanted to be up there ranked amongst the big medical knobs, who make loads of cash, but couldn't pass the necessary qualifications. Are you going to deny it?'

Harriet watched Mathew go redder and redder till she thought he was going to explode.

'Well?' Sandy demanded.

'How dare you,' Mathew repeated, unable to think of anything else to say.

Sandy laid his drink aside when he realised he wasn't going to get an answer. 'I think I'll go for a walk as I have a bit of a headache. Do you mind?'

Harriet simply shook her head.

Things should have calmed down when he returned, Sandy thought as he left the room. He didn't have a headache at all, of course, that had been merely an excuse to get away from his father for a while.

His walk took him straight to the nearest pub.

'I can't stay on after last night, Ma. Do you understand?' Sandy said to Harriet next morning after Mathew had left for the surgery. Breakfast had been a frosty affair.

'I'm sorry about what happened . . .'

'It wasn't your fault,' Sandy interjected. 'It was Pa's. I swear he's worse than he used to be. Or maybe he's still the same and I've forgotten what he was like.'

Harriet glanced away. 'He can be difficult at times, I have to admit.'

Sandy regarded her tenderly. 'I don't know how you put up with him. Honestly I don't.'

Harriet bowed her head slightly. 'He does have his good points, you know. As for putting up with him, marriage is supposed to be for better or worse, don't forget that. And looking on the bright side, if it hadn't been for him I wouldn't have you or Laura.'

'A high price to pay though.'

'We muddle along most of the time,' Harriet said in a quiet voice. 'But he does get upset whenever he thinks about Cakey's money, and of course your being here brings it all back.'

She took a deep breath and drew herself up to her full height. 'So when will you leave?'

'As soon as I can get my things together. I don't want to be here should he come back for lunch.'

'I doubt he will,' Harriet mused. 'But you never know.'

'I am sorry, Ma.'

'I appreciate that, Sandy.' She smiled. 'But at least I have seen you which is something.' She hesitated, then went on, 'One thing?'

'What's that?'

'Would you mind awfully if I came to the station with you and saw you off? That'll give us more time together.'

'Of course you can come, Ma. I'd really like that.' Going to her he kissed her cheek. 'I'll start packing my bits and pieces.'

'Damn you, Mathew McLean,' Harriet muttered vehemently to herself when Sandy had left the room. 'Damn you to hell.'

Laura jumped up from her chair when a tired-looking Sandy appeared. 'So how was it. How were Ma and Pa?' she demanded.

Sandy let out a huge sigh. 'Is there any wine open?'

'I'll get the bottle,' Laura replied, and hurried away. When she returned Sandy was sitting slumped in the chair she'd been occupying. Hurriedly she poured a glass and gave it to him.

'Rough crossing,' he explained. 'I'm afraid I was sick and still haven't fully recovered.'

She pulled a sympathetic face. 'Unusual for this time of year, I'd have thought.'

'That's what everyone said, but it was still rough all the same.'

'Ma and Pa?' she persisted.

He took a large swig of wine which immediately made him feel better. 'They weren't best pleased to hear your news. Pa actually started demanding you go home as that's where your place was, according to him. However, I soon put him straight.'

'And Ma?'

'She'd come to terms with it by the time I said goodbye to her at the station. You'd have left home some day, she said. She just hadn't expected it to be in such an abrupt way without any prior warning. She'll be all right though. But she does worry me.'

Laura frowned. 'In what way?'

'There's a sort of sadness about her nowadays, a deep-down fundamental thing. I found it quite disturbing.'

'Sad about what?'

'No idea, sis. Pa probably; he was even more difficult than I recalled. Turned into a bit of a monster in my opinion. I told Ma I don't know how she puts up with him, and I don't.'

'Poor Ma,' Laura whispered.

Sandy nodded his agreement.

'Anyway,' Laura declared, her whole demeanour changing. 'I have a surprise for you.'

'And what's that?'

'Harald and I have agreed to open a gallery together.'

'A gallery!' That was a surprise.

'A fifty-fifty partnership. I'll put up half the capital, Harald the other half. What do you think?'

'Does he have that sort of capital?'

'According to him he does. All nicely tucked away. He's been thinking about this for a while, but couldn't go it alone. When he suggested the idea to me I jumped at it as it'll give me something to do other than shopping and being round the house all day.'

'And how exactly would it work?' Sandy asked, impressed by her enthusiasm.

'Well, first we find premises, that's Harald's job. When we find them, and both agree on their suitability, we negotiate the lease, after which we'll have them completely refurbished to suit our needs. Approve so far?'

A bemused Sandy nodded.

'Harald will arrange the artists to be exhibited as he knows most of them, certainly the local ones, while I will mainly be in charge of the day-to-day running of the gallery.'

'There's only one small drawback there, sis, you don't speak fluent French,' Sandy pointed out.

'We discussed that problem. I shall have an assistant, one fluent in both languages. She'll deal mainly with the French customers, under my supervision of course, while I deal with the English-speaking ones. And of course my French will improve in time. Harald assures me he'll be able to introduce a great many clients through his various connections.'

Sandy smiled. 'I have no doubt he'll be able to do just that. He has the most amazing contacts, and many of them are extremely well off. He'll get potential buyers in all right, I can guarantee it.'

'Naturally we'll be exhibiting you.'

'I should hope so! I'd be really miffed if you didn't.'

'And guess what?'

'What?'

'Harald and I were out last night and had a drink

with Picasso and Henri Matisse! We ran into them in the Chat Noir.'

'But they're supposed to hate one another.' Sandy protested.

'According to Harald they admire each other's work tremendously, each jealous of the other. Harald says it's a sort of love-hate relationship. Anyway, we joined them and chatted for a while. Well, Harald did most of the chatting as their English is strictly limited. He told them about our plans for the gallery and they both showed an interest in being exhibited. How about that then?'

Sandy was amazed. 'That really would be a coup for you.'

'Harald said afterwards if we'd approached them individually we probably wouldn't have got anywhere, but because they were together neither wanted to be left out. What do you think?'

'As I said, it would be a tremendous coup and a terrific way to kick off. It would certainly make the gallery's name.'

'That's what Harald said. Let's just hope it happens, eh?'

Sandy crossed two fingers. 'Let's hope.' He had a sip of wine, then said quietly, 'I also have news.'

'Oh?'

'I didn't tell you the real reason I went to Glasgow in case I failed in what I wanted to set up. It's directly to do with you and McLatchie.'

Her face darkened with pain and anger. 'Go on.'

'I'll explain fully some other time but I have some friends in low places there, the sort of men who, for the right money, will do almost anything.' He took a deep breath. 'I've paid for McLatchie to be castrated so that he never does to another woman what he did to you.'

'Castrated?' she whispered, blanching.

Sandy nodded.

'Dear God.'

He frowned. 'Do you disapprove?'

She thought about it for a few moments. 'On the contrary, if I was given the chance I'd wield the knife myself. And that's a fact.'

Having said that she burst into tears, her entire body heaving.

Sandy instantly put aside his drink and took her into his arms. 'There there, darling,' he crooned, gently rocking her to and fro. 'There there.'

'I hope it hurts when they do it,' she sobbed. 'I hope it hurts like bloody buggery.'

Sandy had absolutely no doubt it would. And as for afterwards . . . Well, as a man himself it didn't bear thinking about. But McLatchie would only be getting what he fully deserved.

Sandy was about to switch out the light when Laura came into his bedroom. 'I know I'll have a nightmare after what you told me earlier about McLatchie,' she said. 'Can I sleep in your bed?'

She was looking lovely with her face scrubbed bare and her hair neatly combed, Sandy observed. Her night-dress, a pale blue, was also very becoming and elegantly cut. 'Of course you can.'

'Thanks, Sandy.' She smiled and hastily got underneath the covers.

When the light was out she snuggled up to him. 'I

won't have the nightmare now. Not with you beside me.'

And so it proved.

The girl assistant on one of Daly's perfume counters shook her head. 'I'm afraid I've never heard of a Mr Ballantine,' she replied in answer to Harriet's inquiry. 'The general manager is called Mr McColl.'

Harriet's face fell in disappointment. 'I see.'

'But I've only been here a short time. Let me ask one of the longer-serving assistants,' the girl said.

A few seconds later the girl was back with a woman roughly Harriet's own age. 'Are you the lady asking about Mr Ballantine?' she asked politely.

'Yes, I am.'

'I'm afraid he left some years ago. Lovely chap he was, very popular with the staff. We were all very sad when he went.'

'Have you any idea where? I wish to contact him, you see.'

The older assistant studied Harriet intently, having noted the urgency and sense of pleading in her voice. 'Are you a relative perhaps?'

Harriet shook her head. 'A very old and,' she hesitated for a moment, '*close* friend.'

'I'm afraid it's company policy not to give out any personal information on former employees,' the older assistant said. 'It would mean my job if I did.'

A crestfallen look came over Harriet's face, that and one of profound sadness. 'I understand,' she replied, her voice suddenly thick with emotion. 'Thank you for speaking with me.'

'I *am* sorry.'

Harriet somehow managed a weak smile, then turned away. What a fool she'd been to let James go when she'd had the chance of a new life with him. But then, how was she to have known both Sandy and Laura would leave home to go and live abroad? She couldn't possibly have done. But their leaving had changed matters completely.

She wandered aimlessly amongst the counters for a few minutes, trying to regain her composure. When she thought she'd managed that she headed for the door.

'Oh, hello again,' the older assistant greeted her, appearing as though from nowhere. 'Do you know, I was just saying to another customer up from London what a wonderful store Selfridges in Oxford Street is. Have you heard of it?'

A bemused Harriet nodded.

'Selfridges in Oxford Street. Absolutely wonderful.' And with that the older assistant bustled away.

How kind, Harriet thought. How very kind. She'd write to James that very day.

'It's a letter for you from Glasgow. And it isn't Ma's handwriting,' Laura announced, handing it to Sandy who was in his studio waiting for a model to arrive.

He stared at the letter, knowing what it had to be. Slowly he opened the envelope and extracted the single sheet of paper it contained.

JOB DONE
BOB

'Is it what I think?' Laura asked in a strangely neutral voice.

Sandy nodded.

'And?'

'McLatchie's been attended to.'

A look of sheer exultation came into her eyes, that was then quickly extinguished. 'Good,' she whispered.

Sandy refolded the sheet of paper, replaced it in the envelope and slipped that into a pocket. 'Where's that bloody Yvette? She's probably got a hangover or in bed with a new boyfriend, or both, knowing her.'

Laura glanced over at the deckchair Sandy had set up, a multi-patterned towel draped over the nearside leg. 'Is that how you want her? Sitting on that?'

'Side on, reading a magazine. The background a combination of black and grey that'll contrast with her naked body. I think it'll work extremely well.'

So did Laura. In fact the image conjured up in her mind excited her. 'Does it mean you'll lose a day's work if Yvette lets you down?'

'Of course it does. It's too late now to get someone else to pose. For today anyway.'

'I'll do it then,' Laura stated quietly.

That startled Sandy, the possibility never having entered his head. 'You!'

'Why not? Unless you think I'd be unsuitable.'

'No no, you'd be perfect. But it's a nude study, Laura.'

'You've already said that. Well?'

He was stunned. 'Are you absolutely certain?'

'Absolutely,' she declared firmly.

Her firmness decided him. 'All right then. The screen's there,' he replied, pointing.

There were no doubts in Laura's mind. None at all. Going behind the screen, she quickly undressed.

Sandy was waiting for her when she re-emerged. Their eyes locked, and in that moment each knew what the other was thinking, and agreed with it.

Well, it was Montmartre after all. Anything went. Everything was acceptable.

THE END